More Praise for
Picnic in the Ruins

"In this twenty-first-century fusion of Zane Grey, Tony Hillerman, and Craig Childs, Todd Robert Petersen gives us a page-turner of a murder mystery that tackles the ethics of archaeology. Along the way, he dispels a raft of traditional 'exquisite misapprehensions' about the American West."

—STEPHEN TRIMBLE, editor of *Red Rock Stories:*
Three Generations of Writers Speak
on Behalf of Utah's Public Lands

ALSO BY TODD ROBERT PETERSEN

It Needs to Look Like We Tried

PICNIC IN THE RUINS

A Novel

Todd Robert Petersen

COUNTERPOINT
Berkeley, California

For my parents

ISBN: 978-1-64009-322-5

The Library of Congress Cataloging-in-Publication Data is available.

Cover design by Donna Cheng
Book design by Jordan Koluch

COUNTERPOINT
2560 Ninth Street, Suite 318
Berkeley, CA 94710
www.counterpointpress.com

Printed in the United States of America

10 9 8 7 6 5 4 3 2 1

but the end result was the same as everywhere else,
a piece of emptiness left behind

CRAIG CHILDS, Finders Keepers

PART I

Day One

A visit from nobody : Sunday stillness : Vicarious education

Byron Ashdown was twirling the small plastic skull that hung from the rearview mirror of his turquoise Ford F-250 when the old woman shut the front door. He sat up and tried to slap his brother, who dozed with his cheek smeared against the opposite window. His hand wouldn't reach, and Byron wasn't the kind of person to lean, so his hand swiped the air.

"Hey, Lonnie," he said, "she's leaving," but Lonnie didn't wake up. Byron watched her cross the covered porch of the old pioneer home and stop. She opened her handbag and rooted through it.

"Okay, what now? What now?" Byron said.

She walked back to the door, hesitated, looked through her bag again, then opened the door and went back inside the house. Byron cursed once and kicked the floor.

Lonnie bolted awake and looked around, shouting, "What, what?" Then he said, "Come on, I was asleep."

"She came out, then went back inside."

"She still in the house?"

"Do you see her anywhere?"

Lonnie rubbed his eyes, then squinted. The old white house sat back from the street behind a wide strip of lawn with a cluster of tall spiraling dandelions on the north side.

"That's it. We're hosed," Byron said, pounding the steering wheel. "She saw us."

Lonnie turned and looked through the gun rack that covered the rear window. The street was empty. A few cars were parked on the wide gray pavement, but most were garaged. The sun was a thick yellow bead lying on the palisade of red rock that surrounded the town. He looked back through the windshield and saw more of the same. The sky was free of clouds. It was going to be a hot one. "What's to see? Just two guys sitting in a truck. That's pretty much the only thing that happens around here," Lonnie said. "If the cops come, we can tell 'em we had to pull over to read our texts."

"And they'll just think we're a couple of Boy Scouts, right?" Byron checked the time on his banged-up flip phone. It was five to eight.

"You should get a smartphone," Lonnie said.

"So they can find me? No thanks," Byron said. "Look, I just want to get in there, get the stuff, get out, get paid."

"Getting worked up won't do nothing," Lonnie said, frowning at a fast food hash brown patty half-eaten in its crumpled wrapper.

Byron started rocking anxiously in his seat, then unconsciously he took the tip of his thin ponytail and painted it in figure eights across his cheek. Lonnie watched him do it and tried not to comment.

After a few minutes, the old woman reemerged, her handbag snug in the crook of one arm. Byron noticed the addition of a hat. She closed the door and slid her hand along the wrought-iron rail as she stepped carefully down each of the three steps.

"Get down," Byron said, hunching below the dashboard. Lonnie joined him. "What's the hat for? Where's she going? We're screwed," Byron said. Together, they listened to the car start, then to the squeal of the steering pump, then to the silence.

"Man, she's just going to church. Old ladies wear hats," Lonnie said, sitting up first. "The coast is clear."

As Byron sat up, Lonnie unfolded the hash brown wrapper and ate the rest of the patty.

"You eat like a dog," Byron said. "That's why your gut hurts all the time."

"That nurse said my flora was off."

"I'm not getting into a thing about your flora. Can you just stick to the plan so we can make a little money?"

"There's more of them than there is of us," Lonnie said, "like ten times more."

"Of who?"

"Bacteria." Lonnie crumpled the paper and belched. "I should've had a yogurt."

They got out of their truck looking nervous. Byron's head cleared the hood of their truck by a few inches. His body was thick and squared off, like a roast. Lonnie was almost a foot taller, thin and stoop shouldered. His strides were twice as long as his brother's, and he crossed the street before Byron was halfway. When they got up to the house, they tried to look like they were supposed to be there.

"Where's the guy?" Lonnie asked.

"Supposed to be out of town," Byron said. They gathered at the door. "Tell me the plan one more time," Byron ordered.

"Go in, find where he keeps the maps. Grab anything that says Swallow Valley or has that Indian word on it."

"Almost," Byron said. "If we only take one kind of thing, then they'll know what we were after. We need to grab any cash, watches, whatever. Break some stuff. It needs to look like we had no idea what we were doing."

"But we don't."

"Then we're headed in the right direction."

Byron went in first and Lonnie followed, the door opening into a hallway that ran straight back into the house, past a set of stairs on the immediate right, which went up a half flight and turned just above an old color photograph showing a young couple sitting together in the red rock, the man holding up a whole and complete yucca sandal, the woman wearing sunglasses with a scarf tied around her neck, leaning back on her hands, taking it all in.

"Where's the stuff?" Lonnie whispered.

"Shut up," Byron said, creeping forward. He looked into each room as he went past. When they both got to the end of the hall, they saw a kitchen in one direction and more hall in the other. Byron turned and put a finger to his lips.

"But there's nobody here," Lonnie said.

"What's that?" somebody said from an open door at the end of the hall.

Byron and Lonnie froze, then tiptoed toward the sound.

"Did you forget where you were going again, my love?" the voice continued.

Lonnie leaned and looked around the doorframe. He saw a man reading with a large magnifying glass. He was surrounded by pottery, baskets, books, stones, tools, coils of rope, apothecary jars, bundles of papers tied up with brown string, accordion files, and dusty terrariums filled with dirt, gravel, and a multitude of cacti. Many places on the shelves sat empty, though they were cataloged with tiny numbers on small slips of paper.

It took a few seconds before the man thought to pause his reading. "You were on your way to church, dear. If you need me, I can take—" The man glanced up and saw Lonnie staring. "Who in the Sam Hill are you?"

"We're nobody," Lonnie said, stepping into the open doorframe so he wasn't leaning over. Byron squeezed past and into the room. "Leave the questions to us, old man."

Lonnie followed his brother into the room and became instantly distracted by the books. "I'll bet a reader like you knows where that joke came from," he said.

"What joke?" the old man asked.

"The nobody joke."

"It's from the *Odyssey*, you moron," the old man said.

"That's enough about minivans," Byron said. "We're here on business, and you were supposed to be at some Indian pot nerds meeting."

"How would you know that—" The old man's face went red, then changed. "Frangos," he said, huffing. "Frangos sent you. She needs to—you know what—I think you better leave." He stood weakly, his robe open, exposing the scooped neck of his T-shirt and his white chest hair.

"We never heard of anybody called Frangles," Byron said. "So, maybe sit back down and listen." Byron pulled a snub-nosed .38 from the back of his pants.

"Why'd you bring that?" Lonnie asked.

"You take anything," the old man threatened, "and you won't be able to sell it. Dealers know what's mine. Frangos knows that. And she should have told you it's all going back where it belongs."

"Shut it," Byron said, brandishing the gun.

"How is this gonna work, since he wasn't, like, supposed to be here?" Lonnie asked, holding his hands against the sides of his head.

Byron split his attention between the old man and his brother.

"You said it needs to look like we don't know what we're doing, but with him here it will look like we do—you know—know what we're doing. And that's what he'll say," Lonnie said.

The old man cleared his throat, yanking Byron's manic attention back. "You two are obviously idiots," the old man said, his eyes narrowing. "Get out of my house or I'm calling the police." The old man reached for the phone.

Byron jabbed his gun toward him. "Dial and you're dead." The muzzle wavered, then became motionless. His eyes locked with the old man's for an instant, then he turned to Lonnie. "Make yourself useful. I need to think."

Lonnie browsed the study, picking things up and looking them over, which agitated the old man. Lonnie picked up a white pot the size of a cantaloupe. Inside was a red image of a face, something both alien and human, with round eyes and monstrous teeth.

"Put that down," the old man directed. "It's over five hundred years old." He turned back to Byron. "You can tell Frangos the answer is no. It's always going to be no. She can't build a collection with money. You have to earn it. It takes a lifetime."

Lonnie set down the pot and picked up an unbroken geode from the top of a filing cabinet. He tossed it in the air a couple of times to feel its weight. "How come you ain't split it open?" he asked. "The good part is on the inside, like a Tootsie Pop."

"Please, just put it down." The man reached for the phone and started dialing. He had only punched a single number, when Lonnie swung the geode hard against the man's temple, slamming him instantly to the desk. Blood jetted in an arc, startling Lonnie so much that he pressed down on the man's head with the flat of his hand. "Oh jeez," Lonnie said.

"What did you do?" Byron shouted. Lonnie put his other hand on top of the first. "What did you do?" Byron shouted again.

"I was thinking about what would happen if he called the cops. You got two strikes already, Byron." Lonnie leaned on his hands to increase the pressure. Blood seeped through his fingers, and the old man didn't move. "Two strikes. I didn't want you to go back."

"Come here," Byron beckoned, his voice softening.

"I can't," Lonnie said, nodding toward his hands. Byron slipped the gun into his pants and walked toward his brother with his arms opened wide. Lonnie thought it was for a hug, but Byron grabbed him by the hair and pointed his head at the growing pool of blood on the desk. Lonnie flapped and fought against his brother, covering Byron's shirt with red handprints.

"You reach in there and find out if he's still alive," Byron growled.

"How do I do that?"

"You check his pulse."

"How do I do *that*?"

"You've seen it on TV. We all have. Just do it."

Lonnie reached under the man's neck and felt around. "I can't find it," he said.

Byron tightened his grip on his brother's hair. "Keep trying."

"He ain't cold or anything."

"Well, brother. Why would he be cold?" Byron let go of Lonnie, took the old man's wrist, and looked at the ceiling while he tried to find a pulse. After a minute, he tossed the hand away. "Now you've done it," he said. "Ain't gonna be any money in this situation if it stays this way."

"Is he dead?"

"Headed that direction." Byron paced around the room while Lonnie stood dumbfounded, hands dangling at his sides, staring at the old man. Byron took out his phone and flipped it open.

"You're gonna call him?"

"Of course I'm calling him." He dialed the number and looked at the phone while it rang. When the line connected, he put the phone to his ear. "I know you said not to call, but the situation got away from us. Yeah ... Lonnie put him down ... That's correct ... All the way down," he said, then he listened for a while. "It happened before we could ..." he said. "No, we did not get to the list. Not yet."

"Is he saying what to do?" Lonnie asked. "Ask him who this Frangles lady is."

Byron dragged a finger across his neck. "Okay," he said, "we can do that. It should help us cover our tracks. We're on it. Thank you, sir." He flipped the phone shut.

Lonnie looked at him and waited. "'Sir'?"

"Shut up." Byron thought for a second, then said, "Check to see if this guy has a shotgun somewhere."

—

Sheriff Patrick Dalton opened his eyes and saw two people through the windshield of his cruiser staring back at him. One was an EMT he didn't recognize, and the other was Chris Tanner, one of his deputies. The engine was off, but Dalton grabbed the steering wheel, which gave him the fleeting sensation that he was about to run them all down.

Tanner said something to the EMT, then tilted his head and pressed the button on his shoulder mic. "You want us to come back later?" came crackling through the radio. Dalton pulled the key from the ignition but didn't get out. He looked around at the old pioneer home, the crisscrossed police tape, the ambulance, traffic cones, strip of brown lawn, dandelions, wrought-iron handrail, blue sky. Sunday stillness.

An hour ago, he was sitting in church, head bowed, when his phone buzzed. He turned it over and read the text banner. It was from Tanner: SORRY ABOUT THIS, BUT YOU NEED GET DOWN TO THE CLUFF HOME. WE'VE GOT A SITUATION WITH BRUCE. He turned the phone back over and looked around the chapel. The Sacrament was going around. If he left now, people would wonder. So he waited. In a few minutes, the phone buzzed again. All it said was 10-56.

This meant it was a suicide. He thumbed open the lock screen and typed: ON MY WAY.

Bruce Cluff was one of his dad's oldest friends, and he was his mother's prom date. When Dalton's dad passed, Bruce shouldered the coffin. Bruce's wife, Raylene, pulled his mother out of a depression that lasted most of a year. All of this went down while he was on his second tour in Afghanistan. Thinking about Bruce taking his own life yanked the breath out of him.

There was a knock on the cruiser's hood. Tanner shrugged and lifted his eyebrows. Dalton unbuckled his seat belt and got out. As he stood he realized he wasn't in uniform. His dark suit and white shirt stood out against Tanner's khaki and the EMT's white. He pulled his tie off and opened the trunk, taking out the sheriff's department windbreaker he kept in back.

"You gonna be all right?" Tanner asked.

"I'll have to be," he said. "What happened?"

"We've got Dr. Cluff in the study with a shotgun," the EMT said.

Dalton walked past Tanner. "Tell the new guy he can't make it sound like we're playing Clue." Dalton ducked under the yellow tape. "How long until the medical examiner gets here?"

"An hour or so," Tanner said.

"Did Bruce leave a note?"

Tanner shrugged. "Maybe. There's a lot of things on that desk we can't read anymore."

Dalton stopped outside the front door and turned back to look down at the scene. The quiet old street was filled with vehicles now. He looked at his watch. In another hour the neighbors would get back from church, and this would all change from a concern to a calamity.

From where he stood, he could see across the rooftops south toward the red plateau, all the way to the national monument. The blue desert sky was brushed with abstract white clouds gathering at the horizon. He tried to keep ahead of the panic attack, let it hit him head-on like his therapist taught him.

It's the only way to know none of it is real. Don't resist change. That just brings sorrow. Let things flow naturally forward in whatever way they like. Breathe. Follow your outbreath.

"I know you're getting your game face on," Tanner interrupted, "but our window of opportunity is shrinking."

Dalton blinked. "Is Bruce going to get up and walk out of the house?"

"We've got to tag evidence before the ME gets here. You know, and it's June. So, heat."

"Is the A/C on?"

"They've got a swamp cooler, but it's off. It's pretty bad in there already."

Dalton opened the door and went in and led himself down the hall and around the corner to the study. Tanner followed. The EMT was gone. "How's Raylene?"

"At the neighbors'."

"Please tell me she didn't find him."

Tanner nodded sadly. "She came home from church after an hour because Bruce was sick. She said he was supposed to be at a collector's convention, but he canceled."

"Does she know where that meetup was supposed to be?"

Tanner shook his head. "She says she can't remember."

At the doorframe of the study, Dalton stopped and gathered himself. He drew on his childhood memories to map out the space in his head, then he turned the corner.

The blood-soaked desk was covered with numbered plastic A-frames marking the evidence. The top half of the tall leather office chair was blown off, the wood frame serrated like the edge of a flint knife. Somewhere on the floor behind the desk lay the body.

"I told you it was bad," Tanner said.

"I'm a big boy," Dalton answered.

It looked like the shot knocked Bruce out of his chair, spinning it around so it faced away from the desk. He lay sprawled on the ground in a heap, the robe spread behind him, the shotgun flung from his hands, the books in the shelves behind him stuccoed with brown blood and bone. Dalton imagined what happened to the body when the gun went off, the energy of the shot oscillating through the jaw and brain, discharging from the other side of the skull.

A camera flash strobed behind him.

"And nobody's touched anything?" Dalton asked.

"Nobody did," Tanner said.

Dalton surveyed the Navajo rugs, porcupine quill baskets, cedar masks in blue and red, tiny unpainted clay birds, wooden flutes, small irregular petroglyph panels, old green and brown books, maps on wooden stands, bird fossils, purple crystals, whole geodes resting on plastic rings. There were so many treasures in this menagerie: a stuffed weasel, arrowheads in shadow boxes, spearpoints under glass, perfectly round stones of various sizes, framed newspaper clippings about Bruce and his discoveries, antique compasses large and small, steel protractors, and brass telescopes. But he noticed that quite a few shelves had empty spots.

"This place is right out of an old photograph. How would anyone know if something was missing?" Tanner said.

"Raylene might. There used to be a lot more pottery in here." Dalton pointed at a plain bowl. "When I was a kid, this place was full of stuff like that."

Tanner's face became still. "A guy like Bruce with all this Indian stuff in here. I mean some of this has to be in the gray zone as far as the law goes. Are we looking at another Federal pot hunter crackdown?"

"I haven't heard of anything."

"I mean, if the FBI is looking into collectors again, you know, like that guy in Page who drove himself off a cliff once they came after him—if that's coming around again, we'll have all kinds of trouble. The Carver family will go nuts, probably get on YouTube and take over another tortoise refuge."

Dalton walked around the body and tried to make sense of what he was seeing. He thought he'd have some kind of deeper reaction, but it was all flowing around him, like floodwater going around a boulder. He was fine now, but he felt the sand underneath him starting to loosen. "If you're wondering about garbage like that, go talk to Stan Forsythe at the paper," Dalton said. "Crazy talk is his love language."

"I'm not wondering. I'm just thinking. The Feds would let you know if they were coming, right?"

"Feds do what they want."

"That's what the crazies say. I'm asking you."

Dalton's phone buzzed and he looked at it. It was his ex-wife. He lifted his thumb to open the lock screen, but instead he sent her to voice mail.

"The crazies aren't wrong," Dalton said. "I just can't talk to them."

—

Sophia Shepard shut her book, which was bristling with Post-it Notes, and she set it on the orange Formica dinette table. The scholarly title, *UNESCO, World Heritage, and the Human Factor*, set it apart from the whimsical Airstream travel trailer she was living and working in for the summer.

She took her insulated coffee mug and stepped out of the trailer and into the late afternoon air, which was hot and dry and riddled with the trilling of songbirds. The white sun filtered through the canopy of desert trees, mature sycamores, and cottonwoods that sheltered the trailer park from the blazing sky. In one direction lay the street, and beyond it, a self-serve car wash crouching in the open glare next to a run-down laundromat with two duct-tape *X*s running across each of its dust-covered windows. Behind that bleached outbuilding stood an orange sandstone rampart that ran vertically for a hundred feet.

In the opposite direction, the other trailers were arranged in a semicircle like giant silver beetles. Across the way was Mrs. Gladstone's trailer. It was an Airstream like the rest but larger because she was the owner. It had been upgraded with a covered porch, Tibetan prayer flags, and potted succulents, not all of them thriving. Mrs. Gladstone was asleep in a rattan chaise lounge, a Pomeranian perched upon her stomach with its nose in a bag of cookies.

Sophia shouted at the dog, who looked up at her, flicked an ear, and returned to the bag. "Hey, you little monster," she said again, crossing from her trailer to the small patio. She wouldn't call the dog by its name, Cleopatra, but had secretly renamed her Mīkrós Thérion, "the tiny beast." Mikros, for short.

It was one way she tried to keep up on her Greek while she was working in southern Utah.

"Hey, Mikros, knock it off," she shouted, which woke Mrs. Gladstone with a start. Mikros switched from licking the bag to bathing the woman's face with her tongue. "Oh, you tiny starving thing. Did you get all your cookies?" Mrs. Gladstone looked inside, reshaped the bag, tipped the crumbs into one corner, and poured them into her hand.

"Good afternoon, Sophia," Mrs. Gladstone said while the dog snuffled up the last of the crumbs before jumping to the ground and sniffing around the potted plants. On a side table was a can of Diet Coke with a lipstick-printed straw sticking out of it. Behind her, a hummingbird buzzed through the covered porch and landed on a plastic feeder that hung from the edge of the corrugated roof. As it drank the sugar water, other hummingbirds buzzed in and scrapped for a spot. It was vicious for one explosive moment, then they disappeared all at once. The old woman paid them no mind.

"Have you been reading *all day*?" Mrs. Gladstone asked.

Sophia nodded. "Dissertations don't write themselves."

"I don't suppose they would," Mrs. Gladstone said. "I also can't imagine there would be so much to say about—what is it again?"

"The ethics of preserving ancient artifacts."

"Oh, that's right. Museums and national parks and providence. One of these days I'll remember without a hint." She smiled and brushed back stray wisps of hair.

Sophia was about to correct her and say, it's "provenance," not "providence," but she'd done this bit before and wanted to skip it this time.

Mikros barked, sending a lizard across the patio and under Mrs. Gladstone's chair. The dog growled but didn't chase it. Mrs. Gladstone sat up. "I always wanted to be an architect, my dear, but I was told that was for boys. They told me to be a nurse or a teacher. I told them to blow it out their butts."

"So you went to college anyway?"

"I went to Hollywood."

"You're perfect, Mrs. Gladstone," Sophia said. "Absolutely perfect."

"And look at me now. I'm the queen of all I survey." Mrs. Gladstone unfolded her arms and let a dozen bracelets jangle down to the elbow. "But really, a girl like you should be out on the town on a summer night, not holed up. Don't you have plans?"

"I like to get out, but you know there's not much nightlife around here. It's a little dead unless you're up for a milkshake."

Mrs. Gladstone sipped her Diet Coke and set it back on the side table. "Once upon a time, people used to call this hamlet Little Hollywood. Pretty glitzy for southern Utah, don't you think?"

"What was Kanab like before all that?" Sophia asked.

Mrs. Gladstone shrugged. "What you would imagine. Frontier, red rock, tumbleweeds, Indians. Not much else. A whole lot of nothing, really."

"Mrs. Gladstone, Native people aren't nothing," Sophia said.

"Well, you know what I mean," Mrs. Gladstone said with a wave.

Sophia didn't veer. "I'm not sure I do."

Mrs. Gladstone closed her eyes and tilted her head to show she disapproved of this turn in the conversation. "Back in the day, my dear, you might bump into Ronald Reagan, Ernest Borgnine, Sidney Poitier, Raquel Welch. Everyone who was anyone came to town. We were surrounded by stars, and there were a thousand different flavors of nightlife. A girl could get into the right kind of trouble, if that's what she wanted." She looked around, smiled, and shrugged a coy shoulder. "This girl did."

Sophia knew she wasn't ready for a detailed description of the right kind of trouble, so she steered the conversation back to her work. "Tomorrow I'm going into Arizona to check sites in the Antelope Valley. South, near the bluffs. I'll be back by nightfall. Send in the cavalry if I'm not back by Tuesday morning. I'll leave a map in my trailer."

"Speaking of the cavalry, that gorgeous ranger dropped by to see you the other day," Mrs. Gladstone said. She lifted her penciled-in eyebrows and sang: "And he was on a mo-tor-cy-cle."

"Paul?" Sophia asked, hiding a smile with a sip of her coffee.

"There isn't an ounce of fat on that man," Mrs. Gladstone said. "He said he was planning a trip for you two to go off into the backcountry." Mrs. Gladstone smiled. "So, that's what they're calling it these days?"

Sophia sprayed her coffee.

Mrs. Gladstone shrugged dramatically, sending the dozen bracelets clattering in the other direction. "I'm just an old woman, trying to live vicariously through the nomads who stay here with me."

Sophia held up her book. "Well, tonight you'll get the chance to absorb information about UNESCO World Heritage Sites."

"Vicarious education is the best kind, darling," Mrs. Gladstone said.

Sophia laughed. "Did Paul want something specific, like to ask me if I wanted to go into the backcountry?" she asked.

"I don't know," Mrs. Gladstone said, looking around, trying to recall if there was something she was supposed to remember. "He has very good manners for a young man."

"That is true," Sophia said. "If you happen to see him again, could you tell him to email me?"

"Don't the young people just Chap Snap now? Email is so old-fashioned." Mrs. Gladstone took another sip of Diet Coke, and Mikros climbed back into her lap. The phone in her trailer rang. She struggled to get up, until Sophia offered to get it, then she eased back in her chair. "Thank you, dear," she said.

Sophia stepped into the trailer, which was a patchwork of bright color: shelves hand-painted orange, purple, and green, full of self-help books and poetry. Two ceramic parrots stood atop overturned terra-cotta pots, arranged to look as if they were chattering to each other. The space was filled with messages written in script on planks of wood: YOU ARE SUFFICIENT—DON'T TOUCH MY CHOCOLATE—FRIENDSHIP IS FOR KEEPS—SOMETIMES LIFE JUST GIVES YOU THE LEMONADE. The whole place smelled of jasmine and garbage.

"It's next to the fridge!" Mrs. Gladstone called out.

What she meant was that it was under a stack of magazines next to the fridge. Once Sophia found it, she dashed back with the ringing phone and handed it over. As Mrs. Gladstone listened to the caller, her face fell. "You can't be serious?" she said, then she covered her mouth with one hand. "A shotgun?" Her eyes found Sophia's. "That doesn't sound right at all. No, I do not accept it." Sophia heard the woman on the other end say that a neighbor heard the shots. "The police are still there? What about Raylene? I'll come get her." Mrs. Gladstone paused and listened, her face hardening. "Well, how long until the sedation wears off?" she asked.

Mikros trotted back to the porch with a wet sack of trash in her mouth. Sophia tried to take it away, but the dog ran off.

"I don't like it," Mrs. Gladstone said into the phone, then she switched it off and set it carefully on the side table and gripped the arms of her chaise, tears softening her mascara. "I'm sorry for this, Sophia," she said, gesturing to her face. "An old friend took his life today. Bruce Cluff."

Sophia knew the name. "I was introduced to him my first week in town. When I tried to ask about some of the pieces in his collection, he got pretty angry with me."

"Oh, Bruce was angry with everyone." Mrs. Gladstone dabbed at each eye with a fingertip. "But I shouldn't speak ill," she said.

"Seems like he must have had a lot on his mind."

"Bruce had his head in the clouds most of the time—in the dirt, really. I said he was an old friend, that's not quite right. He was not a particularly nice man, if you ask me. But his wife was a dear, dear friend. She's not well. I need to see her as soon as I can."

Day Two

Uncrossed t's : Illegal search and seizure : Fieldwork interrupted

Byron Ashdown clenched a small tactical flashlight in his teeth as he carried two giant sloshing gas cans to the back of the pickup. Lonnie followed with two shovels and a duffel bag slung across his shoulder. The sky was still dark and speckled with stars, Jupiter low against the western horizon, the galaxy core faded down to a single spray of white. As they continued loading their vehicle, dawn tipped the scales, and the stars disappeared.

Lonnie sat on a stump between the truck and their single-wide, and he began to lace his boots. "This isn't a criticism," he said. "I just wanted to say something, and you don't have to do anything about it. But I want you to hear what I have to say."

Byron plucked the flashlight from his teeth and pointed it straight at his brother. "Not now. We're on a time frame."

Lonnie covered his eyes, the light blasting around his fingers. "Money's been tight and I know you're trying to get everything to work out good for us—hey, everything just went purple. Would it be okay if you shined that somewhere else?"

"Now that I've got your attention, I need you to carry what I tell you to carry, put it where I tell you to put it, and sit where I tell you to sit. I don't need a play-by-play or your analysis or any of your regular horseshit, Lonnie. Not today."

Lonnie crisscrossed his hands in front of his face to protect his eyes from the flashlight. "It's just, you know, going out there to dig up pots and stuff instead of taking the maps to the guy like he told us to. I mean, maybe we shouldn't."

"They bought the maps, not the stuff that's *on* the maps. With your logic, I could buy a map of America, and the next thing . . . I'm president. Besides, what if the maps aren't even legit? Wouldn't be the first time."

"Then, I don't know, if that happens, these people would be pretty mad."

"Of course they will, but we ain't in the business of real," Byron said. After a moment, his expression changed and he exhaled. "But then again, what if they *are* real?"

"Now you're confusing me."

"What if they have real treasure in them, then maybe we don't have to settle for the dog scraps here. I mean we know our way around the monument, Lonnie. He don't know nothing about it. What if we just kept one of those maps for ourselves?"

"You know they're not treasure maps. It's not *Pirates of the Caribbean*. It's just a list of ruins. Pots. Whatever. I read them. It's not going to lead us to any gold, you know. We should just get rid of them. Then no one can say we took them."

"Quit making it sound like you're the only one who reads."

"I just never seen you read anything, so I—"

"Can and does are not the same thing. I *can* kick your ass, but I *do* not. Restraint is how I exercise my freedom."

"Is that another lesson you got from jail? Because maybe if we clean out the artifacts from these places first, they're going to be pissed about it and come hunt us down."

"We'll be long gone by then, baby brother, living large in Mexico."

"Yeah," Lonnie said. "I remember." He stood and glanced over his shoulder to the east. The Vermilion Cliffs sat low and black against the horizon, and a pale stripe along their flanks began to glow. The shadows around their home were softening. "Ain't you gonna give me hell?"

"For what?" Byron said.

"I should have just left that geode right where it was."

"It don't make any difference now. None of it does. You got rid of the rock, right?"

Lonnie nodded. "We're going out to the desert so you can—did that guy tell you to . . ."

"What the hell are you talking about? Do you think he told me to put a bullet in you?"

"I mean, maybe," Lonnie said.

Byron dropped a duffel bag into the truck, then lowered his head and touched it to the tailgate.

"You know I was trying to help with the geode and everything. I just was gonna knock him out a little. It was heavier than I thought," Lonnie said.

"Not going to talk about it."

"I know it was a bad thing."

"You can't unspill a beer, Lonnie."

"I know that. It's physics. Energy just wants to spread out and—"

"Stop worrying about that. Yesterday we wanted some money, today we need it. There's just what happens, then what you do next. Ain't no good or evil. That's all made up."

Lonnie stood and looked around. He and his brother grew up in this trailer. He stayed on when Byron quit high school and ran off. He didn't move when his mother died, or when his father disappeared one night. Drove off for groceries and didn't come back. Never turned up. He stayed through it all, working jobs until Byron showed up a year ago, just out of prison, saying he needed a place to stay.

"It means something to me," Lonnie said.

"That's a mistake." Byron climbed up the wood steps, went inside, and came out with the maps rolled up under his arm. He pulled the door shut and put the maps into the gun rack above the deer rifle. "If it don't mean anything to you, nobody will try to take it away."

Byron got in and started the truck. Lonnie buckled himself in. They crawled down the rutted drive and turned onto the dirt road that took them to the gravel county road that turned onto the state highway. As they continued into town, the sky grew brighter.

"You hungry?" Byron asked.

Lonnie nodded.

"What for?"

"Breakfast," Lonnie said.

"I meant what *kind* of breakfast?"

"V8. Donut. Banana."

"No protein?"

After a minute Lonnie said, "V8. Donut. Banana. Cheese stick." Lonnie looked in the side mirror and saw the rolling blue, white, red. "Oh crap. Cops. What do we do? When I get nervous, I say things."

"There is no we. I will do the talking." They came to a stop, and the sheriff's car pulled in behind them.

"I don't mean to say anything, but I get a hook in me that doesn't come out."

"Then don't start."

"But what if I can't?"

The cop walked up behind them, on the passenger's side. His name tag said DALTON.

"Just don't start."

"But I already did."

"Quiet."

"I can't."

"Quiet!" Byron yelled. There was a knock on the window. Lonnie rolled it down.

"Your sticker says February," Dalton said.

"Oh, man. That's right. I did it online. I guess I forgot about it."

"For three months? You have the paper?"

"You mean the one from the website?"

Dalton nodded.

"No, I don't have that. I mean I did it, but I don't have it now."

He handed Byron the ticket.

"Will this violate my parole?" Byron asked.

"It might."

"No, it won't!" Lonnie said. "A ticket is a petty offense."

"Shut it!"

"Your lawyer is right, but if that rifle is loaded," the sheriff said, sliding his pen back into his breast pocket, "then you could be headed back to the big house."

Lonnie began rocking back and forth, muttering to himself. Dalton took note and directed Byron and Lonnie to both get out of the truck and move to the front and place their hands on the hood. He cuffed Byron and said, "You are not under arrest, but I'm detaining you while I check that rifle." He opened the bolt and checked inside. When he saw that it was empty, he replaced the weapon, knocking the maps out of the rack so they bounced from the seat to the floor. Byron went rigid, then stamped one foot on the ground. Dalton replaced the maps and returned to the front of the vehicle. "Mr. Ashdown, you're clear on the gun, but a little advice. A person in your legal situation is going to want to cross his t's."

"Sure," Byron said.

"'Yes, sir' is good enough," Dalton said, then he removed the cuffs and walked back to his car, got in, and switched off the lights.

—

Dalton waited for the turquoise pickup truck to drive off, then he followed it to the light, where it turned north, then turned again into the grocery store parking lot. There were only seven thousand people in the county, so Dalton recognized the brothers, but he only knew bits and pieces of their story. They were Ashdowns. The short one was a prodigal and a cipher. The taller one was more familiar but still mostly someone who kept to the sidelines.

Dalton turned south and drove to the public safety building, turning his thoughts to the moving parts of the Bruce Cluff suicide. He knew Bruce was always fighting with the Bureau of Land Management and the Park Service about something, and he knew Bruce had a reputation with collectors. He was retired and set for money after he sold his dental practice, so he didn't do anything he didn't want to. If Bruce took his own life, it came from a secret he wouldn't want to face in a town that knew everything about everybody.

When Dalton pulled into the public safety building, Stan Forsythe, the editor of the *Red Rock Times*, was leaning against the wall next to the front doors in running shoes, with a purple golf shirt tight across his belly. There was one pair of glasses on his head, another on his face, and a third hanging from a cord around his neck. Stan straightened up when he saw Dalton pull in, which made Dalton want to back out and leave, but as he put the car in gear, another car drove in slowly behind him and tried to park in the spot alongside his. The car stopped and adjusted and started again and adjusted, then started again, boxing Dalton in.

He got out and walked toward Forsythe, who moved into his path.

"Sheriff?" Forsythe said. "There was some pretty interesting chatter on the shortwaves last night. I've got questions."

"About?"

"Don't play coy with me."

"I don't even know what that means, Stan. Some kind of goldfish, right?"

"You're a riot. But why don't you ask yourself why a man Cluff's age would off himself?"

"Been asking that question for the last twenty-four hours."

"So, you're confirming it's a suicide?" Forsythe said, lowering his head so he could see over his glasses. He pulled a small notepad from his pocket.

Dalton massaged both of his eyes and said, "You know I can't comment on an ongoing investigation."

"Yoo-hoo!" a voice called out from behind them. "Sheriff Dalton, yoo-hoo!" It was Janey Gladstone. He turned around and saw her coming toward him in a large-brimmed straw hat and gigantic round sunglasses. She was wrapped in a flowing paisley gown that settled around her when she stopped moving.

"If you don't give me something, people will just make up whatever they want and send it out on social media. You won't be able to get that genie back in the bottle. The internet is dry grass and people are setting off fireworks," Forsythe said.

"Sheriff?" Mrs. Gladstone said. "What are we going to do? It's all so horrible."

Dalton spun around. "What are we going to do about what?" Dalton said, turning again to make sure he knew where Forsythe was.

"About Bruce and Raylene. Mostly Raylene. I mean Bruce is, well . . . there's nothing to be done."

Forsythe raised his eyebrows to say, that's what I'm *talking* about.

Dalton tried to get to the door, but Forsythe stepped in front of him like a defensive end. He sort of wished he could handcuff the guy to the flagpole.

Mrs. Gladstone said, "I could go to the house and help clean up."

"No, Janey. You can't do that."

"It wouldn't be any trouble, Sheriff. I know where Raylene keeps the—"

"It's a crime scene, Janey. The investigators will be there all day."

"That's good. They need to be thorough. But eventually she'll need some things."

"I think she's covered for today. Please don't go to the house."

"Janey, the sheriff doesn't think we should know what's going on," Forsythe said.

"That's not it."

"Oh, Sheriff, everybody knows," Mrs. Gladstone said. "It doesn't take long."

"Look, both of you. Somebody is going to give a statement, but it's not going to be right now, and it's not going to be me who does it."

"Oh, this is all too much," Mrs. Gladstone said. "Our little town. What makes a person so sad?"

"People are thinking this suicide might be connected to the Feds coming back to shake people down for the artifacts they've collected fair and square. Once bitten, twice shy, Sheriff," Forsythe said.

"Look, don't print that, okay? People are amped up enough already. Last thing we need is one of your don't-tread-on-me rallies. This has nothing to do with federal overreach. And it would be a great idea if you wouldn't stir the pot."

"A free press keeps the windows of democracy from getting fogged up," Forsythe said.

Dalton's shoulders drooped. "I'm not going down that road with you."

"It's a shame when people are so scared of their own government. Cluff didn't do anything wrong. He just collected arrowheads and pots and whatnot. He didn't steal anything, but I'll bet he was getting heat over it."

"Nobody is investigating Bruce Cluff for stealing artifacts, Stan. I need you to be the kind of person who won't say that."

"But it's happened before. That guy in Page. He had a collection just like Bruce's. And when the system got through with him, he was dead. It's still an open wound. Last time I checked, the Constitution still has the Fourth and Fifth Amendments."

"Nobody's getting investigated for pot hunting," Dalton said.

"Stanton, which one is the Fourth?" Mrs. Gladstone asked.

"Illegal search and seizure," Forsythe said, pushing up his glasses with a middle finger.

"Oh well, people shouldn't search and seize if it's illegal," she said.

"Very true, Janey," Forsythe said. "Who watches the watchmen?"

Dalton pulled himself out of a slouch and adjusted his belt and holster. "Would it be okay if I went in and got to work?"

"It's a free country," Forsythe said.

"I would just like to help with the effort," Mrs. Gladstone said. "Nobody will tell me where I can find Raylene. Maybe LaRae will." She pushed past Dalton and headed inside the building. He considered chasing after her but didn't.

Dalton leaned into Forsythe's space. He could see the beads of sweat on Stan's brow. "So help me, Stan, this is not a puppet show."

Dalton pushed past Forsythe and went into the building. When he came to the reception area, he found Mrs. Gladstone with her bracelets draped across the high desk. LaRae was on the phone with her free hand resting lightly on Mrs. Gladstone's wrist. As he passed, he heard LaRae tell her that she would ask when they would allow Raylene to have visitors.

As Dalton opened his office door, his phone buzzed. He dug it out of his pocket and saw that it was a text from his ex-wife, Karen: I DON'T SEE THAT YOU'VE LISTED THE HOUSE YET. Three bouncing dots followed. He sat in his chair and waited. The only thing that remained of their marriage was the final paperwork. Her text balloon appeared: THE GIRLS AND I ARE STUCK AT MY PARENTS' HOUSE UNTIL YOU GET THIS DONE.

She moved out right after Christmas, and a month later she came back for the kids. These ongoing conversations seemed like pathetic cartoons. He thought about the right response. What he wanted to say was that he didn't want to sell the house, and since she'd taken everything else, maybe she could leave him something. Maybe it would be enough to remind her that he was a person with responsibilities and his work schedule didn't leave much time for real estate.

His feelings swarmed around the situation. After he came home, the VA doctor gave him some meds for anxiety, but they threw him the wrong direction, sent him into a hellscape, where it felt like somebody else was driving him around with a remote control. He'd bolt awake in the night, babbling, thinking through all the possible scenarios. Waking up dead didn't seem like the worst problem. Somebody might see suicide as a solution, but he didn't see how you'd follow through. Plenty of vets did. Guys he knew. You'd have to be determined to do it, and in a way, you'd also have to believe in something on the other side.

He picked up the phone and typed: BRUCE CLUFF KILLED HIMSELF ON SUNDAY. He watched the message change from "delivered" to "read," then he flipped the phone over and opened the email app on his computer. As his inbox number ascended, he had the feeling that before too long his office wall would be covered with photos, and he'd be connecting them with a ridiculous piece of red string.

—

Sophia stretched awake like a house cat, with a block of sunlight painted across her face and the thin plastic blinds clacking against the interior of the trailer. Birdsong filled the trees. She enjoyed the moment, then her eyes flew open. She grabbed her phone and knocked her UNESCO book to the floor. It was seven thirty. Should have been gone two hours ago.

She tore through the trailer like a cyclone, gathering her sunglasses, multi-tool, water bottle, first aid kit, sunscreen, hat, bandanna, notebook, and camera bag. When she burst through the trailer door, she nearly crushed a small brown paper sack sitting on the rubber mat in front of the folding steps. She stopped and looked across the way to Mrs. Gladstone's trailer and saw that her car was gone. She picked up the bag and opened it. Inside was a tuna salad sandwich on square wheat bread wrapped in plastic, a soft red apple with a brown gouge near the bottom, and a little bag of four Fig Newtons. There was also a note, written on an old card with a drawing of two wispy-haired babies hugging under an umbrella. Across the top it read FRIENDSHIP IS FOR KEEPS. She opened it.

Sophia, here is a lunch for you, honey. I'm sorry I wasn't around, but I had to leave early today to see after my friend, Raylene, who lost her husband. Wake me up when you get home, so I know you're okay. ♡ ♡ ♡ ♡ ♡ *Janey*

Sophia lifted her eyes and saw Mikros pacing back and forth in one of the windows of Mrs. Gladstone's trailer and could faintly hear her yap-growling.

She took the lunch and her backpack and placed them in the bed of the government-issued pickup she had been given for the duration of the grant. It was the plainest kind of vehicle possible. She got in and drove to the BLM depot and fueled up, then she continued to the grocery store. On the way into the parking lot, a turquoise F-250 cut in front of her, the driver flipping her off. She slammed on the brakes and honked, but he gunned the engine and shot in front of her, throwing a cloud of black smoke into the air, half of the truck rolling over the curb as it hit the street.

When her fury passed, she thought about how she'd have to cut corners today to get to the sites she had to measure. It was too far to make two trips, so she'd have to work late, cover everything, and drive back in the dark.

She thought about how she was all by herself in Utah, while her friends from school were doing high-profile fieldwork in Angkor Wat, Cyprus, Peru, and the Gambia. Of course, they hadn't sparred in public with a visiting scholar over cultural nationalism and UNESCO's World Heritage Site designations.

During the seminar, it hadn't seemed like a big deal. Her friends cheered her on. But when her advisor, Dr. Songetay, pulled her aside after the seminar to ask if she really had to call the visitor's work McHeritage, her heart sank.

"Was that an incorrect assessment?" Sophia defended herself.

"No, but it was unwise," he said. "You can't just hand people the tools they'll use to take you apart."

"Truth to power," she quipped.

"Well, okay," he sighed, "I'm an Ojibwe anthropologist, so trust me when I say I've seen how this plays out. You spoke truth to a guy who sits on the UNESCO executive board. Nobody is going to back your Jordan site impact proposal now. I don't like it any better than you do, but now you're a loose cannon. People won't risk that kind of trouble."

"Not even you?" she asked.

Dr. Songetay looked away and shook his head. "Maybe there's something you can do domestically, for the Park Service or BLM or something. I know some people working in Utah. I'll do what I can."

Mrs. Gladstone was so caught up in the idea of getting into the right kind of trouble, but Sophia was starting to believe there was only one kind. She parked and grabbed the lunch Mrs. Gladstone had given her and tossed the tuna sandwich into the garbage can outside the store. She thought about keeping the apple, but it was soft, so she tossed it, too. She might have saved a little time skipping this side trip, but she wasn't going to make a bad day worse by having crummy food.

She moved quickly through the tiny market, picking up a bag of beef jerky, an unblemished Fuji apple, two cans of iced tea, a box of granola bars in green wrappers, and a bag of ice. For breakfast she grabbed a sleeve of powdered sugar donuts, then traded it for a sleeve of chocolate ones, then traded back again. She paid and transferred the ice, tea, and apple into a cooler that already held three jugs of water. She drove south, out of town, past the public safety building and the BLM offices. A few minutes later, she crossed from Utah into Arizona, then a few miles later, she turned onto the Antelope Valley road, the red rock bluffs in her rearview mirror and the unfenced long-grass plains ahead. Forty miles beyond that, at the horizon, a dark stone terrace separated the high hollow sky from the planet's curve.

She had maps and a GPS, but after weeks crisscrossing a million acres, never going to the same site twice, she felt herself growing more and more comfortable navigating on her own. The distances were vast, but she was learning how to measure them by feeling the increments. She would meditate on the high school math of it: distance, rate, and time. The miles she'd already driven this morning would have taken her from Princeton to Baltimore, but she'd only cleared a few small desert towns and only just left the pavement behind. The land here was as wide and open as every cowboy song said it was, the sky immense and impossibly still. The singularity of the colors overwhelmed her, though she thought she might actually be starting to understand it.

Shortly after she had arrived in the spring, she switched from listening to music to audiobooks. The distances were too great to be measured in three-minute pop songs. Books, especially the very longest ones, put time and space into their proper proportions. She began with a memoir about women and wilderness but soon found she wanted something with a patina, so she tried Willa Cather, which was perfect for a time, but when the narration and the landscape and her work all blended together, she quit that book and decided to stay in the past but move across the Atlantic. At this point in the summer, she drove with Thomas Hardy. She was the most comfortable with a story that did not duplicate her day.

All these hours alone crisscrossing the desert weren't spelled out in the grant, but she couldn't ghost the project, not after all the strings Dr. Songetay had pulled for her. She felt lucky (but still bitter) to have found a project that would support her big idea, which was for the profession to abandon its museums and repositories and leave artifacts where they lay. She was beginning to see how professional life would be an unremitting stream of compromises. She had professional contacts here and Mrs. Gladstone, but most days she spent alone, with one exception.

As Mrs. Gladstone observed, she often tried to coordinate her research agenda to be in an area where she knew Paul Thrift, an NPS ranger, was likely to be on patrol. They first met through emails that arrived after her grant funding had come in. Those emails often began with an apology. He was sorry for the late reply. He was not often in the field station. There was no good internet connection on the monument. Cell service was unreliable. He was always willing to help, but his help always came late.

As fall arrived in Princeton, Paul's response time quickened. His answers grew longer, and around Thanksgiving, he began asking about her dissertation. They shared books and articles, maps, names of people she might reach out to. He mentioned a man named Bruce Cluff, a self-taught archeologist, who knew more about the ruins on the monument than anyone he knew. Now, she thought about Mrs. Gladstone and this man and the sadness built into human connections.

Paul Thrift had been fascinated to hear that Sophia wanted to measure the degradation of cultural sites managed by the federal government. She thought it was possible that national parks attracted destruction. He wrote in an email that it was the nature of people. Yellowjackets don't mean to ruin a picnic. They're just doing their thing. Paul admitted that he was amazed that the Department of the Interior would fund this kind of research, but he said he'd help however he could. Deep in the bleak, snow-drifted days of January, Paul told her he wished someone had started this kind of work a hundred years ago. He told her it was almost too late.

When she had finally arrived in May, she arranged to drive to the field station at the far end of the Dellenbaugh Valley at Paul's invitation. It took most of the morning to get there. The directions were good, but the road had been washed out and battered in many places, the destruction focused and intense with wide areas of sand gathered in low sections of the road. She'd been warned to keep going when she felt the wheels strain in these traps. Paul told her if you stop, you're sunk.

Eventually she came into the broad valley filled with blooming orange globe mallow like something from an impressionist painting. The small stone field house was sheltered by the talus apron of a rusty-gray serrated edge of the Kanab Plateau. The rest of the valley stretched off to the west, bisected only by a barren landing strip. The road came in straight, then hooked at a right angle a few hundred feet from the station at a sign that said GREATER DELLENBAUGH METROPOLITAN AREA. Above the house was a water catchment, a solar array, and two frantically spinning turbines. A few miles beyond the station lay a slumbering cinder cone volcano. Beyond that, the eroded blood-orange expanse of the Grand Canyon.

The station was crowded with SUVs, Boy Scouts, and their fathers, who were there for a weekend conservation project. They barely noticed her as she climbed out of the truck and gathered her bearings.

"Hey, you must be Sophia!"

She had turned, looking for a gray-bearded Edward Abbey type, but instead found a grinning bird-faced man with the build of a triathlete. He was tan as a stone, wearing gray shorts, a lightweight green T-shirt, an NPS baseball cap, and wraparound sunglasses dangling from his neck. He extended his hand. "I'm Paul. Great to meet you face-to-face. I hope you didn't have any trouble on the way in."

"No, it was uneventful. But gorgeous."

"Oh, good. Can't wait to catch up."

She noticed a thin transparent snakeskin draped over his shoulder like a dishcloth. He saw her eyes dart to it, and he lifted it carefully and draped it gently across her hands. "That's Daisy—well, actually that's old Daisy. New Daisy is back under the fridge in the equipment shed. She likes the heat from the compressor, and we don't seem to have any mouse trouble down there anymore."

"Must be nice to be able to transform at will," Sophia remembered saying, and she'd written that line in her journal after she'd returned to her trailer in town.

A jackrabbit appeared in the road, zigzagging in front of her truck as she slammed on the brakes. As the terrified thing bounded off, she gripped the wheel, her heart pounding, the remnants of that day at Dellenbaugh dissipating. Sophia held on to the memory of that snakeskin for another few moments, thinking that it was impossibly thin but utterly complete, plain but unique, a thing that would disintegrate at some point and return itself to the earth. Not gone, but something she couldn't name.

She returned to the voice of her audiobook, looking around to see that she was down in a draw. She drove to the top of a rise to get her bearings and found she was near House Rock, which was near site EV-111, the first of two stops she needed to make today. She checked the GPS and drove the last few miles before she stopped and grabbed her pack.

She hiked away from the truck, blindly following the GPS arrow into a draw that narrowed into a shrub-filled slot canyon that swallowed her up. She hiked through the labyrinth, noticing how the scrub oak clung to the rock walls. It was an hour before she climbed out, scrambled across the exposed open rock, then dropped down into another box canyon that flared and opened onto a second plain. As she went on, she fell into a meditative state. Back in Princeton, she'd tried classes and phone apps, and she always found her thoughts bouncing around. Here, mindfulness came without intent, which was a help because these sites were all new to her and her work schedule didn't allow her many opportunities to circle back. She had one chance to take it all in.

She looked at her watch to figure her position: another thirty minutes. The curved layers of sandstone wound past an arroyo, and beyond it was a section of cliff that curved under like something that should collapse but has refused to. She continued down a gentle slope following the cliff, and without warning a delicate stone structure with three dark square windows and a small rectangular doorway appeared. The sight of it raised the hair on her arms.

She unslung her pack and pulled out the paperwork, reread the description to see that it matched. The photocopied black-and-white photograph was identical, taken from almost the same vantage point. She double-checked the GPS unit. The reading also matched. Here she set about her work. She measured plants in the area, checked the soil moisture, took photographs with a digital camera, logged the image numbers on a printed spreadsheet, then sketched the features in the wall that would not show up in the photos. After she gathered the data requested by the NPS archeologist, she zipped up her pack and stood before the dwelling. This site was difficult to get to. She wondered why it was on her list. How could something this remote be at risk?

She put her head through the center window. On the floor, in a shaft of yellow midday light, sat an intact clay vessel, partially buried in the gray sand.

It was pear-shaped with a faded zigzagging chain of squares and lines like the markings on a snake. In the dust alongside the vessel were the complete woven remains of a lone sandal.

She pulled a different notebook from her pack and drew more small sketches. They were quick but remarkably fine. As she drew, she noticed small Y-shaped disturbances in the dust. In the far corner of the room was the random stick assemblage of a pack rat nest. She wanted to get closer, and the door would give her access, but she didn't want to indulge the temptation or explain herself to anyone about how she had damaged the site with a stumble or a wrong step. She would have to record her own impacts.

When she finished drawing, she drank some water and ate a granola bar. She marked the sun's altitude and checked her watch. There would be just enough time to return to her truck and make the second stop. With the sun flaring behind her, she backtracked over the sandstone and through the canyons, this time thinking of the site and the quiet majesty of the remnants of these lives.

When she reached the truck, she was hot and out of water. She pulled one of the canned iced teas from the cooler and rubbed it across her neck in a way that would have been embarrassing if somebody else had seen her doing it. She drank half the tea, dropped her pack behind the seat, adjusted the GPS for the next stop, and drove on, sipping the tea until it was gone.

She drove for thirty minutes to the south, the smaller roads joining successively larger, smoother ones as the hills flattened out. The Hurricane Cliffs emerged from the horizon like a fleet of ships. At one of the triangular crossroads, Sophia came upon the turquoise Ford pickup that had cut her off at the grocery store. The wheel wells and rearview mirrors were over-sprayed with orange dirt. The tailgate was down, showing that the workbox in the back was open on both sides, with its tiny diamond plate wings frozen mid-flap.

During her orientation, she'd been told to always check on a stopped vehicle. It was an ounce-of-prevention approach, they said. Sometimes a pound of cure was too little too late. She slowed and saw that nobody was inside, so she parked in front of it and got out. This section of the monument was multiple-use land, so sometimes there were people running cows, buzzing around on four-wheelers, treasure hunting, flying drones, taking pictures. According to Paul, most of the people out here were looking for something they'd found on Instagram. They had no idea just how dangerous it was to be this far from the pavement in a part of the world the invisible tether of cell towers didn't reach.

The cab of the truck was filled with paper cups and fast food bags. A small plastic skull hung from the rearview mirror. There was a deer rifle on a rack in the back window. She put her hand on the hood. The engine wasn't ticking. She walked to the back and noticed a large map spread on the tailgate, weighed down on each of its four corners with a stone, a thermos, a boot, and an open can of beer in a foam koozie that said ASU SUN DEVILS.

The map was hand drawn with old, delicately inked contour lines of varying thickness that had been rendered with a nib pen. The landforms had been shaded with hairline hatch marks to give them a sense of solidity and weight. In various areas, there were carefully rendered crimson rectangles filled with dots of the same color. Next to each dot was a small number that corresponded to a legend on the left side, which named some sites on the lists given to her by the archeologist. There were two sets of initials—KT and PT—scattered across the maps, with dates next to them. Some of the dates were quite recent. Quite a few of the sites she did not recognize. The map was exquisite, and she felt a larcenous impulse to run off with it. Maybe she could just snap a picture.

"Hey," somebody shouted. She looked up past the truck and saw the silhouettes of two men up on the rim of a layer cake bluff a dozen yards from the vehicles. One was tall and thin and off-kilter. The other one looked like a burnt stump.

"You guys need any help?" she called out. "Looked like you might have broken down or something."

The short one spread his arms to each side and called back, "It's all good. We're prepared for self-rescue. How about you?" His voice was coarse and accusatory.

"I work out here, so yeah, I'm ready. I was wondering if you had a permit for—"

"Okay, lady BLM," the short one interrupted, "if we *were* broke down, could you call out of here on your radio?"

Sophia didn't want to tell them that she did not have a radio, but she didn't want to remain silent either, especially if she could stop them from doing something that couldn't be fixed. The truck outed her as a Fed, but they didn't know she had no real authority. She looked back at her truck, then remembered she'd been told to leave the scene if there was trouble.

"It's so easy to get hurt out here," the short one shouted.

"Specially when you're all by yourself," the tall one finished. "Two's better than one."

Sophia stepped back so their truck was between them, offering some cover if the bottom dropped out of this thing. She considered getting out of there right away, but she hesitated, trying to work out a plan to get another look at that map.

After a moment, the short one barked, "She's nobody. Get her away from the truck."

The tall one stumbled down one side of the bluff, collapsing the ground under his feet as he went. He dropped, howling, in a cloud of dust, and in the confusion, Sophia ran back to her truck and drove off.

She checked her mirrors every few seconds, thinking maybe she could give these two the slip if she pulled onto a side road, but she decided it was safer to stay out in the open. When the road straightened out, she sped up but backed off when she imagined what getting a flat would do to this situation.

After thirty minutes of empty rearview mirror, she pulled over and wrote everything down, scribbling for nearly a page until she realized she didn't get the license plate. There was no way she could make her report and get to the rest of sites on her list, which meant she was going to have to come back on her day off. Furious, she opened her cooler and ate while she drove.

Two hours later she walked into the BLM offices, and the only person there was a bored intern, who handed her an incident form.

"Do you get a lot of these reports?" Sophia asked.

"Nope. I mean, I don't, but they say this kind of thing happens all the time."

"And nobody reports it?"

The intern shrugged. "That's how it goes out there. It's, like, the Wild West, right?"

"Where is everybody, anyway?"

"At meetings in St. George."

Sophia frowned and filled out the report, transcribing her notes onto the form. When she handed it back, the intern took it and set it on the left side of her desk, then decided it was better to put it in an empty basket on the other side.

Sophia drove back to her trailer and took a shower, but she really wanted a bath. She drank a beer, emailed Paul about her experience, and told him to watch out for a turquoise Ford. Who knew when he would get the message, but she sent it anyway. Her head dropped to the pillow, then she remembered Mrs. Gladstone's request, so she pulled herself out of bed and slipped her feet into her sandals.

The summer twilight was still luminous as she crossed to the other trailer. Mikros barked and then retreated as she knocked. Mrs. Gladstone was asleep in her chair with her mouth open and her head back. Mikros was now on top of the chair, and she scrambled up to the counter and began eating something out of a green ceramic bowl. Sophia carefully opened the door and crept inside. She found some paper and a pen and wrote:

Mrs. G—I made it back safe and sound. It got a little crazy out there. I'll tell you about it later. Thanks for the lunch. Tomorrow I go up to Bryce for my big presentation in the lodge. I hope you were able to take care of your friend, and I'm sorry for her loss.
Sophia

She tucked the note under the television remote that sat on the table next to Mrs. Gladstone's chair. Mikros turned her head from the bowl, lowered it, and growled. Sophia backed her way to the door and let herself out.

Day Three

Fake news : *Far from the Madding Crowd* : A time of reinvention : Death by PowerPoint

S heriff Dalton stood outside the HooDoo Diner, staring through the window, shading his eyes with one hand. He carried a copy of the *Red Rock Times* folded in thirds under his arm. The door opened, a bell jingled, and a heavyset man in denim overalls came out, working a toothpick in his mouth. "Stan's in his regular spot," he said, trundling past.

"Am I that obvious, Pete?"

"Pretty much," he said without stopping.

Dalton yanked open the door and went through.

"It's a heck of a thing," the woman behind the register said.

Dalton held up the paper. "I know."

"I meant Bruce. Didn't figure him for it," she said. "They say his wife found him. Is that true? Because if it is, I don't know what kind of world we're living in anymore."

"Can't talk about it," Dalton said.

"It's okay. I understand. I just wanted to say something."

"Jenny, I'd speak to it if I could."

"I know. You're a good man. Can I get you something?"

"How 'bout a piece of Stan Forsythe?"

Jenny slapped Dalton's shoulder and pointed to where Stan was sitting.

Forsythe was spread out across the whole table, an iPad on one side, a legal pad on the other, a plate with the remnants of his breakfast in the middle. He was scraping the last of his hash browns through a streak of ketchup. When he saw Dalton, he sat up and said, "Let me explain," right as Dalton lobbed a copy of the paper into the center of Forsythe's plate.

"There was still good food on there," Forsythe said.

Dalton pointed to the headline: ARE THE FEDS BACK FOR YOUR POTS? Stan looked down with a fork and knife sticking out of his fists.

"*That* is garbage, Stan," Dalton said. "Completely false."

"Garbage and falsehood are not contraries, Sheriff, and besides, a question can't be true or false. This is meant to provide my readers an opportunity to ask questions and reflect. It's called critical thinking. Backbone of a free democracy."

"I'm not here to split hairs."

Stan lifted the paper from his plate and turned it over, ketchup side up. "Splitting hairs requires a delicacy that is missing from this morning's repartee." He folded the paper in half the other way and set it aside, then looked at his plate and decided he was done.

"I told you we'd be issuing a statement," Dalton said.

"I'm sure you will, but in the vacuum caused by your bureaucratic punctiliousness, a whole town is wondering why a pillar of their community took his own life on a morning he might normally have been found in church." Stan gestured to the diner. Dalton looked around to see everyone frozen, watching him. Stan lifted a half-empty glass of orange juice and toasted Dalton.

"Don't you have some oath to do no harm?"

"I'm a newspaperman, not a Greek physician. I ran a story with the best information available at the time. And if you had read past the lede, you might have noticed that the article doesn't point a finger at anyone, it merely recalls comparable events from a few years ago in an attempt to make certain the citizens of our community don't jump to any rash or uninformed conclusions. I mean, really, Sheriff. Those who do not remember the past are doomed to repeat it."

Someone in the diner shouted, "Yes!"

Dalton looked around and lowered his voice, "There's all kinds of reasons for a person to take his life that have nothing to do with federal government. You planted that idea in people's heads, and now you're responsible for it. Couple of months ago I went to the doctor for a pain in my eye. Thought I was going blind. Doctor said when you hear hoofbeats, think horses, not zebras."

Forsythe made a show of thinking about what Dalton said. "What was wrong with your eye?" he eventually asked.

"That ain't the point."

"You brought it up."

"Plugged tear duct."

"That's awful. I had that happen to a salivary gland once. Fixed it with some of those sour candies."

Dalton scowled. "This is an ongoing investigation."

"I never said Bruce killed himself *because* of the Feds. That story was just a little history to provide context. When you've got something for me to print, I'll print it. Were it left to me to decide whether we should have a government without newspapers or newspapers without a government, I should not hesitate a moment to prefer the latter," Forsythe said.

Dalton threw up his hands. "I don't know what you're talking about."

"You know who said that?"

Dalton shrugged.

"Thomas Jefferson. The primary author of the Declaration of Independence. Governor of Virginia. Secretary of state. Third president of—"

"I know who Thomas Jefferson was," Dalton shouted, then he composed himself. "I'm just saying you made my job about a thousand times more difficult. You get this town tied up in knots, and we'll have more grief on our hands than what we've got right now." Dalton didn't wait for a response. He walked to the register. Before he could ask for it, Jenny had a Diet Coke ready in a to-go cup with a straw. He took a twenty out of his wallet and said, "Thank you. This is for that muckraker's breakfast. Please keep the change."

On the counter by the register was a line of business cards in little plastic holders. He noticed that three of them were for real estate agents. He took one of each and stuffed them into his shirt pocket. "I'm sorry for turning your place into a dinner theater," he said.

"It's okay. We're still doing breakfast," Jenny said with a wink.

—

Sophia turned off the highway and followed the long line of taillights that led through the crowded cluster of hotels, gas stations, and fake frontier buildings outside of Bryce Canyon. She was listening to the audiobook of *Far from the Madding Crowd*, and she thought to herself how ironic it was that the only traffic she dealt with anymore was in national parks.

She had been listening to a section of the book where Bathsheba and Troy encountered a pregnant woman on the road who was destitute and making her way painfully toward the Casterbridge workhouse. She was Fanny, Troy's old love. Troy sent Bathsheba ahead in the carriage before she could recognize the woman, then he gave Fanny all the money in his pocket. She spent the last of her strength reaching her destination, and a few hours later, she died in childbirth, along with the baby. Their coffin was later brought to Troy and Bathsheba, who discovered the two bodies inside.

As Sophia sat in the backed-up traffic, waiting to get through the entry station, she thought about the bodies she'd seen in museums, mummies desiccated and sometimes entwined. She thought about the ones she'd seen in photographs curled together in stone burial cists. One pairing from Mexico was layered in yellow and blue feathers, the bodies decorated with turquoise. Sophia realized that behind all the data, context, and information, there was a great sadness to the ruins she studied, a sorrow the artifacts would only sometimes reveal. The rest of the stories came from what Dr. Songetay called a historical imagination. He caught hell for that term from his colleagues but never walked it back.

The swirl of thoughts triggered by her book, and the idea of mummies trapped forever in museums, made her eyes misty. The whole purpose of Thomas Hardy was to give her something to think about that wasn't archeological, but at this point in her life, her work was a black hole that pulled everything into it. At the entry station to Bryce Canyon, she could have used her government plate to skirt the line, but she wanted to talk to her friend Lucy, who was working the gate today. She even moved over, so she'd be in her lane, then she rolled down her window and waited. The two of them met during the seasonal employee orientation. Lucy smiled when she saw her.

While Lucy helped visitors on the other side, Sophia checked her phone for messages.

"Oh crap, are you crying?" Lucy asked, pointing to Sophia's face.

"Me?" Sophia said, dabbing her eye with the pad of her finger. "No. Well, yes. It's this stupid audiobook I'm listening to. I should stick with the Shins, right?"

"How's the research?"

"It's good. I need to crunch some numbers, though."

"I'd love to get out in the field," Lucy said, gesturing to her sandstone enclosure and the lines of cars. "What book is it?"

"*Far from the Madding Crowd*," Sophia said.

"I love that book. Well, I saw the movie," Lucy said.

Sophia sat straight. "Both are good. I better get moving before they honk. It's been a crazy couple of days. I'll take you out sometime and we can catch up. Text me."

"Yes. You're doing a talk at the lodge today, right?"

"Yep. I'm supposed to share my research project with the taxpayers. Here's to transparency."

"Right? I will be stuck out here. So, break a leg." Lucy gave her a double thumbs-up.

Sophia passed through the entry gate, crossing the threshold from the regular world to the front country of the park, the most artificial of transitions. She pulled ahead, plodding along with the rest of the traffic past the visitor's center with its stone, timber, and glass architecture—half college campus, half shopping mall—designed for the visitor who can't be without amenities for even an afternoon.

Sophia meandered through the parking lot and turned down the incline to the drab backside of the building where the staff parked. It reminded her of the false front sets on a movie backlot; with two and a half million pairs of eyes on the front, there's no sense wasting money where it won't be seen. In 1916, when they set up the National Park Service, they couldn't have imagined all this.

As she was parking, she ran the legislative language through her head: parks were meant to preserve the scenery and nature and historical objects, and somehow also leave them unimpaired. All these buildings and roads and buses seemed like the opposite of preservation. Not all the parks were circuses like this one, though. Where she was doing her fieldwork, there was only back-country, no offices or kiosks, no pavement or parking lots. The contrast was extreme. Everyone working for the Park Service or the BLM seemed to understand these contradictions, but all of it was complicated. Learning the ins and outs clarified very little.

She took her backpack to the door, where she punched in a key code. The air was filled with a deep pine scent and the hush of the ponderosas. It seemed like a shame to come up here just to go inside, but she had paperwork to complete before her presentation, or she wouldn't get paid. She was also hoping to grab a few minutes of the park archeologist's time.

She headed upstairs and checked her small mail cubby. Inside was a news-letter, an invitation to a potluck for seasonal employees, and a schedule of her interpretive presentations for the rest of the summer. There were three more to do after this one. She stuffed everything into her backpack and went down the hall to the archeologist's office, whose door was open.

"Hi, Dalinda," Sophia said. "You got a minute?"

Dalinda looked up and cracked a smile, followed by an eye roll that Sophia wasn't sure how to interpret. She was wearing the gray-and-green uniform, her hair in a bun. Sophia's eyes lingered on Dalinda's silver, turquoise, and coral earrings. When Dalinda relaxed her smile, her crow's feet disappeared. Sophia then noticed her desk, which was strewn with three-ring binders. "Come in and sit," Dalinda said. "I'm just finishing an email."

"If you're busy, I can—"

"It'll be worse later," Dalinda said, beckoning.

Sophia set her backpack on the floor and sat down while Dalinda returned to her typing.

The office walls were covered in maps. A few were framed watercolors capturing the exquisite misapprehensions nineteenth-century cartographers had about the American West. The rest were working maps thumbtacked to the wall and flagged with notes on colored squares. They were plain but beautiful in their own way, like mathematical formulas, exact where the others were imagined. One displayed the distribution of debitage in lithic scatters. Another revealed stratigraphic layers of Indigenous habitations. Each map told a different story of the people who once lived here. Sophia thought about how maps charted space but also invoked time. Every map described a place but also told a story about the thoughts and attitudes of the age that produced it.

Sophia unzipped her backpack, took out a notebook, and wrote that idea down.

Another of Dalinda's maps showed an array of sacred sites in the park. This one had been marked and amended by hand many times. It was part of an ethnographic project Dalinda was working on with tribal liaisons. Native people had been bitten by the government so many times, the project was constantly at risk. So much of the information here was protected. Somebody couldn't just walk in and get access to it, even with a Freedom of Information Act request.

A confidentiality clause had been built into Sophia's grant project. She would have to redact sensitive information about cultural sites when she wrote her dissertation. The complexity of the laws and regulations pertaining to federal land made her head spin. It was a whirlwind of acronyms. It was all meant to protect park resources from looters and vandals and the negligence of tourists, but these directives often looked backward, overlooking contemporary Native peoples, the way their lives and concerns were unfolding. An exhibit in a visitor's center might present traditional agriculture methods, but it won't say a thing about a tribe's struggle with diabetes.

Her mind jumped to a lecture where she remembered the professor saying that our laws were simply a catalog of our injustices to one another. Legislation is always written in hindsight, by the victors, who revere the vanquished but turn a blind eye to the survivors.

She nodded to herself and wrote that down, too.

"Okay," Dalinda said. "Sophia Shepard, it is good to see you. What's up?"

"I'm freaking out a little about this presentation," Sophia said, a little nervous about skipping the small talk. She tucked her notebook back in the bag and zipped it up. "I mean, I teach undergrad classes at Princeton, but doing this is just—I don't know—it feels like some armchair archeologist is going to pounce on me and wreck everything."

"That is one-hundred-percent guaranteed to happen. An hour on the internet beats an advanced degree." Dalinda stretched in her chair. "I took a look at the slides you sent. You're going to do fine."

"I'm not just worried about the visitors. It's having you and the superintendent there."

Dalinda's face dropped. "About that. The superintendent can't come. He has a funeral down in Kanab today. It's a sad story."

"Is it for the guy who—"

"Bruce Cluff," Dalinda said. "He was an amateur collector who knew everybody. Apparently, he took his own life Sunday."

"I heard. That's terrible," Sophia said.

Dalinda motioned for Sophia to close her door. When it was shut, Dalinda leaned forward and said, "I don't want to speak ill of the dead, but Cluff has been a problem for us for a very long time."

"Oh," Sophia said. "I didn't know."

"Cluff was tight with his senators, so he got special consideration he didn't deserve. He did whatever he wanted and never checked with us. And he never got busted for it. If the Paiutes had Cluff's access and influence, we'd be doing very different jobs right now."

"That drives me out of my mind," Sophia said.

"It is what it is," Dalinda said, leaning back in her chair. "You've seen what it's like around here, white guys calling the shots, sweeping Native people under the rug. When the tribes push back, they're told to sit down, shut up, and mind their own business. Status quo is as status quo does."

Sophia froze, her jaw set and her mouth a straight line.

"You know the Native population of the county you're working in is less than two percent," Dalinda continued.

"What?"

"Yes, one point five five percent, actually. It's not a mistake that you don't see them. It's a hundred and fifty years of concerted effort. For a while in the eighties, tribes had a seat at the table, but they've been shut out again."

"But it's *their* table," Sophia said.

Dalinda nodded. "You are correct. Congress is ready to sell off the parks to energy companies for pennies on the dollar, but if anyone starts talking about giving it back . . ."

"How do you keep going?" Sophia asked.

"I'm an optimist. That's why I sit all day, sending emails into the void," Dalinda said, gesturing around her. She made an exasperated face that softened into a crooked kind of half smile. "We're doing good work, Sophia. It's hard, but it's worth it. We make progress despite everything. It's not a straight line, but it's something."

Sophia sat up and thought about the coils of bureaucracy that were looping silently around her. It was a strange world, equal parts hope and cynicism. How could you ever survive it? Sophia realized time was getting away from her, and she had much to do, so she queued up her other question. "Dalinda, have you ever been threatened when you're working? Sorry to just change direction on you." Sophia was nervous about putting the question out there. She didn't want to seem naïve, but she also realized maybe this wasn't something to fool around with.

"That's okay. You mean, like, out in the field?"

"Yeah. Yesterday a couple of guys near Antelope Flats made some threats."

"I'm sorry," she said. "It's pretty common, I'm afraid. What did they look like?"

"One was tall. The other short. They were weird, like cartoons. Drove a turquoise pickup. I forgot to get the plate."

"Don't worry about that. It sounds like you came across the Ashdowns. They're poachers and pot hunters—goons. A month ago, somebody reported them trying to yank a petroglyph panel off a cliff wall with that truck and a tow chain."

"You've got to be kidding. How come they're not in jail?"

"We've got bigger fish to fry and not enough evidence to build a case. All it takes is money, which is in short supply these days. Did those knuckle draggers shoot at you?"

"No. Just verbal threats. Intimidation. They suggested that I could get hurt out there. It was so stupid. I filed a report at the BLM offices in Kanab."

"Okay, that's good, but they are so shorthanded down there, who knows if anything will come out of it. If you see those two again, call dispatch, okay?"

"I don't have a radio."

"What? They didn't . . ." Dalinda was beside herself. She pulled a notepad close and wrote something down.

"They had this hand-drawn map, which they were obviously using to dig stuff up."

"The thing is, everybody's got a map," Dalinda sighed. "And they all think they're going to strike it rich. I've only seen a couple maps that are even in the ballpark. Leave those guys to law enforcement."

"All right," Sophia said.

"But I am going to get you a radio. We've got policies about that. And I'm pissed that they sent you off without one."

"I am, too, now that I know they were supposed to give me one but didn't. Thank you."

There was a ping from Dalinda's computer, and she cursed under her breath. "I'm so sorry," she said. "I've got to respond to this. Another fire. Some ranger broke into a meeting in Denver—never mind. Good luck, Sophia. You'll do us proud. I'll try to make it over, but if this Denver thing comes off the rails, it'll wreck my whole afternoon."

"It sounds awful," Sophia said, gathering her stuff. She took another look around Dalinda's office and tried to imagine herself in the archeologist's place, juggling fieldwork and bureaucracy. It didn't feel like a good fit for her.

"And really," Dalinda said, "I'm going to get you a radio. I'm the worst mentor."

"No, you're amazing," Sophia said. On the way out, she asked if Dalinda wanted the door open or closed.

"Closed," she said. "All the way, please."

—

The Ashdown brothers barreled down the winding double lanes of the Virgin River Highway. The steep gray stone walls of the gorge shot skyward as they descended. Lonnie watched for the open spaces that would momentarily reveal terraces of Joshua trees receding into the sunlit alcoves. The view would open for a second, then disappear.

As they dropped in elevation, the air temperature rose. Lonnie tested it by laying the back of his hand against the windshield. It was still desert here but completely unlike their home in Cane Beds. They rode together in silence with the stereo off and Byron hunched over the wheel, his jaw clenching and releasing without pattern. When Lonnie reached for the radio knob, Byron slapped his hand without looking.

"It's a long time to have zero music," Lonnie said.

"I need quiet. I'm thinking," Byron answered.

"About what?"

Byron turned his head and glowered at him. Lonnie got nervous and pointed to the road ahead of them, which was curving. When the rumble strip buzzed, Byron turned his attention back to the road without speaking. After a spell, he said, "I'm thinking about what that girl's gonna say."

"She didn't know what we were doing."

"But she'll probably say something, right? You know, since she works for the Feds."

"Nobody will find us because we're not there anymore."

They both squinted as the sun broke through the mouth of the canyon and they shot out into the open desert. The light was blinding on the open plain, which ran unobstructed to the dark hulking mountains at the horizon. Byron pulled a pair of cheap orange-and-black sunglasses from the visor. Lonnie lowered his visor and tested the heat again.

"At least we got the maps, and you put them in something for protection," Lonnie said, reaching his hand back to knock on a cardboard tube sitting in the gun rack. "And they work. I mean, we found a couple pots without really trying. That's something. Plus the money we're gonna get from this guy. I'm just worried about what happened to that old man."

"Yep, the maps worked. That's what I was trying to figure out." Byron shook his head. Three birds followed each other through the air in front of the truck and disappeared through the raised arms of a Joshua tree. "What happened to the old guy is why we need more money now. We're gonna have to lay low. We'd be okay if we were just trading this stuff for cash, because it was supposed to be break and enter, take the maps, steal some other household things, couple of pots, a rug, get out, and nobody knows nothing. Now there's a dead guy and we didn't negotiate for that. How long you think it's gonna be before somebody figures out none of it is what it looks like?"

"I don't know. Couple of weeks?" Lonnie said.

"You really don't get it? What that guy had us do was just to slow them down. Once they start doing the science on us, we're screwed."

"DNA?" Lonnie asked.

"DNA, chemistry, microscopes, you name it. They're going to figure it out, so if you quit talking to me for a minute, maybe I can think."

"So, no radio, then?"

Byron hit the brakes and yanked the truck over to the side of the road. A minivan behind them blared its horn and swerved around the truck. Byron gripped the wheel and stared straight ahead, snorting and sucking air through his nose like a bull.

"You want me to get out and walk?" Lonnie asked.

"Walk to where?" Byron yelled back.

"I don't know, you pulled over, just like Mom."

"You realize we're not playing a video game, right? You know there's no reset button on this thing."

"I'm not stupid."

"Braining that guy is pretty much the definition of stupid."

"I know it. But saying the word 'stupid' doesn't help."

"Jail is full of morons, Lonnie. Overflowing with them."

"Doing something stupid is not the same thing as *being* stupid. Remember, I said if they put you back in jail I'd be alone again. Dad's gone. So is Mom. So. I had to do something. If we got caught, okay. Then maybe I could just go back there with you."

Byron looked across the interstate at the abandoned two-story house and the cluster of mobile homes that squatted behind it. "Alone is better than that place, little brother." He rolled down the window, spat once, then rolled the window back up.

"I take it back, then," Lonnie said.

"Well, you can't."

"Not what I did, just what I meant by it." Lonnie turned toward the window. "Maybe jail is a good place for you."

Byron checked his mirror. He waited for a semi to pass, then he lurched back onto the road. After they got up to eighty, Lonnie reached for the radio. Byron didn't stop him. They drove that way, listening to classic rock, for another fifteen minutes, then they exited the freeway on the south end of town and parked in the CasaBlanca Casino, where they were supposed to meet the guy who would take the maps and pay them off.

"We're early," Lonnie said.

"Early is on time." Byron fished a small spearmint tin out of his pocket and twisted off the lid. He leaned over and opened the glove box and took out a banged-up empty ballpoint pen barrel.

"Oh, man," Lonnie said. "Do you have to?"

"Don't want to hear it."

"Meth makes you crazy."

Byron stuck the pen down into the tin and snorted quickly, rubbing the side of his nose with a knuckle. He did it again on the other side, stuck the empty pen into his shirt pocket, and closed up the tin. "Let's do it," Byron said, sniffing rapidly.

"He ain't gonna be here for, like, an hour."

"Early bird gets the worm."

"Maybe." Lonnie said. "But the second mouse gets the cheese."

Byron laughed, then let it decay to a frown. Lonnie knew his brother was starting to feel okay, but he also knew that feeling would change into something horrible.

"Second mouse. That's a good one," Byron said.

"It's not me. Some guy had it on a T-shirt," Lonnie said.

They got out of the truck and looked around. Byron carried the cardboard tube with the maps. Lonnie walked along, with his hands in his front pockets. There was no sidewalk, so they headed through the heat toward the front doors. As they drew closer, they heard the patter of a waterfall that marked the end of the covered valet parking zone. The whole area was blooming with bright red flowers and surrounded by dwarf palm trees. A dry wind blew through the brittle fronds. Lonnie reached over and pulled off some flower petals to see if they were real. He cupped them in his hand and sniffed. They smelled like his mother's perfume.

They went in through the sliding doors and were accosted by the clamor. Instantly, they were hit with the smell of cigarettes and air conditioning, and they were overwhelmed by the sheer number of slot machines, each one playing its own repetitive melody that gathered into a flapping, clicking, boinging sonic wave. Lonnie thought it sounded like a gigantic toy orchestra tuning in a great, infinite loop, but he kept that idea to himself because his brother wouldn't understand it.

Byron stopped, sizing up the room. Almost everyone there was stone-faced with small plastic buckets of coins. The real gambling was farther in, where no-body would be distracted by people coming and going. Lonnie started to look around. "Hey," Byron said. "We need to pick the right place."

"Didn't you tell him where to meet us?"

"I said in the bar. He doesn't get to decide the details. I set this part up."

"Han Solo would choose there." Lonnie pointed to a corner with a round table and a booth against the wall.

"That's a good pick," Byron said, and he followed his brother but sped past him so he could sit in the corner. "You get the chair."

They sat, and Byron arranged the cardboard tube so it could be seen at a distance. He set his truck keys on the table with a clunk, the heavy brass skull keychain lying on its side, the twin ruby eyes glinting. A pair of fake palm trees curved through the stale air overhead, and their table gave them a panorama of the entry. "This'll be good," Byron said, nodding over and over in a way that started looking crazy. A minute or so later, a waitress in a tight black skirt and pantyhose stopped at their table and set down a couple of coasters. Her name tag said CJ, HOMETOWN NASHVILLE.

"How about a shot of Lord Calvert?" Byron said, both hands curled into fists on the table.

"No Calvert, but we've got Jim Beam," she said. "Will that work?"

Byron's face fell. "Fine," he said, spitting the *f*.

"How about you?" she said, turning to Lonnie.

"Beer is all."

"Oh, honey, don't make me run through the list."

"Hamm's, I guess," Lonnie said.

"How about a Coors? It's on tap."

"It's not my favorite, but okay. And some cheese fries—chili cheese fries."

"Y'all are so metal," she said.

After she left, Byron leaned forward with his elbows on the table. "I don't need you crapping your pants from all that grease."

"I'm starving. What good is being here early if we just have to sit here dealing with a skipped breakfast."

"Being hungry keeps you sharp."

"Agree to disagree," Lonnie said.

The drinks came. One shot glass. One beer. Napkins. Lonnie filled one cheek with air, passed it over to the other. Byron bit his nails, took out a pocketknife, cut his cuticles with the scissors. A group of people in the same color jackets moved through the space, heads pointed in every direction. Walls staying in one place. Lights just sitting there. People twitching at the slots, moving like broken machines. Chili cheese fries. Hot, salty, soft. Byron didn't want any. Pushed the plate away when Lonnie offered it. A person stood behind someone at the slot machine. She set a hand on his shoulder. Jackpot. Coins spilled into the bucket but it was too much and overflowed. The rest went into an empty glass. She went away and came back, handed him a drink, took the coin glass. Their waitress appeared, waved her hand. Byron sat up and handed her his shot glass. She came back with a beer, set it down, took the empty glass, plate, napkins. A group of girlfriends moved across the room. The one in the middle pulled up her shirt for a photo. Lonnie pointed. The girls vanished. Lonnie looked again. The space suddenly filled with friends with white beach towels draped around their necks. In the distance a guy was checking in at the front desk with fat arms, a mullet, and a spray tan. A guy in a silver suit walked past, sizing him up, a small box of chips under one arm and a highball glass in the other. Some guy kicked a slot machine. His stool went over. Nobody seemed to notice. One waitress (not theirs) started yelling at another waitress (also not theirs). She just stood there and took it. Byron's jaw muscles flexed, and he took hold of the tip of his ponytail and tickled it across his cheeks.

"I've got a bad feeling about this," Byron said. He moved the tip of his ponytail over to his lips.

"You should quit playing with your hair if you want this guy to think you're somebody to worry about," Lonnie said, then he looked down for his fries and realized the plate had already been taken.

"It's soothing," Byron said.

"Also, not tough."

"Am I supposed to skip my self-care?"

"Maybe you wouldn't need so much self-care if you weren't always gearing yourself up."

"Really?" Byron said. "You're going to lay that on me?"

Lonnie shrugged.

"I should have done this by myself," Byron said.

"How will we know it's him?" Lonnie asked, trying to change the subject.

"He said he'll know *us*."

"And you don't think that's weird?" Lonnie said. "What if this guy is the cops?"

"Would the cops have told us how to clean up your mess?"

Lonnie thought about it, but before he could answer, Byron did it for him. "One thing—I always know when it's the cops."

"Must have picked that up in prison," Lonnie said.

Byron leapt across the table and grabbed his brother by the shirt. "Enough," he said. "No more talking. We're gonna do our business, then we're out of here." When people looked over, Byron let go and sat back. After a few seconds, things returned to normal.

Lonnie pointed out all the people. "Maybe our kind of business needs a private place."

"We do this in private, and he'll kneel us down and put a bullet in the back of our skulls. I picked this spot on purpose. It's strategic."

There was a crash, and the Ashdowns turned. A guy with sculpted sideburns and his cap on backward lurched through the crowd. Two casino bulls were behind him. They grabbed him by the shirt and pushed him out the front doors, knocking his cap to the ground. One of the bulls stopped and picked up the cap, carried it to the door, and threw it after the man, who didn't even pick it up. He just stood there, screaming, flipping them off with both hands.

"That's me on the inside," Lonnie said.

"What?" Byron said.

Lonnie checked for the missing plate again. "Never mind," he said.

The waitress appeared. "Can I get you guys anything else?"

But before either of them could answer, a man in a silver suit handed the waitress two twenties and said, "They're all done." The man was neither small nor large, and his face was tan, like a hide. His chin was lowered, and he stared out from the tops of his eyes. The fabric of his suit caught the lights of the room and made him look like someone who ought to be on stage. He set a Walmart sack on the table, pulled out a chair, and sat down without saying hello, interlacing his fingers to make a single, giant fist.

"You must be Byron and Lonnie," he said.

"Maybe," Byron said.

The man opened his hands and said, "Well, I'm Nick Scissors."

"What's in the bag?" Byron asked.

"A surprise," Scissors said. "For the both of you."

"From Walmart? Nice," Byron scoffed.

"You go to war with the big-box retailer you have, not the one you wish you had," Scissors said, leaning forward. "A news item in your local paper confirms that you two followed my instructions. I had my doubts, but I stand corrected. Consider this a bonus." He patted the bag and smiled.

"You mean, like employees of the month?" Lonnie asked.

"Something like that. You have the maps?"

Byron pointed to the tube.

"Well, that's just a tube, isn't it?" Scissors said.

"They're in there. You can check," Byron said. "Besides, that's how you told me to do it."

Scissors kept his eyes on Byron. "I want you to look around this room, up at the ceiling. Start at one o'clock. Don't move your head, just the eyes." Byron looked. "Okay, now three, seven, nine, and eleven. I realize you can't see your seven."

"Cameras?" Lonnie asked.

"This location was not a stupid choice, Mr. Ashdown," Scissors said. "The anonymity of this carnival, and the panopticon surrounding us makes certain everyone minds their p's and q's."

"What does panopticon mean?" Byron said.

"It means, we're not going to roll out this transaction in plain sight, but . . . an exchange will take place," Scissors said.

"It's simpler than you're saying. You give us the money. I leave the maps sitting right here." Byron said, gesturing to the tube with a nod. "We take off, then you stick around for a while."

Scissors reached into the side pocket of his suit coat and held out his hand. He relaxed his grip slightly; a brass skull dropped and spun on its chain.

"Hey, wait," Byron said, a look of panic streaking across his face.

"You'll leave when I decide you can go," Scissors said.

"When did you—" Byron said.

"Trade secrets, friend. A magician never tells you how the trick is done. Feel around on the floor," Scissors directed.

Byron moved his boots from side to side and he kicked a small package. "What's that?" he said.

"There are two envelopes, one for each of you. I took the liberty of dividing your fee up front . . . in the interest of family harmony."

Lonnie smiled and gave a tiny fist pump. Byron glared at his brother. Lonnie lifted his eyebrows and said, "What? I trust you." When Byron looked back at Scissors, he was holding the cardboard tube.

"Hold on a minute," Byron said.

Scissors stood and slipped the tube almost invisibly inside his jacket. "Open your bag," he said.

Lonnie grabbed the bag and ripped it open. Inside was a pair of blue swim trunks covered in red, green, and orange popsicles. He lifted it out and held it up. There was a second pair inside and a small key card folder from the casino.

"I'm going to have you two stay here for a couple of weeks, let things cool down. You've got a room, paid through the end of the month. Two king beds. And there's a prepaid credit card in there too, with five hundred on it. For incidentals."

"That's cool," Lonnie said. "But what about my job back in—"

"Shut it," Byron said.

"Consider this a time to reinvent yourselves. Sit by the pool. Read a book. Binge-watch something. Stare at the walls. But don't go home. I'm serious about this." Scissors then turned and walked through the slot machines. A man in the row got a jackpot, and his machine lit up. A second later, Scissors was gone. A huge grin came across Byron's face, and Lonnie thought his brother had gone crazy.

—

Sophia spent the rest of the morning and early afternoon in a conference room, doing paperwork and finishing up the last of her PowerPoint presentation on the ethics of preservation and the problem of restoration. To clear her head before the program, she dashed to the shuttle stop and hopped on a bus right as it was leaving. It was packed with people in a way that was familiar to her as someone from the East Coast who was still somewhat uncomfortable in the openness of this western landscape.

There were no seats, so she took hold of an overhead bar and listened to the bits and pieces of conversation: a jambalaya of Japanese, Korean, Italian, French, German, Polish, and a little English, but not much. Because of her research on the impact of archeological sites under different jurisdictions, she constantly thought about the numbers of people who came here. The National Park Service was one agency among many in the United States, which was one of many governments around the world trying to manage the erosion of history.

Her interest came from a course on the history of UNESCO, the United Nations Educational, Scientific and Cultural Organization. It was an organization that seemed amazing from one perspective, but over the course of those fifteen weeks it had been unpacked and reformed into a complex colonial force that left her unsure if there were any good institutions at all anymore. It was one thing to study theories in the classroom and something else entirely to watch power and money in action.

Sophia let her eyes drift through the bus. She watched a father in a nearby seat tracing the path of the Fairyland Loop on a map for his daughter. She asked questions in Cantonese and sucked on the rubber straw of her water bottle as he answered. Sophia could only guess what a trip like this might cost. Surely less than Disneyland. What experience did he hope for her? For himself? What memories did he want her to have of this place when she was old and he was gone? This was the question that fueled all of her studies, the work she felt driven to do. Would that girl treasure the water bottle and its memories when she left for college? Would she find the map in her father's things when he passed away? Which stories seep into the everyday things we leave behind? Which ones evaporate?

She looked up and down the aisle of the bus as it stopped, some people stepping off, new people climbing on. She wondered if any of these people would be coming to her presentation, or if they were just interested in snapshots of the scenery. So many people think an archeologist wears a fedora and a leather jacket, cracks a bullwhip, and jumps from trains onto the backs of galloping horses. But so much of the work is slow and meticulous, the gathering of information, the sifting of it. Mountains and mountains of paperwork, so much of it digital these days.

One of her professors would read Shelley's poem "Ozymandias" to her students, tell them that living memory dies and our knowledge of the past survives only through the trace of physical things, which eventually crumble and blow away, leaving us with two stone legs, a partially buried face, and a single half-crazed witness. This professor was fond of saying that the only thing left behind to speak of us will be the Statue of Liberty buried to the waist with the surf crashing all around it. Even this reference, Sophia thought, was almost lost, gone like Charlton Heston, French science fiction, Romantic poetry, and every other good and noble thing.

The shuttle stopped at the lodge, and Sophia waited while everyone in front of her stood and filed off. She stepped down the bus steps and back into the fresh air, surrounded by towering ponderosas. The buildings, shingled in brown and green, came from another age, like buildings imagined for a film.

Across the parking lot was a white tour bus with a massive red swoosh across the side. In the front window was a cling banner that said RANCHES, RELICS, AND RUINS in a gaudy Egyptian font. Tourists spilled from the doors of that bus as well and filed into the lodge under the direction of staff people with clipboards and palm-sized walkie-talkies. She couldn't imagine having your first encounter with a place like this be something like that, but maybe it's better this way than not at all. Maybe it's better than turning them loose on the place like shoppers on Black Friday. She didn't know anymore. The lodge was packed, and if she didn't have to be there, she would have gone right past it and out to Bryce Canyon itself, the majestic red-rock amphitheater that sells this park to the world. The sculpted expanse makes the lodge a mere curiosity by comparison.

When she finally made it to the auditorium, she found the room empty except for a young ranger in a uniform and the broad-brimmed campaign hat. He switched on a computer projector and motioned for Sophia to come on in. The room was large and open and entirely built from wood, glass, and stone. The wood was glazed with varnish that made it glow. The glass doors along the back caused a rippling reflection. The stonework made the room look like it had been there forever. She examined the vaulted ceiling with its open crisscrossing timbers that gave it the appearance of a country church.

The ranger glanced up and hailed Sophia. "I'm Thad. Dalinda sent me your slides. I have them loaded on the laptop," he said.

"Thanks, but I've made some changes, so I have it here on a USB drive." She dug it out of her backpack and crossed the room to hand it to him. "It's on a file called Mission Impossible."

"Oh, no," Thad said with real alarm. "We called it Preserving the Past. It's on all the posters."

"It's okay," Sophia said. "It's a joke. Preserving the Past is correct." Thad kept staring at her like she was going to say something else, but she didn't.

Eventually Thad said, "Phew. That's good because we put up posters everywhere." He laughed a bit nervously. "But I get it. Preservation can be a hard sell sometimes." Thad looked like he might have more to say about that if he were off duty.

Sophia watched him nod and swap the files on the computer and start the slideshow. An image of a glowing orange sandstone cliff appeared with streaks of dark brown desert varnish running top to bottom. On that wall was a line of anthropomorphic petroglyphs: tall figures with radiating headdresses or wide horns. Beneath those figures was a cluster of gorgeous white spirals and below them, scrawled in black, were the words LLOYD ♡ AUBRI 4EVER. Superimposed over everything in white Times New Roman was the title "Preserving the Past: The Impact of National Parks and Tourists on Cultural Heritage Sites." Sophia caught Thad's eye, smiled, and pointed to the screen. Thad gave her the thumbs-up.

Sophia moved to the back of the room to get a look at the slide. She felt the words and images could be easily seen. Her heart was starting to pound, and she felt restless thinking about what she was going to say today about museums and parks and the impact of millions of people on cultural sites. She wanted to leave these visitors with a sense of what it takes to preserve and protect these treasures. She wanted them to know it doesn't happen on its own.

As the first visitors entered, Sophia made her way through to the front of the auditorium. By the time she got there, she saw that people were lined up and flowing in quickly from their tour buses. Thad handed her the clicker. "Dalinda gave me some notes for an introduction." He looked at his watch. "When you're ready, I'll get things started, then get a head count, then I've got to run over to the Fairyland Loop Trail."

"That would be great," Sophia said, looking out at the people gathering in the room, who were all sitting and turning in her direction. So, nobody from the park would be there. She knew it was because they were all stretched thin, but part of her wondered why. Maybe they wanted to separate themselves from her presentation, or maybe they thought they had already heard it a thousand times before. Maybe they trusted her. She didn't know for sure.

Soon, the seats were filled. Thad stepped between the aisles and without fanfare took out a small sheet of folded paper and read, "Good afternoon, ladies and gentlemen. Thank you all for coming to Bryce Canyon National Park and for making this interpretive presentation part of your experience today. We have a special treat for you. One of our seasonal employees, Sophia Shepard, will present some of her research on the preservation of cultural history sites that exist on federal land in the area. This work is part of ongoing efforts by the NPS to preserve important resources for your present and future enjoyment. Ms. Shepard comes to us from Princeton, New Jersey, where she is a doctoral student, doing work to help us document the ruins of the Indigenous peoples who disappeared from the Southwest around seven hundred years ago. As I said, the data she collects will go into the archeological record to help guide policy and decision-making as it relates to the use of our public lands and resources."

From the middle of the crowd a hand went up.

Thad looked at Sophia, who shrugged. "Yes?" Thad asked.

A man with a French accent said, "You have said that the Native peoples used to live here. Will she speak of those who remain? They seem to be hidden, you know?"

"Good question, aaand . . ." Thad said, turning to check with Sophia, who nodded. "That is a yes, this will definitely be part of today's presentation. But we should save all other questions until the end."

Thad stepped to the side of the room, and the audience's attention landed on Sophia. "Before I begin," she said, "I'd like to recognize the fact that Bryce Canyon National Park is located on the seasonal hunting and gathering ground of the Paiute Indian people, who first occupied this area around 1200 C.E. Before them, this region was the home of the Fremont and Ancestral Puebloans. We also recognize the continuing presence of the Paiute people, the Utes, the Diné, and all Indigenous peoples who are represented by the National Park Service."

The man who raised his hand before raised it again.

"Could we wait for comments?" she asked.

"But you said *continuing* presence, which I do not see here in the park," he gestured around the room. "We have not seen any—"

"We will get to that very important point," Sophia said, scanning the varied rows of faces before directing everyone's attention to the image on the screen. "As you can see from this first slide, the past and the present are always colliding. We often think of the past as a single thing, maybe because it has already happened, but history is a complex mosaic of people and their intersections through time. Often one group of people would arrive in a place new to them only to find the previous residents gone. Sometimes, as we see in this image, we're able to see how different groups of people left their marks on a single cliff." She used the laser on the clicker to guide their attention to the row of figures, then to the carved spirals, and finally to the names of the two lovers who left their recent mark with some charcoal.

"More often we see cultural intersection—and some may call it vandalism— from another perspective." She advanced to an image of three pots lit harshly behind the glare of plate glass. "These Pueblo and Zuni artifacts were found a little over a hundred years ago in places that are less than three hundred miles from here, as the crow flies. They are now located in Cambridge, Massachusetts, which is about two thousand miles from here, as the crow flies. You will find artifacts like these scattered across the globe, some in museums and some in private collections. Some we know about, most we don't."

Sophia felt her pulse accelerate. The auditorium was close to full, and with the reflections of the people in the window glass, the room seemed twice the size, which made her neck and shoulders tense a little. She tried to calm herself and muster some courage by thinking about how important it was to share some of her fundamental ideas about museums and parks and ethics. Her talk had to be the right balance of sermon and seduction and she wondered if she would achieve it. She advanced the slide again to a photo of a large brick building with tall windows, pilasters, and cornices. It looked like a blue-collar version of a Greek temple.

"This is the Peabody Museum of Archaeology and Ethnology, which is part of Harvard University. The Peabody was founded in 1866, and it is one of the oldest and largest museums focused on ethnography and archeology. In the last one hundred and fifty years, the Peabody's collection of artifacts has grown so much that there is little space to contain them. The work of cataloging and organizing everything—even with the help of computers, bar codes, scanners, and a massive endowment—is absolutely overwhelming. The Peabody's website has this to say about its collection: 'The Peabody is well known for its significant collections of archeological and ethnographic materials from around the world, many of which were acquired during the era of European and American expansion, exploration, and colonization.' This is good self-awareness on the Peabody's part, but it doesn't change the fact that they brought these things from the four corners of the world, and now they can't manage it. Most of this massive collection of millions of artifacts is—as the man who spoke earlier said—hidden."

Sophia walked them through a series of images. Human bones loose in a cardboard box. Human bones laid out on a table in the shape of a person. An Egyptian mummy in a gold-and-lapis sarcophagus. Two semicircle groupings of stone spearpoints and arrowheads fanned out on felt. Some were made of flint, some jasper, and others were knapped from obsidian. There was a magnificent robe made of blue and gold feathers, a grouping of six human jawbones, then a cedar burial box carved with bird and beaver faces.

She watched the audience carefully, the light changing on the multitude of their faces with each advancing image. Some leaned forward. Others nudged a neighbor. From time to time a phone rose, obscuring a face for a moment, replacing it with a blue glow while they posted pictures they'd taken. She tried to imagine what this photography might look like as it ascended into the cloud in real time. Then an idea came.

Sophia checked the room and saw that Thad was gone. She pointed to the image of the burial box and said, "There's only one of these boxes. Two hundred years ago, you'd have to travel to the box to see it, and you'd have to know where to find it. In all likelihood, the Coast Salish people wouldn't take you to see it. Travel to British Columbia at that time was difficult. You can imagine the way people must have thought that it would be so much more efficient to bring these things to the places where there were people instead of the other way around. Of course, that would be for people with money to pay the price of admission and the leisure time to attend."

She advanced the slide to an image of the Moon House ruins, with its beautiful overhang and delicate rooms, which was threatened by over-visitation. But this image didn't fit the new script, so she backed up to the burial box.

"This is where we get the Peabody and events like the Chicago World's Fair and all the marvels of the Gilded Age. Suddenly thousands of people had trolley access to the world. If you think about it, museums were the internet of the nineteenth century. They gave some people—a certain kind of person— access to ethnographic treasures, but to accomplish this, they had to remove them from where they belonged and ship them off."

Sophia could hear the people creaking in their chairs. The audience had stopped taking pictures and she could see the small white pinpoints of the projector light repeated in their eyes. She was no longer certain where she was in her presentation, but she meant to move them from the problems of museums to the half solution of national parks, and from there to the new problems parks have created.

"Let me back up," she said. "The real first internet was probably a sixteenth-century German compendium, maybe the Library of Alexandria, but museums made a real splash. They unlocked the wonders of the world. Today, it seems hard to understand the impact because, with a cell phone, people can look at the Rosetta Stone from close up. You can hear a Sioux war song, see Indonesian dancers. You can fly virtually through the Grand Canyon, over and over and over again. Before all this, the experience had to be physical, and that took a lot of money. It was an amazing feat of the age to organize and fund explorations to send wealthy white Europeans across the globe in search of your antiquities. There's a reason the movie was called *Raiders . . .*" she paused for effect, ". . . *of the Lost Ark.*"

Sophia wished she were recording this talk. It felt like ideas that had been rolling around loose in a box were finally coming together. She paused for a second to try to keep track, then she dove in again.

"Museums are amazing places, but they are . . ." Sophia hesitated while she tried to find the right word. This was the danger of improvisation. The right word for a graduate seminar would have been that museums were "racist" or "ethnocentric." One of her professors would always say "Gordian," which was only the right word for him. The correct word for this when meeting with Dalinda or other Parks or BLM people would be "multi-jurisdictional." The term "tricky" came to mind. "Convoluted." Maybe something folksy like "messed up." But in the end, she settled on "complicated." She picked up again: "Museums can be complicated. One person's artifact is another person's ancestor. The presence of something in a museum only points to its absence from the place it left. And this is the thing museums don't want to say out loud. All of their holdings came from somewhere else. So, the most important questions anyone can ask are Who did this amazing thing belong to? And who had it before it was here? Who took it away from them? How did it even get here? Who had it first? And like the man in front asked before, Where are these people now? We have a word for the answers to these questions, and it is 'provenance.'"

Sophia drank some water and scanned the room to see if anyone from the park had slipped in. She felt these visitors deserved to know what lurked behind their vacations. As she looked around the room, she met people's eyes, and some motioned to the screen behind her.

"I've heard people talk about museums like they are some kind of pirate ship, but in reality, they are privateers, since their theft is so often sanctioned by the state. My father is from Alabama, but my mother comes from Iran. I grew up hearing her talk about the way her own country—and Syria, Egypt, Lebanon—was systematically plundered by the British and French. This is true of Central America, China, and Ireland—pretty much every place on the planet has had its heritage stolen and relocated somewhere else, usually accompanied by people talking about how the civilized world can help let light into the dark areas of the globe. Sometimes those places were called backward sectors. The U.S. president has other names for those parts of the world."

A woman near the back stood and excused herself. Her husband followed a few seconds later. He stood in the doorway looking back at the screen for a lingering moment before she called for him to come.

"Some people argue that artifacts should remain in place. They can be documented best right where they are. Some say artifacts should be documented, then removed to repositories so they aren't destroyed. Some say it's finders keepers. Some say the people making these decisions don't have the right to make them."

Sophia looked down at the laptop to get her bearings, and when she looked up, she saw a raised hand. The man who raised it was slim, balding, wearing a fleece vest. He looked like the kind of person with an NPR travel mug and a Subaru. "But a park," he said, "like this one, is just a museum in reverse, right? You aren't taking these things anywhere, but you're bringing all of us here to see them."

"That is a good summary," Sophia said, realizing too late that she'd allowed the lid on Pandora's box to be lifted. Her presentation had just become a Q&A. "The national parks have dual responsibilities. They are supposed to protect the resources for right now and make sure what's available right now will be also available to people in the future. Some people call them the dueling mandates."

"Like dueling banjos," somebody called out. In the murmur that followed his joke, Sophia tried to gather the group's attention back.

"Does that make sense?" she said to the NPR man, who nodded, sort of. She went on. "For many years these sites were plundered by the people who settled here, and 'settled' isn't really the right word. They took what they wanted, destroyed much of it outright, saved a little, sold the rest. They erased the people who were here. Now it's impossible to know what really happened, what it was really like. Because it is not our history, what we are able to show you is inaccurate."

Another hand went up. He looked European, with a sweatshirt tied around his shoulders. He didn't wait to be called on. Instead, he stood and spoke. "Who owns history, then?" he asked in a German accent. "Is it the people of the present day or the people of the past? This is a question I often ask myself, and the more I think about it, the more I am unsure. German people are enchanted with the American Indian, and these western lands, but perhaps we love something that no longer exists. I'm sorry if this is an unhelpful question. Perhaps it is not even a question at all."

Sophia felt the room narrow. This was what she secretly hoped her digression might open up. His question was the key to her work, and she loved how he put it so simply.

"What is your name?" she asked.

"Reinhardt," he said.

"Reinhardt, I don't know if I have an answer, but a good archeologist is always asking herself that question. The answer depends on so many things."

"I am a physician, so I lack the necessary training to ask myself this as a professional. But I pursue these things as a hobby. I study the American Indian only as an amateur, as a lover of such things. I will take my answer from this chair. I did not mean to create a distraction." He sat down and tilted his head slightly to one side.

As Sophia began to formulate her answer, another hand shot up. It was a man with a giant red maple leaf on his shirt. He didn't wait to be called on either. "A guy at work says Indians came from spaceships that crashed, like, ten thousand years ago. They just got stuck here. He says when they all disappeared it's because that's when the rescue ships came."

"Oh, don't. Please don't say things like that. First off, they didn't just disappear. Second, it's already hard enough—"

"You don't really think we're the only intelligent life forms in the universe," the man replied. There was some laughter, and Sophia was furious that he had stolen the room. Her jaw clenched, and everything seemed to get louder.

Just as Sophia was about to launch her counterattack, the German spoke again without rising. "Perhaps there are no intelligent life forms anywhere." The audience laughed, and the man waited for it to grow quiet again. "But in reality, given the immensity of space, the chances of us existing in the same small window of time as other intelligent life is immeasurably small. That doesn't even factor in the time delay of such cosmic distances."

"Look," the maple leaf guy said, "the U.S. Navy has seen UFOs. They've got pictures."

Reinhardt smiled and shrugged.

From another corner of the room a man's voice called out. She couldn't see his face. "They came across the land bridge from Russia."

"Okay," Sophia said, "that may not be true either. It's just one story and it's not set in stone. Genetic data is showing us other possibilities—"

Another hand went up. It was a woman, finally. Her jacket matched the one her husband next to her was wearing. "Do you know anything about the man from Kanab who killed himself? They say his house was a kind of museum. How does he fit into all of this? Nobody gets to see his stuff."

Sophia was advancing through her slides to get to the one that outlined the main points of the Antiquities Act of 1906. People in the audience began talking back and forth. Soon there was a rising, confounding cacophony of languages. When she came to the slide she was looking for, she had clicked too many times, overshot it, and had to back up. As she did, a Korean man, who had been sitting quietly through the presentation next to his wife, sat up straight in his chair on the aisle. His eyes went wide with alarm as he gasped, tipped forward, and fell. The people around him moved away as he hit the floor. His wife knelt immediately at his side and looked around pleading for help in her language. Sophia couldn't see what was going on, but she began to run for the door to get help.

"Let me through. Let me through," said Reinhardt. "Clear the way." He knelt and checked the man's breathing and pulse, then looked at Sophia, held up two fingers, and pointed to his eyes. "You. I believe he is in cardiac arrest. Call for help, then come back here. If there is a defibrillator in this lodge, please bring it back."

Sophia rushed from the room and wove through the crowded corridor. She cut the line at the front desk, which triggered a series of disgruntled complaints. "We've got a heart attack in the auditorium. He looks older. I didn't get a good look, so I don't have a description."

The desk clerk was young. Her name tag said SILVIA, HOMETOWN TRNAVA, SLOVAKIA. Sophia could see that the girl couldn't process what she was saying. She reached over the desk and grabbed the phone, dialed the number, and called it in. When she was done, she handed the phone back to Silvia, who held it without hanging it up.

"Do you know where a defibrillator is?" She pantomimed placing the paddles on a chest and the jolt that followed. Silvia's face fell, and she started to panic. "Never mind," Sophia said.

She ran back to the auditorium and found the crowd gathered in a circle around the fallen man. The German doctor was on his knees performing CPR, singing softly to himself as he leaned into the compressions. It was the Bee Gees. "Stayin' Alive." After many strokes, he leaned down and gave two deep rescue breaths.

Someone from the crowd called out: "They're saying don't do mouth-to-mouth anymore."

The doctor returned to his compressions. "Danke," he said to his critic. "Physicians receive different training." Then he returned to his song.

A woman in a rhinestone shirt turned to her husband and asked, "Is he singing *Saturday Night Fever*?"

Her husband shrugged. "Maybe. I haven't seen it in a long time."

"Do you think he should? I mean a man is dying right there. Maybe it's tacky," the woman replied.

Someone standing next to Sophia said, "Lady, I think whoever does the CPR gets to pick the music."

The doctor continued to give compressions and rescue breaths. He checked the man's pulse at regular intervals. Sophia heard the sirens and started pulling chairs aside to make a path. In a few minutes, the park EMTs burst into the room with a rolling stretcher. When the doctor saw them, he stood immediately and let them do their work.

"I began CPR within ten seconds," Reinhardt said. "He has a pulse, and he's breathing on his own."

"We've got it," one of the EMTs said.

"I'm a doctor."

"Congratulations," the other EMT said, shouldering past Reinhardt so he could transfer the man to the stretcher.

Sophia looked around and stood on one of the chairs. "Ladies and gentlemen, could you all please step to the side? Maybe just right up against the walls?"

A tour guide wearing a Ranches, Relics, and Ruins T-shirt approached the EMTs with her arm around a frightened woman. She said, "This is that guy's wife. You should take her with you. Mr. Kwon doesn't speak any English. Do you?" she asked Mrs. Kwon, who nodded.

"Only a little," she said. "Not so much."

"They're going to take you both to a hospital," the tour guide said. The crowd parted, the EMTs left with the Kwons, and the space closed up behind.

One of the other people in a tour group T-shirt said, "Okay, everybody, let's break into our small groups and carry on. Make sure you have enough water."

Another tour group person said, "Don't worry. Mr. Kwon will be just fine."

People who were not part of the group milled around for a while, then disappeared. A third tour group person said, "Before we go, a round of applause for Dr. Kupfer. He's the hero of the day." The remaining people clapped and cheered. Reinhardt looked up surprised, and he waved off the applause. As the room continued to empty, Reinhardt sat in one of the scattered chairs, and he hung his head.

Eventually the only people left in the auditorium were Sophia and Reinhardt. As she shut down the projector and ejected her USB drive, she watched Reinhardt stand and walk around the place where Mr. Kwon had fallen. He took out a small bundle of sage tied in string. As he circled the area, he shook the bundle once in each of the four directions, then held the sage to his nose and breathed in deeply. He lowered his head and said a few words so quietly Sophia couldn't hear them. When he was done, she said, "He's probably going to be okay."

"Cardiac arrest is very serious."

"But you're a doctor, right?"

"A dermatologist."

"Oh," Sophia said. "A doctor anyway. Nobody else knew what to do. I didn't."

"I better continue on to the next event," he said.

"You're on the tour?" Sophia asked.

"Yes. It is a very bad one. I made a mistake. Their website was misleading."

"I'm sorry."

"Everything they show us here is a cartoon. Bright colors. Strings of flags. Hot dogs with ketchup. I would rather see something quiet and real and true, not always a Schauspiel." He paused for a second. "Not always a . . . pageant, you know?"

"It's even hard for me to know what stories to tell, and I have an advanced degree," Sophia said.

Reinhardt tapped his fist against his sternum. "The stories should come from here."

Sophia did not agree with him on this point. The heart has a habit of falling in love with beautiful falsehoods, but this guy had just saved somebody's life, so she gave him his moment. Instead of rebutting, she said, "Hey, there's a lot of amazing stuff to see around here. Keep your eyes open."

"Danke," the man said, shouldering his backpack. As he was leaving, Thad returned.

"Oh, wow," he said. "How are you doing?"

"I'm okay."

"It's not normally like this," Thad said.

"How could it be?"

"They're taking the Kwons to Cedar City. Regional is going to send you a link for an incident report, but you should sit down as soon as you can and take some notes. Details get slippery as you come down."

Sophia wandered out of the lodge and walked through the pines to the edge of the amphitheater. As she took in the intricate expanse, her phone buzzed. It was a VIP email notification from Paul. She tapped the email and it opened.

Sophia, good news. I've got some days off this week that I have to take before the end of the fiscal year or I'll lose them. I was wondering if I could interest you in an adventure. Do you remember that site we talked about when we were climbing a couple of weeks ago, a place called Swallow Valley? It's the one that requires a technical approach. There's a lot of scrambling and some pitches we'll have to climb. Keeps most people out. Nothing too gnarly. I know you could do it. It would take two days to get there and back again. What do you think?

She closed her eyes and tried not to smile as tourists passed her on either side. So, it was true, he did have plans, along with the presence of mind to share them. Climbing with him was the best thing she'd done since she got here. She didn't know how she would do outside the gym, but it turned out she was good at it, and Paul was like nobody else. A flutter expanded inside her chest, and she calmly tried to gather it back up, but it billowed like a parachute, which made her all the more aware of each breath.

She lifted her phone and wrote: *Gnarly?* Paul said corny things like that all the time, innocent, naïve, endearing things. He was one of the only men she'd ever met who seemed almost entirely without guile. She stared at the phone for a moment, thinking about what he'd do when he read her message, so she hit the delete key seven times and wrote:

> *I will answer your call to adventure, but only if you promise to never, ever use the G-word again in my presence. I am ready to climb again. The harness and shoes you loaned me were fantastic. Send me a packing list for everything else and remind me to tell you about how I gave some guy a heart attack today.*

Day Four

All the world's a stage : Ninety-five in the shade : Let's hope
today is bullet free : The cowboy variety show

Nick Scissors sat by himself in the breakfast room of his hotel. He had
one of each kind of Danish separated on small Styrofoam plates: lemon,
cherry, blueberry, and plain. He sipped his coffee and watched a Fox
News story about the secretary of the interior saying he supported the president's plans to help the United States become energy independent. While the
story ran, he ate two of the Danishes, wiping his fingers with a paper napkin
he took from a stack.

At the table next to him, a couple worked out the itinerary of their vacation. Next stop, Zion National Park, then a day in St. George and down to
Phoenix. The man pushed the map away and looked at his wife. "This would
be a hell of a lot easier if there was a bridge across the Grand Canyon," he said.

In his mind, Scissors imagined a scene where he leaned over and said, "I
don't mean to interrupt, but there are already a number of bridges across the
Colorado River. One at Page. The other at Boulder City." Next, he had the
man saying, "I'm talking about a bridge that goes right across the middle." Or
maybe the man would say, "In 1969 we put a man on the moon. Ever since
then, we've been okay with being number two." And then the man's wife would

interrupt, saying, "I'd never drive across that bridge. Can you think what something crazy like that would cost us in taxes?"

And then the scene was over. The couple was eating in silence. Scissors looked back at Fox News, which had moved on to sports. He ate a third Danish and wrapped the fourth in a napkin and cleared his space. He rode the elevator to the third floor and let himself back into his room. The cardboard tube was on the bed and the maps were rolled out on top of each other and held down by two empty water glasses, the room's travel iron, and a copy of the Gideon Bible.

The room clock said 8:20, so he took a seat and started playing with a deck of cards. He shuffled, fanned, and flipped the cards. He cut them with one hand and tossed them effortlessly, so they spun like the edged facets of a kaleidoscope. With his hand cupped, he sent the cards through the air, gathered them, and repeated, then he took a card—the two of clubs—from the top of the deck and slipped it into the middle, then he shuffled the cards, tapped them square, and cut the deck, going right to the two of clubs again. He repeated this trick a half dozen times.

When the clock read 8:29, he set down the cards and pulled a cell phone toward him. At 8:30 it buzzed. He answered it. A woman spoke without identifying herself. "One of my maps is missing. They're a numbered set, and the fifth of seven isn't there. It's the map that shows the entire Swallow Valley site, including the approach. Did you send me all the photos?"

"I'll check." Scissors got up and looked through each one. She was right: he hadn't seen them before, but there were small numbers in the lower left-hand corner of each map. "What do we do?" he asked.

"Well, Nicholas, I'd like you to circle back."

"It's a crime scene. I can't just come and go."

"You'll have to. At my back I always hear time's wingèd chariot hurrying near. The oil and gas auctions are in a month. I have already put an entire machine in motion."

"You've been clear about that."

"None of this goes back into the bottle."

"Ms. Frangos, we should walk away from this one."

"Impossible."

"I might have to."

"If this mess gets back to me, you're coming along for the ride."

"I see," he said.

"Retrieve the missing map, and you're released from your obligations. You were made for this job. I've seen you vanish into thin air."

"That was on stage. This is different."

"All the world's a stage, Mr. Scissors, so it's too bad your career as an illusionist stalled out."

"Like you said, it was good training, and this is better pay."

Scissors parted the vertical blinds and looked across the valley at the massive CasaBlanca sign sticking up against the white haze and the jagged black mountains in the background. He opened up the napkin holding the last Danish from downstairs. He picked it up and took a bite.

"Nicholas?" she asked. "Are you there?"

"It's difficult for me to measure the weight of my actions when I don't know what you're trying to accomplish."

"Well," she said, "I'm not the villain in this story."

"Villains don't usually cop to it, but whatever."

"You are a cog in a larger machine. What we are doing is bigger than those two pinheads, or either of us, really. Just get me the map. I will compensate you for this adjustment in the arrangements."

"If something goes wrong, Dumb and Dumber won't be our patsies anymore. The whole idea from the start was to throw them under the bus. I worry they'll do it to us."

"Don't get caught and we'll be fine."

"Thanks, I'll put that in my notes." He reached for the deck of cards and fanned it out on the table.

He drew the seventeenth card from the left and flipped it over. It was the two of clubs. He finished what was left of the last Danish and wished he had another.

—

The casino pool was shallow and wide, surrounded by chaise lounges on one side and a fabricated fiberglass cliff face on the other. The sun was just high enough to crest the trees. It was too early for Byron, especially after cutting loose all night, but Lonnie convinced him they wouldn't get a spot if they waited, and he was right. The place was teeming with people.

On one side, a short water slide emerged from under the trees. Lonnie, flanked by children, lowered himself into place and scooted himself into the flow with a strawberry daiquiri in his hand. The slide dumped him into the shallow receiving pool. His head went completely under, but he managed to keep his drink aloft, like a red periscope.

He popped up with his hair flat against his face and crossed the pool to the seat where Byron was lying out, faceup, in his popsicle swim trunks. His eyes were closed, his fingers interlaced across his chest, cradling a blue aluminum beer can-bottle that looked like alien technology emerging from his breastbone. Alongside the chair was a folded-up towel with both of the manila envelopes of money sitting on top. Byron knew it was a risk, but he wanted to keep the money close. When Byron heard Lonnie approach, he kept his eyes closed but slid his hand down and rested it on the cash.

"This place is great," Lonnie said, setting his drink on the pool deck. He used his hands to squeegee the water from his beard and hair. "You gotta do the slide."

"Don't gotta do nothing," Byron said, taking a swig of his beer.

"You don't know what you're missing."

"I know exactly what I'm missing. I've watched you go down that thing like a dozen times."

"I don't know why you brought that money down here," Lonnie said in a whisper voice. "There's a safe in the room. I figured out how to use it."

"They're worthless."

"What?"

"When you get back up there, press the lock button until it says SUPER, then press all nines," Byron said.

"Then what?"

"Then you lose your money. Anyone can get into those things."

"Whoa. How'd you learn that?"

"Cellmate. He says everybody working here knows it." He patted the money. "That's why the cash stays right here."

Lonnie took his drink and pushed off the pool wall and drifted to the fake waterfall. He turned under the cascade and watched people of all shapes and sizes move around. Most of them were on a cheap vacation, not on the lam. Lonnie felt safe here, like nobody would dare do anything right out in the middle of it all. Byron was just lying there, not moving, which made sense because he was crashing. Lonnie watched his brother set his beer on the concrete next to his chair. He looked at the old palm trees, which were starting to blow around as the day heated up.

Lonnie took a few more trips down the slide, then swam over and told Byron he was going to unwind in the hot tub.

"It's ninety-five degrees, numb nuts."

"I like it anyway," Lonnie said, then he swam across the pool like a skinny white frog and disappeared into the grove of trees that surrounded the hot tub. Byron felt the dryness of his mouth and sucked on his teeth to get the saliva going. He was bonking hard, but he didn't want Lonnie to see it. He settled himself and thought about how he got here.

A guy he knew inside gave his name to Scissors, who called him on the phone, out of the blue, like some telemarketer. He said his employer was out of options and needed some help that lay somewhat outside of the law. Byron said he wasn't interested to see if he could crank up the price. When Scissors assured him it was good pay, Byron asked, "How far outside?"

Scissors explained that Bruce Cluff, some local guy, was in the possession of certain maps and catalogs he had made of an area called the Swallow Valley. This guy's employer was interested in purchasing said maps and catalogs, but Cluff refused to even hear his employer's offer. The employer had already set certain processes in motion, processes that the employer was not interested in shutting down.

"They got maps on the internet," Byron said.

"These maps are . . . unique," Scissors said. "You will be compensated for your time."

"For stealing some maps?"

"Let's think of it as liberation."

"I haven't told you my rate," Byron said. He was stone broke and wondered if the man on the phone knew that.

"The rate is not what you say it is, but it's market price. Trust me. It is fair."

"And you get to say what's fair?"

"There are other names on our list."

"And since mine's Ashdown, you're starting with me."

"Abernathy, Aguirre, Albertson, Alsopp, Anderson, then you."

"I get it," Byron said.

"The thing is, it can't look like the maps were singled out to be stolen. My employer requires discretion."

"You can have 'em fast, cheap, or secret. Pick two."

Scissors named the fee, which was so high Byron didn't think to negotiate, which was exactly the plan, and when he figured that part of it out, it got under his skin. Eventually, once everything bent over and went south, Byron began hatching a plan of his own, a kind of insurance policy. After they tested the map, he took that one from the roll and left it in his closet back home. Some of that treasure was going to be his no matter what else happened.

Across the pool, a lifeguard gave three short whistles. Byron looked over and saw Lonnie running along the deck. He jumped into the pool and ran through the shallow water. A second lifeguard shouted, "Hey, man! You don't run. Everybody knows that." Lonnie slowed, but his face remained panicked.

"He's still here!" Lonnie shouted, pointing behind.

"Who?"

"Scissors. Over by the fence."

"Inside or outside?" Byron tried not to panic.

"Out. Watching me. Come look."

"I'm not going over there. That's what he wants."

"You have to, so I know I'm not crazy."

"You've been drunk since last night."

"You've been tweaking since—never mind. Come look. If it's not him, I'll shut up forever."

"Forever?" Byron pulled himself up from the lounge, bent down and took the envelopes, then he followed Lonnie. As they walked, one of the lifeguards took off his sunglasses and said, "Keep him under control."

At the midway point, Lonnie said, "There he is." A hundred feet past the pool deck was a ten-foot-high iron fence that separated the end of the court-yard from the parking lot. Scissors stood right in the middle, gripping the bars. He was in different clothes: a yellow golf shirt and white slacks. When he saw that they had seen him, he waved, then put his hands in his pockets and strolled away without looking back.

"Why'd he do that?" Lonnie asked.

"He's a freak."

"Well, it sure freaks *me* out."

"He's just trying to make us think he's onto us. But he's got to take the maps to his *employer*." Byron put the last word in air quotes. "He just wants us to lay low."

"Why wouldn't we? This is awesome," Lonnie said.

"Let's go back," Byron said.

"Back home? Is that a good idea?"

"Back to the chairs, you idiot."

When they got to their place at the pool, a woman was standing next to one of the lounge chairs. She was wearing a navy blue one-piece with fishnet across the cleavage. "What is she doing here?" Byron asked.

"Don't you remember? She stayed the night with us," Lonnie said. "Her friend is here, too." He pointed to a skinny woman lying facedown a couple of lounges over. The first woman was bent over, undoing the buckles of her sandals. Byron copped a look down her swimsuit and thought about last night. Across her chest was a tattoo of the word DESTINY interwoven with thorns and flowers that looked like they'd come from another planet. They had par-tied. Very little of it was clear. When she could not undo the buckles on her shoes, she sat, leaned over and tugged them off.

When she noticed Byron and Lonnie, she said, "We showered."

"Sure. So did we," Byron said, stepping astride his chair and collapsing backward into it, which startled the woman who was lying on her stomach.

Her frizzed-out hair was dull, with a green dye job that was faded almost all the way out.

Lonnie got situated in his chair, and the four of them were set out in a row: girl, boy, boy, girl. Byron undid his ponytail and regathered it. He put the envelopes behind him, in the small of his back. The woman on Byron's side put her hand on Byron's thigh. Her acrylic nails were covered in tiny flowers and jewels, and she used them to tickle the hair on Byron's leg. Byron looked over at her and saw the names BRADEN and HAILEE inscribed on the inside of her forearm.

"I didn't bring any sunscreen," she said. "I'm gonna burn."

"We all are," Byron said, watching to see if Scissors would show.

Lonnie tapped the other woman on her bare shoulder. "Hey," he said, "I don't remember your name."

"Leia," she said. "Like the princess."

"She's a general now," Lonnie said.

———

After three o'clock, the sun drilled through the west windows of Dalton's office and started burning up the wall from floor to ceiling. He'd been trying to do paperwork for hours, but the day had been chewed up by interruptions. At three thirty, the white bar of light came even with Dalton's eyebrows, and the glare disturbed his work enough that he wrote a note reminding himself to request an awning.

In an attempt to save himself, he left his office, drove to town, got a late lunch, and ate it in his Bronco. Before he was finished, the phone rang. It was Karen.

"Pat," she said. "I'm trying not to be that person."

"It's okay."

"It's okay that I have to keep calling you about the house or okay that I'm trying not to be the person who has to keep calling to remind you about selling the house?"

Dalton set down his pickle. "Both?"

"Please remember that this is what we agreed to."

"You need to have a little charity."

"Do not do this, Patrick."

"It's going to happen, but not today." He lifted his potato chip bag and looked inside: all that was left were crumbs and pieces. He poured them into his mouth. "You can come back and live in it," he said. "I'll move out."

"That's not what we want. I've been through that."

"We? I haven't heard the kids say they don't want to live here. Put them on. I want to hear it from them. If that's what they really want, I'll list it this afternoon."

"They're at ballet."

"Okay, then tonight."

"Patrick."

"Have them call me. I'm sorry. I've got to go find out how my dad's best friend died."

"I thought it was a suicide."

"I'll get to the realtor as soon as I can," he said, then ended the call.

On the way back to work, Dalton watched a guy in a silver Sebring roll through his stop. Normally, he wouldn't have worried about it, but he was procrastinating and this was a perfect distraction.

The man's name was Nicholas Szczesny, from Las Vegas. He wore a yellow shirt and white pants, like he'd just come off the golf course. He was polite and soft-spoken, said he liked this little town, but he was used to driving in Vegas, which is a bit more aggressive.

Dalton said that's how it was for him after driving in Iraq.

"When were you there?" Szczesny asked.

"2010," Dalton said. "Did a second tour in Afghanistan. You?"

"2004, a little before that, a little after."

Dalton looked down and saw a small tattoo of a skull with a bayonet sticking out of the top on the man's forearm and decided not to ask any more questions. He took his license and registration, looked him up, and saw that his record was clear. He came back and said, "I'm going to let you go with a warning. People around here aren't always paying attention, so a full stop can make a difference."

The man smiled. "Attention must be paid."

"Have a good trip."

The man drove off, and Dalton returned to the public safety building. When he got back to his desk, he found a stack of requisitions and a Post-it reminding him not to forget to sign the overtime. Ten emails later, he tried getting back to work when a call came through from LaRae. It was five o'clock. "I'm sorry," she said.

"Sorry for what?" Dalton asked.

"I know you asked not to be bothered, but it's Janey Gladstone. She insists."

"On what?"

"Talking to you."

"About?"

"She says something weird is going on at Raylene Cluff's house." Dalton made two fists—one he set on the desk and the other tightened around the phone. He wasn't much of a decorator, but he'd set up a few things directly in his line of sight: a picture of Karen and the kids, a shelf with some trophies from high school, a shadow box with his military medals, a photo collage of him holding up a variety of fish he'd caught over the years, and one large photo of a coho salmon he caught in Nunatak Fiord in Alaska. He'd set all these things up to be a place for his eyes to go when he didn't want to yell, punch, or kick anything. Today he focused on the coho. He caught that thing eight years ago, right after he got back from Afghanistan. It took him forty-five minutes to land it. Weighed thirty-three pounds. The guides shipped it home for him on ice. Cost him a hundred bucks to do it, but he didn't care. He never ate it. It was still in the freezer.

"Sheriff," LaRae asked, "are you there?"

"Yeah, put Janey through," he said.

There was a click, a span of silence, then the sound of rapid breathing. "Janey, this is Sheriff Dalton."

"I am at their house, not really at, but in—inside it," she whispered.

"Whose house?"

"The Cluff home."

"After I said not to?"

"I came over to get some personal things for Raylene."

"We could have sent somebody over."

"Well, there's a reason they call them personal things, Patrick."

"Fair enough."

"I believe I have found myself in an extraordinary situation. Somebody is here who should not be."

"Somebody besides you?"

"I came down here to the basement because that's where the laundry is, and I heard a clatter outside, so I went to the top of the stairs and looked around and saw that somebody was climbing up the outside of the house. There was no ladder, just his legs. I went back down, but I can hear him clomping around up there. It comes through the ductwork."

"Where are you now?"

"By the chest freezer."

"Hang up and hide," Dalton said.

"Hide? Where?"

"Someplace you can get comfortable. You might have to be there awhile."

"Now you're scaring me," Mrs. Gladstone said.

"I am hanging up now so we can get someone over there."

"Can't someone keep talking to me?" Mrs. Gladstone's voice was thin.

"How about LaRae Knowles? Would you talk to her?"

"Yes, I can do that," Janey said.

"Okay, hang on." Dalton put her on hold and rang LaRae. When she answered, she said, "I am so sorry. I know you said to hold your calls."

"That's fine. I need you to keep talking to Mrs. Gladstone. Tanner and I need to get to the Cluff house. Sounds like somebody is breaking in."

"That's really weird," LaRae said.

"It is."

"I've got it," she said and pulled the call back to her phone.

Dalton hung up and left through a side entrance. He radioed Tanner from the Bronco and told him where to meet. He tore through town with his lights on but no siren. Time stretched out as he worried. In cop shows they always cut this part down to a couple of shots, never showing how the drive gives a person enough time to suffer through a hundred possible outcomes, catastrophe piled on top of catastrophe. There were more ways for this situation to go wrong than he was willing to imagine.

Tanner was waiting for him when he arrived. He had his sidearm unholstered and was wearing his body armor, which amped up Dalton even more. "The street is clear. Nothing weird going on. I ran the plates on these cars." He pointed to the three vehicles on the street. "They all belong to the people who live here. That one is Janey Gladstone's," he said, pointing to a white Buick.

"Tell me this is nothing," Dalton said.

Tanner shrugged. "I'd rather be ready."

Dalton called in the situation, and the dispatcher asked if they needed backup. Dalton said, "I got everybody here with me at the moment." Tanner chuckled.

They walked up to the house and split. Dalton continued down the driveway toward the carport, and Tanner went through the bushes and around. After a few minutes, Tanner came across the radio. "There's a ladder here, hanging in the garage. You think the burglar returned it to where it goes?"

"Not likely," Dalton answered.

"Then it looks like we're dealing with somebody who can climb better than I can, which means we're also looking at a different story than the one we thought."

"Don't say it."

"You think the guy is still in there?"

"I don't want to find out by having him shoot first," Dalton said.

"If we crouch here all day, we'll regret it," Tanner said. "Meet me at the back door."

Dalton came around the house, and Tanner was standing at the back stairs with his weapon pointed in the air. "Who goes first?" he said.

"You got here first," Dalton said.

"A leader's gotta lead."

"If I get shot, who does the paperwork?"

"You're seriously the worst boss ever."

"There's an old lady in there."

"All-time worst," Tanner said.

"Fine," Dalton said. He cracked open the back door and went inside. They went room to room on the ground floor, passing through the crime scene, which still hadn't been cleaned. The stench of it was uncomfortable. One of the evidence numbers on the desk had been tipped over. He walked up to it and noticed an empty rectangular spot in the dust and blood spray, not quite the size of a sheet of paper. He took a picture of it with his phone, then looked around more carefully until Tanner joined him. He showed Tanner the spot and said, "Let's find Janey, then come through here a second time."

"Come here first." Tanner brought Dalton over to the shelves, and he showed him a new blank spot in the dust. This one was round, about eight inches across. Dalton took a picture of it as well.

They went upstairs and searched each room, calling each one clear when they were done. Nothing seemed to be out of order.

"You still think we've got a suicide?" Tanner asked.

"I'm not sure I want to know what's going on," Dalton said.

They went back downstairs and found Mrs. Gladstone sitting on an old couch in the far corner of the basement. She was wrapped up in an unfinished quilt, talking to LaRae on the telephone with the cord stretching to the wall. When she heard them, she said, "Oh, they're here now. I better hang up." She got up and placed the phone on the hook. "He left," she said.

"When?" Dalton asked.

"Well, a while ago. He went through a window and came down one of those trees. He's quite the climber. I told that to LaRae."

Dalton and Tanner looked at each other. "Can you describe him?" Dalton asked.

"Well I only heard him thumping around and shaking the trees."

Dalton sent Janey with Tanner to give a statement, then he went back to Cluff's study. He'd seen plenty of burglaries, and there was always a trail of destruction. There was nothing like that here. Whoever came here was looking for something specific. He went to Bruce's desk and lined himself up with the dried blood. He squinted to imagine the physics of it, trying to understand how it fit with the story. To the left of the bookshelves was a small standing table with a number of maps rolled out on it, the paper curled up around four large glass electrical insulators that held the maps in place. As he got closer, he saw that the top map was clean, and everything around it was misted in a fine brown spray. Two or three layers down, the maps were slightly rippled, like they'd been wet and dried back out. He lifted the insulators and the top three maps rolled up, taking back their original shapes. The fourth map down was covered in the same spray. Things had been moved around after the shooting.

These maps were hand-drawn renderings of places on the monument. He'd heard about Bruce's maps. His dad had talked about them, but Bruce kept them out of the public eye. He left notes all over the maps with pencil marks so fine and faint they looked like they'd been scratched into the paper with a needle. At the base of the table was an empty cardboard tube, also unsprayed. On the side, in black marker, Cluff had written *Swallow Valley*.

—

Reinhardt Kupfer boarded the Bryce Canyon shuttle bus at the Agua Canyon stop. Hot and dusty, he found a seat near the back and scooted next to the window. A large man with muttonchops sat next to him, a walking stick with a half dozen fantastic human faces carved into its length resting between his knees. When the bus pulled out, Reinhardt opened his shirt pocket and dug out a small obsidian arrowhead, which he held in the palm of his hand and admired. It was a jet-black, nearly perfect, side-notched triangle flake, roughly the size of his thumbnail, more like a fighter jet than he would have imagined. He turned it over and over, testing the edge with the tip of his thumb.

"Where'd you get that?" the man next to him asked.

"I found it. On my hike."

"Can I see it?"

Reinhardt set it in the man's wide hand and watched him as he poked it with his finger. "It looks real," he said.

"It is, I think. I'm going to find the ranger who spoke to us yesterday and ask her," Reinhardt said, reaching for the artifact.

The man's hand veered away. "I never saw one up close like this," he said. "My cousin found one once, said it was real, but we all thought it was just some broken rock. I mean that's what it looked like, but this one is for real." Reinhardt set his hand lightly on the man's wrist. "I'm not going to steal it," he said. "It's just cool to hold."

"Of course you wouldn't," Reinhardt said. "It's just that I—I would hate for it to drop."

The man returned the arrowhead to Reinhardt's hand.

They went along the slow road, watching red rock flash through breaks in the pines. Reinhardt took out his phone and framed up a picture of the arrowhead as he pinched it between two fingers trying to catch the perfect light. He snapped the picture, then uploaded it to Instagram, typing the caption ENDLICH EIN GUTER TAG NACH EINEM ANSONSTEN KOMPLETT BESCHISSENEN URLAUB. ICH HABE AUSSERDEM EIN MENSCHENLEBEN GERETTET. It was true that this was the first good day of an otherwise completely crappy vacation. Yesterday, he had been a very good Samaritan, but he thought that perhaps it was unseemly to mention that he had also saved a human life, so he deleted the second sentence, tagged the location, and added #indiancountry, which Reinhardt noticed had over 16,000 uses already. He had only one bar of service, so the image uploaded slowly.

He dozed a little during the ride, his muscles sore from the hike. His long sleeves and pants left him feeling hot but protected from the intense sun. In his daydream, he replayed moments of his hike as short video clips, and as the bus came into a wide-open meadow, he woke, checked his phone again, and saw there was one Instagram notification for his post. It was from @doktor_tomahawk, Wolf, Reinhardt's medical partner back in Germany.

Wolf Messer had been in his sixties and looking to bring on a young doctor to help him prepare for retirement. As they sat in Wolf's office, Reinhardt commented on the decor: a Haida moon mask, a hand drum with the painting of a buffalo skin on the head, a red Navajo blanket with two left-turning swastikas at the center, and many other treasures. Reinhardt was so distracted he couldn't speak of his residency. He told Wolf that his own apartment was filled with posters of similar things, photographs taken by Ansel Adams of the American Southwest. He had purchased a few small items in gatherings he'd been to in Baden-Württemberg: buckskin trousers and a pair of beaded moccasins. At this, Wolf left all talk of dermatology. Their conversation carried on through dinner and well into the night. The next morning, Wolf called him personally to invite him to join the practice. When Reinhardt came to sign the papers, Wolf emerged from his office in a lab coat and a full Lakota warbonnet, the feathers fanning out around his balding head. He had spread out each hand dramatically and said, "Welcome, welcome, welcome."

The bus came to a stop at Sunset Point, and the others began filing off. The man sitting next to him said, "Have a good one," and Reinhardt nodded to him.

"You also," he said.

On the sidewalk, he checked his phone again. Wolf had sent him a photo of the walnut shadow box he kept on his desk. It was filled with a dozen stone points, each one a different material and shape. The message said this was an auspicious beginning. Reinhardt put his phone away and continued along the sidewalk, following the brown signs that pointed the way to the rim.

In the gaps between the pines, white clouds piled on top of each other, and in the negative space of the clouds, cerulean pools of sky gathered. It was a color he'd seen many times in paintings, but never this intensely. With his eyes focused on the sky, Reinhardt approached the rim of what the park pamphlets called a "hoodoo-filled amphitheater." From those quaint words he expected to find a mere curiosity, a playground of geologic novelties. Instead, what he saw was hewn straight from the earth and scattered across the horizon like something built and abandoned by giants at play. In a single sweep of his vision lay every possible variation of standing rock: fingers, columns, teeth, pillars, knobs, turrets, toadstools, minarets, pilasters, and pylons. His breath left him all at once, and as he inched forward, the parallax of the scene shifted, and he began to sense, in the core of his belly before he actually saw it, the precipitous drop of the rim, hidden by an innocuous patch of tawny tufted grass. As he lifted his gaze, he took in each successive plane, the closer formations crisp and defined, and those at a distance becoming, by intervals, more impressionistic. At the horizon was a great silent dome, fading slowly in and out of the atmospheric haze. A hundred miles southward across the expanse, a hard black rain fell into the dry air, evaporating on the way down. A soundless arc of white electricity pulsed from the cloud and forked delicately against the flat colors in the distance. Reinhardt waited for a second strike, but it did not come. A few seconds later, the faintest rumble.

A couple passed Reinhardt on the left, talking excitedly about the sublime view. Their teenage son lagged behind, typing something into his phone. Without looking up he said, "We came all the way here, for this?"

"Put your phone away, Miles," his dad said, but the boy ignored him.

Reinhardt soon became aware of people passing him on either side. He followed the rim to the left and saw a great throng from the tour coming toward him. He looked for an escape route, but it was too late, people waved and shouted his name, so he waved back lifelessly. When the group came closer, they called out. "Hey, it's Doctor Hero," somebody shouted. Reinhardt smiled and waved. A man in a T-shirt that said IT'S NOT MY FAULT / I WAS UNSUPERVISED asked where he'd been all day.

"I went down into the hoodoos," Reinhardt said.

"Too much hiking for me," the man's wife said. She wore a large-brimmed straw sun hat, a fanny pack, and white sandals.

"Those are the hoodoos that you do so well," the man said, chortling at his own joke.

His wife said flatly, "Make him stop. He's been telling that dud all day."

"You coming to the dinner? There's supposed to be a whole show and everything."

"I'll have to clean up first," Reinhardt said.

"Well, I hope I see you, so I can buy a hero a beer," the man said.

"Danke," Reinhardt said. "I'll see you there perhaps."

Reinhardt left the sidewalk and wove through the trees to the lodge and caught the shuttle back to the visitor's center. The ride was short, so he stood. He stepped off the bus quickly and went into the building, looking for Sophia. He was thinking about the idea of provenance, how she had told them that the most important question anyone can ask of a thing is Who did it once belong to and who does it belong to now? His thought, who owns history, was at the forefront of it all, matched now with the question of who owns this park and the things inside it. He wanted to let her know that what she said hadn't fallen on deaf ears.

There was a desk in the center, near the back, past the T-shirts, baseball hats, and children's toys, by the cash registers and the day's weather report. A ranger with clear cat-eye glasses and a green tattoo of a Celtic knot on her forearm was sharing information about a trail with a young couple. From the green, white, and red tricolor patch on the tourist's backpack he could see that they were Italian. When they were done, Reinhardt stepped to the desk, removed the arrowhead and placed it in front of the ranger. She looked down at it, then at Reinhardt over her glasses.

"Hello," he said. "Yesterday I was at the lodge for a presentation on antiquities. There was a young archeologist there, and I would like to ask her some questions about this arrowhead I found today on my hike in Agua Canyon."

The ranger picked up the arrowhead and turned it over a couple of times. "Sir," she said, "it's against the law to take things from the park. We have over two million visitors to this park every year. If everybody pocketed one thing, there wouldn't be much of this park left to visit."

"I'm sorry. I didn't know," he said.

She set the arrowhead back down on the counter, and Reinhardt was not sure if he should take it back. "This is what we mean when we tell people to leave no trace, but in this particular case, I'm not going to cite you. This arrowhead actually comes from right over there." She pointed to a rack of costume jewelry a dozen feet away in the gift shop, next to some multicolored scorpion refrigerator magnets. She pushed the arrowhead toward Reinhardt. "It's okay," she said. "Take a look."

Reinhardt accepted the false treasure and walked over to the display of necklaces made of fake leather cord and an arrowhead in the same perfect black triangle shape, with identical chips and ridges. He ran his hand behind them, like they were strands in a beaded curtain. He glanced back at the ranger, who smiled slightly and shrugged. "Sorry," she said, "but thank you for leaving the trail cleaner than you found it."

Reinhardt left the visitor's center, and on the way to the shuttle stop, tossed the arrowhead into the mouth of a green metal trash can. A small boy watched him do it. Reinhardt wanted to say something to him about the way this world can beguile and deceive us, but he spared the boy his nihilism.

When the shuttle came, he boarded and went straight to the back. The bus left the front gates, and soon they were out of the park and on their way to the small town that lay outside of it. He watched the tourists, each one concluding the day's adventures. They all seemed happy, thirsty, and satisfied.

Reinhardt opened his phone and found the photo of the arrowhead and deleted it, then he went to Instagram and deleted his post. He thought about returning home and having to explain to Wolf how he'd been taken in by the false front of America. He wanted more from this trip than it promised, and now he was ashamed at his naïveté. He might as well have spent the afternoon looking at dioramas or IMAX films. He could have done these things without leaving Berlin.

The bus pulled off and stopped in front of a cheap amusement park version of an Old West main street. The bus emptied, and when Reinhardt stayed brooding in his seat, the bus driver's voice came over the PA. "End of the line," he said. "That's it. This bus is going out of service."

Reinhardt waved and stepped onto the pavement and wandered numbly to his hotel. There was no smell of pine, and the air conditioning chilled him. He bought two bottles of water at the front desk and went to his room, drinking one bottle on the elevator. As he showered, he thought about calling the whole thing off, but the idea of leaving was just as overwhelming as the thought of continuing on through a B-movie rendition of America. He dried off and lay on his bed, and before he could gather his thoughts, a knock at the door jolted him from his melancholy. "Dr. Kupfer. It's time for the chuckwagon dinner," the voice said. It was someone perky from the tour. There was a pause followed by more knocking. "Dr. Kupfer?"

"Ja," he said. "I am almost ready."

"Oh, good. We'd hate for you to miss it," the annoying voice said.

Reinhardt dressed, thinking that perhaps spending the evening alone in this depressing motel room would do him more harm than good. He met with the group in the lobby, and they all walked together in a gaggle across the motel parking lot, toward the back-lot town, which was the gateway to an establishment called the Young Family Chuck Wagon Dinner Theater and Country Emporium.

The air was filled with the scent of roasting meat and the din of guitars and cowboy song. To one side was a stage featuring a covered wagon and a theatrical campfire made from red, orange, and white LEDs, pulsing in a slow, hypnotic rhythm, not at all like the quick dance of real flame. The band was clearly not cowboys but theater students from a nearby university doing their summer internships. Reinhardt imagined this was probably very exciting and fresh for them a month ago, but as he looked around, he could see that they and everyone else in the Emporium were on autopilot.

The Korean contingent of the tour had formed a subgroup. So had the Poles, and everyone else, all lapsing into the comfort and familiarity of their own languages, showing each other pictures of their version of the day on their phones. There were plenty of faces he did not recognize. Families with small children. Older couples, and a long-haired Japanese man wearing a leather jacket despite the lingering heat of the day. This man sat at a table by himself, sketching in a black notebook, his plate of food untouched.

The rest of the Emporium looked like a movie set seen from the wrong angle. The wood was new and bright, and the fake fences built with shiny brass drywall screws. Reinhardt queued up for his meal, and as the line advanced, the songs gave way to a melodrama. A college kid with a glued-on black mustache tried to steal the gal of a different college kid who was clean-shaven with a blue bandanna tied swaggeringly around his boyish neck.

The whole thing escalated quickly. There were words, a shove, and a flamboyant stepping back. More words. Hand gestures. The bad guy drew on the good guy, and while the good guy's hand was going to his gun belt, there was a shot. The bad guy clutched his stomach and sank to his knees. The girl's skirt was up, a thigh holster exposed, and a smoking nickel-plated derringer in one hand.

"Clementine," the villain said, "my only crime was loving you too"—he coughed and fell forward—"much."

The girl and the dandy embraced and sang a duet of a pop song Reinhardt did not recognize from the cowboy canon.

As he came to the buffet, he took a coarse paper plate. Dollops of food appeared on that plate with neither grace nor ceremony: meat, red beans, half a corn cob, a square of corn bread, another square of sheet cake, with a shot of whipped cream from a can. He took his plate to the only empty seat in the Emporium, which was next to the sullen Japanese man, who did not notice him when he sat. Reinhardt ate one bite of everything, then pushed the plate away.

The Japanese man leaned forward. "Some show," he said without taking a break in his sketching.

"It's the only way this particular day could end."

"But it's not very cowboy."

Reinhardt laughed and shook his head. "No, it's not, is it?"

"It's okay though. I'm here for all this corny stuff. My name is Kenji," he said, extending his hand. "I am from Osaka."

"I am Reinhardt. From Berlin." They shook hands.

"Wow," Kenji said. "What a world where the Axis powers can be on vacation together right in the heartbeat of America." He looked down and wrote a note to himself.

"Your English is excellent," Reinhardt said.

"My father hired a tutor for me and my sister. He wanted us to follow him into business. I used English to watch old cowboy movies. I love John Ford, Sam Peckinpah. Your English is also good, but you're German, so it makes sense."

"Thank you?" Reinhardt said.

"Every German I know can speak excellent English." Kenji closed his notebook and stood. "I would love to stay and chat it up with you, but I have preparations to make for a big meeting. It was nice to make your acquaintance."

When he walked past, Reinhardt saw that Kenji had a large image of Hello Kitty painted on the back of his leather jacket. As the Emporium closed back around him, Reinhardt pulled his plate back and tried another bite of the thick beans, then the corn bread, then the cake. The band returned to the stage and started playing a song about cool, clear water.

Day Five

They did not go to town for beers : It's from a movie you
never saw : There's no bad ideas in brainstorming : The
elusive *Antilocapra americana* : Just ask Bruce : Complex
questions usually require complex answers

B yron woke to the sound of peeing. He lay still, waited for it to stop, then
listened to the bobbling of the toilet paper roll. Moonlight filled the
room, and he wanted to shut the blackout curtains, but he didn't want
anyone to know he was awake. He felt the spot next to him, which was empty.
The room's A/C unit kicked on. Lonnie was asleep in the other bed, and Leia,
the woman next to him, sat up.

"Is that you?" she said.

"Yeah. What time is it?" the other woman said from the bathroom.

"2:12."

"How long were we supposed to keep an eye on these guys?"

"Till that Scissors guy comes back. Maybe this afternoon."

"Come smoke with me."

"He said we have to stay *with* them."

"They're sleeping. How's he gonna know?"

The toilet flushed, and he heard a zipper close. "Come smoke with me,"
she repeated.

Byron listened as the women dressed and left the room. When they were gone, he crawled across the bed, opened the drawer of the nightstand, and reached inside.

"No," he said, sitting up. "No, no, no."

He stood and tore through the room naked, opening all the drawers and slamming them shut. Lonnie awoke and rolled over. "What's wrong?" he groaned.

"The money! Where's the money?"

"You're naked, man," Lonnie said. "Where's the girls?"

"I put the money in the nightstand last night."

Lonnie pointed to the safe, which sat above the minifridge.

"Why's it in there? Never mind." Byron squatted in front of it. "What's the combo?"

"Mom's birthday."

"I mean what's the number?"

"You don't know Mom's birthday?"

Byron pushed LOCK and held the button until the word SUPER appeared, then he tapped the 9 button until the safe opened. Inside were both envelopes. He opened them and thumbed through the bills.

"It's February fourteenth. Valentine's Day. You should know that," Lonnie said.

"I don't need a lecture."

"Where are the girls?" Lonnie asked.

"Smoking."

"They could smoke in here. It's that kind of room."

"I'm just telling you what they said."

"Do you think they'll be back?"

"Yeah," Byron said, "I think they will. They're working for Scissors."

"Like us?"

"This is different. We need to get out of here."

"It's, like, the middle of the night."

"We've gotta go home."

"That's the one thing Scissors said not to do."

"We ain't listening to him no more."

While the girls were out, the brothers snuck through the casino, crossed the parking lot, and drove away. Lonnie slept through most of the trip. Byron kept himself awake with another snort of meth and a Mountain Dew chaser he bought while he gassed up the truck using the Visa card Scissors gave him.

At some point he'd have to come clean on the fact that he kept one of the maps, but for the moment he focused his attention on getting home, getting that map, and gathering up the gear they'd need to make their own way onto the monument and start digging. He thought about how he'd make his parole check-ins and how the only thing a person like him could do for a living when he came out of prison was go right back into the life that put him there. He was glad Lonnie was asleep or he'd have to talk to him about jellyfish or Myanmar or anvil lightning or electric airplanes or the *Guinness Book of World Records*. What he wanted was some quiet so he could make a plan without being interrupted.

They climbed through the gorge, blew through each of the towns along the way, and slipped back into the quiet desert. The stars reappeared when they were away from the lights of the city, and the Milky Way presided over the dark expanse.

Byron knew the turnoff to their home by feel. The change in direction woke Lonnie up. He overshot their rutted driveway slightly, then looked behind and backed in. The sky was starting to lighten in the east. When they got close to the single-wide prefab house, Lonnie hopped out and guided Byron as he backed the truck past it, stopping him a few inches away from the tongue of their small travel trailer that looked like a shabby canned ham, even in the half light of the morning. Byron hopped out of the truck and ran straight into the house as Lonnie unfolded the crank and lowered it down. He set to work securing the hitch and connecting the travel trailer's lights to the truck's wire harness. When Byron reemerged, he said, "We get ten minutes, then we're gone."

"How does he even know where we live?"

Byron pointed to the end of the drive. "It says ASHDOWN on the mailbox. You painted it there, you idiot."

Lonnie stood and lurched up the stairs after his brother. "Quit calling me that," he shouted. Byron jumped into the house and tried to close the door, but Lonnie leaned against it with his shoulder and slowly gained leverage.

"We don't have time for this," Byron growled.

Lonnie wedged his shoulder against the door, then he reached around and grabbed Byron's ponytail. Byron roared and tried to grab his brother's hand, which caused him to lose control of the door. Lonnie pushed in a few more inches and was able to yank on the ponytail even harder. Byron cursed and fell to the ground, pulling his hair free of Lonnie's fist but also allowing the door to jump forward and pinch him on his back fat. "I'm sorry I'm sorry I'm sorry I'm sorry. All right! What's wrong with you?" Byron shouted.

"Nothing's wrong with me," Lonnie said, stepping over his brother's body. Lonnie went into his room and took an old canvas duffel and filled it with clothes and the pillow from his bed. He stripped and put on new underwear and socks, then he dressed the rest of the way. He took a hat and a pair of old aviation goggles he used in the desert. From a shelf above his bed, he selected two books and a spiral notebook with a pen jammed into the wire coil. He closed up the bag and took it to the front room.

Byron carried two smaller bags of his own, one in each hand. He had the map rolled up under one arm.

Lonnie walked past him with his bag and tossed it on top of the tools. "What's that?" he asked.

"It's one of the maps. That one we tried out. I kept it." He leaned the map against the side of the single-wide.

"Maybe that's why he sent those girls. We need to find him and give it back."

"And what? Apologize?"

"If that's what it takes."

"Guys like Scissors don't just say, 'No biggie, it's water under the bridge.' They throw you off the bridge. What's done is done. Let's go."

Lonnie went back to the travel trailer and pulled a piece of stovewood that chocked the wheels. "We're just gonna keep running, then? Like the cat in those cartoons?"

"What cat?"

"The one that gets a skunk stripe, then she gets chased the whole time. Scissors is going to keep coming for us like that skunk."

"That's why we're doing this. Down there we're sitting ducks. Now we've got insurance."

"I don't like running. And it's Pepé, by the way."

"Who is?"

"The skunk. His name is Pepé. I forgot the name before."

"Seriously? You know this guy might just kill us—I'm not going to even—look. We ain't running, we're hiding. Plenty of people have done it. Butch Cassidy, Sundance, Billy the Kid, the James Gang."

"The James Gang is a band."

"I'm talking about Jesse James, you moron."

"They got that guy from the Eagles in it."

"I don't know how I start off talking about us getting killed and you end up talking about the Eagles."

"You said James Gang. It got me off track. Stress gets my wires crossed," Lonnie said.

Byron changed his posture; it looked like he was lowering his center of gravity. He set down his things on the ground next to the truck, and he did it so gently that Lonnie grew nervous. "Brother, this moment in time is not about your word associations or idea showers, or your—"

"Chains," Lonnie said, and he knew it was a mistake, but he had to finish the thought. "They're idea *chains*. And I don't try to do it. It just happens."

Byron shook his head and held up a finger. "The only advantage we have over Scissors is we know this place. You've seen how he dresses. He might be city tough, but off-roading isn't one of his skills. I don't have time to get into it with you about physics or chaos theory or any of it, Lonnie. We have time for you to put some food and ice in a cooler or we're dead."

"You came back for the map," Lonnie said, ignoring the rest of it. "That's why we aren't, like, on our way to Mexico or something."

"So what?" Byron said. "You've counted that money. It's ten grand for each of us. How long you think that will carry us?"

Lonnie shrugged. "I can stretch it."

"That map is the goose that laid the golden egg. When things get tight, we'll head out, dig something up, turn it into cash."

Byron went back into the house and returned with a Phoenix Suns duffel bag and his rifle. Then he went back inside and came out with a spotting scope and a tripod. He put the rifle in the rack and packed the duffel bag, scope, and tripod behind his seat in the truck. Lonnie went in for the food. "Don't take everything," Byron said. "Do something to make it look like we're coming back." Lonnie took every other box from the pantry, and a few things out of the fridge: some cheese, a couple of limes, a thing of baloney. He packed it all away, then sat down at the table. He took an envelope and flipped it over and wrote:

Dear ladies, make yourselves at home. Went to town for beers. Be back soon. Byron and Lonnie.

He took the envelope and slid it into the thin aluminum frame that went around the window. Byron made one more pass through the house, came out and picked up the map, stopped to read the note, nodded, then got in the truck. He put the map in the top slot of the gun rack and checked on the trailer behind them, then he turned and put the truck in gear.

—

Sophia rose in the dark five minutes before the alarm on her phone went off. She went into the trailer's Spartan galley and started a pot of coffee. While she was waiting, her phone flashed and buzzed, and she lifted the screen to see the calendar banner, which read BACKCOUNTRY ADVENTURE WITH PAUL. This was going to be a welcome break from gathering data.

As she drove, she remembered a course she took as an undergraduate about ecosystems. The professor told a story about a trip he'd taken with students the summer before into the jungles of Costa Rica. He said that while he was lecturing about climax ecosystems his voice just vanished. Everyone's attention turned to the space left behind by his silence. They noticed that the chatter of the birds and monkeys also ceased. Somebody asked what was going on, and the professor whispered, "Jaguar," as he spread his arms and tried to sweep them back down the trail. The professor said they all looked up and saw the dark symmetry of the cat crouched upon a tree that had fallen but was still suspended by the neighboring trunks, a narrow shaft of daylight painting a stripe of black-and-orange prints in the fur across the shoulders of the beast. The animal lowered its head and pulled back its ears. They watched its chest expand and collapse like the bellows of a forge, and then, without warning, it leapt from the fallen tree away from them to the floor of the jungle. They heard leaves rustle, then the return of their own breathing, and after a time, bird calls and the chittering of a monkey somewhere overhead.

"I've been researching this place for fifteen years," their professor said, "and that was the first time I'd seen something like this."

Sophia hoped she might return to school with such a tale to tell. Something that would give her work some field credibility. Most of the time graduate students returned from fieldwork with ribald drinking stories or tales of bribing officials. They'd regale each other with stories of insects eaten, inclement weather endured, equipment stolen, equipment damaged, data lost. There were volumes on diarrhea, the diameters of spiders, the lengths of snakes, "Why did it have to be snakes?" Most stories were wild, but light on true adventure and with very little romance. Now that she was in the field, she realized that the stories were there to offset the banal repetition of gathering data. What she was doing with the impact of tourism wasn't going to stop any hearts, but maybe something worth telling could happen on a side trip with a certain local legend.

Paul Thrift never spoke of his own exploits, but others did. She'd heard of how Paul once dove out of an airplane and parachuted into a slot canyon that had been unexplored because any other approach would have taken too long. He traveled the deserts with almost nothing. He could feed himself out there, find water with a forked stick. She worried, a little, that this trip would be too austere. She'd gone over her gear obsessively, packing it, trying the backpack for weight, unpacking it, winnowing, packing it again. In addition to food, clothes, tarp, first aid kit, notebook, pencil, and camera, she had her phone (for the audiobooks), a sharp multi-tool (in case she had to cut off her own arm), a hat, bug net, compass, tiny jet stove, and backpacking pot that belonged to her father. All of that.

In addition to her gear, she was bringing a few things for Paul, who could walk from the North Rim to the South Rim for meetings but who had trouble making it to town. Paul had sent her an ascetic list: pecans, sunblock, wet wipes, brewer's yeast, some kind of bodybuilding protein powder, and two books that had come for him at his post office box. One was Loren Eiseley's *The Firmament of Time* and the other was called *Altered States: Buddhism and Psychedelic Spirituality in America.*

The Eiseley was a book she'd recommended to him. Seeing it here in his resupply box made her smile and quickened her pulse ever so slightly. She'd read it in a paleontology course she'd taken as an elective, and she'd mentioned it to him only once, weeks ago when they first met. The only other thing on his list was so strange it gave her pause. He asked for Jolly Ranchers, which seemed antithetical to the mythology surrounding Paul: sugar, plastic, artificial flavor?

She loaded everything into the truck and noticed that the sky was beginning to glow, and through the trees a few wisps of cirrus clouds soaked up the pink dawn glow. She closed and locked the door of her trailer, then saw a light come on at Mrs. Gladstone's. The door opened, and she stood behind the screen, wrapped in a quilt. Mikros leapt up at Mrs. Gladstone's feet and began yapping at her.

"Going out again?" Mrs. Gladstone said. "You're a workaholic." Her hair was wrapped in a flowered silk scarf.

"Oh no. This trip is for pleasure."

Mrs. Gladstone picked up Mikros and held her next to her face. "Good for you. All work and no play makes Jill a dull girl."

"I'm still going out to the monument."

"Boring. I thought you were going to say Las Vegas."

"Paul is taking me to a place called the Swallow Valley," she said.

"Swallow Valley, huh? People have been talking about that place for as long as I can remember. I think it's a fantasy."

"Paul said he thinks he's found it. We'll have to climb to get there."

"Sounds dangerous."

"It could be," Sophia said, smiling nervously.

"A little peril always got my propellers turning," Mrs. Gladstone said, "but it'll probably be safer out there than it would be here, what with some cat burglar running loose in town."

"Cat burglar?"

"He broke into the Cluffs' house while I was there yesterday. As if there hasn't been enough tragedy for Raylene lately. I'm glad nobody got hurt."

"Well, I hope you're okay."

"Nothing a Valium can't fix. And I have Cleopatra in case he tries anything here." The dog barked boldly from the safety of Mrs. Gladstone's arms.

"Be safe," Sophia said. "We'll be in the Antelope Flats area. Paul says it's near the junction of County Roads 16 and 14. I wrote it all down." She handed Mrs. Gladstone a slip of paper, which she tucked inside her brassiere. "If we're not back in forty-eight hours, send in the cavalry."

"I'm sure you've thought of everything. Girls have to these days." Mrs. Gladstone re-hoisted the dog and re-gathered the quilt around her.

Sophia said goodbye and drove to the grocery store. She picked up some rice, bouillon cubes, jerky, raisins, Dr Pepper, and B vitamins. At this hour, the store was almost empty. A few employees were stocking the last of the night freight. She worked through her list, and the last thing on it was ChapStick. In Princeton, she'd lose a tube before it ran out. Here in the desert she went through it so fast it caught her off guard. Her hair, skin, and lips felt stiff, like clothes left out on the line.

As she came around the end of the vitamin aisle, she saw the two jerks from a couple of days ago on the monument. The tall one with slumped shoulders had his arms filled with cans of beans. The shorter one was squatting down to get at the cans that were near the back of the shelf.

"Not that kind," one of them said.

"This is the kind I like. They've already got seasoning."

"It's too salty."

"The salt is what I like."

Sophia turned, backed up until she was out of sight, and stopped to listen.

"Now's not the time to get picky. We've got bigger problems right now than salty beans."

The other one chuckled, then said, "The problems of three little people don't amount to a hill of beans in this crazy world."

"Three who? What are you talking about?"

"Nothing. It's from a movie. You never saw it."

"Well, there's only two of us. So shut up and get a cart."

She went up the next aisle and hoped to stay away from these two. It was becoming clear how the walls of a small town were always up. She was the stranger, and they were locals. The store employees were locals, too. What must it be like to live in a place where you knew everyone but mostly only interacted with the steady flow of tourists who might only spend an hour or two in your hometown? She remembered once waiting for a table at a restaurant and seeing four kids from the university on a double date saying hello to an older woman who was leaving the restaurant. When the woman and her husband left, the students talked about how weird it was to run into a professor out in the world. One of them said, "I know it's dumb, but I guess I never think about how they have, like, this whole other life."

A whole other life.

She made her way to the back of the store and turned to consider the lip balm. She grabbed her go-to basic, then noticed all the choices. Some had SPF protection, some had color, the whole gamut of shades from plum to rose to aubergine. She picked a color she liked and held it in her hands for a few seconds before putting it back, feeling a little crazy about lingering like this. Eventually she picked an unscented tube that offered sun protection and would be less likely to attract pests. Boring but useful.

She asked for a bag of ice, paid, went to the truck, put the ice and soda into her cooler, loaded everything into her pack, then stopped at McDonald's for breakfast. She ate, leaning against her truck in the morning light, then she threw away all the trash so Paul wouldn't know about her culinary indiscretion. She liked the greasy comfort of the sandwich but felt the shame of Paul's paleo-super-macro diet, a practice that would possibly keep him alive forever. She poured her coffee from the Styrofoam cup into her vacuum mug and drove south toward the monument.

—

The Ashdowns left the grocery store and drove out to the state highway, then went twenty-five miles west before turning onto a road that was close to invisible until you were right on top of it. Byron followed each turn of the road with absolute certainty, following a series of branching dirt tracks that shrank down to a pair of ruts in the underbrush. Lonnie pointed to a red rock alcove fifty yards into the sagebrush.

"We camped there once," he said.

"Not here," Byron said, and he kept driving.

"I like that spot."

"This ain't about liking it. We need a place where we can see our house without anybody seeing us."

"An ugly hideout isn't, you know, like some mark of quality. Plus, we can get a line of sight from a bunch of places." Lonnie folded his arms. They bounced in the cab for a couple more miles before Lonnie asked how much gas was left.

"There's enough," Byron snapped. "Plus, we brought the gas can. I don't need a backseat driver right now."

"I'm sitting shotgun, though," Lonnie said.

Byron slammed on the brakes, which bounced Lonnie's face off the dashboard. He came up holding his nose with both hands. "Uncool," Lonnie said, examining the blood on his palms. He massaged the sides of his nose with his middle fingers.

Byron's eyes were tight and dark like the cut ends of a steel rod. "How many times do I have to remind you that we are running for our lives right now?"

Lonnie shrugged.

"I thought you would have a little more focus."

"Thinking about us getting killed gets me weird, so I let my mind think about other things. I let it go where it wants to like my meditation DVD says to."

"One of us needs to be on task, don't you think?"

"Probably." Lonnie reached up for the handle above his window. "I don't know what I'm supposed to think about since I've never been killed before. You know, or had somebody trying to kill me because his brother stole a map he wasn't supposed to steal."

"No wonder Mom worried about you." Byron started driving again. Out of the corner of his eye, he noticed Lonnie had both pinkies up his nose and he was trying to adjust something. Neither of them said anything about it. In a few minutes, Lonnie noticed a bare patch of sun-dried dirt next to a single mature juniper tree, and he pointed to it. Byron slowed and rolled down the window. He raised himself up a little, looked into the distance, and said, "Yeah, we'll have a good view from here."

Byron pulled over, and they worked together silently to unhitch the trailer and chock the tires. When they were done, Byron said, "That Las Vegas SOB ain't going to sneak up on us here."

"We should get a bag of rattlesnakes and throw them in his car," Lonnie suggested. "I brought a pillowcase, so we could if we wanted to."

"Who's gonna fill it with snakes?"

Lonnie shrugged. "There's not supposed to be any bad ideas in brainstorming."

"Is that what we're doing?" Byron asked.

Lonnie set down his duffel. "Well, we don't have any ideas other than being here, do we?"

Byron spat on the ground. "Not yet. Come take a look." He walked past the truck, up a gentle incline, and stood on a bluff that overlooked the tiny cluster of ranch houses, mobile homes, and trailers that made up their outpost neighborhood. From this distance, everything was tiny, the size of Matchbox cars. "If he comes looking for us at the house, we'll see him before he sees us."

"Then what?"

"We've been hunting before," Byron said. "We'll set up the soft blind," then he closed one eye and pantomimed firing a rifle. Byron went back to the truck and pulled the soft blind out and began erecting it. They brought two camp chairs, a cooler, the gun case, and the spotting scope over to the blind, then made themselves comfortable and dug in for the duration. Byron opened the cooler and handed his brother a beer. "I'm finally calming down," he said.

After a few sips of beer Lonnie said, "How do we know he's coming?"

"Because that's how people like him make money. Nobody's going to pay him for leaving loose ends. That's why he's called a cleaner, because he does the dirty work."

Lonnie and Byron sat back in their chairs and watched the valley through the slit in the blind with their eyes unfocused to take in everything at once. They'd learned this as boys, when they were poaching deer with their father. They had to keep an eye out for the bucks and for State Fish and Game. He told them when you're watching for something in particular, you won't really see anything.

As they sat, time broke down into segments, the way ice clears a stream in springtime. They each drank a second beer, then they nodded off, woke and slept, woke and slept. Still nothing out there. Clouds spread across the sky, gathering, boiling, pushing shadows across the valley floor. A crescendo and decrescendo of sunlight. Another beer. Handful of salted nuts. Checking the spotting scope. Nothing but the door to their house, everything unmoving. One distant crack of thunder. No rain. Lonnie got up to pee and came back. Then Byron went. The shadows shortened, and with the sun overhead, they put on wide-brimmed camouflage hats. Above them at intervals the white trails of jets skimmed the belly of the stratosphere.

Byron crashed. His whole body collapsed as if the connective tissue had been removed. His head flopped back, hands dangling almost to the ground. Lonnie pulled the spotting scope over and focused again on their house, down in the valley. In the bright disk, at the center of the crosshairs, he watched a silver Chrysler Sebring creep up the driveway. Lonnie nosed the scope over so the windshield was right at the middle. It was Scissors.

Byron snuffled and settled a little deeper into his chair. Lonnie wasn't sure he should wake him right away. Maybe the whole thing was like hornets. Stay still and they'll fly away. If Byron woke up, he'd try to take him out, and there was no way he'd make that shot from here. There would only be one chance, and Lonnie didn't like the odds.

Through the scope he saw the car door open. Scissors got out, reached into his jacket and pulled a pistol from a shoulder holster, then closed the car door with his foot. He looked around, stooped, and took a pinch of dirt in his fingers, dropped it, and stood again. He went up the stairs to the front door, stooped to peer inside, then without hesitating, he broke the glass with the barrel of the gun and reached inside to open the door.

"Hey," Lonnie said without thinking.

Byron heard him and started awake. "What's going on? Is he here?"

"Down there."

Lonnie didn't take his eye from the spotting scope, so Byron took the rifle and pointed it toward the trailer, using it to see. "Is that his stupid car?"

"Yep. He's inside the house," Lonnie said.

"Give me the clip," Byron said, holding out his hand.

"I don't have it."

"We've got a gun and no bullets?"

"I mean, maybe. It's not my gun, so how would I know?" Lonnie said.

"Seriously, there's no bullets? At all?"

"There could be some in the truck. You're not supposed to keep it loaded. We went through that with the cop."

"Don't lecture me on the law," Byron said.

"I don't think shooting at him is a good plan," Lonnie said.

"I don't plan to shoot *at him.*"

"I'm not sure anyone could make that shot the first time."

Byron kept looking through the rifle scope and swearing in a steady stream. "What's he doing in there?"

He watched Scissors emerge from the single-wide and head to the shelter where they kept their travel trailer. He searched around until he found a red gas can, which he lifted and shook to take stock of how much fuel was left.

"I guess we forgot the gas can, too," Lonnie said.

"Shut up," Byron said.

They watched as Scissors doused their house and the rickety front porch, and they both swore when he lifted the cover of their gas grill and lit it with the piezo switch.

"You got anything in there that matters?" Byron asked.

"My winter coat. Picture of Mom and her sisters. Books. A box of football cards," Lonnie said, his eye still on the spotting scope. "It's a good coat. How about you?"

Scissors carefully tipped the grill over on its side. Flames leapt out of the interior and raced across the patio, turning at a right angle when they hit the wall.

"I got what I need. Prison teaches you to strip down."

"I think that's maybe not exactly what you meant to say."

Byron ignored the comment and adjusted his position, then dry fired the rifle with a click. "I know a couple of guys who could make a shot like this. They'd do it just to see if they had it in them."

"I really don't think jail made you a better person," Lonnie said.

"No, it did not," Byron said, sitting back and setting the rifle in his lap. "But that's not what prison is for, little brother. It's just another way for some rich guys to get richer."

"It's burning pretty fast, huh?" Lonnie said.

"What's he doing now?"

"Getting into his car."

"This lets you know what that guy was gonna to do to us," Byron said.

Lonnie sat back in his chair. He got two beers out of the cooler and passed one over. They cracked them open at the same time and drank in silence. Above the top of the blind, they could see the billowing column of black smoke coiling skyward.

—

An hour into the drive, Sophia crumpled the wrapper of a small caramel and glanced in her mirrors. Behind her was a column of black smoke, to the northwest near Cane Beds, near the Paiute reservation. While she was watching the smoke, a pronghorn antelope bounded alongside the truck, keeping pace through the golden mesh of grass. Its stark white face ignored her. This was a creature so present in its own motion, the world was an afterthought. As she reached for her phone to snap a picture, the antelope pulled ahead, cut in front of her, and burst diagonally across the open ground, following the receding line of steel giants carrying power from the hydroelectric dams on the Colorado River to Las Vegas and L.A.

After so many weeks in this new place, Sophia realized that even though she was meant to be studying the past, she was, in fact, deeply involved in a long sequence of present moments that served as historical muses, creating a rhythm for the long view. Clouds would gather and dissipate. A snake would uncoil itself across the road. Dry grasses would oscillate in the breeze. Birds would chase one another beneath the open sky. Each moment gone in the instance of its unfolding. Each day so much like the others that had come and gone before.

The terrain changed. Flat roads gave way to gentle undulations. After a time, she came across a rise and saw a white NPS Jeep parked at the junction of two county roads. Paul was wearing regular clothes, stretching his hamstrings. As she slowed and approached, he looked up to greet her. He looked exhausted, but immediately asked about her voyage. The word threw her. Why not say "trip"? "Street clothes, huh?" she asked instead of answering his question.

He shrugged, "All work and no play. That's why I'm leaving the Jeep here."

She watched him close up the Jeep and lock it. He moved deliberately, like someone doing Tai Chi.

She circled back to his question and said her "voyage" was uneventful except for her encounter with an antelope.

"Pronghorn," he said. "*Antilocapra americana.*"

"I can't believe how fast it was. I must have been going forty."

"Fastest creature in North America. Amazing stamina." Paul transferred his gear to her truck and said he hoped it was okay if she drove. He'd been doing a lot of it lately. Then he switched topics and asked about the resupply.

She said she got everything on the list. "You can go through it while we drive."

"I'll wait. We should just catch up," he said. "That's what I'm looking forward to."

Within a few minutes, they were under way. The sky that was empty in the morning had filled with clouds during the day, and a few dumped dark patches of virga into the air. They drove out of the open into a different place, where the rocks emerged from the soil like the bones of something buried eons ago.

They spoke of the land and the weather. Paul talked about the mundanities of the monument, the complications of politics and budgets. Sophia talked about her research and how she was trying to clarify, for herself, at least, what the work of archeology should be. This led to a discussion of museums and repositories and eventually they returned to parks. She told Paul about her presentation at Bryce and the idea that people should have access. At the same time, people have a habit of ruining what they love. She told Paul about the man's heart attack and the doctor who had saved him. Paul asked her what mattered to her most, and she said it was the truth. She wanted her work to cut through the bogus ideas that museums have put into people's heads. She was also worried that sometimes parks are sacrificial. You have to let people ruin part of a place so you can save the rest of it.

Paul nodded. "We think about that a lot," he said. "It's a hard call. I don't think we always get it right. I mean, we didn't used to, when a park meant a lodge. I mean, we don't do it like that anymore. It's not supposed to be Jellystone. Some people in charge don't know that."

As they drove on, they spoke less frequently. Paul would point out a remarkable red-rock fin or an anomalous tree on the dry plain tapping into some scarce underground water. After a time, Paul pointed to a spot in the distance where the low cliffs gathered into a kind of promontory. "Up there," Paul said. "That's the trailhead."

"Here?" she asked. "But there's no road."

"Where we're going, Sophia, we don't need roads," Paul said, grinning.

Sophia took note of the odd rhythms of his speech. His language was graceful when he spoke on the subject of the natural world, but it was an odd grab bag of movie and TV quotations when it came to anything else. She decided to meet him halfway. "Since this truck doesn't fly, I wouldn't mind a good road," she said.

"If people had flying cars there wouldn't be any place left worth going to," he said, turning to look out the window.

Sophia put the truck into four-wheel drive and abruptly turned off the road, which banged Paul's head against the window. He sat back and adjusted his seat belt.

"Sorry," she said, trying not to laugh.

The truck whined as it climbed and bounced over the rocks. In a few hundred feet, she came to dry open ground scattered with bone-colored rocks. Around the perimeter were a number of small blooming cacti. Paul said they could park there. "You can't do this up at Bryce, but the monument is different, and parking here helps hide the vehicle," he said.

They got out of the truck, stretched, and started pulling gear out of the bed.

"How come we're hiding?" Sophia asked.

"I don't like people to know about these sensitive sites."

"But it's public land. I'm not criticizing, I'm just trying to figure out what places like this are for. I've got my ideas, but I'm interested in yours."

"Well," he said, opening the top of his pack, "it is public, but that doesn't mean we have to advertise. We're supposed to preserve the resource, and sometimes the best offense is not even being on the map. GPS coordinates don't come with safety instructions." Sophia looked at him with a squint that Paul noticed. "Swallow Valley is special because it was lost," he said.

"It's not on any of the official maps or the inventories I'm working with, but it's everywhere in the oral history," she said.

"Not anymore. Everyone around here has gone silent. They'll talk your ear off about UFOs and Aztec gold, but ask them about Swallow Valley, you get nothing." Paul said. "Only one guy would talk to me about it, but he just died. I thought we might come up here to honor him. He had maps he drew himself. Wouldn't let anybody see them. You had to be on the inside. The Paiutes are the only ones who know more about this place than him, and they aren't talking to anybody either. I don't blame them. Every time they do, they get burned."

"With nobody talking, we're going to lose the knowledge," Sophia said. "In a generation it'll be gone. This is our Library of Alexandria."

Paul looked at her and grinned.

"What?" she said, then she opened her pack. "I have a tent. I thought we could split the weight between us."

"Maybe we could do without a tent on this one," Paul said. "We'll be hauling these bags up a lot of cliff faces. Any extra weight we take in there should be water."

Sophia frowned and pulled out her tent and stowed it in the cab. Sophia showed Paul his box of things, and he quickly parceled out what he needed, taking note of the books. He held up the one she'd recommended. "I'm looking forward to this," he said, "and to these." He held up the Jolly Ranchers. "Thank you. These are my weakness."

They loaded the water into the center of the packs, then packed around it. Paul carefully loaded one last red stuff sack into his bag, checked it, and cinched everything down.

After an initial scramble over some boulders and a low cliff, they made their way through the high chaparral. Paul navigated by sight toward a mesa in the distance that was flanked on either side by miles of running cliffs forming what would have, from the air, looked like a long funnel. Small clusters of sage and agave transitioned to larger juniper, which burst into the mechanical racket of cicadas as they passed.

Paul's pace was indomitable. Even so, Sophia sensed that he was throttling back. She tried not to take it personally. He'd have to throttle back for just about everyone. He looked like a creature who could walk forever. *Antilocapra parkrangerus*. As they hiked, Paul asked her to say more about her research, what she'd been seeing in the data she was gathering about the degradation of sites on the monument.

"It's complicated," she said. "And I'm trying to avoid confirmation bias."

"Bias about what?"

"The belief that people ruin everything."

"They do," Paul said, then he corrected himself. "We do, and I hate that there's a term for it."

"Right? I feel like I'm a scorekeeper for the Anthropocene. It's like watching a house burn down."

"And taking notes."

"Crazy notes. Never-ending notes."

Paul stopped and turned. He bit the rubber tube of his hydration bladder and sipped. Without a word, he pointed toward the west, where they'd come from. They'd gained enough elevation to bring them high above the valley floor. From this position, they could see the high voltage lines in the distance, small now like toys, running to the horizon where the dark green of the mountains was broken only by the defiant red escarpments of the cliffs to the north. Paul noticed the tiniest thread of smoke rising in front of the Vermilion Cliffs. "Huh," he said. "A fire in Cane Beds."

"I saw that earlier."

"I hope they get it under control, or it'll run wild across that grassland and up into the Kaibab Reservation."

Paul turned to the south and the ridge dropped away precipitously, revealing at some distance a lava field that drew a sharp line of contrast against the tawny desert floor. "This whole area has seen volcanic activity in the last two hundred years. If you look across the plateau to the first escarpment there, you'll see the cinder cones. They're like the most geometric landforms out there."

In her mind, Sophia repeated the word, "geometric." These were the sentences she liked.

"What?" Paul said, distracted by her pause.

"Keep going," she said. "Talking, I mean. I'm okay to hear more about all this."

"That lava flow has some interesting history. Paiutes used it as an escape route or a place for ceremonies. They have almost invisible pathways through the middle of the lava that they made by carrying tens of thousands of basket loads of cinders in there. And over there, a few miles past, that's where a crazy old hermit lives in a school bus. This place is a lot of things."

"What's that?" Sophia asked, pointing to a cluster of houses.

"Carvertown," Paul said. "It's a little bit militia, and a little bit rock and roll. Just kidding, the Carver family's been ranching out there since the 1880s. They think of us as the intruders. Over there across from Fandango Wash is another recent volcano. People call it El Sombrero, you know, for 'hat,' but the root word actually comes from the Spanish word for shade."

"Ha," she said, "I'll bet it throws great shade."

"Not at midday," Paul said.

She was about to explain her joke, but instead she said, "I think most people imagine you as some kind of stoic protector, but really you've got some solid natural history standup moves."

"I'll be here all week," Paul said, sipping from his tube and continuing on. After a time, she thought about how easily her body assumed the pace and the weight of her pack. She felt as strong as she had ever been in her life, and she thought about how this research project would be over before she knew it, another passing moment among many. She wished she could more easily switch to geologic time and recalibrate. These bursts of pressing human concern needed proper perspective.

They hiked on through the scrub, climbing higher and higher, boots crunching in the sandy soil.

"How do you know we're going the right way with no trail?" she asked.

"The layers," he said. "Each band is a different kind of rock that cuts through the whole area. If you know the shapes of the exposed layers, it's kind of like a map, or a slice of a map." He held his hands out like he was casting a spell. "We're on the Kayenta Formation right now. It's the blocky stuff, kind of crumbly. Lots of broken ledges. The Navajo Sandstone—which is a lot thicker—that's above us. It used to be part of a massive sand desert." He pointed to the high cliffs ahead with tall vertical cracks. "It starts red and turns gray at the top. Above that is the Carmel Formation. We came up through the Wingate. You can kind of piece the whole area together in your mind and see where we're supposed to be going."

"So, you've been there before?"

"Not really. But it's been described to me."

"So, you're in the know?"

"A little bit. More than I would have thought." Paul stopped and unzipped a pouch on the belt of his pack. He took out two Jolly Rancher candies and handed one over. She got grape. "You have a green apple?" she asked, handing hers back. Paul dug around until he found one. She took the tiny brick, unwrapped it, and slipped it into her mouth. The acidity drew saliva into her mouth like a pump, and she closed her eyes to focus on the sensation. In the dry air, the effect was like a sugary sweet heartbeat against her tongue. She opened her eyes and saw Paul watching her over his lowered sunglasses.

"Shut up," she said.

"It's good, right?"

"I had no idea," she said.

Paul pushed his sunglasses back up onto the bridge of his nose and held out his hand. "I've got a place for the plastic," he said. His hand stayed out until she placed the wrapper in his palm.

The sun dropped halfway to the horizon as they came to a vertical cliff that went up about twenty feet. It was flat with no obvious handholds except for a corner that was almost ninety degrees. Paul carefully set down his pack and tied one end of a length of parachute cord to the top loop and took the other end in his teeth. He placed both hands against the rock, then one foot, followed by the other. Before she could process how he was doing it, he was at the top, sitting on the edge, hauling up his bag.

When he untied his pack, he dropped one end of the cord. "Tie it on. I'll haul it up."

Once her bag was clear, Paul said, "It's called stemming. The trick is to get the friction from your feet. You'll think it won't work, but if you get out of your head you'll be fine." She started the same way: hand, hand, foot, foot. Her weight pressed her palms and soles against the sides of the corner. Bit by bit she inched her way up. When she came to the top, Paul's voice broke her focus. "Inch your feet up and you'll come right over."

She didn't think it would work, but suddenly she was sitting on the edge looking down. She noticed that the massive boulder they had just climbed was not brown like the surrounding stone. It matched the red rock from above.

"Nice climb. I knew you wouldn't have a problem," Paul said.

"I wasn't so sure," Sophia replied.

"You're really good . . . for a gym rat," Paul said.

"Thanks?" she said, and he shrugged, grinning.

She could see they were now in the new layer of Navajo Sandstone, and the whole environment had changed. The shapes, scale, colors, and rhythms of the fractures in the rock were different. Across the expanse to the east were a series of buttes, the color bands matching the rock she was on: orange separated by gray, topped by a buff-colored layer at the top.

They hiked on. After a few minutes, Sophia asked, "Is it true that you jumped into the Colorado River in some kind of sea monster outfit?"

"Who told you that?"

"Everybody."

Paul paused. "It was a dry suit with hand paddles. I wanted to see if I could go rim to rim on my own without a bridge."

"I see," she said. "And the pilots say they take you and your bike places and just drop you off, you know, in the middle of nowhere."

Paul filled his cheeks with air, then let them deflate. "Yeah, I wish they'd stop telling those stories."

"It's a pretty wild mythology."

"Honestly, it makes me feel self-conscious. I should tone it down."

"You know they're not making fun of you. You're like their Captain America. I didn't mean to make it feel weird. I wanted to see if it was truth or legend."

"Everybody's a hero," Paul said. "That's my message."

She watched his face when he said it, and she could see that he was telling the truth. As the way rose higher, they came to a boulder field and hopscotched across the stones' bald backs. After the boulders, they traversed a long ridge of stone that curved past protean columns of rock that seemed more like frozen gas than eroded solids. Eventually, they arrived at the mouth of a slot canyon that was plugged with rockfall.

"This is the technical part," Paul said.

"What have we been doing for the last three hours?"

"The approach. This is as far as I've come before."

Paul opened his pack, removed a red stuff sack, and set it aside. He then hauled out ropes, harnesses, and an array of other equipment. He arranged all of it carefully on a black nylon drop cloth. He carefully repacked the stuff sack into his bag. "This is the route we talked about. We'll climb two pitches here, then on into the great unknown."

As he set up for the climb, he talked through the route, suggesting that he'd climb lead, and she would clean. She mostly climbed routes that were top roped, so this would be a new challenge, something she had wanted to try for a while. Paul handed her a harness and shoes, then looked upward. "The first pitch will end at the midpoint of that rubble." He pointed to a place where the rock curved under, casting the faintest of shadows. Sophia nodded and donned her gear and stowed her boots and socks in her pack. They went over their belay signals, then roped up.

Paul climbed easily and with a lightness. He moved so quickly she had to work constantly to keep the rope from going slack, but her hands fell easily into the quick rhythm of it, the pull of the ascending rope offset by the weight of the brake side threaded through the figure eight. At intervals, Paul would stop, select one of the wired nuts, slip it into a crack, test it, clip the rope into place, and climb on. When he completed the first pitch, the rope went slack, and they began hauling up their packs on the length of static cord Paul sent down. Sophia tied on Paul's pack and tugged the line. The pack floated into the air and spun as it rose. Moments later the unknotted cord descended.

"Now yours," Paul called out.

She repeated the process.

With both packs up, Sophia then tied into the rope and felt the slack come out of it, the tension transferring to her pelvis. She loved how the climbing shoes transformed the smallest protrusion or horn of rock into a platform with its own kind of certainty. By moving slowly and methodically, she found herself rising quickly, the tightness of the rope giving her confidence. Climbing made her acutely aware of her balance and strength, but she was always surprised at how engaged her mind was. She didn't zone out. It was like solving a massive three-dimensional puzzle. When she came to one of the colored wire stoppers with its carabiner, she removed it and clipped it to her harness. She did not feel an immediate mastery in this cycle, but she found a peace in it.

The belay ledge was small, but Paul had everything organized, and they were able to reset and trade places. In a few minutes, Paul was climbing again, setting protection, clipping in, and climbing on. Soon he disappeared from view, and Sophia only knew he was there by the tugging and resistance on the other end of the rope. The process repeated itself, bags first, Sophia's leading the way, since it was the last one tied. Because of the angle of the cliff face, her pack swung out into space and spun in the air as it ascended. When the cord returned, she tied on Paul's pack. As his pack went out and up and across the overhang, it caught on a small tree growing impossibly from a void in the sandstone. He raised and lowered the pack a number of times to no avail.

"Hey," Paul yelled down. "My pack is caught. I think if you lean out, you might be able to unsnag it."

"I don't know if I can," she said.

"It should be okay," Paul replied.

"How about I get up there, then we figure it out?"

"It should be okay if you just nudge it a little," he repeated.

She climbed up to the overhang and strained to reach the pack, which was just out of reach. "Can you just pull harder?" she said.

"I don't want it flying around," he shouted.

She tried again and almost reached one of the straps before she lost her grip and fell. The rope caught her, stretched, and yanked her against the rock. Immediately, she was upside down, heart pounding, her whole body electrified with adrenaline. The swinging of the rope dislodged Paul's pack, and the small tree that snagged it fell past Sophia and into the space below before hitting the ground. After a few inverted seconds, she fought her way back into position and found new hand- and footholds. She clung there with the belay line slack as Paul hauled his pack to the top.

When the belay was ready, Sophia shouted, "Climbing!"

"Climb on," he called back.

As she climbed, she ignored the suggestions Paul made, using the anger to help her focus.

At the top, Paul apologized for the accident.

"Was it an accident?" she said. "Because—I don't know—it seemed like something else." Sophia untied the rope and sat on a rock to remove her climbing shoes. Her heartbeat felt audible, her jaw tight. After a few moments, once she relaxed, she began to hear the insects again, and then the taffeta of the wind through the vegetation, and finally, somewhere farther up the canyon, the dry croak of a raven.

—

Dalton told LaRae that he had to run a personal errand, and after that he was going to stop by the Beehive House and pay Raylene Cluff a visit.

"You want me to call ahead?" LaRae asked.

"It's better if I just drop in," he said.

"They told me they'd prefer a heads-up."

"That's why I like to drop in," Dalton said, winking.

"Before you go, I wanted to let you know the trailer fire over in Cane Beds is out. They also said they're okay if you still want to take a look at what's left."

"Thanks. I've got my eye on it."

"But Cane Beds is in Arizona," she said.

"When two weird events pop up in the same week, I lose interest in jurisdictions."

LaRae thought about Dalton's answer and looked like she might ask another question, then decided not to. "I'll hold down the fort," she said.

Dalton drove into town, letting his to-do list wash over him until he got to Red Cliffs Realty. He looked up and down the street to see if anyone was watching, and there was nobody he knew on the sidewalk, so he went inside. The only person in the office was the receptionist. She was young and he didn't know her.

"Can I help you?" she asked.

"I guess I need to sell my house," Dalton said.

"Oh, fantastic. Can you fill out our online form?"

"Is Jim Gardner still here?"

"No, Jim's retired."

"Oh, I hadn't heard. Maybe I could leave my name and number." Dalton took out a pen and looked for a slip of paper.

"The web form is really easy, though."

"But I don't like web forms," Dalton said.

"But then you'll know the information we have on you is right," she said.

Dalton stared at her and she stared back.

"I guess you'll want me to do that from home." Dalton put the pen back.

"Or you could do it on your phone," she said.

Dalton walked out of the office without saying goodbye and drove to the Beehive House, where social services had temporarily relocated Raylene Cluff. It was an assisted care facility in a pioneer home with a large brick addition attached to the back. A hand-painted sign out front featured a logo with a blue beehive surrounded by a few simple bees. Dalton's mother had lived here until his sister moved her to Salt Lake to have her close at hand. Bruce and Raylene had no children, so this is where she landed, too.

Dalton wanted to talk to Raylene about the missing items and the break-in. He hoped she might be able to shed some light.

The orderly at the front desk greeted him.

"I'm here to check on Raylene Cluff, ask her a couple of questions. She ready for something like that?"

"I'll have to get permission," he said and excused himself.

Dalton took in the surroundings. They hadn't changed much in five years. It was cramped, full of oddly matched donated furniture that had come from several different decades. The orderly returned with a harried woman wearing a Kane County Fun Run T-shirt over her blouse and blue half-moon reading glasses on a chain around her neck. She had a wild arrangement of white hair tied back with a flowered scarf. Her name was Catherine Mowbley.

"What do you need to see Raylene for?" she asked.

"I'm trying to clear up some things for the report on her husband."

"You know she's not lucid," she said. "The stress of the situation isn't settling well with her. We've had her on sedatives since she came in."

"Catherine, this is one of the big pieces of the puzzle."

She looked at him. "You might not get much out of her. She hasn't said more than a couple of words. They also just gave Raylene her meds. She'll be out of it pretty quick."

"Can I give it a shot?" Dalton said.

The orderly sent them through to a common room, and in a few minutes, Catherine appeared with Raylene in a wheelchair. Dalton noticed she was strapped at the wrists, a blanket tucked around her legs.

Dalton took a chair from one of the tables and brought it closer to Raylene.

An orderly locked the wheels on the chair and stepped back. Raylene looked ashen and exhausted. Her silver hair was unkempt. Her thin arms pulled at the restraints.

"Sheriff," Raylene said. "These assholes think I'm going to run off and join the circus."

Dalton was surprised by her cursing. He'd known her for a long time. She worked as a librarian, and she'd dress down rowdy teenagers for 10 percent of the language he'd just heard. When Catherine saw his face, she told him this kind of language was a new development for Raylene but not uncommon for people in her situation.

He nodded, then said, "All this could just be a safety concern, Raylene."

"They've got me locked up so they can steal from me and Bruce. While I'm here, they're off ransacking my house. You talk to anyone. They'll tell you."

"Raylene, you've known me and my parents for a long time."

"You're the one married to Olma. I didn't know you were a cop."

"Olma's my mother," Dalton said, looking at Catherine, who had her hands on her hips. "I'm Patrick, Henry Dalton's boy."

Raylene blinked and turned her head a few degrees.

"Yesterday there was a break-in at your house—"

"I told you they were trying to rob me."

"Now, I'm pretty sure it wasn't any of these people. It was in the middle of the day, and I'll bet they were all working. It seems like the people who broke in were after some of Bruce's things. I found a couple of spots where it looks like things used to be, but now they're gone. A lot of artifacts Bruce used to have in his study, it looks like they're gone, too. I mean, all the pots are gone, Raylene. I have some photographs. Could you take a look and—"

She waved him off with a dismissive hand. "You should just ask Bruce. He's got all of that stuff cataloged."

"I'd like to ask Bruce, but he's—"

"Sheriff," Catherine interrupted. "Let's talk, over here."

"Bruce is what? He's supposed to be coming to pick me up."

As Dalton and Catherine stepped away, the orderly tried to make Raylene comfortable. "She doesn't know what happened. We thought maybe it was the shock. Maybe she was in denial about what happened, but I think we might be looking at the onset of dementia."

"You mean, like Alzheimer's or something?"

"I'm not a doctor, but yeah. I think that's what we're looking at. If you drop anything about Bruce taking his own life, she might withdraw again."

"I've got to ask about the break-in. Is she going to have trouble remembering that?"

"Why was there a break-in if Bruce killed himself?" Catherine asked.

"Well, that's a good question, isn't it?"

"A lot of times people with dementia have trouble with new memories. Older stuff, well, there's more connections in the brain. It's better encoded. She might forget today altogether. She doesn't know why she's here. Last in, first out," she said.

"Then I better get cracking." Dalton took out his phone and went to the photos app. "Am I okay to show her these pictures?" He thumbed through to pictures of the empty spots he'd found in the dust.

"Sometimes old memories are fine. Sometimes they're not. Give it your best shot."

Dalton went back to Raylene and sat in his chair. "Can I show you a couple of pictures? I'm wondering if you could tell me what is supposed to be in these spaces."

"What's wrong with Bruce?" Raylene asked, her eyes soft and unblinking. "I'm not stupid."

"He's had an accident," Dalton said.

"Well, I want to see him."

Dalton looked to Catherine for guidance. She shrugged and touched Raylene softly on the shoulder, which didn't soothe her.

"He wants to see you, too," Dalton said.

Dalton showed her the first photo of a small disk left in the dust.

"That's where the Swallow Valley bowl goes, the one with a monster inside. It's one of Bruce's favorites. It doesn't look like much from the outside, but what a surprise when you look into it."

"Was it valuable?"

"Oh, yes. But he'd never sell it. Those things mean so much to him. He's had a hard time letting that one go. He's saving it for last."

Dalton wrote himself a note that said: *Saving it for what?*

"Okay. How about this one?" Dalton showed her the next photo with the square space in the dust. On one side was a large agate bookend, and on the other was a potted cactus.

"That's where his inventory goes. It's his whole book of everything. The list of all the things. Everything with a catalog card and everything on one of his maps is in that book."

"Could you tell me what it looks like?"

"It's a blue thing with a stiff back, like we used to use in chemistry."

"It sounds important."

"It used to be."

"Tell me what that means."

"A while ago Bruce started taking everything back."

"Is that what you meant when you said Bruce is having a hard time letting things go?"

"That's right."

"So, what's going back?"

"All of it. His whole collection. A few years ago, he had a change of heart. He said he thought that when he died all his things would lose their meaning. They'd just be something for somebody to sell. That's why he's doing it. He's old, though, and he's been getting help."

"Do you know who that helper would be?" Dalton asked.

"Oh, some young man. He's not from around here."

Raylene's eyes drooped, and Dalton could see that her meds were starting to set in. Dalton reached over and put his hand on hers. He noticed an ornate turquoise ring. There was a second ring on the other hand. "Are these in that blue book?" he asked, gesturing to the jewelry.

"Bruce found the turquoise for this one in a burial pit," she said, extending her left hand. "Ever since he was a teenager, he found things nobody else could. He had a nose for it. He said he found these stones folded together in a piece of hide and stuck in a mummy's fist. It was covered in blue feathers, and there was a crown of yellow feathers all around the head. He said it looked like a leather sun. The whole thing was lying in a little room full of sand and stones. Imagine that. A human head like a tiny little star in there. He brought the stones home and turned them out on the kitchen table. He had a Navajo he knew in Chinle make this one for me, then he gave it to me for my twenty-fifth birthday." She wiggled the fingers on her other hand. "This one was made in Mexico. I don't remember the story for it."

Dalton thanked her and said, "It helps to hear your perspective, Raylene." Then he stood and returned the chair to the table, thinking about someone far in the future finding Raylene's rings loose in the loam of her remains, no story, no body, just the stones and silver. What would she think of that person slipping the ring on their own finger, trying to imagine her?

"When are they going to let me go?" Raylene asked.

"Once they know you're not going to run off and party with your girl-friends," Dalton said.

"When Bruce comes home—he's going to come get me, right?"

"He will," Dalton said.

The orderly took Raylene away, and Catherine showed Dalton out of the room. "I shouldn't have let you in here."

"I'm glad you did, though. I have to ask you not to talk about it, though. Especially not to Stan Forsythe."

"I don't talk to that man unless I have to," Catherine said.

Dalton knocked on the door, and he was buzzed out. "Hey, Sheriff," Catherine called after him. "If Bruce didn't kill himself, then what the heck is going on?"

Dalton shrugged. "I'd sure like to find out."

—

The way from their climb to the white sandstone domes led them through thick, luminescent chollas, bristling with light. Where there had been no trail before, a subtle path emerged from the random placement of stone and vegeta-tion, and they followed it for the ease of the passage. They moved into shadow, and the sunlight became a white corona behind the stone ramparts. They hiked for another hour through this rough architecture, climbing upward until they stepped at last into the cool space of a sandstone amphitheater at the center of which was a series of small connected brick structures nestled under a thick natural overhang. Off to the side was a miraculous pool of standing water, fed by an invisible spring.

Sophia gasped. Paul turned around, beaming. She dropped her pack and began digging around for her camera.

"No pictures, okay?" Paul asked.

"Why not? The grant gives me clearance," Sophia said.

"This trip is not quite on the books." Paul made a face that was neither smile nor grimace. "Actually, it's one hundred percent off the books. You can't tell anyone we came here."

"Are you kidding me? This isn't on any of the maps. It's like the discovery of a lifetime."

"It's really just a rediscovery," Paul said.

She looked at the silent cliff dwellings with their thin black windows and narrow slotted doors. "This site could help me establish a baseline for my research. I'd have a pre-tourism basis for comparison."

"Maybe," Paul said. "Maybe. But if you write about it, people will come. And if people come, then we'll have to file a management plan, and once we do that, it's probably over for this place. I can take you to sites that have essentially the same features, and—"

"But if this is really Swallow Valley, we'd be able to make important connections that are just educated guesses right now."

"The Paiutes don't need us to interpret this place for them, and tourists don't need an explanation for something they aren't going to see." Sophia noticed a look of uncertainty flash across Paul's face. "It would be a huge favor to me if you just soaked this place in, without recording it. The USGS is pulling sites like these from their maps because they feel like they are aiding and abetting the looters. Some people think we should redact everything from the maps and write in 'here be dragons' like in the good old days."

Sophia stopped digging through her bag. "You know I agree with you about the trouble with tourism, but being able to gather data on this site would change everything for me when I get back to Princeton."

"And it would change everything for this place. Tourism here would be catastrophic. That's what you're researching, right? Can you imagine a ladder bolted into that cliff? With everything that's going on in D.C. right now, climate denial, all the push to let energy companies in here, anonymity is the most efficient way to save this place."

"Efficient?" Sophia said with no attempt to mask her anger. "There are a lot of efficiencies in this world that make it a worse place to live. And there's a world of difference between studying a place and posting it on Instagram."

"Okay, 'efficient' was the wrong word. But it's just me and a million acres out here. I can only be in one place at a time. They cut our budgets every chance they get. We're being led by bureaucrats who hate the idea of public land. This is a no-win situation. If I can redefine even a couple of the parameters—reduce the number of people, keep it hard to access a site, make sure the legislature doesn't even know what's out here, and quit painting a target on every amazing thing—if I can do that, then maybe I'll stand a chance." Paul was going to say something else but he stopped and took out a blue hardback lab notebook from his pack. "Let me show you something. The guy I talked about who'd been up here fifty years ago, he cataloged it, drew pictures of what he found. He came back twenty or thirty times over the course of a decade. Never told anyone about this place, except for his wife."

"And you."

"That's right. He took things out of here, said he was rescuing them." He handed her the notebook. "This will give you a sense of what he was up to. Take a look."

She opened the book, which was filled with studious notes and sketches of artifacts. Each entry featured a drawing with careful crosshatching that gave the images a heft; around these flowed physical descriptions written in an impeccable hand, all of it done with thin black and red lines. The meticulous descriptions told the dimensions of each object and the conditions in which it was found. For some entries there was a second sketch showing the proximity to other artifacts in the inventory, the orientation within a room, chamber, or kiva, or there was a rendering from the side showing the depth of the object in the ground. Sophia stopped at a page featuring a detailed sketch of a clay jar with a corrugated outer surface. The notes said: *White slip clay body, quartz sand temper with beautiful tool-dented corrugated surface design. Moenkopi style.* Each entry gave a date of discovery, some going as far back as the 1970s. Many of the entries had a second date written in the margins in pencil, and there were initials, too: KT and PT. The pencil dates were all in the last five years.

"The level of detail here is amazing."

"He was self-taught."

"What are these dates in pencil?" Sophia asked.

"He's been reviewing his collection. That's where I've been helping."

Sophia closed the book. It was old but in good condition, meant to last. She noticed a fine stippling of brown across the back cover. "Helping how?" she asked.

Paul retrieved the notebook and put it away. "Let's look around," he said. Paul led the way across the amphitheater down near the pueblo structures. The wind bent the grasses lightly, and as they drew closer the sun moved through a notch in the cliffs, illuminating the rock with a warm golden light while the buildings remained in shadow.

As they crossed, Sophia noticed the shallow depressions of irrigation ditches that had been almost completely refilled with rock and soil. If she hadn't known what she was looking at, she wouldn't have noticed anything, but as they walked on, they skirted the midden and she spotted potsherds and lithic fragments among the vegetation. She knew there would be more if she had the time to work through the area, but Paul pushed toward the circular pits ahead.

Their roofs had collapsed, and a quick look inside showed the stone pilasters against the walls that marked them as kivas and the whole site as late Pueblo II, maybe early Pueblo III. Her arms and hands filled with electricity. In the rubble at the bottom, she could easily make out the hearth ring and the remnants of a ladder. Again she wanted to linger, but the tangible lure of the cliff dwellings drew them on. The plaza was filled with sage and rabbit brush. What she had seen so often depicted as an abstract delineation on a flat diagram was now a real space with wind and sound and the scent of pinyon and juniper in the air.

The first row of freestanding ruins transformed from shapes to textures as they approached. The adobe had flaked off, and the precise angular stone masonry beneath it showed its intricate patterns. They stopped and allowed their eyes to float up beyond these broken structures to the horizon, where this frozen curve of striated sandstone blended seamlessly into these stacked linear rooms. At the center of the structure was a tower with three doors facing outward. These buildings spoke with their stillness, vibrating like the soundboard of an ancient instrument. She wanted to explore everything at once but she knew she had to measure out her excitement. To take it all in at once would be to take in nothing at all.

"There are so many sites like this out here. But the thrill of finding a new one never goes away. Parks can be a problem, but they are also pretty good harbors, sometimes . . . when they let us do our jobs," Paul said.

Sophia was gone, her attention returned to the first block of rooms, which were decimated because they had been too exposed to the elements. Luckily, most of the vertical planes remained in place, giving a sense of the organization and size of the original structure. Sophia allowed her hands to rest upon the walls as she moved throughout the spaces, though she knew she should be wearing gloves. Above this structure was a higher level of buildings, constructed in a secondary alcove. They looked like something from a story told to amuse an emperor. Any attempt at a description would always be insufficient. You could not do it with data or with poetry. It was simply impossible.

"I have to go back for something," Paul said. "You keep exploring. I'll catch up with you."

"Yeah, um, sure. I'm just going to . . ." Sophia drifted past the closest structure to those built into the rock under the massive cliff brow. She drew close and peered through the narrow door, the wood lintel and doorframes still in place, smooth and lithe, holding their former shapes as limbs and branches. They were low enough that she had to stoop. The interior space was cool. Her eyes had to adjust to the dim light. When they did, she saw that the space inside was small by modern standards but proportioned in a purposeful way.

In the opposite corner, she saw a haphazard cluster of sticks leaning against the wall. Next to them was a pile of desiccated corn cobs and a wooden ladder leading from this space through a square hole in the roof. No baskets or pottery. No tools. The room was devoid of what she'd seen in many years of slideshows, drawings, photographs, textbook descriptions, and exhibits in museums and repositories. Nonetheless, it left Sophia with the singular thought that any claim of newness for this continent, any sense of it as a "new world," was undeniably and irredeemably false.

Sophia skirted the rest of the buildings in the block, and she turned at the corner, where she discovered a natural approach on the rock itself that gave her access to the second story. From this vantage, she could see back along the path from the overhead view, which revealed the genius of the people who planned and built this place. The line of roofs revealed four ladders spaced at nearly even intervals. More than anything she wanted time to explore and document these spaces. She also knew that trying to gain entry would risk catastrophe. Along the rock floor of the alcove was a room with the perfect right-angled shadow of a door.

Overhead, cliff swallows swooped back and forth. The entire overhang was filled with the churring calls of these acrobatic birds. Perhaps the alveolar clusters of bulbous daubed nests above were the inspiration for these adobe buildings, or perhaps it was a deeper design. She looked out again, her position granting her a clear view of the amphitheater and back across the desert from which they had ascended. Through notches in the ridgelines looking west she could see Antelope Flats, and behind that, the Vermilion Cliffs. The sun had dropped just below the horizon, holding its intensity. Dusk would soon follow.

Sophia moved to the door and looked inside. Again, she waited for her eyes to adjust, hoping for the slow materialization of objects: pot, basket, metate, something. But the room was barren except for an indistinct pile in one corner. She looked around and did not see Paul, so she stepped through the threshold and into the darkness. The pile turned out to be a heap of seashells of all sizes, most broken, but many intact. Sophia began to understand that Swallow Valley had already been picked clean by others. The shells had likely been held in some other vessel, upended and stolen years ago. She withdrew from the room, scanned the area, and saw Paul looking around before descending on a ladder into one of the kivas whose roof remained intact.

He said he left something behind. Sophia descended the cliff trying to decide whether or not to call out to Paul or to keep the element of surprise in her favor. In the end, she decided she wanted to see what he was up to for herself.

The kiva was off to one side, set above the ground on a brick-and-adobe rim rather than lying flush to the ground. Three roof poles emerged from one side, extending three feet past the short walls. Sophia lay on her belly and peered down into the kiva entry. She spied Paul crouching in the far corner, awash in the yellow glare of his head lamp, his knees splayed out frog-like to either side, a small bowl in one hand. With the other hand, he moved the soil aside, set the bowl into the well, and turned it. From his shirt pocket, he took a small branch and feathered out the soil to erase his presence.

"What the hell?" Sophia said. "I'm coming down there!"

"Nothing. No. Don't. I'm coming out," Paul said.

"Is that pottery?"

Sophia turned and came down the ladder, the thick wood stable, showing no signs of weakness or wear. Her attention was split between the interlocked wood poles that comprised the cribbed roof and Paul standing up and brushing off his hands.

"Put your light on it," Sophia instructed.

Paul turned his head until the bowl was illuminated. The exterior was undecorated but starting at the rim there was a red band, and after that, diagonal lines that covered the interior. She stepped forward and dropped to her knees to see inside the bowl. There was a striking humanoid face there, red with large obovate eyes and an open mouth set on the top and bottom with rows of triangular teeth.

"Is it intact?"

"Yes."

"Where did it come from?"

Paul didn't answer.

"Did you move it from somewhere else?"

"That's a complicated question."

"No, Paul. It's pretty simple."

"Okay, well, then it's got a complicated answer." Paul stepped around the bowl, picked up a scrub oak branch and cleared his tracks as he came past Sophia, mounted the ladder, and climbed past, switching off his head lamp.

"You're not going to leave that here," she said.

"Yep. That's what I'm doing." Paul stepped out of the portal and was gone.

Sophia followed Paul out of the kiva. He was walking away from her toward the plaza and their backpacks. The amphitheater was in the full shadow of evening, and while it wasn't cool yet, the blue sky was deepening, and the rock was turning from orange to purple.

She called after Paul, but he kept going.

"You weren't supposed to see that," he said.

"Then why bring me on a super-secret site-destruction mission that you knew would infuriate me?"

Paul stopped and turned. "For all the rest of it," he said, spreading his arms. "And because you told me you were missing out on some cool summer international dig in Jordan, and this was your consolation prize research. I thought maybe you'd like the adventure. And who knows . . ." Paul stopped and crouched next to his pack and returned a red stuff sack to the interior. He took out the blue lab book and made a notation.

With so much theft and vandalism, the idea that somebody might return an artifact was unthinkable to most people. It would be a high-risk move for him as a government employee. Part of her wanted to dive right into that conversation. Another part of her wanted to stay on the moral high ground. What she couldn't do was walk away. "You know, anyone who finds that pot will discover a lie."

"Sort of."

"They'll think it's something it isn't. This place has been stripped, Paul. There's nothing here but that bowl."

"But that bowl is where it belongs."

"How do you know that?"

Paul held up the notebook. He flipped through the pages and stopped at a rendering of the bowl, a detailed description of its location in the kiva, even a sketch of the exterior with its low wall and ladder. "I know it was taken in October 1973. And I know he asked me to return it six weeks ago because he knew he would never make it back."

"Who has you doing this? It goes against so many regulations—it was Cluff, wasn't it?"

Paul nodded.

"So, you're up here for him, not because you wanted to spend time with me."

"Well, can't it be both?"

"I'm glad I can be another one of your efficiencies."

"It's not like that."

"It's exactly like that. You dragged me up here to kill two birds with one stone. That bowl was in your pack, which is why I swung around upside down on a rope. So, what am I supposed to do now, report you? I thought we were doing something else."

"Something else? Look, you don't have to file a—"

"Of course I do. Dammit, Paul. And I have to take that bowl with me. I have a professional obligation."

"And put it where? It's right where it belongs. It's just been on loan. But isn't that what you want? Aren't you the one who says museums are complicated?"

"They are, and all this—whatever it is, a date or a field trip or some kind of backward heist movie—did not un-complicate any part of it, for me."

"It's what Bruce wanted. His death changed the timeline."

"But it's not Bruce's bowl, Paul. It belongs to the people from this place."

"They moved and left it. There's no sign of violence in this place. It was abandoned."

"No violence *in* this place, yes. Violence *to* this place? That's a different story."

"Well, like I said, you weren't supposed to see this," Paul said. He swung the pack onto his shoulders. "I'm going to set up camp for the night." Sophia stood and put on her pack.

She walked out of the amphitheater, watching where Paul stopped on a ridge facing west. Eastward the clouds were blazing red and orange, tall kachina clouds full of rain and lightning. Beneath them were the cliff walls of Swallow Valley, the dwellings tiny and delicate at the base.

Sophia made her camp away from Paul. She ate without speaking to him, watched the sunset burn away and the stars prick the firmament. After twilight had dissolved, a meteor arced across the belly of sky through the constellation Leo. It burned for a full second before pulsing once and fading.

"Paiutes call that putsuywitcapi. It means star excrement," Paul called out.

Sophia lay back and slapped a mosquito. "You ruin everything," she called back.

PART II

Day Six

A rain delay : A hero twice in one day : Growth mind-set : The destination is on your right : They always run : Additional variables

A clap of thunder woke Sophia. She sat up straight in her sleeping bag and listened as the boom echoed through the canyons and decayed to a hollow rumble. It was dawn, but Swallow Valley was still mostly in shadow. Wind rattled the cottonwood and willow leaves, and the air was much colder than she would have expected.

She climbed out of her sleeping bag and slipped her boots on. Paul's gear was packed, and his bag leaned against a rock. He wasn't anywhere in the amphitheater. She walked around, checked the kiva from yesterday, and went up to Paul's backpack, where she found a note stuck into one of the inch clips like a tiny flag:

Checking the trail.
Filtered water from the pool in those bags →
PT

She followed the arrow with her eyes and saw a dual-bag filtering system hanging in the branches of a tree, the lower bag bulging. Beyond that tree lay the amphitheater, the overhang, and the silent dwellings. It was no less amazing on the second day, though today's light was more subdued, cooler, filtered through the clouds, and the cliff faces seemed more rounded and smooth. Sophia thought about what it would have been like to have inhabited this place, to have emerged every morning of your life into this.

The lightning came first—a white etching in the grayness. She counted out the interval of twenty-three seconds, then the thunder followed. She couldn't remember how that translated to miles. Longer was safer. She knew that, but she didn't know how to interpret thunderclaps coming so close together.

She turned again and beheld the ruins until the urge to pee was overwhelming. She imagined that Paul would return the moment her pants were down, so she sought some privacy in a semicircle of scrub oak.

When she finished, she returned to her pack and pulled out two granola bars, then she went to the water bags and filled her bottle. After that, she pulled out her notebook and a pen, and saw her camera partially wrapped in a sweatshirt. She remembered Paul's plea not to take pictures, then thought about how scandalized he looked when she caught him in the kiva. Screw him and the horse he rode in on, she thought. It was her father's pet phrase, and it delighted her to use it now. She pulled out the camera and turned it on, then located an extra memory card and stood. Somebody's got to do this, she said to herself. She wasn't going to leave empty-handed. If this trip was off the books, then he'd never bust her. She could leverage that.

The notebook went into a cargo pocket in her pants, the camera around her neck. She began taking wide-angle photos of the area, one of them using the panorama function that stitched together slices of the Swallow Valley into a wide ribbon of landscape. She worked quickly, systematically cataloging the midden area, the pit houses, showing details of the collapsed roofs. She captured each of the rooms in the main structure, moving from east to west, noting the shot numbers in her notebook and writing small notations to go with them. Each time she captured an image she thought about how she would want to return to see what it was like in different seasons.

It was one thing to explore a site that was already on the books, but to be the first, maybe that was no longer even possible. You'd just be the most recent to discover something. And that was the problem: the race of archeology, the carving out of one's career, setting that priority over the site, the artifacts coming in ahead of the people who had lived and died there. The best solution was to get out of the way, but the building of a career had so much mass, so much gravitational pull. She tried to make sure her motivation was people over things, but she could wrestle with that after she got the photos.

Once she'd documented the room block, she returned to the kiva she was in yesterday and photographed the interior, including the bowl Paul replaced. She looked for voids that would suggest the activity of other thieves, and found nothing, even when she shot with the flash. There were no other footsteps beyond her own. She considered removing the bowl and carrying it out in her pack, but decided, in the end, that she'd likely destroy the pot in the process.

Instead, she climbed out of the kiva and, following Bruce Cluff's lead, wrote down details of the replacement using Paul's initials instead of his name. When she closed her notebook, she noticed the clamor of the cliff swallows, and switched her camera to video mode. She shot over a minute of the birds swooping into and out of their nests. When that was done, she took a breath and considered her choices. She knew where this place was. Paul was in way over his head. This was a bona fide opportunity.

Another flash filled the sky, and the wind picked up, bringing a rich resinous essence to Sophia's nose. She scanned the area, looking for Paul, and finding him still gone, she closed her eyes and tried to identify each of the olfactory notes: desert earth, juniper, pine, and a hint of her mother's perfume, something of the Persian part of her. A splintering crack of thunder startled her and sent her eyes racing around the amphitheater.

She had been taking photos for nearly an hour. She returned to the cliff to check on the storm and saw it moving across the far end of the valley floor. Twenty miles, maybe more. She felt one or two drops of rain on her forearm and decided to pack her gear away.

As she finished the second granola bar, Paul came through the sage, saw her, and waved like nothing at all had happened. "Did you find the water okay?" he asked. She pointed to the bottle at her feet. "I didn't want to wake you."

"Yeah," she said. "I kind of wanted to sleep, so that's what I did. Slept. It felt great."

"That's good." Paul looked around and gave her a crooked smile. "So, how about this place?"

"It's good," she said, wondering how long this fake conversation would carry on.

"This is one of those sites people don't like to talk about. They figure it'll turn into a circus like Moon House or the Citadel. I'd heard about it for years, but nobody would give me a location. People don't trust the government much around here," Paul said.

"Can't blame them," Sophia said. She wondered why he was pretending like yesterday hadn't happened, but she knew.

"About that . . ." he said.

"Yeah, about that," she said, taking her opportunity. "You know what you've done to this site? It's not just me talking. There's laws."

"Thoreau said sometimes you've got to let your life be a counter-friction to stop the machine," Paul said.

"You are the machine, Paul."

"Cluff got the bowl when this land was private. The law lets him do that."

"Everyone's an archeologist, I guess," Sophia said.

"Everyone's a ranger, too, apparently," Paul countered.

"Democracy sucks sometimes."

"Speaking of democracy, let's talk about what we should do next. Our circumstances have changed a little." Paul walked over to the cliff edge and motioned for Sophia to follow. It was an abrupt, graceless transition. "That storm is going to cross over to here, then bump up against the mesa we're on right now. It'll drop a lot of water so it can climb over, and that water needs to go somewhere," he said, tracing the path down the talus slope and into the maze of rock they had come through yesterday.

Sophia nodded. She could see how it would gather.

"I think we should stay here another night."

Sophia's face twisted into a shape of disapproval.

"I've hauled bodies out of those canyons. When they go in, it's dry. Hot. Blue sky. Then all hell breaks loose."

Sophia's shoulders slumped, and Paul sat cross-legged and picked up small stones one at a time, collecting them in his palm. Sophia sat as well, unscrewed the cap of her water bottle, and drank.

"I shouldn't have kept my reasons for coming here from you," he said. "I can see that now."

"None of my business," she said.

"No, it is a lot of your business. My secrets aren't fair to you. You're out here to measure impact on this place. I'm one of those impacts."

"We all are." She folded her arms.

Paul nodded, looked at her, and said, "The threads we don't see are the strongest."

"Come on," she said. "You don't have to turn this into a nature meme."

"I'm not being literal. We're part of a whole system," he said.

Sophia nodded in a way that didn't mean she agreed. The wind picked up and a raven coasted by them at eye level, its wings curled and its wiry black feet extended underneath. From the horizon came another flash, deep inside one of the clouds.

"Can I show you something?" he asked. "I found it this morning." Paul stood and offered his hand. Sophia capped her bottle and got up on her own.

"Is it something else you returned?" she said.

Paul ignored the comment and started down the path they'd come up but drifted to the left into a thicket of scrub oak. Sophia followed. The rumble of thunder filled in around them, the echo decaying over the vastness of the monument.

"Sounds like it's moving away," she said, pushing a branch aside. Paul kept going.

In front of them was a continuation of the back side of the cliff wall that held the amphitheater. It went up almost vertically for a hundred feet, long striations of desert varnish painting the surface. The cliff had weathered in the center, leaving a nautilus-shaped void in the surface of the rock, which had been invisible on the hike in because of the direction of the light. Paul scrambled up a boulder and motioned for Sophia to join him.

"What are we looking at?" she asked.

"You see that spiral shape in the rock? Let your eyes drop just beneath it."

Sophia saw a thin ledge, perhaps thirty feet long, with a small masonry wall above it. She gasped involuntarily. "A granary?"

"It's got to be. I scouted it this morning, and there's a good nontechnical approach. Shall we?" he asked.

It came across as a peace offering, but she didn't care.

They found their way through the brush to the talus slope and scrambled up. They were able to zigzag their way farther up until they were on a wide shelf just below the granary ledge. The next level up was eight or nine feet away, the height of a regular ceiling. Paul studied the space and found a thin vertical crack. Right above it were a number of good, obvious handholds.

"Go up my back and stand on my shoulders." He crouched down and tapped his thigh.

Sophia grabbed Paul's neck and shoulder and climbed him like a ladder. She balanced herself against the rock and repositioned her feet so she was standing with one foot on each shoulder.

"I kind of want to step on your face," she said.

"That would be fine. I deserve it." Paul extended himself and stood taller, and Sophia rose another six inches, high enough to pull herself onto the ledge.

"I don't know how we're going to get down," she said.

"We'll cross that bridge when we come to it."

Sophia was about to ask Paul how he was going to get up, when he reached over the ledge and pulled himself over like he was climbing out of a swimming pool.

The granary wall was made of shaped stone bricks that had been mortared into place. The structure stood proud of the cliff wall about one foot, and there was enough space that they could cross to the other side without concern. Sophia looked back and realized they were now fifty feet or more above their starting point. They were above the tops of the cottonwoods, and they could see across the expanse to the storm clouds in the distance. It was a complete view of her research area.

"It's such an interesting question why they put their corn all the way up here," she said.

"Aesthetically, it's the most gorgeous pantry in the world. Some theories

say it was a theft deterrent, but it could be to protect the contents from flooding. Practically though, it's bananas how hard it is to get up here."

"Maybe they wanted to make sure people only broke into the stash if they
were really hungry, like hiding the Oreos. Sorry," she said, "Oreos are a sugary
snack some people are obsessed with."

"I know what Oreos are," Paul said.

On the far side of the granary, there was a square half door with a Douglas
fir doorframe. Paul stepped aside and let Sophia have the first look. She peered
in. The interior was empty, but the floor was a latticework of sticks.

"There's a ventilation system in here," she said, "for humidity control." She
looked up and confirmed that this granary had been built using an alcove in the
cliff for the main structure. In the dim light, she could not see how the adobe was
connected to the sandstone of the cliff. She stepped back and gave Paul a look.

"Wow," he said. "Just wow."

Sophia sat down on the ledge and wrapped her knees with her arms and
watched the clouds part enough to show patches of blue sky.

Paul stepped around and sat next to her. "As far as I can tell," he said,
"nobody has recorded this structure. Cluff didn't. I've read what I could about
this site, and they talk about an amphitheater and the dwellings, but not in this
kind of detail. That makes us the first."

"On record."

"Well, right. On record," he repeated, making air quotes around the last
two words. "It's pretty amazing, though. This whole plateau is full of sites like
this. It seems empty, but it's not."

"My heart is racing," Sophia said, looking around. "I want to shout, but
that seems stupid."

"It's not," he said. "I get it."

"What you just said about this place being empty. I feel like I've seen all
kinds of empty since I left Princeton."

Paul nodded. He fell into thought and after a time nodded again. "If I
tell you something, do you promise not to tell anyone? I mean it doesn't really
matter anymore, but out of respect would you keep it to yourself?"

Sophia did not like this arrangement or any of the other times he asked for her secrecy, but she was beginning to see that furtiveness was the lingua franca of the times. She traced an *X* across her chest but she wasn't sure she meant it.

"Before this place became public land, Cluff knew people would come. He knew they had come before and cleaned it out. He'd done his share of damage, and he admitted it. Before it all changed hands, he came up here on horseback with some dynamite. He told me he meant to make this one of the hardest places to get into, because most pot hunters would be too lazy to climb." Paul stretched each of his legs and brought them back into the same position as Sophia's. She looked at him as he stared out across the monument. "It is pretty hard to get here, but who knows how long that will last. Most days, I think we're doing this work all wrong," he said, lowering his head onto his knees, "but I'm not sure if there's any better way to get it done."

———

Reinhardt Kupfer awoke in his motel room from a dream in which he had been fitted with a pair of giant wings fashioned from buffalo skin and a frame of bent willow branches. They had been laced to his body on something like a corset. As he stared at the barren ceiling, with white glare pouring in around the curtains, he recalled that he could control the crude flapping of his rough and halting flight with two knobs of gnarled juniper that protruded from each side. He had been using these wings to view the desert from above.

Without moving Reinhardt thought about how he was not yet halfway through his Ranches, Relics, and Ruins adventure. In the last five days he'd seen collections of baskets, pots, kachinas, masks, flutes, real arrowheads under glass, fake arrowheads on the trail, atlatls in the hands of one-quarter-size hunters, theatrical lights in museum dioramas, re-creations of kivas cut away to reveal the inside architecture, scale models of geological features, video presentations about the changing seasons, push-button lectures about ethnobotany, voices reading pioneer journals, wheels children could turn to depict the water cycle, signage, quotations, wall-sized facsimiles of historical documents, enlarged photographs, and kiosks. But there had been neither ranches, nor relics, nor ruins.

He rose and folded his clothes, thinking again about the cost of cutting it all short and flying home. The logistics weren't a problem, but he didn't know how to tell Wolf that this country was just a cheap illusion. As a boy, Reinhardt was enraptured by the Indian novels of Sigmund F. Krause. They fueled his dreams of the American Southwest. But this was nothing like the books.

He left his packing and stood in the bathroom under the blue-tinged fluorescent light. As he lathered his face, he considered his red-and-black dreamcatcher tattoo with a saying written underneath. It had been a North Star for him since before medical school. The first time someone read the tattoo and asked him, "What does 'your land is where your dead lie buried' mean?" Reinhardt told him it was his plan for fighting the modern world. Not much of a plan, he thought, then shaved, rinsed his face, and finished dressing.

He brought his packed bag to the motel lobby, which was full of polished rocks and rubber tomahawks. The rest of his group were eating their pasteboard breakfasts and checking their schedules, their luggage herded together next to the bus outside. He added his bag to the mass and decided he would skip the paltry meal. Next to him, two of the tour organizers began a hushed conversation.

"The Korean guy bought the farm last night."

"Kwon?"

"Yeah."

"I thought he was fine."

"So did everybody."

"I think they want us to re-route through Cedar City to deliver their luggage to Mrs. Kwon. She thought they were going to come back to the tour once he was given a clean bill of health."

"Re-routing will throw everything off."

"Right?"

"We'll never hear the end of it."

Reinhardt tapped one of them on the shoulder.

"Yes?" he said, turning around.

"That man was an entire life, not just something on your checklist," Reinhardt said. He didn't wait for an answer but sped past the buses, crossed the parking lot, and walked down the sidewalk until he came upon a campground made of teepees set on concrete pads. A small boy emerged from a teepee wearing Spider-Man pajamas and a green Incredible Hulk mask. In his right hand, he held a stick that was taller than he was. He pounded it against the cement, then hurled his bludgeon into the road.

Someone said, "This is the wrong place for teepees."

Reinhardt turned to find Kenji wearing the same clothes from before, leather jacket and everything. "This is all wrong for many reasons. We have enthusiasts in Germany, and we camp in teepees that we have made and decorated ourselves. Seeing something like this is hard on the heart."

"I spent the night in a similar false teepee once, in Nikko, Japan. It was in a place called Western Village."

"Did you enjoy it? What did you say the other night at the dinner? Was it corny?" Reinhardt asked.

"Western Village is abandoned. Now it is—what's the phrase—a ghost city?"

"On the tour they call it a ghost town. We haven't been to one but we have talked about them."

Kenji lit a cigarette. "Nikko has people in it. I'm just talking about Western Village. Listen, I heard you're the hero who saved a man's life in the lodge. Nice work. I saw you walking, and I thought I would say something about it."

"He died last night."

Kenji exhaled and flicked his ash. "I'm sorry to hear that."

"I wish I could tell his wife that I did what I could."

"You should."

"She is alone now in another town with none of her things."

"You should deliver them to her."

"How? I have to get on that bus going to Faketown, U.S.A. And I don't want to say anything in front of these people."

"I can drive you," Kenji said, stubbing out his cigarette on the sole of his boot.

"But I've paid for everything," Reinhardt said.

"Eat a bad meal and you suffer twice. Let's do it."

Kenji stared at Reinhardt until Reinhardt nodded, then he nodded back.

They returned and saw the buses loading. Reinhardt pulled his duffel bag from the pile just before someone grabbed it for loading. Kenji reached out for Reinhardt's bag and sent him for the Kwons' luggage. As he approached a small group of tour organizers, one of them spoke through a tiny megaphone: "I HAVE GOOD NEWS AND BAD NEWS. THE BAD NEWS IS THAT MR. KWON HAD A SECOND HEART ATTACK IN THE HOSPITAL IN CEDAR CITY LAST NIGHT AND HE DID NOT SURVIVE IT." The crowd interpreted the message to themselves, and a few seconds later, an audible sound of lamentation moved throughout the group. "THE GOOD NEWS IS WE'RE NOT GOING TO THE GRAND CANYON TODAY, BUT INSTEAD WE'RE GOING TO RE-ROUTE TO CEDAR CITY, HOME OF THE UTAH SHAKESPEARE FESTIVAL. THIS WAY WE CAN DELIVER THE KWONS' LUGGAGE TO MRS. KWON." This time the crowd was silent.

"Is there a Target in Cedar City?" someone asked.

The tour organizers looked around at each other, and before they could answer, Reinhardt said, "I will take the luggage."

"Really?" the woman with the tiny megaphone said, but not through the megaphone.

"I will go."

"DR. KUPFER IS A HERO TWICE IN ONE DAY," she said, and the crowd cheered.

"Well it was actually once on Tuesday, and then now," he said, but nobody heard.

While people shook his hand and clapped Reinhardt on the back, another tour organizer wheeled a great black suitcase across the parking lot and set it in front of him.

"You really saved our bacon," she said.

"Where do I take this?" Reinhardt asked.

"DOES ANYBODY KNOW WHERE HE SHOULD TAKE—" the woman asked through the megaphone.

"To the hospital," someone else on the tour staff interrupted. "There's only one."

As Reinhardt hauled the roller bag, Kenji pulled up behind him in a red Mustang convertible. "Put that in the back seat," he said. "Our things are in the trunk."

Kenji pulled out of the parking lot so fast Reinhardt's body flattened against the seat. The rest of the traffic was keeping to the speed limit, so the car's engine growled and purred a dozen times in the half-mile drive to the state highway. Some kind of Japanese heavy metal was playing, which disappeared into the wind once Kenji got the car going.

The small municipal airstrip and ramshackle trailers and billboards and small independent motels appeared in the distance, grew to full size, and pulsed by in rapid succession. Once they passed these vestiges of civilization, Reinhardt let his gaze lift to the horizon, something he could never really do in Germany because one was always surrounded by forest. Here you were out on the surface. Over the eons, the skin of everything had gone thin, and the earth's orange bones jutted like they'd worn through the dry olive-green garments of the high desert. In the blue distance, clouds piled on themselves with an orderliness that kept him from comprehending the distances. Reinhardt took out his phone, trying and failing to take pictures of the vast landscape.

"It never works," Kenji shouted.

"I know, but you have to try," Reinhardt said, and posted a shot of the clouds and a small gas station to Instagram. He geotagged it with BRYCE CAN-YON, UTAH, and added the caption SKYSCRAPER CLOUDS.

They drove on, the hills dropping to the road on the west and the valley spreading for a dozen miles to the plateaus to the east. Orange hulking cliffs faded into the distance. There was a turn and the highway ran for a while parallel to a sinuous river. They drove for some time with the racket of the music radiating into the dry mountain air before Kenji reached up to switch off the stereo. "As a doctor, you must be well acquainted with death," he said.

"Did you say death?"

"The mortal coil."

"I am a dermatologist."

"For the skin?" Kenji asked.

"Yes."

"Like rashes and pimples?"

"And cancer," Reinhardt said. "Skin cancer is no small thing."

Kenji nodded. "Not so common in Japan. We have other ways to die."

Reinhardt looked out the window at the green valley and the sparse habitations. He thought of Mr. Kwon and the crowd of people surrounding him as he performed the chest compressions. Reinhardt's patients often died under another doctor's care, leaving him to consider death at a distance. He referred the problems away.

"Death creates sorrow for the living, not for those who are gone," Kenji said, then after a pause, he broke his attention and pointed to a gas station ahead. "Shall we refresh ourselves?" He downshifted, and the car's engine roared. The deceleration flung a book forward from the back seat, which Reinhardt picked up. It was called *The Hero's Journey for Screenwriters*. When Kenji noticed Reinhardt had rescued the book, he asked him to return it to the back seat, then signaled and pulled off the road, stopping next to a gas pump. Reinhardt spotted three more books just like the first in the space next to the Kwons' gigantic suitcase: *The Monomyth on Screen*, *Mythstructures for Blockbusters*, and *There and Back Again: The Hero's Journey Case Studies Vol. 4*. He set the book on top and got out to help wash the window.

"So, you're a screenwriter?" Reinhardt asked.

Kenji squinted at him. "Sort of. I make video games."

"Oh, like *Doom* and *Grand Theft Auto*?"

Kenji laughed and shook his head as he inserted his credit card. "I made *River Horse*."

Reinhardt's face lit up. "With the hippopotamus? I have that on my phone."

"You and fifty million other people."

"You must be rich, then."

Kenji shrugged.

"I'm not very good at the game. It's harder than it seems. I haven't ever won."

"You should play to play, not to be finished playing. What is the longest you've floated your River Horse?"

"Twelve, maybe thirteen minutes."

"Not bad," Kenji said. "Top twenty percent."

"Well, that's incredible. What are you doing with all these screenwriting books, then?"

"A studio wants to make the game into a film. Animated. For children."

"Interesting. You must be excited."

"The first round of meetings did not go very well. They gave me these books, and I rented this car. I told them I needed a week."

The gas nozzle clicked off and Kenji hung it back up, tore off the receipt, and folded it carefully. Reinhardt finished cleaning the window and returned the squeegee to its bucket. They went inside, used the restroom, and chose snacks. At the register Kenji motioned for Reinhardt to add his Coke and cashews to his gummy worms and cigarettes.

"Thank you, but I can take care of my own snacks."

"I know you can, but I am the programmer who brought *River Horse* to the world, and you are making the sacrifice today. I am just your helper, so let me help."

When Kenji looked up at the cashier, he was snapping a picture of them with his phone. "*River Horse* is cool." He smiled at them. "I love your game." Kenji reached into his jacket pocket and tossed an enamel pin of a purple hippopotamus to the boy. "Hey, thanks, mister," he said.

"That is one hundred percent authentic, man," Kenji said. "Keep on floating."

"You keep on floating, too."

They returned to the car, and as they buckled their seat belts, Kenji looked at Reinhardt and squinted. "You are on a quest. I could see that earlier at the teepees."

"It's just a vacation."

"I think this is more than a vacation. On this drive, I have been thinking about these books I am reading, and perhaps I am your first threshold gate-keeper, or a mentor. I don't yet know the difference." He reached into the back and brought forth *Mythstructures for Blockbusters* and handed it to Reinhardt. "You'll see it in there."

Kenji drove back onto the highway, then, checking the maps application on his phone, turned right and headed west. Reinhardt leafed through the pages. Chapter One was called "Ordinary World." Chapter Two, "The Call to Adventure." Reinhardt stopped and read about the mentor. The book explained that after the rejection of the call to adventure the hero desperately needs guidance. The mentor is of great importance and provides wisdom or practical training. Often sustenance. Reinhardt looked down at his Coke and sleeve of nuts.

Reinhardt closed the book. "I am the hero?" he asked.

"I think there can be many heroes, maybe everyone is a hero. I might be a hero for my own story, just like every player is their own hippo. My job is to get you from the ordinary world into the new one. I think I am beginning to see how it works. You met me to be transported. I met you to be the transporter."

Reinhardt opened the Coke and took a sip. "But transported where?"

"Who knows. To there, so you have someplace to come back from. There and back again. A hero will encounter obstacles. You will be thwarted. You will be tested. There will be some time in the underworld. The innermost cave. You will emerge with wisdom."

"Are all the books helping you make a movie about hippos floating in a river?"

"Perhaps that is my quest, and I will find a mentor for that. But these books all quote a man who said to follow your bliss. What is your bliss, Reinhardt?"

"To go swimming in the desert."

"Why that?"

"It's something I read about once in a book when I was a child."

"Okay, start small and build," Kenji said, tearing open the gummy worms with his teeth.

———

Byron's attention was split between the road and the cars passing in the other lane. Lonnie held the grab handle and rested his head against his forearm. "How do you know Scissors isn't going to find our camp while we're out here and sit there waiting for us to come back?" he asked.

"Because if he was gonna find it, he already would have," Byron said.

"I'm not trying to argue with you—"

"Then don't."

"But this guy seems like the kind of person to just keep, you know . . . trying."

"Let me say something to you, and I'm going to try using the crazy talk that seems to make sense to you. In the joint they had a book group. I did it a couple of times before it got too stupid. There was this one book called *Mindset*—"

"You read a book?"

"Not all of it. Didn't have to. It said some people think they come as is and some people think they can make improvements. Fixed versus growth. The prison shrink thought all of us were fixed."

Lonnie laughed. "Like puppies."

"Not that kind of fixed. Dammit. Listen to me. I'm trying to be serious."

Byron pulled off the highway and drove under a ponderosa-pine-log entryway with a sign at the top that read ASHDOWN'S cut into a ten-foot ripsaw blade. They drove through the huge circular turnaround in front of the house, came past the garage with the RV slot at the end, and stopped at a fenced equipment yard back at the bottom of the hill. A vinyl banner on the fence read ASHDOWN CONSTRUCTION & EXCAVATION.

"Every criminal I know believes two things. One, the world is trying to screw him over personally. And two, he's got a plan to get himself ahead. Even guys who are locked up think that. So, that makes them what? Fixed or growth?"

"Growth?" Lonnie said.

Byron slapped the steering wheel. "Damn right. Growth mind-set. That shrink was dead wrong. This bastard Scissors has got a growth mind-set. Whoever he's working for has got it. I sure as hell got it."

"Maybe we both got it," Lonnie said.

Byron put the truck in park. "This is what I'm trying to say, little brother. The way you're acting right now, I'm afraid that's the fixed mind-set." Lonnie's face fell. "You don't want nothing to change. I'm trying to show you how to fix that."

"Okay," Lonnie said, getting out.

"You gotta call your own shots, man." Byron shut off the truck, fetched a pair of rusty bolt cutters from the back, and walked straight to the chain link gate.

"I thought you said you had a key," Lonnie said.

"I said I had a *way in*," Byron said, struggling to open the bolt cutter jaws.

"Uncle Pete is going to flip his wig."

"Uncle Pete ain't gonna know. It's June twenty-first. That means he's in Carvertown with Aunt Linda for the Freedom Jamboree. They won't be back until Monday."

"I mean the lock. He's gonna see that it's been cut."

"Look. We put the backhoe right where it came from, take the lock with us, and he'll blame it on one of the dumbasses that works for him and—boom!" Byron made an explosion with his right hand and let it drop slowly down to his side. "Nothing out of the ordinary."

"Yeah, boom." Lonnie mimicked the pantomime. "So, why are we doing this in the middle of the day?"

"So we don't *look* like we're stealing it."

"But we are stealing it."

"Borrowing. When you're planning to bring something back, it ain't stealing."

Lonnie looked around and could not see another house in any direction. Byron placed the padlock between the blades of the bolt cutters, and he struggled to move the handles. Lonnie watched his brother strain, and stamp his feet, and curse the tool. He tried moving the jaws into a couple of different positions. Lonnie made a mental note that this is what a growth mind-set looked like.

"That lock is probably made out of stainless. It's pretty hard stuff," Lonnie said.

"You should probably quit talking to me," Byron said through clenched teeth. He strained and re-grabbed the tool, then strained again.

"Okay. I'm just saying."

"Just saying what?" Byron grunted.

"I'm just saying you probably need a longer tool." After a second Lonnie smiled and snorted twice.

Byron stopped what he was doing and looked up. He let the lock slip out of the blades, and it smacked against the fence. Lonnie tried not to smile. "I'm really sorry," he said. "It's just funny, that's all."

"You know that sumbitch Scissors is out there looking for us, right? That's what he's choosing to do with his day. We are his entire focus."

Lonnie covered his mouth and tried to stop laughing, but he couldn't. "You know I do weird stuff when I'm nervous. I can't help it."

"Since you're full of suggestions, why don't you do it?" He threw the bolt cutters at his feet.

Lonnie picked them up and tested out their rusty pivot point. He took them to the truck and fished out a blue can of WD-40 and sprayed it into the jaw joint and handle bolts, then he worked the action until it was smooth. He stepped past his brother, pinched the blades down on the shackle, and clipped the lock in a single quick movement. The lock clattered to the ground, and each side of the chain fell away.

Lonnie handed the cutters back to Byron and said, "Don't feel bad, B. I've just got longer arms."

"I don't give a shit about your arms." He picked up the bolt cutters. "Just open the gate." Byron threw the bolt cutters in the back of the truck and got in. He backed the truck up to a trailered CASE backhoe. Byron dropped it onto the hitch and chained it up. Lonnie attached the brake harness.

As they got into the cab, they both watched the weather system southward at the horizon. The stratus clouds were thick and dark out there, but the sky above was white with high cirrus.

Lonnie said, "You sure we want to go out there with weather like that coming in?"

"That don't mean nothing. Probably won't even get to us."

"We could still just leave that map somewhere for him. We've got his number. We could leave it and lay low. We could camp, and I can get another job. It's no big deal."

"You remember that old Sunday school lesson about the ten talents?" Byron said.

Lonnie thought about it for a bit. "No. It's been a long time since I went to church."

"Well, it pretty much says go big or stay home."

"That doesn't sound like any kind of Sunday idea to me."

"It is, and that's one hundred percent growth mind-set, baby. Lemme put it this way. If you and I would have stayed home, we'd be burned to a crisp. This way, we're about to strike it rich."

———

Reinhardt asked for Mrs. Kwon at the information desk of the hospital in Cedar City. "I am the physician who administered CPR Tuesday, and I have some personal items for her." The volunteer lifted the glasses from the chain around her neck, put them on, picked up the phone, and called around.

Kenji dismissed himself to smoke, and Reinhardt said, "Don't leave yet."

Kenji gave him the thumbs-up and went outside.

A few moments later, the volunteer told them that she is not supposed to give out any personal information. Reinhardt gripped his temples with a thumb and finger and closed his eyes. When he'd gathered himself, he looked at the volunteer, who stood up while his eyes were closed. "I changed my vacation plans to bring this woman her suitcase. The other day, my mouth was on Mr. Kwon's mouth, I was breathing my air into his lungs, and my chest compressions broke a number of ribs. That man is now dead. His family are all in Korea, so none of them are likely to arrive here in this town. So, are you telling me you are planning to deliver this suitcase to Mrs. Kwon and relieve me of my obligation?"

"I, actually, well . . ." the volunteer said, removing her glasses and letting them dangle from their beaded chain. She was visibly upset. "She is probably at the funeral home at this point."

"Thank you. Could you give me directions?"

"I better not."

"But it says 'information,'" Reinhardt said, pointing to the sign.

The woman looked at him. "Swindlehurst," she sighed. "I'd try Swindlehurst Funeral Home."

Reinhardt left, typing that name into his phone. He gathered up Kenji, who squinted when he learned they had another stop. They drove a short distance to the address, which was a log cabin on Main Street. Reinhardt dinged the small service bell at the front desk, which summoned a young, heavyset man in a black suit to the front. He was wearing a dingy white apron over his clothes. His red hair was cut short, and his hands looked large enough to span a dinner plate. "Can I help you?"

"I have a delivery for Mrs. Kwon. Her husband died last night."

"I cremated him this morning," the young mortician said. "But we're out of urns. I'm waiting for UPS."

"Cremating him?" Reinhardt asked.

"Yeah, for the trip home. That way he'll fit under the seat." The young mortician smiled, and when he saw that Reinhardt did not return the smile, he lowered his eyes. "Sorry, this is a really tough job, you know, emotionally, so I try to keep it light," he said.

"We are just trying to deliver a suitcase to Mrs. Kwon. We're from the tour company," Reinhardt said.

"No, we are not," Kenji said, putting his hand on Reinhardt's neck. "He is liberated from the tour."

"Normally at Swindlehurst we try to maintain the confidentiality of our clients, but you two seem like Good Samaritans. And I am trying to reconstruct a nose and cheek for a viewing this afternoon, so if you could take the suitcase to Mrs. Kwon and this paperwork and that bag," he said, removing a manila envelope and a Ziploc bag from a drawer and setting it on the desk, "it would help me out. I'm by myself today."

Inside the Ziploc bag was a metallic hip joint and a number of small screws. "Okay?" Reinhardt said, looking at Kenji. Kenji nodded.

"It was a really strange nose to begin with," the young mortician said. "And when the putty softens, it's hard to work with." Kenji nodded. "This is commercial putty though," he said. Reinhardt waited to see if the young mortician was going to keep talking. When he didn't, Reinhardt asked for an address, and the young mortician said, "It's on the envelope."

Reinhardt looked down. "Very good. Thank you."

Back at the car, Reinhardt said, "One more stop on our quest." Kenji shrugged, and Reinhardt typed the address into his phone, and they drove through town to a motel called the El Rey. The voice on the phone said, "You have arrived. The destination is on your right."

"Enchanted helpers," Kenji said, gesturing to the phone. "You see, this is a quest, complete with magic." When Reinhardt narrowed his eyes, Kenji said, "The best technology is simply magic by another name." As they pulled into the motel, they passed through the covered entry, and Kenji said, "This is the gateway. The first threshold. Don't you see?"

Reinhardt said, "It says she's in room two thirty-seven, so keep going." They drove past ordinary cars, dust and dirt-speckled, some with plastic shells mounted on the roof, some with bike racks on the back, some with telltale bar codes revealing them as rentals. As they drove past the swimming pool, they saw an older woman sitting alone in a chair with a Ranches, Relics, and Ruins T-shirt on. Her head was down. Her arms crossed. A half dozen children screamed and jumped into the water, swam back to the edge, climbed out, and jumped again.

"Is that her?" Kenji asked.

Reinhardt nodded.

"The time has come, then." Kenji put the car in park but left it running. "This is where we part ways. I must return to Hollywood. You must follow your bliss." He handed Reinhardt his copy of *Mythstructures for Blockbusters*. "This is the owner's manual."

Reinhardt refused the offer. "I couldn't," he said, but he took the gift when Kenji insisted.

Kenji popped the trunk and got out of the car. He set Reinhardt's duffel bag on the ground and hauled the Kwons' suitcase out of the back and wheeled it around to him. Then, without warning, Kenji threw his arms around Reinhardt and hugged him, lifting him slightly from the ground. Kenji clapped him on the shoulders and said, "Go. Be a hero."

Kenji drove through the turnaround and came back the other way. He lifted his fist into the air and left it there as he drove to the street and turned south.

Reinhardt came to the swimming pool gate and waited for a line of children to waddle through. When the gate clanked shut behind him, he thought that Kenji had been wrong. Perhaps this was the real gate, a small and nearly unnoticed thing. Then he looked at the book in his arms, put it in his bag, and shook off the thought.

He rolled the suitcase along the pool deck and stopped in front of Mrs. Kwon, who had moved to the edge of the pool now that the children were gone. She sat with her pant legs rolled up and her feet on the first step.

"Mrs. Kwon?"

She looked up and didn't recognize Reinhardt, but her face changed when she saw the suitcase. She put a hand over her heart to ask, Is this mine? Reinhardt nodded yes and offered her the envelope and bag of hip parts. "All of this belongs to you," he said.

Mrs. Kwon stood but remained on the swimming pool step. Reinhardt still held out the bag of medical remnants and the envelope, but Mrs. Kwon gestured to a side table with an elegant slow sweep of her open hand. She said something to him in a few sentences of Korean, and Reinhardt said, "Es tut mir leid für deinen Verlust." He stepped aside and set the items on the designated table. Mrs. Kwon reached out with both of her hands. Reinhardt understood that he was to grasp them, which he did. She squeezed his hands softly, with almost no pressure at all.

Reinhardt did not wait for anything else to happen. He took himself back out the gate and let it close behind him. Was this returning to the ordinary world? Did the owner's manual in his bag talk about a path that returned to itself like a Möbius strip? He wondered if he now had a role in Mrs. Kwon's journey as Kenji had a role in his.

He slung his duffel across his shoulder and walked through the motel driveway entry. When he reached the street, he looked up at the mountains and the thunderheads rising behind them, their tops shearing off. He typed RENTAL CAR into his phone and waited for the results.

—

Dalton and Tanner walked in from the road. When they got to the place, they ducked under the yellow police tape that was held up with bamboo poles and took stock of how little was left of the single-wide. The smell of smoke hung heavy in the air, and what remained looked like it had been bled of its color. Dalton kicked through the ashes and the toe of his boot tinkled against a blackened knife and fork, then he found the springs of an easy chair. As his eyes adjusted, he found an upright refrigerator and an oven. There were some twisted lengths of conduit, too. Everything else had burned or fused itself to something.

Tanner followed the concentric rings of destruction outward past the carport and the gnarled cottonwoods until he came to the edge of the property itself. None of the neighboring land looked damaged, though it was a close call. The burn became a crosshatch in the tan grass at about thirty feet. The nearest structure was a green-and-white travel trailer on blocks with the windows bashed out. A sign on it said FOR SALE 50 BUCKS.

"It's a shame the fire didn't clear out some of this other crap," Tanner called out.

"Careful what you wish for," Dalton called back.

Dalton and Tanner questioned the neighbors, who said two brothers lived here, but they'd been scarce lately. They kept to themselves, so there wasn't much to say. One of them had been away for a while. The tall one had been around more. On the phone, the Mohave County sheriff told them the utilities were all in the name of Lonnie Ashdown.

To the south and west, clouds gathered into a massive gray shadow, the force of the rain evident in the acute angle of the squall line. Rain, if it got this far, would turn everything into a slick black mess, washing away any evidence that might be left. Dalton kicked the sooty ground again and shook his head.

Tanner circled back and joined up with Dalton. "What do you think the fire marshal's going to say about this?"

Dalton took off his hat and dusted his thigh with it. "He'll say it's no accident."

"I mean, it could be. Doesn't take much work to start a fire out here," Tanner said.

"These Ashdown fellas don't come across as the kind of folks partial to working."

"They aren't."

"I haven't heard much about them since they moved over to Cane Beds. I pulled them over a couple days ago for out-of-date tags. They're out of my county now and out of Utah. Not my circus, not supposed to be my monkeys," Dalton said.

"What did the Arizona report say?"

"Byron's the older one, been all through the system. Petty theft, possession of meth with the intent to sell. Recently it's been cars. Seems like he took the fall for an operation out of Reno. It doesn't look like they honored his sacrifice. The other day he was worried I was going to violate his parole."

"Still no honor among thieves?"

"I was a couple years ahead of Byron in school. He wasn't much of anything back then. We weren't friends. His file says the Army wouldn't take him, and that's when the trouble started," Dalton said.

Tanner lifted his eyebrows. "I mean, if the Army won't take you," he said.

"Apparently he couldn't pass the vocational aptitude test. Didn't finish high school."

"What about the brother? People say he's kind of slow, or something," Tanner said.

"He's clean. And he's a known quantity, I guess. Doesn't cause much trouble. Apparently, he spends a lotta time at the library."

"Libraries keep a file?"

"No. LaRae says she sees him there, in the back. Reading."

"Reading?"

"That's what she says." Dalton walked past the black outline of the trailer and went far enough toward the mailbox to get to where the burned marks ended. He stooped, pulled off his sunglasses, and squinted at the tire tracks. After a minute, he stood and put the glasses back on.

"After I got out of the service," Dalton said, "I started working here. Had the same job as you. A situation came up with this guy named Wes Carnaby. He was a little bit off like these two. Lived with his sister. She was a lunch lady for the middle school. One day, about a week after Thanksgiving, we get this call from the library. They said Carnaby was asking for information on where you can and can't bury human remains."

"He was asking for a friend, right?"

"Yeah, right. Librarian told him he might have some luck checking the county code. It was Raylene Cluff told him that, just for the small world of it all. Apparently, Carnaby didn't like the idea of looking something up for himself. He threw a fit, and she suggested he ask a funeral home."

"You gotta love a librarian."

"He stormed off to a table and started scribbling in a notebook, holding on to the side of his head, talking to himself. Swearing. She asked us to come down, but by the time we got there, he was gone."

"I can see where this is headed."

"Maybe not," Dalton said. "We paid him a visit, and he was right in the middle of the driveway, loading the sister's body into the back of his pickup, pulling her up a ramp he'd made out of a plywood Dr Pepper sign. She was rolled inside a piece of carpet he'd tied up with twine."

"Dammit." Tanner's mouth shrank.

"When he saw us, he stopped and asked if we were going to just stand there or if we could lend a hand. We asked him what was in the carpet. He told us it was just carpet all the way through. We asked him if he wanted to amend his answer, and he told us it was none of our business. We told him we thought it was maybe just a little bit of our business, then he up and ran off, straight through the backyard. Threw himself over the fence, or he tried anyway. He popped up on the other side and limped through the vacant lot. Came out on Ninth East, then we picked him up."

"They always run."

"Well, he was just walking. Told us later that he found her like that."

"In the carpet?"

"No, dead. We asked him why he didn't call us, and he said he didn't want us thinking he did it. We asked him if he was worried about it because he did kill her, and he said he didn't but he wanted to."

"This is *not* the way I thought it was going."

"We kept him in jail until the autopsy came back. She died of a stroke. So, we opened the door, told him he was off the hook, and we let him go. On the way out, he stopped and stared at a plate of cookies somebody brought in for something, a birthday maybe. We told him to help himself. He took the whole plate, just dumped it into his coat pocket. Then he walked out. Didn't say anything. And he left the plate."

"He left the plate?"

"Set it right back where it was." Dalton kicked the dirt and spat. "Maybe what we're looking at here is an accident or a mix-up. Maybe it's sinister. Maybe worse. Did these guys kill Bruce and steal his pots? I don't know. Thinking about what people are capable of can really mess up your week."

Dalton walked back toward the ruins of the carport, where more things remained intact. He sized up a collapsed fifty-five-gallon drum and a metal tool chest. "Part of me hopes all of this is connected, then it's only one villain at a time." Dalton lowered himself down and took an interest in the ground.

"I see what you're saying, but how would that work? These guys break in, planning to steal pots from Bruce. He's there. They kill him and just take the pots. Nothing else. Then they make it look like suicide, come back and burn down their own house to cover their tracks? It doesn't make sense. The criminal element around here didn't grow up playing chess."

"Yep. They're barely thinking about their last move."

"Sometimes there's no thinking at all."

"That's right." Dalton pulled a Leatherman from his belt and opened it up and used it to flip over a board that had been pressed down into the mud, revealing a two-foot strip of unburned ground underneath.

"You find something?"

"Nope."

Tanner took off his hat and reshaped the crown. "Maybe there's something to what Stan Forsythe is saying, you know, about Feds moving in, confiscating people's collections. Maybe they were onto Bruce, and the event you're investigating was a preemptive strike."

"That sound like Bruce to you?"

"White males have pretty much cornered the suicide market around here."

"Doesn't explain these Ashdowns."

"Maybe this place was full of pots."

"Pots have been fired before. We'd see something left in the ashes if they were here." Dalton inched closer to the ground that hadn't been scorched. "If Cluff's house had been the one to burn, I'd think you were on the right track. Can't figure out why here."

"Maybe they pissed off the neighbors."

Dalton stood and turned slowly in a semicircle. "One of these pissed-off neighbors called it in."

"I need a nap," Tanner said.

"Come here," Dalton said, taking Tanner with him down toward the mailbox end of the driveway, where they both squatted down. "These tire tracks. It's a truck with a trailer. They come out from where the carport was, head through the burn, then go out to the road."

"Okay."

"These other tracks . . . they're coming back in and sit right on top of the others. See how the front wheels turn? And one of these front tires is a spare. The passenger side up front is skinnier."

"Somebody came in after the Ashdowns left?" Tanner said.

"That's the story I'm telling myself," Dalton said.

"So, looking for cars driving on a spare?"

"It's a start." Dalton stood and stamped his boots and looked toward the southern horizon. The cluster of clouds in that wedge of sky had grown darker, turning deep purple, and the angle of the rain had sharpened. The rest of the sky was belted in gray nimbostratus, and the temperature had dropped. They could both feel it.

"Afghanistan taught me there's no winners." He started toward the vehicle. "Let's take some pictures before that storm gets here."

—

Scissors dropped eight quarters into the car wash control box and dialed the toggle switch to PRE-WASH. The machinery engaged and the nozzle hissed. He unsheathed it and began to rinse the Sebring systematically from top to bottom. He spent extra time on the wheels, stopping to check the condition of the spare he'd been driving on for the last day and a half. It seemed to be holding up. After the pre-wash, he applied the suds, rinsed, and sprayed on a finish he knew wouldn't do anything, but there were forty-five seconds left that he couldn't let himself throw away.

When he was done, he drove the rest of the way into Kanab and stopped at the China House restaurant. There were a few other customers spread throughout the place. When the waiter brought him a menu, he held up his hand and said, "A bowl of hot-and-sour soup, kung pao beef, and iced tea. No rice, please."

"Really? No rice?" the waiter asked.

"I'm trying to watch my figure."

"We all should," the waiter said, then dismissed himself.

When the man was gone, Scissors took out his phone and dialed.

"It's been two days," Frangos said.

"Yes, ma'am. It has."

"When were you planning to fill me in on this carnival of errors?"

Scissors looked around and straightened the two bottles of soy sauce in front of him. "I was hoping to wait for good news, but that's been in short supply," he said, then he began reorganizing the sugar packets by color. "I've had bad weather, a flat tire, some cat and mouse with local law enforcement. Somebody was in that house before I got to it. Not the cops."

"Not the simpletons?"

"I don't think so. It wasn't a pro, but he was more careful than these yahoos. He moved all kinds of things. Maps were out of place, an upstairs window was jimmied, footprints on the siding. I still think the Swallow Valley map is with Dumb and Dumber, though."

"Tell me more about this other thief," she said.

"I didn't see him or anything."

The waiter brought Scissors his soup and iced tea. He nodded a thank-you.

"I can't say I like the addition of this variable."

"The whole thing has turned into a goat rodeo as far as I'm concerned."

"Then we have some common ground. People on my end don't want to move until I can assure them that Swallow Valley should be part of the roll-back. That can't happen without the map. Bruce Cluff was one of the last people who even knew how to get there, and he wouldn't have anything to do with me."

Scissors blew on the soup, then tasted it.

"Do you think these mooncalves have the resources to get themselves to Swallow Valley?"

"No," Scissors said. "Did you say 'mooncalf'?"

Frangos ignored the question. "I want them out of the picture before they get caught."

"I'm looking for them, but there's a lot of places they could have gone. We're talking about a million acres."

"A million is not a large number for everyone, Nicholas."

"This place barely has roads."

"Get a horse," she said.

The waiter slid the kung pao in front of Scissors, and he pantomimed a request for chopsticks.

"All of this matters a great deal," Frangos said. "You have done good work for me in the past. I'd like to keep you around."

"That's a kind sentiment," Scissors said.

"Everything we are doing is time sensitive. Critically so."

"Since when does government move fast? I mean, they're not known for it. I've had an inside look."

"As have I," she said. "Do you think our stooges were stupid enough to have destroyed the map, perhaps to spite you?"

"It's hard to say. I don't think either of them did too well in school."

"Were you a savant of some kind, Nicholas?"

"No, ma'am, but it was for different reasons."

"Don't tell me you were a restless spirit."

"Independent is more like it."

"An autodidact, then?" she said.

"That's right. One of those."

The waiter set the chopsticks next to Scissors, who picked them up, slid off the paper, and split them apart with one hand.

"So, what is your assessment of the situation?" she asked.

"I think they're just trying to double-cross us," he said, taking a bite. "Me, really. I don't think they even know you're part of this."

"And it needs to stay that way. The window of opportunity will close on us without notice," she said.

"Can you buy us some time?"

"I'm already doing that, but at some point, my people in Washington, D.C., will have to stop looking the other way. When that happens, you cannot be out there. If you're not gone, you'll be on your own."

"Like *Mission Impossible*?"

"I'll do more than disavow my knowledge of your activities. You'll go under the bus. Isn't that how one says it?"

"I've always come through," Scissors said, taking another spoonful of soup. "It'll be the same this time."

"I expect as much. This isn't meant to be a pep talk."

"Didn't sound like one." Scissors waited for her to say something else, and after a moment he looked at the phone and saw that the call had ended. He pocketed his phone and took another spoonful of the soup, then looked outside at the Main Street of this tiny town. By tomorrow, he figured he will have tried all of the restaurants, and he wanted to be done before he had to start doubling back.

Day Seven

An easier way to make money : Dynamite : Inauthenticity :
There's people in here : Pok-pok-pok : With winged boots :
Vexations : Plan D

The sheriff's deputy returned Reinhardt's driver's license and the rental car's registration papers. "That German license doesn't give you diplomatic immunity, Mr. Kupfer," he said.

"No, of course not, Sheriff—" Reinhardt looked up at the man's name tag. "—Sheriff Tanner."

"Deputy. It's just deputy."

"It is very difficult to obtain a German driving license, but I understand you, and I will slow down."

"That sign isn't a suggestion."

"I understand."

Reinhardt watched Tanner return to his car, then he continued following his phone's instructions to a diner for breakfast. He drove past the Kanab Chamber of Commerce until he came to a sign with three large columns of orange rock surrounding the name HooDoo Diner in red neon.

The waitress told him to sit wherever he wanted. There was a man in the first booth with a plate of eggs, link sausages, and hash browns covered in ketchup. Alongside his meal was a gray laptop, and he was reading the newspaper as he ate. Most of the other tables were taken, so Reinhardt took a booth near the back. As he sat, the waitress showed up with a tall, red glass of ice water. She asked Reinhardt if he'd like something to drink. He asked for coffee, and she set down a menu. "Specials are on the board," she said.

There was a Belgian waffle for $5.99 and a Navajo taco for $6.50. When she returned, he asked about the Navajo taco. "We don't serve that until 11:30, hon," she said.

He chose the Denver omelet and biscuits, then took out his phone and started going through his photos. There was one of the kid at the rental car place giving him the peace sign with his two front teeth protruding from under his top lip, a picture of the black Mustang he rented, then blurry pictures he should not have taken while driving from Cedar City to Kanab.

There were pictures of towering sandstone walls and smaller minarets. Travel trailers and small clusters of cattle. There were many images of old buildings, contrails crossing the open sky. Thunderheads on the horizon, and the massive storm cloud he'd seen yesterday while driving from Cedar City as it opened up to the south on the monument, the dark tatters of rain localized and intense. On either side of that storm was calm blue sky as far as he could see. Next was a picture of his own two feet plunged into the blue waters of the Virgin River, then photos of vivid Indian paintbrush and pale sage. He was looking for the one image he could use to announce that he'd reached escape velocity and left the oppressive tour. None of yesterday's photos were right. They looked like loafing.

The last photo, one he'd taken in the middle of the night, was a rectangle of black and pixel noise. This was the experience he wanted to share. It happened late last night when he'd arrived in Kanab to find all the motel signs lit to say NO VACANCY. He ventured inside their shabby offices once or twice to inquire, but they all shook their heads and said they were sorry. He drove out of town, branching off onto a series of ever-narrowing dirt roads, then he parked the car behind a dark clump of rustling bushes, retrieved his cheap new sleeping bag from its box, and tried to fold down the back seats and arrange himself inside the trunk compartment. Eventually, he curled into the fetal position and managed to fall asleep.

When he woke in the night, he heard what he thought was a group of girls talking. He was embarrassed, and he thrashed around in the car until he could look out into the surrounding terrain. There was nothing but darkness. He lay back down and again heard the voices. His head popped up a number of times, and he scanned the darkness, then lay back down. When the voices returned, they were louder. The sky was lighter, but he couldn't see anything. Even though it was ridiculous, Reinhardt lifted his phone and took a picture.

As he looked at the photo, he saw something in it, and he tapped the edit button. When he dragged the brightness slider to the left, three pixelated coyotes materialized in the middle of a blue field. They were nearly white, like creatures from another planet, and their metallic eyes glowed. They were trotting along the road, their legs blurred. One coyote stared straight into the lens. Reinhardt gasped, then checked to see if anyone was watching. They were all eating and staring blankly at their own cell phones.

He selected this ragged image for upload. He tagged @doktor_tomahawk and added the caption MEET YOUR COUSINS, THE COYOTES. He thought Wolf would laugh at the joke, but mostly he wanted to document something about his new quest. He tapped the map icon and located the image in Kanab, Utah, at @thehoodoodiner, then he uploaded the image. He watched the blue bar span the width of his phone, and then the image appeared in his feed. Wolf, in far-off Berlin, would see it at suppertime.

Just as he closed his phone, the waitress slid a massive plate in front of him, and with the other hand refilled his coffee.

A bell hanging on the door jangled. Reinhardt glanced over his shoulder when he heard it and saw two filthy men enter. One was tall with a slow, simian gait. The other was short, with a ponytail and a massive hunting knife on his belt. The short one carried a large roll of paper under his arm. The cook glanced at the waitress and the waitress shrugged.

The two men sat at the booth right behind Reinhardt and resumed an argument that seemed to have been under way for a while. Reinhardt set his phone down and began to work on his meal. The men made a racket rolling out the paper and holding it down with various items from the table.

"Why do you get to have it right side up?" one of the men complained.

"Because I can't read it upside down."

"And I can?"

"I'm the one driving."

"If you turn it a little, then it's halfway for both of us."

Reinhardt twisted around to ask them if they could be a little quieter, and the short one said, "Mind your own business, jackass." Reinhardt tried to make eye contact with someone else in the diner to verify that the man had actually talked to him like that. Everyone was keeping their heads down.

The waitress said, "The cook wants you boys to mind your p's and q's."

Reinhardt craned his neck back to the window above the grill and watched the cook fold his massive arms and frown. His neck sloped directly into his shoulders like a tree trunk just above the roots. "I'm letting you Ashdowns eat here out of respect for your Uncle Pete," he said, pointing at them. "You hear me, Lonnie?"

"We're cool," Lonnie said.

"Byron?" the cook said. "You're the one I'm really talking to."

"Yeah, we're cool. How about some coffee?" Byron said.

The two men went right back to their conversation. The taller one, who sat directly behind Reinhardt, said, "What do you think we're going to find out there?"

"Those little circles show where the pots are."

"Pots?"

"Yes, Lonnie. Pots."

"We don't need pots. We need, you know, like some place to . . ." There was a pause, then Lonnie lowered his voice, making what he said inaudible.

"I told you what we're doing. We sell the pots to that guy in Fredonia," Byron said, "which'll get us that tacos-and-cervezas-on-the-beach cash money. There's all kinds of circles up there around Swallow Valley."

"But there's no roads," Lonnie said. "I don't want to have to hike in, B. My knees are crap."

"This is the place Uncle Pete and Dad used to talk about. Dad said the Aztec gold was up there, not in Johnson Canyon like everyone thinks."

"There ain't no Aztec gold, even I know that. People been looking for it since, like, forever. Don't tell me you stole this off Scissors because of gold fever."

"Shut up and listen. This map has all the old places on it. Antelope Flats. Dutch John's Butte. Las Casas Altas. Swallow Valley. Since they put in the monument, people don't go to the old places anymore. They just follow the signs. Only a couple of guys know where any of these places are, and one of them was you know who. I feel like I keep telling you this."

"Right," Lonnie said, then more softly, "yeah, okay. I don't want to talk about it."

Reinhardt ate more of his breakfast and washed it down with the coffee. He noticed the waitress and the cook whispering to each other through the grill window, which made him nervous.

"Can't drive to Swallow Valley," Lonnie pointed out. "It's up on the plateau. Plus, after the rain last night, who knows what's washed out up there."

"I know that, but we can get to here, here, or here," Byron said, thumping the table three times. "I say we try Las Casas Altas or Antelope Flats. It's a good road, and there's tons of them little circles. We could make short work of it. We got all weekend."

"Well that's good luck, for once, I guess," Lonnie said.

"Right?" Byron said. "Where's that coffee? Man, I'm starving." He got up, approached the waitress, and asked when she was going to get to them.

Reinhardt turned on his phone and switched to the selfie mode so he could spy on them over the table. With a little tilt of the wrist, he was able to get a good picture of the map. He shot a quick burst, then ate more of his breakfast, trying to look nonchalant.

Byron sat back down and rolled up the map.

"There's gotta be easier ways to make money, rob a bank or something," Lonnie said.

"But we need clean cash at this point. Ain't no time for a real job, Lonnie. Ain't no time for paychecks or taxes or dye packs blowing up in our faces."

"How come you rolled it up?" Lonnie asked.

"Cause they're bringing the coffee. Last thing we need is you spilling something all over it."

"Last thing we need is *you* spilling something on it," Lonnie said. Reinhardt heard him skootch out of the booth. "I gotta see a man about a horse."

"What should I order?"

"Ranch breakfast and some yogurt, like a parfait or something. My guts aren't feeling great."

The taller one walked past Reinhardt, his long arms swinging slowly. Reinhardt finished his breakfast, and when the waitress passed, he asked for his check. "I'll get you at the register, hon," she said.

Reinhardt left a tip, paid the bill, and went to the car. From behind the wheel, he pulled up the first image and zoomed in. He could see the map with pretty good detail: the roads, the contour lines, the little circles, all skewed because of the angle, but all there, hand drawn, and amazing. In the Antelope Flats area, he could see five treasure circles. In faint handwriting, there were the words *Pueblo II, five vessels returned,* and *burial site—human remains.*

A treasure map, he thought, a real treasure map. He set down his phone and picked up *Mythstructures for Blockbusters,* thumbing through it to the chapter on the first threshold gatekeeper. He skimmed until he came to the term "herald," where he slowed, learning about how people or objects or letters can announce the need for change and point the hero in the right direction. He looked up and took stock of himself sitting alone in a strange town and began to create a mental list: the woman lecturing at Bryce, the Kwons, his flying dream, Kenji, the coyotes, and now this map. He was normally a rational person, but here it was, all lined up.

Just then his phone buzzed. It was a text from Wolf: I SAW THAT PHOTO OF YOUR SPIRIT GUIDES. FOLLOW YOUR BLISS, MY FRIEND. WE'LL TALK WHEN YOU RETURN.

Yes, Reinhardt thought, and he began to lay plans for an adventure to Antelope Flats.

———

When they came to the spot where the canyon narrowed to a high-walled chute flanked on each side by pines, Sophia noticed the slick rock transitioning to cobble and larger stones. Beyond that was a massive boulder, and after that, the sixty-foot drop to the level below.

Paul stopped by a pinyon pine and pulled on it from a number of different directions.

"We climbed that? It looks worse from up here," she said.

"It does. But don't worry, we'll rappel down." Paul removed his pack and pulled out his rope along with the other gear.

While he tied a series of arcane knots around the pine, Sophia said, "So, I'm putting it together, I think." She pointed to a section of the canyon wall above and behind them. There was a pathway smashed through the trees and a trail of rubble behind. "Cluff blasted this boulder out from up there." She pointed to a spot halfway up the side of the canyon.

"Yep," Paul said.

"I'm surprised he didn't kill himself in the process."

"So was he," Paul said.

They harnessed up, then lowered their packs and prepared for the belay, and after a moment, Sophia swallowed hard and backed over the brow of the rock, hopping a few feet at a time, past an empty spot where the tiny tenacious pine tree had grown. At the bottom, when she was clear of the rope, she called to Paul, who whistled over the edge, then lowered himself with the delicacy of an aerialist.

"Fun, huh?" he said, uncoupling from the rope.

"Don't push it," she said. "You still occupy a complicated place in my head."

Paul's face grew sad, then he exhaled and performed some kind of magic with one end of the rope, and the length of it fell, unspooling, to the ground. The ease with which it came free made Sophia unsure about wanting to repeat the process.

Once the gear was repacked, they continued on. The sky above them was blue, and there was no sign of flooding in any of the canyons. The view of the return hike was disorienting. The descent was beginning to take its toll on her knees and ankles, but she distracted herself by thinking through her photos and notes and by justifying her feelings about Paul and his stupid off-the-books project. No wonder he kept going on about hiding the vehicle and having her drive. Returning artifacts this way would probably cost him his job. The whole ends-justify-the-means attitude was common in archeology. You see it in salvage divers and in Howard Carter's journals from the Valley of the Kings. Their belief in the greater good was overpowering. She felt science was the only way to keep self-interest out of it, but even the science was accomplished by politics and bureaucracy and personalities. In graduate school, they talked about the emic and etic. There were insiders and outsiders. The more she moved about in this desert landscape, exploring these ruins, the more she felt like a foreigner. You could try to grow close to another culture, but that wouldn't make you part of it. You'd always be an observer. And if you were exploring the past, then that rift would become a gulf.

Her thoughts flowed through these channels all morning. As the hours passed, the sky became white, and the landscape around them went specular as the sun blazed down. Sophia thought about people who sought out a life in this environment, the ones who did not gather with others in the larger pueblos but instead retreated here. These lives were not accidental; neither could they be known except by the people who lived here and passed on. What she felt now was another aspect of the emptiness and absence she felt yesterday at the granary.

She paused at a switchback and sipped her water. As she adjusted the sternum strap on her pack, she realized that she had one Jolly Rancher left in the breast pocket of her shirt. Paul had rationed them out that morning, and she'd gone through them. She quickly popped the candy into her mouth only to discover it was grape. She would have to deal with it. She wrapped the luxurious rectangle in her tongue, and as she hiked, she turned it over and over until it was nothing more than a purple ribbon.

And then it was gone.

They came again to the vista of the lava field. Paul was waiting for her. "You doing okay?"

"I'm fine."

"Okay."

"You've been quiet."

"I've got a lot on my mind. Obviously."

They hiked on, stopping regularly to stretch and drink.

During one break, Paul said, "You're not going to tell anyone about what happened up there—you know—with the bowl, are you?"

"I haven't decided," Sophia said, adjusting her backpack.

Paul moved his hands to his hips and adjusted his sunglasses. "You're still mad."

"Very observant."

"I really hoped this trip might go in an entirely different direction."

"Me too."

"I was thinking if I had a chance to meet the me going up the trail two days ago, I'd pull him aside and give him some advice."

"Like, don't ruin everything?" she said.

"Well, more like don't lie to Sophia."

Sophia exhaled and tried not to roll her eyes. "Not lying to people is really important. I hope this isn't a brand-new insight for you."

"I made a promise to Bruce, and I wanted to see it through. But it's bigger than that. Political stuff. We all know it's coming, but we don't know when. It's like the bad guys are gaining on us, trying to unwrite a hundred years of hard work, sell it all off to the highest bidder. Sometimes, when you're here in the middle, the only thing you can do to make a difference is break the rules. It's just hard to be the one who has to enforce them at the same time."

Sophia did not know what to say and what to hold back, so instead of speaking, she looked through a gap in the low hills toward Antelope Flats and then back up at the way they'd come down. She felt many responses come to the surface of her mind, then depart. During her silence, she saw Paul's impeccable posture eroding, and she felt as if her message was coming across just fine.

"How much longer do we have?"

"At this pace, maybe an hour."

They continued on, her feet growing sore from the hammering of the trail. The way flattened out, and eventually her truck materialized out of the junipers. She dropped her pack in the truck bed and opened her cooler, which was full of ice water. She removed two cans of Dr Pepper and placed one on the back of her neck. She offered the other to Paul, who declined.

"Suit yourself. More for me," she said. She cracked open the soda and drank half of it in a single, long, burning, delicious stream, then unlocked the truck.

They drove in welcome silence down the steadily widening paths to the county road, until they came to Paul's Jeep.

"I'm sorry I ruined everything," he said.

Sophia shrugged. "I'm sorry I set my expectations so high." Sophia got out of the truck but left it idling.

Paul unbuckled his seatbelt and said, "At least you got to prove that people actually do suck. It's not just confirmation bias." He smiled weakly, got out, and started transferring his gear from Sophia's truck into his vehicle. After a couple of trips, he stopped, swore, and began hurriedly checking his vehicle top to bottom, saying, "This isn't possible. No. No. No. It couldn't just disappear."

"What's gone?"

"My weapon—the M16—it's gone."

"Are you sure you brought it?"

"The SIG Sauer and the Remington are here, still locked up. The vehicle was locked." He checked the doors and windows and threw his arms in the air.

"Maybe your mind was somewhere else. When was the last time you saw it?" Sophia said, not minding at all that she came across as smug.

"I serviced it last week," he said, slumping against the vehicle. "So, it's got to be back on my workbench. It's the only thing that makes sense. With all the crap going on right now, I'm just not on top of things."

"It's okay to be imperfect," Sophia said.

"Not right now it's not, not for me," Paul said. "I'm going to have to hustle back to Dellenbaugh Station. I'm so sorry. I'll be in touch. We should talk about all of this at some point."

"We should," Sophia said and watched Paul speed off to the south.

—

Reinhardt arrived at a gas station that perched on the edge of the Paiute Indian Reservation, thirty miles southwest of Kanab. It was a standard American highway oasis with a massive open roof sheltering eight self-service fuel pumps. He had seen so many photographs of places like this that it did not seem foreign to him at all. During the drive, the wind had picked up, and percussive gusts shoved his car with enough force to make him veer out of his lane. As he pulled into the station from the side road, dust exploded into the air like waves breaking on a dry beach. In the open, flat ground between the station and the highway stood a huge green fiberglass brontosaurus.

As Reinhardt parked, he noticed more dinosaurs printed on every sign and pump, and he thought how strange it was for people to cling to the fiction that our oil came from these creatures. Another gust buffeted the car, and across the way, an old man with a wispy white beard and no mustache labored outside in the turbulence to fuel his old camper. Reinhardt watched him carry a step stool, which he stood on to clean the windshield. As he began his work, the wind snatched the paper towels from his hand and carried them off.

Reinhardt got out of the car to throw his trash into the garbage, and the old man saw him. He climbed down from his stool, looked to where the towels had gone, then approached Reinhardt with a fury in his small eyes. "Supposed to rain again," he said without preamble. "Like to be the monsoons."

Reinhardt nodded and turned to scan the southward expanse where the dark and distant mountains lay derelict against the sky, which was blue at its zenith and populated by a dozen or more clouds heaped in bales that dwindled in size as they approached the tan haze of the horizon. "Rain? But it's so clear now," Reinhardt said.

The old man gestured to all sides, the wind blowing his hair and beard around. "Winds of change, son," he said. "Winds of change." Then the man walked back to his camper, a slight limp in his right leg. He stowed the stool in the back camper, then disappeared around the other side. When he reappeared, the man shouted, "Don't fool with the rain."

Reinhardt nodded and thanked him.

"It looks like a desert now," the old man said, "but this whole place was created with water."

"I will remember your advice," Reinhardt called back.

"Not advice," the man said. "It's a warning." Then he limped across the concrete to the convenience store, the wind picking up again so that he struggled to open the door. After several attempts, he pounded on the glass with his fist. The door opened slowly, and a teenage girl with long straight black hair pushed against it until the old man could enter, then she guided the door closed. It looked like she was used to the task.

Reinhardt began pumping his gas, and a burst of dust blasted him in the face, so he hunched behind the pump and looked past it toward the open desert. A wall of dust formed in the air and billowed across the open ground, targeting him. Inside the dark roller, debris lifted into the air and fell scattered behind. The wall cloud swelled as it approached and surged across the highway. Reinhardt ducked, pulling his face down into the neck of his shirt right as he and the gas station were engulfed. He squatted and waited until the roar of the wind had passed, then he stood.

A half-powered wind lingered, then the gas dispenser clicked off. Reinhardt replaced the nozzle and saw the gas station door opening slowly against the wind, the teenage girl turning her shoulder into it, pushing with everything she had, like someone in a silent movie. While she leaned against the glass, the old man limped past her and crossed to his camper, then the girl walked the door backward carefully so it wouldn't slam.

Reinhardt walked past the camper as it drove off, noticing the Arkansas license plates and the bumper sticker that said I ♥ ATHENS. He pried open the gas station door and eased it shut. Inside, the girl sat on a stool behind the register, inspecting the tips of her hair. His breath caught in his chest as he recognized that she was an Indian. "Rote Indianer," he whispered to himself, and she looked up.

"Can I help you?" she said.

He shook his head, embarrassed and surprised and a little confused by the girl's red plastic hoop earrings and her black hoodie. Naturally, she wouldn't be wearing eagle feathers or beadwork, but he was expecting something else. She returned to her hair, and Reinhardt continued to look at her, noticing the acne on her cheeks, and the dermatologist in him thought perhaps he might recommend a retinoid cream.

But he said nothing and continued on to the restroom. He used the toilet, then washed his hands and face. Out there was a real flesh-and-blood Indian, bored like any teenager with a bad job, surrounded by cigarettes and lottery tickets and a flimsy display of unsold LED flashlights. He was disappointed in himself for confusing her with his idea of Native people. She was not playing Indian like Wolf and his friends from the teepee camps back home.

He dried his face and returned to the store and saw her sitting in the same position but now playing a game on her phone. He picked up a few bottles of Cherry Coke, a few bottles of water, and set them on the counter, then went back down the aisles for potato chips, nuts, and candy. From different parts of the store, he watched her until the guilt of it overpowered him. He looked for a back door, but there wasn't one, so he approached the register and set his purchases down. The girl rang him up and put everything into a plastic sack. He had so many questions he wanted to ask her, but he knew he would be clumsy and embarrass himself even more, so he settled for directions. "I'm looking for the road that leads to Antelope Flats," he asked.

"Where?" she asked.

"Antelope Flats."

"I don't know where that is. Is it on the monument or something?"

"It is supposed to be near here, or out there," Reinhardt said, pointing through the window. "Let me show you the map I—"

"Hey, Ronnie?" the girl called out.

After a second, "What?" The voice was quiet.

"Where's a place called Antelope Flats?"

"Where's what?"

"Antelope Flats, like somewhere on the monument." The girl sighed, then a skinny kid came out of the back wearing a Limp Bizkit T-shirt and saggy gray jeans. His ears were gauged and he had a round face with square glasses. "Antelope what?" he said, still quiet.

"Flats," she said.

"Is that a place?" They both looked at each other for a moment.

"He says it is," she said, pointing to Reinhardt.

"Hello, yes," Reinhardt said. "My map says the turnoff is close. I am supposed to find a road called Sundown."

"Ah, okay," Ronnie said. "Sundown is what my grandma calls . . ." The boy thought for a moment. "If you've got a map, how come you can't find it?"

Reinhardt shrugged. "It's not a very good one. And I am not from around here."

The girl laughed.

"My grandma used to talk about Sundown. Maybe it's just County Road 16. It's like three miles that way," he said, pointing east. "There's a tiny little sign, but you won't see it if you're going fast." Ronnie squinted out the window at Reinhardt's Mustang. "No four-wheel drive?"

"This is my only transportation," Reinhardt said.

"Okay, but Sundown is only graded for a few miles. Then it gets pretty bad."

"Yeah," the girl said. "And you should fill up first, though."

"For reals. Get gas now. People run out of gas out there all the time. Tow truck will rip you off. Maybe you should get a better map."

"He already paid," the girl said.

Reinhardt held up the bags, then he thanked them and pushed against the door. The wind had dropped off enough that it worked easily.

He looked back at the windows of the store and saw Ronnie and the girl staring at him. After a few seconds the girl covered her mouth and turned away. He thought he could see Ronnie smiling. As Reinhardt took another step, his angle of view changed and the sun struck the glass, turning it into an opaque flare of white. When he left the tour group, he was hoping to find something real that hadn't been staged, but now he knew that they'd only been shown what the tour company wanted them to see. He moved his two bags into one hand and opened the car door. An empty plastic sack blew past him like a ghost. Gazing into the vault of the sky, he saw himself as a creature given over to and divided by vanity; his cheeks burned with shame and anger for the tour and for believing Krause and Wolf and the web pages that planted these ideas in his head about what he'd find out here. He regretted having to pay so much for the truth. Then he corrected himself. Anyone with the truth, he thought, should not be willing to sell it.

He sat behind the wheel and considered aborting the trip, then looked down at *Mythstructures for Blockbusters* and he thought about the call to adventure and how a refusal follows it. If the hero stays home, there is no story. He set the key fob into the ashtray and looked around, thinking of everything that had brought him here to this *X* on the map, and he made the choice to press on.

Before he left the gas station, he rolled down the window and snapped a picture of the glossy brontosaurus with a vast desert panorama stretching out behind it, and he posted it to Instagram and geotagged the image with PIPE SPRING GAS AND GROCERY, ARIZONA. The caption: INTO THE GREAT WIDE OPEN.

Reinhardt found County Road 16 after passing it twice. He wanted to drive with the top down, but the wind made it impossible. Enveloped in air conditioning, he opened one of his Cherry Cokes and drove on. His attention drifted outward to the mesas in the empty distance. The lack of green gave Reinhardt the impression of moving through a landscape drawn in chalk on a sheet of packing paper.

Eventually the wind died down, and being the only movement in such stillness made him question the passing of time. Every few miles he stopped and took more photographs with his phone. At some point there was no longer cell service. Eventually the road was blocked by three cows: two females and a calf. One of them swung her head and stared at him, white-faced, like somebody waiting their turn to speak. He took a photo of her through the dust-spotted windshield, then he honked, but it did not disperse them, so he got out and ran them off with shouts and waving arms.

He drove on, watching the steady unbroken, unchanging view, listening to the rumble of the tires and the hum of the engine. He noticed that his body had relaxed, so he rearranged his limbs. This was better than what he planned. Perhaps that was the mistake, thinking he could imagine this place from his apartment in Berlin after a few clicks on the internet. Even Sigmund F. Krause's books didn't have the full feeling of the space, and a map is never anything more than a finger pointing the way. Above all else, this mess of a trip made Reinhardt feel possibilities that had been veiled before.

He heard a horn and noticed a turquoise pickup bursting forth from the dust behind him. The truck pulled a trailer carrying a large yellow excavation machine with a blade on the front and a digging arm in the back. The English word for it escaped him, and as the truck zoomed past, leaving him in the wash of its dust, he thought of the German: Löffelbagger. After a few minutes, he drove clear of the cloud and saw the truck was gone. He was glad to be alone again.

The next photograph he stopped to take was of a derelict truck from the forties that lay a hundred feet from the road, swallowed by creosote bushes. As he approached the vehicle, he saw that it was riddled with bullet holes. Sunlight lanced the interior with slender white beams, each one filled with swirling dust. The inside was littered with broken bottles and old cans. As he returned to the car, he thought for a moment about the difference between Bryce Canyon, which was a national park, and this national monument. One was an amusement park full of noise and tourists, the other something frozen in its own time.

After a while, Reinhardt dug into his bag looking for the packets of pemmican he had brought from Germany. He'd tasted it for the first time sitting around a fire in buckskins at a hobby club encampment in the Black Forest. It was before he'd met Wolf, at the start of it all. Friends from college took him and a woman he thought he might marry—Greta; her Indian name was The Blue Sky Girl. He'd loved Krause's books as a child, but so did everyone. The camps unlocked something in him, an escape from the anxieties of school and the mounting waves of digital connections. According to his friends, Indian people lived authentic lives, which he and his friends imitated, hoping to escape the modern world.

He opened the pemmican and took a bite, remembering the games and drum circles, the teepees and dances. He thought about how, much later, Wolf had taken him to other camps and introduced him to Germans who had transformed themselves completely into what they thought an Indian was. As he drove, he began to see how false those gatherings had been, how misguided and ill conceived. Taking the thinnest possible slice of the truth, they had concocted their own mythology from afar, using Native people as props and side characters. The Krause Museum was a sham. Their powwows and trinkets like so many cardboard cutouts. The kids in that gas station were real; he was fake. Wolf was fake, though he called himself a practical anthropologist. All of it was an idea of an idea of an idea.

Reinhardt set the unfinished pemmican down on the seat and drove on. He did not know how to have this conversation with Wolf when he returned to Germany, but he knew he must. It was overwhelming enough to have this dialogue with himself. Was this his quest? Was he to return home with this new knowledge?

Reinhardt took many photographs on the drive, saving them in his phone for uploading later. A single cloud separated from the others, casting a massive shadow across the expanse. A ramshackle homestead collapsed back into the crumbling hillside it was built into. He drove and snacked and looked for more things to photograph. Eventually he came to a section of the road where the high-voltage lines crossed overhead. The towers were massive, and as Reinhardt considered them, he tried to guide his thinking to something more Teutonic and less borrowed. He imagined them as golems given the task to guide power from the country to the city. He dreamed up a story where a boy was given magic metallic seeds and told not to plant them until there was a full moon. The boy, of course, rejected this counsel and that night these giants grew and wreaked havoc on the nearby village. A wizard gave them all magic rope to carry, which froze the golems in their tracks.

Reinhardt crested a rise to find a man standing alongside the road, next to a silver Sebring convertible. His clothes were not a hiker's. He wore a loose-fitting Hawaiian shirt, green pants, and white loafers with no socks, and he was waving Reinhardt down.

Reinhardt stopped, and a thick tan cloud of dust immediately engulfed the both of them. The man approached the car, motioning for him to roll down the window by cranking his hand. Reinhardt lowered the window with a button, then he turned off the car.

"It's odd," the man said, repeating his pantomime and looking at it. There was a tattoo of a dagger-pierced skull on his arm. "We do this gesture, even when there's no crank to turn."

"Excuse me?" Reinhardt said.

"Like how we say that we hang up the phone when there is just a button, and even then, often there is no button at all, just an image of a button."

Reinhardt looked all around to see if there was anyone else. There wasn't.

"But we didn't come here to philosophize," the man said. "I am looking for some business associates. One tall, the other short. They drive a turquoise Ford, I believe."

"That truck passed me a while ago," Reinhardt said.

"Which way?"

Reinhardt pointed backward with his thumb. "They passed me back there, then I didn't see them again. It would be easy to get lost out here."

"It is very easy. I've been beating myself up about losing these two." The man noticed the snacks on his seat. "Is that pemmican?" he asked.

"It is," Reinhardt said. "But I am embarrassed to say I bought it on the internet."

"No shame in that. Using the internet is not really a choice anymore."

"My friend Wolf makes his own. Mine is inauthentic. It has raisins and walnuts."

"I stand corrected. Shame on you for raisins and walnuts." The man stood and looked up the road and back again.

"Can I help you find them?" Reinhardt asked.

"You came in on 16, then. Not sure what road we're on now."

Reinhardt said he did. "I can show you my map," he said, reaching for his phone.

"That isn't necessary," the man said.

"Do you think they are okay?"

"For now," he said. "They know their way around here. I'm just following."

"If I see them should I say that you are looking for them?"

"Ah, no. I'd like to surprise them," the man said, looking at his wristwatch. "I appreciate your time." He thumped the roof of the car and stepped back. Reinhardt looked over and saw that the man's car was using its undersized spare tire. He thought about pointing out that such a small tire would cause problems on these roads, but instead he put the car in gear and drove on, with the man waving him past, like somebody guiding planes at the airport.

Reinhardt watched the man in his rearview mirror. He crossed the road to his car and got in.

A hill rose in front of him, and after crossing it, he lost sight of the man completely.

He sped up, dropping down into another dry valley, then rose over another hill. In the near distance rose a fantastic palisade of orange rock that folded upon itself like the ruffle on a costume. The road carved through the sagebrush, toward the cliffs. He opened his phone and flipped to the map. By his best reckoning, he was close to a place called Las Casas Altas.

He drove on, stopping to take photos of each new thing. At one stop, he got out of the car to get a closer photograph of a cluster of small humanoid orange rocks, and bursting through the general buzz of insects, he heard the sudden blasting racket of a rattlesnake. Before he could think, he jumped back and saw the snake coiled under a bush, watching him, its black tongue whipping the air. Everything else was motionless.

When Reinhardt moved, the snake cautioned him with a quick burst of sound, then walked its looped body back over itself as it retreated farther into the vegetation. Soon, it was entirely gone.

Reinhardt took his own pulse at the neck. It was about 125, double his resting rate. A clammy feeling moved across his skin. He felt tired, then nauseous, then elated. He wanted, for some reason, to chase the snake, but he kept himself from it. Instead he looked to the sky. This, he thought, is what I came here for.

He returned to the car and emptied one of his water bottles. He tried to orient himself again on the photograph of the map and verified that Las Casas Altas was a cliff dwelling, and he was close by. He drove on, with the undulating cliff wall on his left. Soon he could make out a high row of small, dark squares on the cliff face, higher up than anyone could climb without help.

A deafening bang jolted the car. The steering wheel wrenched out of Reinhardt's hands and the vehicle swerved into the cut side of the road with enough force to deploy the airbag, which exploded against his face in a blinding white flash. He sat in the seat, stunned for a moment, his ears ringing, surrounded by the smell of something burning. He gathered himself together and opened the car door. The fiberglass bumper was splintered, and the engine ticked with dissipating heat. He bent down to get a look under the car and saw a lacerated rock and a line of reddish fluid streaming from the transmission into the dirt.

He looked around at his surroundings, then up into the sky, which was filling with clouds. In the midst of it, a tiny jet airplane flew diagonally across the blue vault. He noticed that there were no vultures, then quickly realized that there would be no vultures yet. In that tumble of thinking, queasiness came first, then panic, then tears. After it had all passed, he said to himself, "Listen, Dr. Kupfer. You need a plan, not hysterics." He stood, brushed himself off, and started looking through the car for anything useful.

—

The Ashdowns were parked on County Road 16 a few hundred feet into the sagebrush in a place called Antelope Flats with the truck windows open, the borrowed backhoe off the trailer, and Bruce Cluff's fifth map unrolled on the hood and held down with a pair of toolbox magnets. The other two corners flapped in the wind. A scant number of junipers and creosote were scattered about in this tight dish of land. A low palisade of dark basalt hemmed them in on the east and gave way to a box canyon that dropped fifteen abrupt feet to a concavity with a natural dirt ramp that led back to the level of the road. Beyond that area, farther to the north, was a single hill rising out of the chaparral. The county road rose up to the base of the hill and followed its contour and continued farther into the monument. They were sixty-five miles from the state highway. Another thirty-five miles of dirt road lay between them and the north rim of the Grand Canyon.

Byron sat inside his uncle's backhoe at the bottom of the draw with the black stone wall of the box canyon wrapped around him on one side and a steep dirt slope on the other. The steel boom curled behind the machine like the segmented tail of a massive yellow scorpion. Lonnie stood next to him holding the roll cage while Byron worked the loader down into the rocky ground. The bucket came up, quivered, then dropped, and the monstrous tines bit into the dirt. As Byron cranked the control levers, the front rode up slightly, the pitch of the pumps rising. The loader bucket sank into the ground, and the machine spasmed, throwing Lonnie off. He screamed and rolled out of the way, then jumped up and tried to flap his arms to get Byron's attention, but Byron kept digging.

"Hey," Lonnie shouted. "Hey, Byron!" He waved his hands until Byron turned off the machine.

"What?" Byron said, spitting through the open side of the cab.

"Aren't the pots and whatever gonna be worth more if they're, like, you know, all in one piece?"

"You and me and a couple shovels ain't gonna cut it. We'll make it up in volume," Byron said.

Lonnie shook his head. "I don't think it works like that."

"Let me remind you that we're at *this* particular crossroads because of your problem-solving skills, not mine. Get out of the way. The clock is running."

"I feel it too, you know. This guy isn't going to just lay off and let us go."

"He'll lose interest."

"I'm starting to lose interest," Lonnie said. "I guess that's what I'm saying."

"Then you're free to go. But I'm tired of eating scraps with the dogs."

"I know. You've said that before."

Byron turned on the machine, lifted the bucket, pulled back, swiveled around, and dumped its contents at Lonnie's feet. A large white thing tumbled out of the dark cascade of dirt and rocks. When it came to rest, Lonnie saw two eye sockets and a row of small flat teeth.

He looked up to see if his brother had noticed, but Byron was already turning the machine around. He drove ahead a dozen feet and dug again. Lonnie reached down and pulled the skull out of the dirt, considering it. His first thought was surprise that the map was right when it said this spot had human remains, then he thought maybe there wasn't just one person here. Lonnie turned the skull around and saw, behind the eye, a radiating web of cracks. His eyes unfocused, and for a moment, he thought he might pass out. "We can't do this," he said, but the sound of his voice was swallowed up by the backhoe. He dug into the loose earth with his hands, which was still damp from the recent rain, and kicked up the curved tines of a rib cage. As he scanned the mound, he saw the crusted dome and serpentine cracks of a second skull, which he pulled out and set alongside the first. He wanted to get these people away from Byron and the random tires of the backhoe. Lonnie dropped to his knees and started digging. He quickly found the parallel bones of a forearm. At the end of it was a curled fist held together by the clumped dirt.

He stood, and when Byron swung the bucket back around, Lonnie lifted up the bones, and when Byron saw them, he shut down the machine. "What's that?" he shouted.

Lonnie pointed to the mound of dirt. "There's people in here. You have to stop."

Byron smiled and whooped and climbed down from the machine. "Gimme that," he said, snatching the bone away from his brother. Lonnie scrambled, picking up the two skulls, as Byron tossed the arm bones aside. "You know what those mean?" Byron said.

"This is a graveyard?"

"It means we hit the jackpot."

"I don't think that's what it means, Byron. This is the opposite of a jackpot."

"What would *you* call it, then?"

"Well, disaster comes to mind," Lonnie said. "Maybe a curse." He showed Byron the fractured skull. He wanted his brother to see there was something going on here that was more important than money. He thought about his own mother buried in Kanab, and he knew his brother wouldn't even consider digging in that cemetery. "These are somebody's ancestors, Byron. Please, let's just go," he said.

His brother was unmoved. "Oh, shut up and get the shovels," Byron said, and he headed back to the machine.

—

As Sophia drove back to town, she tried to listen to her book, but she was too mad about what happened on the trip to follow the story. She tried music, but even the angry songs were angry in the wrong way, so she switched to silence and let herself stew. Yes, Paul lied to her, but that was not exactly right; he kept information back—he was playing a role. It was supposed to be a trip for them—that's what it was, right?—but it turned out to be a disguise. A ruse— that was the word she wanted. He obviously had no plans to tell her about anything until he was caught—the double-dipping bastard.

When the road straightened, she checked the signal on her phone: NO SERVICE.

Over the summer, she had discovered some of the places on the monument with coverage: on top of Mt. Logan and west of the Hurricane Cliffs. In Antelope Flats, a little ways from here, you could get a sliver of signal if you were high enough, not enough for data, but you could make a call or send a text. She weighed it all out, and given the work she was doing, she decided to stop at Antelope Flats and call Bryce Canyon and see if Dalinda could walk her through the procedure for something like this. Then she could focus on what to say instead of how to say it.

As she came around the corner and dropped down the hill, she saw the turquoise Ford again parked off the road in a sparse area of juniper. There was a trailer there, too. She slowed, and when she didn't see anybody, she pulled in behind the truck and stopped to give the place a closer look. Beyond the truck, a yellow backhoe arm flashed into view, then disappeared. She got out. This time she was going to at least get the license plate number.

On the hood of the Ford was the same hand-drawn map she'd seen last week. She groaned and scanned the map more carefully to see if she could figure out what they were doing. Swallow Valley was on it, as well as a spot nestled in a canyon, marked with a small square surrounding an *X*. Next to it was the note *2 sticks dynamite set here in 1981. Access controlled.* She recognized the handwriting from the blue book Paul had with him, and she thought of everything Paul told her about Cluff. Her pulse jumped as the dots connected. She pulled out her phone, checked again for a signal. When she failed to get one, she snapped a picture of the license plate and the map, ran back to her truck, and hopped into the bed. Still no signal, so she stepped up, stood above the cab, and picked up 1X, which was enough to connect. But from that height, she could see the two guys moving earth with the backhoe, which meant they could see her.

She hopped down and sprinted to their truck, plucking the map from the hood, tearing it where the magnets held it down. On her way back to her own truck, a voice called out, "Hey! We seen you a couple days ago." It was the taller one. He looked exhausted, and he carried a human skull carefully in each hand. It looked like he'd been crying.

"Disturbing a burial site is a federal offense," she shouted, standing tall, to make herself seem larger, because she had been trained in mountain lion safety but not for anything like this.

Lonnie looked down at the skulls in his hands. "I tried to stop him," he said, then he lifted his face.

Sophia took out her phone and pointed it at him. "I'm filming this. My name is Sophia Shepard, and this man is—"

"Won't do any good if you can't send it. No reception out here."

She looked down and still had the 1X. "I'm good. We can use it in court," she said, then continued narrating the scene. When she did, Lonnie raised both hands and the skulls over his head. She looked around for something she could use to defend herself, but she had a phone in one hand and a map in the other, so she jumped down and reached for her truck's door, thinking she'd lock herself in. Then a light flashed on the scrubby hill north of them, and an instant later Lonnie's face burst into a kaleidoscope of blood and sunlight, which fanned into a mist as he dropped to his knees and fell forward into the dirt. The skulls leapt free of his grasp, rolled for a few inches, then came to a stop.

The surrounding space collapsed around Sophia, and she could no longer hear the straining of the backhoe's engine. One second later, a staggered line of holes burst across the center of her windshield, each impact followed immediately by a burst of scintillating glass and the dull thud of the bullet burying itself in the back of her vehicle. Sophia dove to the ground and covered her head. A series of metallic pings came in triplets. During a pause she spotted the dead man through the tires of her truck and saw his back lurch as a bullet struck him across the shoulder. After a few seconds, another string of bullets rang across the fender of the other truck.

Her father, who had been a Marine in Iraq during Desert Storm, had taught her combat tactical breathing to help her with anxiety attacks in middle school. He said it's how you can get in control of your parasympathetic nervous system. She did not know what that was, but they were the right words to show he wasn't making any of it up. He told her this is how she can pull her head back in the game when she loses it. Breathe in, hold, exhale, repeat. After three cycles, she could feel her vision sharpen. Another few rounds and her thoughts started making sense. She could hear the backhoe again.

She turned on her phone and checked that she still had a connection. She thought about calling 911, realized their response time would be two hours or more, then with one hand she typed a hurried text to Paul: IM BEING SHOT AT ROAD 16 ENVELOPE FLATS. The second she sent it, she saw the autocorrect error and fixed it with a second text: ANTELOPE. The delivery message appeared and another round of pok-pok-pok rang out somewhere in the sheet metal above. She crouched.

While the backhoe growled and groaned, Sophia lay on the ground with the map next to her and the phone cradled in both hands, waiting for "delivered" to change to "read." She tried to process what was happening. It seemed like some kind of drug deal in a movie going bad. Was this random or planned? Was it a turf war? Was one of these guys double-crossing the others? Two against one? Pottery was worth money, but not that much. Her thoughts stopped sprinting when another flash popped on the hill. She tensed, anticipating the incoming bullets, until she realized the glint wasn't shots at all, but it had come off the windshield of a car crawling down the road toward her. The delivery message switched to "read," and her pulse jumped. A new balloon appeared on the screen followed by three bouncing dots, but there were no words in it yet. If the shooter was in the car, she had just a sliver of time.

She rolled up the map and slipped it into her pack, then she stood, opened the truck door and grabbed her water bottle, and somehow in the middle of her reaching, the phone slipped from her hand and fell, hard. She looked up and around at the hill and the surrounding bluffs, then crouched and turned over the phone. The screen was shattered, entirely, pieces of glass sliding off and dropping to the ground. When she pressed the on button, the phone did not light up. The glass would shred everything, so she zipped her pack shut and threw her phone into the truck, shards flying everywhere. Taking her bearings, she pulled her pack onto her shoulders and ran straight for the curving terrace of rock that lay thirty yards east of their vehicles. As she ran, she stopped to check behind her just as the car pulled off the road and rolled slowly in her direction.

When she came to the basalt wall, she realized there was no way around it. She wedged herself into one of the angled corners and climbed straight up like she had on the way into Swallow Valley. In a few quick moves, she made it to the top and rolled across the rocks to the dirt on the other side. From this shallow depression she returned to her combat breathing. Then the car door slammed, barely audible over the rumble of the backhoe.

She knew she should keep her head down, but she didn't want the man to sneak up on her, so she peered over the edge and saw him strutting around her truck with a military weapon slung across his back. He wore a pair of blue medical gloves, a white panama hat, and a garish Hawaiian shirt. After a quick inspection of the area, he stopped and removed his sunglasses, then he continued to the dead man, toed the body, placed the muzzle of the gun against the back of his head, and fired.

The backhoe kept working. The man walked down the incline, lifting the weapon to his shoulder. A few seconds after he disappeared, she heard the backhoe stop, and then the desert sounds filled in: an insectile shriek from the junipers and undulating clap-clap-clap pulse coming from all directions. Two more gunshots echoed across the space, then silence filled in as a group of wrens zipped past her and disappeared into the space beyond.

Sophia watched the man climb back up the draw and walk straight toward the turquoise pickup. After he searched the cab and bed completely, he began systematically tearing the truck apart, pulling the seats forward and cutting them open with a folding knife. When he finished, he shot out the tires, then moved on to her truck, which he dismantled in the same fashion. When he was done, he stood to one side and held up a can of her Dr Pepper, popped it open, and chugged it, wiping his mouth with the back of his forearm. Once it was gone, he shot out the tires of her truck, crushed the can with the heel of his shoe, then took it to his own car and left it on the seat.

"Thank you for the soft drink, Sophia," the man shouted. "I found the so-das and the wallet you left behind. It surprises me how perfectly those twenty-three flavors quench my thirst. Wouldn't you like to be a Pepper, too?" He paused and moved his gun to one shoulder. "I realize it is entirely possible that you have run off. Someone in good physical condition could be half a mile from here by now, which would be the safest thing. No doubt. Then again, a reasonable person might be wondering if running might reveal her position. Such a tremendous thing to weigh out. The whole situation makes you a little bit like Schrödinger's cat, doesn't it? To me, you are both alive and dead." He paused, and Sophia closed her eyes, squeezing out the tears she'd been fighting against.

Sophia felt herself losing it again.

"A few moments ago, as a final gesture, the gentleman on the backhoe informed me that the map I am looking for was on the hood of his truck. I see now that it's missing. Since it is not in your truck, and since it doesn't appear to have blown off—there are some torn pieces here under the magnets—I imagine the map is with you. So, I am giving you a one-time offer to set things right."

From the south, she heard a vehicle. She imagined that it must be Paul. She hoped it was. The vehicle stopped, and she heard the echo of the door slamming.

"Hands where I can see them," Paul directed.

"What seems to be the problem?"

"For starters, that's my weapon, which means ten years of federal time for you."

"How strange," the man said. "I found this here, right in the middle of a tragic situation. I'm glad I have the opportunity to return it to you directly."

Sophia rolled over and peered across the rocks and saw Paul, now in uniform, advancing with his pistol leveled at the man, who held Paul's gun awkwardly out to the side with one hand.

"This escalated quickly," the man said.

"Lace your fingers behind your head and get down on your knees," Paul shouted.

Sophia was emboldened by Paul's command of the situation, and she called out. "I'm up here."

"Are you hurt?" Paul asked.

"I'm fine."

The man looked in her direction and stared.

"Eyes over here," Paul said. "Set that weapon on the ground."

The man went down on his knees, relaxed his shoulder, and the gun dropped.

"Stay on your knees and move back," Paul ordered.

"That will ruin my outfit," the man said.

"Just the pants," Paul said.

Sophia laughed a little to release some pressure. She stood and watched Paul pick up his weapon and set it on the hood of the turquoise pickup.

"I notice you have a radio," the man said, "but I haven't heard you call anything in."

"This isn't a performance evaluation," Paul said, walking around the man, who kept his bent arms rigid like fins on an old car. Paul checked on the body lying facedown, then moved to where he could see into the draw.

"Sophia. I've got two guys down. Is that right?" he called out.

"I think so," she shouted back.

"Sophia?" the man said, toying with Paul. "So you know each other."

"Shut up," Paul said, returning to the man with a pair of handcuffs. Sophia watched Paul as he cuffed one hand, then the other, and stood the man up. As Paul turned the man around, he struck out with his forehead and knocked Paul backward. The man dropped to the ground, slipping his cuffed hands behind him as he fell. In a single motion, he pulled his feet through the ring of his arms and reappeared standing, with a pistol he'd pulled from an ankle holster.

Paul was still reeling from the head butt when the man shot him point-blank in the chest. Paul staggered back. The man shot him again, and Paul disappeared over the sheer stone edge of the box canyon.

Sophia screamed, drawing the man's attention. He turned, with his hands still cuffed, and shot at her until the pistol emptied. Bullets ricocheted off the cliffs, and she ran away through the sage in a straight line, leaping over boulders. The man's voice followed her, now amplified through the speaker in Paul's vehicle. "SOPHIA! I RESCIND THE PREVIOUS OFFER!" She cut through a row of dense bushes that tore at her clothes. Ahead of her was a wash that might lead to a hiding place. She ducked into it.

"ONCE I NEUTRALIZE THESE VEHICLES, I'LL COME FOR YOU AND MY MAP!"

—

Reinhardt figured he was about eight kilometers from his Mustang, going in what seemed like the right direction. The sameness of this sage flat would have turned him around if not for the sun burning in its transit across the sky. With all this walking, he hadn't even made it back to the place where he'd encountered the strange man wearing golf pants. He crinkled the water bottles he carried in each hand and felt the dryness in his mouth modulate to a dull throbbing ache. He stopped and selected a white stone from the side of the road and placed it into his mouth. This lozenge was warm and rasping on his tongue. Saliva gathered around it, which he swallowed, knowing there would be only so many times he could recirculate his water this way.

The sky was filled with proportional white clouds. Behind them was a belt of gray. Rain fell from two of the clouds in separate sectors of the sky, neither of them near. He told himself that this road led to the state highway, and if he could just keep going, he would meet up with a vehicle. It was a national monument after all. As he trudged, the sun dropped steadily from its zenith toward the west. When his eyes went out of focus, he rubbed them only to discover they were crusted in salt. He dabbed a finger to his tongue to confirm. The flavor made his stomach growl.

He kept walking, checking his phone periodically for a signal, noting that it was after 16:00. Eventually, he switched the phone off to preserve what battery was left. For the last two hours he'd been talking to himself in German. He told himself that he was in good physical condition, and that he would know enough to be able to monitor his own vital signs.

As he walked, he took note of the distant cliff formation and the occasional relics of recent human occupation. Everything was so vast and still and bright that the space was difficult at times to look into, so he kept his eyes to the ground. The most common signs of humanity aside from the road were the wind-blown plastic bags. He noted glinting fragments of broken glass, and the flattened bodies of small birds, snakes, lizards, and mice. So, people did come down this road. All was not lost.

Occasionally, a beetle moved deliberately through the gravel of the road, a single crisp point of blackness trundling toward some objective. Reinhardt tried to imagine what it was heading for, but he applauded its singleness of purpose. At random intervals, a bar of shadow would sweep across the landscape. His skin could sense the transitions from light to dark with the sensitivity of a phonograph needle. He was also acutely aware of his sunburn. The hat he'd fashioned from a few thin branches and the same grocery sacks he saw blowing around did little to offer shade.

Eventually Reinhardt looked up and realized that he could sense no visible progress. He did some quick calculations and decided that, if no one came along, continuing on would certainly kill him. He set his backpack on the ground and opened *Mythstructures for Blockbusters* and skimmed the section on The Ordeal, part of The Descent. As powerful as this mythology felt to him, Reinhardt rejected the idea that a hero must die and be reborn. If he was unable to save Kwon, how could he save himself? So, he turned back to retrace his path.

In the distance, he focused on a gray mesa and the green backs of pine-covered mountains. He began walking, though each step was agony. He lapsed into a meditation so deep, his wrecked car surprised him when he came upon it.

He opened all the doors and sat inside with the seat fully reclined. It was scorchingly hot, but his body savored the rest. After a few minutes, he went through every inch of the car. There was a red-and-white-striped candy wrapped in plastic deep in the crack of one of the back seats. He placed it in his mouth and felt a zing of Christmas.

He imagined that with a tarp he could build a solar water collector. He'd built one once, as a boy, for a school project, and it worked. He thought about how Wolf would take the news that he'd left the tour and died in the desert like an outlaw. He tried to remember if he'd learned anything useful from any of the teepee gatherings he had been to in college and with Wolf. They had learned archery, how to shoot guns, and he could make fire without matches, but these skills all seemed ridiculous now. He did not need to build a fire using a bow, a spindle, and a length of leather cord. He was useless out here. He had learned nothing, and he would be remembered as a fool. The tour group would use him as a cautionary tale. "Remember Reinhardt Kupfer, who was devoured by vultures and coyotes?" At that moment, Reinhardt took solace in the fact that he was unmarried and childless.

A breeze picked up, and Reinhardt felt some relief. He reviewed the order in which his body would close down: his urine would darken from the color of a pilsner, to an ale, to a porter, to a stout. His heart rate would spike because of his thickened blood. Then his body would shut down any organs that were not key to survival. He would be unconscious when his liver failed. Animals would feast upon his remains. They would have to identify him by the rental car paperwork.

Reinhardt looked over at *Mythstructures for Blockbusters* and thought about how this should be the time for supernatural helpers to arrive. He picked up his phone and recalled what Kenji said about the digital assistant and powered the phone on. There was no signal, so he stared at it until he decided to check the photograph of the map. He saw the circles of Antelope Flats, which he felt like he passed long ago. Everything was so close on the map and so far apart in reality. At this point, he was closest to the ruins called Las Casas Altas and a cluster of three wavy lines with a word he couldn't read, but it ended with "tsuvats." The map had a number of these glyphs spread across it, difficult to see while pinching and dragging. He had 4 percent battery left. The tsuvats-glyphs were nearby, close to the road, so he powered the phone down, took his empty bottles, some jerky, and walked southward.

He could see a long way down the length of road, and there was nothing but a smaller road, unnoticeable to anyone in a vehicle. He followed it to an abandoned homestead. In the harsh light, he saw an old wood barn collapsing on itself and a fence line that ran for thirty feet. Past the fence was a cluster of green trees and shrubs at the base of a large rounded hill, popping out against the brown and the blown-out white sky.

At the center of this oasis, in the shade, was a moss-covered cluster of rocks. From the bearded chin of the lowermost rock, a single clear drop of water swelled, broke free, and fell into the mud at the bottom. The land reclaimed the water into its own secret cache. Another drop gathered immediately, not quite, but almost, forming a trickle.

Reinhardt found that he could lie next to the glorious damp rocks in such a way that the droplets would land in his mouth. His mouth would fill every twenty minutes. He wouldn't die of thirst this way, but this was certainly no way to solve his problem quickly. After two mouthfuls, he set up his bottles and let them fill.

The day was waning, and he did not think he would die of thirst tonight.

From the shade, Reinhardt watched a jet cross the sky, the contrail miraculously threading its way through the many clouds. He thought about how strange it was to be absolutely and utterly alone and also in plain view of two hundred people, close enough to be seen but as unreachable as people on their way to Mars. With winged boots, it would be a six-mile walk to that airplane. In a couple of hours, he could be up there with his thumb out, and soon after, hitching his way to Los Angeles, where he would crawl into the crisp sheets of a hotel on Sunset Boulevard with bottles of San Pellegrino scattered about. He would cash in all of his frequent flyer miles then and fly home first class. What good is money if you can't use it to save your own life?

He untied his boot laces and ate some of the very dry jerky that remained in the bag. The pemmican was gone. Venus appeared in the deepening blue, and without preamble, one of the clouds lit up, the interior flashing twice, with the faint tracery of electric blue following after.

—

By midafternoon, Dalton quit working and drove home to tackle the repairs his house would need before he could sell it. He started weeks ago but let it sit until he had a free day, which never came. It's always easier to resist a chore near the beginning than it is at the end. Now it was clear that the shower would not re-grout and seal itself, no handyman would straighten the gutter and nail it in place, and the weeds would continue to encroach. Dalton felt he'd been set before the crank of a massive dynamo that powered everything around him. He could turn this crank and keep everything going or rest and enjoy the darkness.

Each chore on his list began as a plain and innocent task that quickly became a vexation for which he did not have the proper tools, know-how, or patience to complete in a single afternoon. He originally thought he might cross a half dozen or more items off his list, but he ended up finishing two.

When hunger and the long shadows of evening stopped him, he realized he had nothing to show for his labor, so he threw in the towel and drove to the Shake Stop for a cheeseburger, fries, and a strawberry malt. He paid, and the girl handed him a number on a small plastic A-frame.

A woman standing behind him in line asked, "Sheriff? Is it true? All that stuff they're saying in the paper?"

Dalton turned around. He felt suddenly self-conscious wearing a T-shirt, cargo shorts, and running shoes instead of his uniform. "I haven't been keeping up," he said.

"You know, about Bruce taking his own life because the government is coming after his Indian stuff."

"Does that sound like something Bruce would do?" he said.

"No," she said. "It doesn't sound like him. Suicide doesn't sound right either, a good church member like him."

"Lots of people take their own lives, Emmalene."

"Not in Utah."

"I wish that was true," he said. "We get more than our share of that trouble."

"But, you know. This kind of thing has happened before. Down in Page. Anyone that knows anything about when the FBI came looking for pots and arrowheads says this is just like it was then. It's too much government."

"I know that's what Stan Forsythe says, but I don't see it like that, and I'd be in the know if that's what was happening. But it's not. So, don't worry about it."

"Stan's been talking to people."

"I'm sure he has," Dalton said.

The girl called Dalton's number and he went up to get his food, which they gave to him on a plastic tray. "Could I get this to go?" he asked.

"We've got the liberals to thank for it. Never should have been parks or monuments in the first place. Nobody wanted it. We finally have someone in Washington who can get these parks straightened out. We should get the land back in the hands of people who've lived here and raised their families on it."

"You mean the Indians?" Dalton asked.

The woman laughed and gestured to the buildings and streets around them. "None of this was built by Indians." Her arm settled at her side, and she smiled.

"The Paiutes have a different story about that," Dalton said. The girl slid Dalton's food through the window in a pulp-fiber tray, the malt jammed into one of the cutout slots, the food warm in a paper sack. He thanked her and turned back to Emmalene, nodded, and left before she had a chance to say anything else.

He got right in the car and decided he didn't want to go home and surround himself with failed projects, so he drove to the office. He thought he might just sit at the computer and start the listing on the real estate website. The next time Karen called, he wanted to be able to show some progress. As he drove, he spotted a cluster of thunderheads to the south. They were deeply shadowed at the base and almost specular at the top, the light shearing them into flat stacked planes. A thin flicker of lightning pulsed twice in the core of the cloud, and in the gathering dusk, the evening star came on in a single pulse. It was a little early for monsoons, but it was nice to have things cooling off.

Dalton pulled into the building, unlocked the door, and found LaRae inside, sitting at her desk. "I didn't think anyone would be here after hours."

"I'm getting some work done. No sense sitting at home thinking about all this, you know," she said. "Plus, it feels better being here, you know, with everything coming in at once. I mean, I know none of it is official."

"Yeah. I get it," he said.

"Most people think it was the one thing, but now we know it's something else." She moved her hands around her head to show a process. "It makes me crazy watching all the bits and pieces whiz by, and I can't say anything about it. It's just a lot, you know."

"More than I was expecting."

"Have you read the ME's report?" she asked.

"Not yet."

"Well, you should. I mean, I peeked at it. I don't know if that was okay. But you should read it."

"You're fine."

"Doesn't help me being home alone, thinking about it. You brought your dinner, and I'm stopping you," she said.

"Yeah. I was going to—I was going to come here to list the house tonight. They want me to use a website."

"I know you're supposed to," LaRae said. "Karen's been calling here all week."

"I'm sorry."

"I told her you're underwater. I could help you with some of it," she said.

"You don't have to. This is my thing."

"After what you did for me when Thom left, I figure I owe you."

"I appreciate that. You don't owe me. And you don't have to worry."

"I didn't tell her anything specific. Karen, I mean."

"That's good."

"She asked, but I didn't tell her."

"She's used to knowing."

"But she did say something weird. She asked if I thought everything Stan Forsythe's been saying would make it hard to sell a house. I guess she's been following his blog or something. Maybe it's on Twitter."

"You can't put any stock in it."

"He's stirring the pot."

"I know it. I'm old-fashioned, I don't use my phone for anything but calls. Keeps my blood pressure down."

"You should eat your dinner before it gets cold," she said.

"I'm starving." Dalton went past her and looked down at the stack of papers and mail on her desk. "Is that all for me?"

LaRae nodded. "Let me know when you want it, and I'll bring it to you. But you should look at the ME's report, but maybe after you eat. It's got pictures. Also, I called the Beehive House about Raylene. They say you can pick her up tomorrow. They aren't sure what you're hoping to get out of it."

"A lot of Bruce's stuff is missing. More was taken during that last break-in. I'm trying to see what she remembers. I was thinking maybe a Sunday drive onto the monument might bring something to light. They said old memories aren't all the way gone at first."

Dalton let himself into his office and logged into his computer. He spread his food out on the desk and googled Red Cliffs Realty. As he ate, he filled out the fields and clicked the check boxes, but each one made him more and more furious.

He switched over to his email and opened the secure link to the ME's report. He scanned down to find the cause of death. It said homicide. He pushed the food aside and leaned in.

The report described two wounds. The first was an impact to the side of the head, a traumatic blow to the pterion, rupturing the middle meningeal artery. Blood from this wound had begun to gelify when it was over-sprayed by a second event, a gunshot that entered between the eyes at the glabella and exited through the occipital bone at the base of the skull, an angle difficult or impossible to self-inflict.

—

Sophia ran until she could not continue, stopped, and leaned against a boulder. When she looked up, the world around her darkened at the edges, forming a vignette. At the center was a pool of blue against orange against buff. She stepped forward and turned and steadied herself, moved the hair out of her eyes, and said, "You can keep going. I believe in you." Then she felt herself jerk upright and continue on. At first her feet did not know where to land, and she was too muddled to place them. Then they began to understand the trail, allowing her to shut that part of the thinking down and watch the stones along each side of her path drift out of the way. She smiled at them, and they nodded silently back at her.

When she became thirsty, she saw the water bottle emerge from the pack and received it. "Careful. Careful," she said. "Stop running. It all needs to go inside of you." She felt her legs stiffen, so she handed the bottle back and ran on.

Ahead of her, at the top of an incline, she saw two women sitting together wearing chadors. They looked like her aunts back in Iran. When they saw Sophia, they lifted their arms and beckoned her. She ran to the top, using the stones as steps, and she stopped when she saw that it was only the top of a ridgeline, dropping away at the other side. The women reached out and held her hands. She saw the fine tracery of the henna tattoos on their hands, the silver rings. Their hands slipped away, and when she turned to thank them, they were gone.

The valley filled with thunder, then the echo of it drained slowly out.

Behind Sophia was the ground she'd crossed, the cinder cone, and the miniature backhoe jerking silently in the distance, a tiny pickup truck carried in the bucket, lifted high into the air. The scene looked like toys photographed with a tilt-shift lens, focused at the center and foggy at the edges. She sat on a flat orange stone, hands braced on her knees, and she tried to process what was happening. Three stories played simultaneously: the one where a man she did not know was killed in front of her, the one where the invincible Paul Thrift was murdered, and the one where the killer was now coming after her. Stacked on top of those stories were three more: how she interrupted two grave robbers, how another man was killed offscreen, and how she was now running for her life with a map valuable enough to set all of this off.

Each time a story would come at her, she would gently relax and let its own momentum carry it beyond her. Eventually, they struck at her and regrouped enough times to make her grow tired and confused. During this slowness, she reached out and chose the running-for-her-life story and the finding-a-map story, then she tied these long, rippling streamers together as they fought against the wind. When she pulled the knot tight, she felt the sounds of the desert returning: wind, the thrumming of insects, the rustle of hair against the collar of her shirt, and in the distance, the crash of a pickup truck dropping to the ground.

Her skin drew taut. Her eyes came back into focus. Her Plan A was to wait, get back to the truck, and drive out, which was probably the man's Plan A, which is why he was destroying the vehicles. So Plan B was hiking out, back to the state highway. She unzipped her backpack and sized up the not-quite-one-liter of water she had in there. This guy would be on the road, so she'd have to go overland, which would be a death sentence. She dropped her head into her hands and decided Plan C would be to make her way to the Dellenbaugh ranger station, which was twenty miles away. This would be the least likely plan to be on his list and the most likely to put her in touch with people. Dellenbaugh Station was the population center around here. She would wait until night, find her way to the road, and hike in the cool hours to minimize her water loss.

Lightning flickered in the clouds again, leaping and pulsing from the column of the clouds like the bones of a bat wing. A cool breeze riffled the leaves and carried petrichor to her nose. When she realized it would rain, she felt options opening. She'd be able to replenish her water, and the man would be out of his element. He was, after all, wearing a panama hat. She kept to Plan C, wanting to stack the odds in her favor.

She had some food, but she didn't want it. After two sips of water, she dug in her bag and found, to her surprise, one more loose watermelon Jolly Rancher, which triggered the memory of Paul staggering backward over the cliff. She caught the panic loop before it knocked the wind out of her. Eventually, when Paul did not report in, someone would take notice, and they would investigate. But given Paul's habit of disappearing into the desert and his reputation for being a master of this landscape, waiting to be rescued was no plan at all.

She stood, stepped away from the rock, and turned her back on the catastrophe to look over the other side of the ridge. Now that her vision had come back into focus, she saw a thin road running down through the bones of the canyon. That road split into a pair of smaller ones. She pulled out the map and unrolled it. She saw the spot where she was standing circled in ballpoint pen and all the names and dates clustered in this area. With her index finger, she traced the curve of the mesa that ran all the way into the Dellenbaugh Valley. She turned the map to match it to north and guessed that the smaller of the two forking roads would take her to the station. After returning the map to her pack, she noticed a strange momentary glint. It was a car, a black car parked down there. Okay, on to Plan D.

Without thinking, she clambered down the ridge, skating on the loose stone, catching herself on scrawny junipers and pinyons until she realized she just might kill herself trying to get to safety. She thought of something her mother always said, "Slow is fast, baby." The sky surrounding her was darkening, turning the color of blue she thought only happened in Spielberg movies. There wasn't a lot of time until darkness would come, but she imagined a timeline where she fell, shattered her knee, and had to crawl to the road on her belly. She thought about the phone call she'd make when this was all over. Mom, Dad, I'm okay. I just wanted to let you know that I remembered combat breathing and I remembered slow is fast.

As she descended, she realized she was crying and thought it was stupid. She had also lost sight of the car but kept moving in the same direction, hoping to find it again. In the dimming light, something flew toward her. She crouched and looked up in surprise as an owl revealed itself in its passage overhead, its wide wings and round head unmistakable. She expected to hear the pulsing of its wings as it passed over, but there was nothing but the sound of her own breathing.

When she stood, she saw a bright orange section of cliff in the midst of the shadowed valley, and in a straight line across the middle of the façade, she saw a line of rectangular windows, like the granary. Five of them in a row. Las Casas Altas, she thought. They were on her list of sites to record, but she hadn't gotten to them yet. She was two weeks from that section of the monument.

At the bottom of the slope, she crossed a short flat shoulder and jumped from a low berm onto the road. The black car was a Mustang. The hood was up and the doors open. The driver's side seat was reclined, and a single leg emerged from the interior, the calf resting in the notch formed by the car frame and the open door. The man in the car was whistling a simple five-note tune, something familiar. She remembered it from middle school dances. Was it "Wind of Change" by the Scorpions? She followed along in her head, and when he sang the chorus aloud, she let out a chuckle that made the man sit up.

"Wolf, is that you?" a voice called out.

"Are you okay?" she asked.

"Oh," he said. "Not Wolf. Someone else."

"No, not Wolf."

The man stood weakly and supported himself with the car. He was scarlet red with a mad look in his eyes. "Wolf is my medical partner back in Germany." He blinked and looked around, held up an empty water bottle, and crinkled it. "Oh, that is right. I am still in America on this adventure. The dream was vivid."

In the dim light, it took a moment, but she soon realized she knew this man. "You're the doctor from Bryce Canyon," she said.

"Berlin. I'm actually from elsewhere. The home of Alexanderplatz and the Brandenburg Gate. Not jelly donuts. That is a great goof—blown out of proportion."

He came across as drunk, but it was clear that he was reeling from dehydration and exposure. "Why don't you stand here," she said, taking his hand and placing it on the car. The black metal was still hot.

Sophia looked at the car to size things up. A mire of black fluid flowed a few inches from under the front of the car, then soaked into the dust. In the failing light she could barely see it. The man cleared his throat. "Excuse me, but I was wondering if you had a vehicle we might use for a rescue. It is all mixed up though. This is the road of trials, but I thought I was through the first gate, but you are obviously the supernatural aid. It is all out of order."

"Supernatural what?"

"Aid. You know. But that is for act one. You were the one who told me about these places, that they existed. That was the call to adventure, but I didn't heed it. Kenji was there, too, for the second call. He said he was a gatekeeper, but perhaps not. This ordeal seems more appropriate for—" The man doubled over with his hands on his knees, and he growled through his teeth. "Oh, this is not good."

"Are you okay?" When he nodded, she asked, "More appropriate for what?"

The man breathed deeply a few times, then stood again. "For act two. I cannot tell which part of the story we are in right now."

Sophia realized that this poor man was trying to talk to her about Joseph Campbell. She tried to refocus him. "What happened to your car?"

"This is not my car," he said, trying to take a few steps.

"How did you get out here, then?"

"It's a rental."

"Oh no," Sophia said, "there's really no time for this."

"It's okay. I paid for the insurance," he said with absolute seriousness.

She intercepted the man and took hold of his shoulders. "Do you have any water? We are both in a life-and-death situation."

The man laughed and ducked back into the car for his backpack. He then walked past her, beckoning with his hand. He looked as if he might collapse at any moment. As he walked along, he babbled incoherently about someone called Kwon or maybe Krause or maybe he was talking about two people. He said Kwon died, that it was now his time, and he walked on.

"Where are we going?"

"To the water," he said, shambling. He mentioned Wolf again and talked about the sisterhood of coyotes, who were also supernatural helpers. So many supernatural helpers. He talked about all these things as if Sophia were familiar with them. Soon they arrived at a cluster of green trees and shrubs at the base of a large rounded hill. Even in the gloaming, the green stood out against the dryness and the clouds gathering around them. At the center of this oasis was a cluster of moss-covered rocks. The man sat on them and placed his hand under the drip. "Here is the water. We'll have to be patient," he said, then he toppled over.

Sophia ran to his side, knelt down, and lifted his head, setting it on her thigh. She opened her pack and took out her water bottle. Only twenty ounces remained. She remembered that when she was growing up, her mother would tell any guests they brought bliss to her home, so she swirled the water and took a sip, then put the bottle to his lips. "Drink this," she said, and when the water touched his lips, she watched them curl and open. He stopped himself.

"This is yours," he said.

"My water belongs to the tribe," she said.

"Yes, we are all one tribe," Reinhardt said.

"No, it's not that, it's something my dad used to always quote from his favorite book."

Reinhardt nodded, then reached up and lifted the bottle and drank some more. "Not too much," she said, "you'll get sick."

"Hyponatremia," Reinhardt croaked. "You are correct. I am a doctor, which makes all of this worse because I know what is happening to me on the inside. I will sip. Sip, sip, sip, sip." He took another small amount, then licked his lips and handed her the bottle. "Take this from me. I will not be able to stop myself."

She screwed the lid back on and the man collapsed more fully. Her leg was starting to tingle with numbness, and she strained her ears for the sounds of a car. The trees above them shook in the growing breeze, and the air temperature dropped. She heard a pap, pap, pap of raindrops in the dirt and looked up. The sky above them was a swirl of purple, gray, and abalone.

"Have you seen a man in a silver car? Dressed funny, like for the golf course or something?"

"If I were tiny, I could slip into this bottle for a little swim," he said.

"A silver car," she repeated. "Have you seen anyone out here like that?"

"Yes," he said. "He was lost, I think. Or his friends were lost. Maybe we could take your car back to town."

"Mine is out of commission. What is wrong with yours?"

"The transmission is gone, which is my fault."

"Do you have a phone?"

"I do, but the battery is now dead."

"Can we charge it with the car?"

"That is dead, too. It is also my fault, but I don't know how I did it. I think I was trying to use the fan."

"Can you sit up? My leg is going to sleep."

He lifted himself and sat cross-legged. "Put your bottle under there. It'll be full in a few hours."

There was a flash in the sky, and a clap of thunder cracked overhead, the echo bouncing from wall to wall like stones in a giant metal box. The wind picked up even more as the squall line came closer. Rain began to fall with greater frequency. Sophia could feel it on her skin. Three small birds passed above the car and flew in undulating lines toward the cliff dwellings at Las Casas Altas.

"This is a gift from the goddess," Reinhardt said.

The rain picked up, pelting them. "We should look for shelter," she said.

Large raindrops peppered the ground, coming in half notes at first, then the tempo sped up. Initially, Sophia thought they might be able to wait out the storm in the Mustang but realized they were right on a road, too visible, so she led the way across the sage flats toward the cliff dwellings. There were no channels to fill with flood waters, and the cliff would make sure nobody could come up behind them. Reinhardt marched on with his arms out to the side to maximize his exposure to the rain. Overhead was another stroke of lightning, the flash painting the junipers and cholla bone white.

"Hey, we need to get to the cliff," she said. "This isn't safe."

"But it feels wonderful. I am renewed. Perhaps reborn."

Thunder crashed through the space, startling the man.

"The lightning is the least of our worries," she said.

Reinhardt spun and ran in wobbly circles. Sophia chased him, attempting to capture his attention, like someone trying to gather up a loose chicken. "Look, mister. There's a crazy person out there trying to kill us. Not us, but me."

Reinhardt stopped. "I know about this part. This is the initiation. After the road of trials, I am supposed to meet the goddess." He pointed at Sophia, then at himself. "And we emerge from the abyss transformed." He stopped spinning, and the rain grew more intense. "It is absurd," he said, patting his backpack, "but everything in the book keeps happening."

"What book?"

He pointed to the rock overhang. "I will show you under the cover of these cliffs." Then he ran. Sophia followed. She realized that any plans she had for getting to the ranger station were going to depend on having water, and they were soon going to have the problem of too much water and nowhere to put it. When they got to the overhang, they huddled on the dry flank of dirt at the base of the cliff. To one side were a series of openings, like the orbits in a massive skull. "There," she said, and they scurried inside.

They stood as they dripped. Reinhardt put his pack on frontways and opened it. He withdrew a large book and showed it to her.

"It's too dark. What does it say?"

"*Mythstructures for Blockbusters*," he announced. "It is a book for writers."

"Blockbusters? You think we're in a movie?"

"No. It's about how our story is all stories." In what remained of the daylight, she saw Reinhardt's teeth. His voice sounded like a smile.

"You're dehydrated, and we have to hide."

"From what?"

"From the man in the silver car."

"You saw him, too?"

"Yes," she snapped. Sophia began to shiver, so she hugged herself and rubbed her arms. She watched the world outside the cave tiptoe into darkness. In the west, a single bleached-out vortex punched through the black sky, which was only a shade lighter than the black of the cliffs, which was a bit lighter than the black of the ground.

Reinhardt looked at Sophia for a moment, then he ran into the rain and returned with a small bundle of sticks. "Wolf gave me a small fire starter, which I have with me in my pack."

"That guy would see a fire," Sophia said.

"We could build it back here, in the innermost cave."

"No fire. And I can see what you're trying to do here. I have a master's degree in cultural anthropology. We're not doing the monomyth, and I'm starting to lose my mind."

"And yet the cave is right here, around us," he said. "I feel much better by the way, though I think some diarrhea is coming." Reinhardt reached into his open pack and withdrew a head lamp, which he slipped around his head and switched on. As he looked around, he saw pictographs. "Look," he said, walking up to the wall.

"Don't touch them," Sophia yelled. "The oils in your hands—" When Sophia saw the images, her breath stopped. On the wall was a series of six enshrouded purple figures, each the length of her forearm. A seventh figure was over to one side with considerable space between. It was the same size as the others but lighter, faded. This figure was robed in stripes, with a long beard running down the front. Its eyes were wide and round like rings and its mouth was drawn with two parallel horizontal stripes.

"It looks like a robot," Reinhardt said.

"Shhh," Sophia said. "Let me borrow your light."

Reinhardt handed it to her, and she placed it on her forehead. The panel contained other images: a crescent moon, stars, water glyphs, and spirals. To the left of the figures, below them, someone had carved J. NYE 1954 and below that NEPHI P. -67. She looked around the cave and found charred wood, a pack rat nest, a tin can smashed flat and rusted almost black. The ceiling was black from smoke that came from an unknowable number of fires. She reached for her phone to take a photo, then remembered it was broken. She did not have her other camera with her, so she took out her notebook and sketched the whole panel quickly and deftly, then she drew each figure more slowly and carefully.

When she was done, they were both shivering. "Let's go outside and try to catch some water," she said, "then we can build a fire, okay?"

They left the cave and heard a great crashing of water all around them in the darkness. Massive sheets of water came over the cliff tops. Sophia took her empty water bottle and held it in the rimfall. The bottle filled swiftly. She drank half and gave the bottle to Reinhardt, who drank the rest. She refilled the bottle and traded it with the cheap disposable bottles Reinhardt handed to her. Once they filled everything they had, they stood and listened to the immensity of it.

"This rain was foretold," Reinhardt said. "I promised that man at the gas station that I would remember his warning, but I didn't."

Sophia looked at Reinhardt, afraid to answer him and unlock the full story.

After a while, they lit a fire and curled up in the sand to sleep. From time to time, Reinhardt rose and bolted from the cave into the darkness, returning after a few minutes. This happened over and over. Soon he began shivering again and asked if Sophia would get his sleeping bag from the car. He had other useful things there, too. Sophia jogged back to the car with the head lamp, which she kept dark. The rain had stopped, and her motion through the night helped warm her up and dry her off.

She returned with his sleeping bag, a fleece jacket, and an inflatable pad. The small fire had burned down to embers. She helped Reinhardt into the bag and zipped herself into the jacket, keeping the pad for herself.

She tried to sleep, but when it didn't work, she sat up, listening for intrusions. Reinhardt drifted into an uneasy sleep, like a giant blue caterpillar writhing in the sand. She thought of the Caterpillar from *Alice's Adventures in Wonderland*, a book she loved as a child. The Caterpillar posed a nagging question that Sophia often thought about: "Who are you?" Alice gave the best of all possible answers: "I knew who I was when I got up this morning, but I think I've changed several times since then."

Day Eight

An extra charge : Plenty of law and order : Staying upwind :
Fried chicken and arrowheads : Untröstlich : Into thin air :
Patsy Cline : The hermit's inholding : A black hole

Scissors stood next to a rattling ice freezer outside of a travel oasis dialing a number on his phone. Despite the downpour last night, the pavement was dry, save for a few puddles gathered in the low spots of the concrete. Next to him was the silver Sebring, the wheel wells splattered again in mud, the single spare tire looking like a withered limb.

"Yes?" Frangos answered.

"The local bumblers are out of the picture."

"But not out of the equation," she said. "You just moved them to the other side." Scissors took the phone from his ear, stared at it, then put it back. "This hasn't been what you might call a surgical operation," she continued.

"I know it. When I found them, they were tearing up the Antelope Flats site with a backhoe."

"With a what? Who does that?"

"They aren't going to do it again—can I back up to what you said before? Did you make a math joke?"

"It wasn't over your head, was it?"

"Almost, but I think I got it now." A woman came up to him and motioned to the freezer. Scissors stepped back and waited until she was done and gone.

"I staged the situation to come across like our boys got interrupted by some law enforcement and decided to shoot their way out of it. It rained last night. The roads are a nightmare. I don't think anyone will get out there for a couple of days."

"I don't want the details."

"Okay. I got that. Let me say, though, it's been impossible to execute a plan with these morons going off script."

"Do you have my map?" Scissors looked up at the clear sky, then over at a car that was just pulling up for gas. A man and a woman in fresh hiking clothes got out. Before he could answer, Frangos asked, "Who *does* have it, Nicholas?"

He took a driver's license from his shorts pocket.

"Somebody named Sophia Shepard. She's from Princeton, New Jersey. Born in 1991."

"I will call you back."

Scissors closed his phone and pocketed the driver's license. On the ground, by his feet, was a white plastic sack, out of which he removed a Little Debbie lemon pie. He opened the box and slid the pastry out and began eating it as the young couple fueled and cleaned their windshield. Beyond them lay the monument with its buttes and mesas. He thought about what that place looked like close up, and he decided there was a reason nobody lived out there. Those two were on a jaunt, but soon enough they'd be back to—he leaned enough so he could see their license plate—Illinois.

The phone buzzed, and he finished the last two bites of his pie and flicked the crumbs from his fingers before answering.

"That was fast," he said.

"I'm changing the plan. Bring Sophia Shepard to me."

Scissors looked at the ground and opened his grocery sack. There were two more pies in there, and a bottle of iced coffee. "Kidnapping is extra."

"Do you think I'll shortchange you?"

"I'm a contract man, right? What we're doing is a contract renegotiation."

"What are you asking me for?"

"Twenty-five," he said.

She paused. "Okay."

"In addition."

"Wait, what? No. Absolutely not. Twenty."

Scissors let his arm drop when Frangos began reading him the riot act, and when she finished, he put the phone back to his ear and said, "One thing about free-market types like yourself—you don't really want freedom for everybody."

"Fine. Twenty-five."

"I can't guarantee a delivery date," he said.

"Why not?"

"This isn't factory work. I have to hunt her down."

"Then I want status reports."

"That'll slow things down. I have to drive forever to get cell service."

"Then you'll drive forever."

"Understood." Scissors looked down into his open bag and pushed it with the tip of his shoe. "I got one more thing," Scissors said. "There was an unintended amplification with a park ranger."

"Who was it?"

"A guy named Paul Thrift."

"He's a troublemaker. A stunt he pulled in Denver has set me back months."

"He's not a troublemaker anymore," Scissors said.

She paused for a long stretch. "Okay," she said. "This will raise some red flags, but it is what it is."

"It couldn't be helped, but it should look like the two dingdongs did it."

"This is what you staged?"

"That's right. The average person is not hard to mystify," he said.

"Well, that's that," she said, then hung up.

He closed the phone, put it in his pocket, picked up his bag, and went inside. There was a teenage girl at the register, looking at her phone. "Excuse me. I need to get a tire replaced. Does anyone around here do that?"

Without looking up, the girl said, "They got people in Fredonia or Colorado City. Take your pick."

—

Dalton rang the bell at the front desk of the Beehive House, and after a short pause the receptionist stepped out of the break room brushing crumbs from the front of her blouse.

"I'm here to pick up Mrs. Cluff," Dalton said. He kept one hand on his belt and handed a form to the woman. "We need Raylene to go over some evidence, but we can't bring it here. Everything's on the request. I had someone call over last week."

"Evidence?" the receptionist asked. "Suicide doesn't usually require evidence. That's, like, for court, isn't it? Seeing as how the victim is the perp."

"Perp?" Dalton asked.

"Don't you call them that? I'm a big *Law and Order* fan."

"Oh," Dalton said. "Didn't know they still had that on."

"You can stream anything now."

"I get plenty of law and order in my day-to-day."

"Right?" she laughed.

Dalton smiled, but he felt like he was showing too much teeth, so he relaxed his lips.

"So, you need her on the Sabbath?" the woman asked.

"We do."

"Okay." She took the paper, read it, put it into the top of a small desktop scanner and pulled it out of the bottom when it had gone through, then she handed it back. "That stuff they're saying in the paper? That's not true, is it?"

"I can't say anything. I'm sorry."

"Oh, sure," she said. "It's just got people talking."

"That's people for you. You probably know from your show that talk like this can mess up an investigation. I told Forsythe that myself."

The receptionist picked up the phone and said, "Could you get Mrs. Cluff ready to go outside?"

"I appreciate it," Dalton said. "We hate to put her through it, but we're not sure what kind of memories we're getting from her."

"People not remembering is our day-to-day," she said.

Dalton watched an old man through the wire-grill windows behind the desk. He was trying to evade two orderlies in light blue scrubs. The man crept along behind an aluminum walker. The orderlies kept their distance, advancing when he did. "Karl, that's the puzzle corner. It's a dead end," one of them said. Karl looked back, heaved the walker out in front of him, and pulled himself toward it.

"Come on, Karl," the other said, "you'll miss *American Ninja*."

The receptionist tidied her desk and did a little work at the computer. After a few minutes, she got a quick phone call. "Mrs. Cluff will be out in a minute. You can have a seat if you'd like."

Dalton folded up his document and slipped it into his back pocket. He sat in an uncomfortable chair and looked around the room. The facility looked like somebody tried to make it nice back in the 1980s, then spent the next thirty-five years scrubbing the color out of it. A wood sign on the other side of the room read I TRY TO SEE THE GOOD IN EVERYBODY, AND I DON'T CARE WHO PEOPLE ARE AS LONG AS THEY'RE THEMSELVES, WHATEVER THAT IS. —DOLLY PARTON. He wondered about the person who thought that was the perfect message for this place. It obviously wasn't for the residents. Dalton wondered if he tried to see the good in people. He wasn't sure he did anymore. Mostly he saw behavior. Motive wasn't relevant. That was for the lawyers.

He heard Raylene before he saw her. "Well, I don't want to go anywhere. This isn't North Korea. People are still allowed to choose!"

The orderly set the brake on her wheelchair. "It's the sheriff, ma'am. We can't really tell him no."

"Where is he? I'll tell him to blow it out his ass."

Dalton stood and smiled. "I can blow it out my what?"

Raylene stopped trying to escape and sat back in the chair. "Patrick," she said. "You weren't supposed to hear that."

"I've heard worse."

"Well, it's a good thing you can't read minds," she said.

The orderly said she needed to be back by five.

Dalton acknowledged the schedule, then wheeled Raylene down the ramp and helped her climb into the Bronco. She was slow and careful, shunning help at first, but finally giving in after a couple of valiant attempts. When she settled into her seat, she said, "Bruce has a step stool for me. It's easier to get in that way."

"He's a man for all seasons," Dalton said. "So, did Bruce take you onto the monument much?"

"Wasn't a monument then."

"True."

When she noticed that Dalton wouldn't accept that answer, she said, "We went out all the time. That place was his first love."

"Not you?"

"We have different passions."

Dalton made sure she was buckled in, then he pulled around in a half circle and drove on. "Where did he take you?"

She seemed to be more at ease outside of the facility. "Everywhere," she said. "When we were young, we went everywhere. A lot of it on horses. It's a lot nicer than these four-wheelers. What a racket."

"I don't like them either." Dalton was unsure how direct he should be or if that would make her withdraw. If he beat around the bush, she'd think he was up to something. He looked at her with her hands folded on her lap, her head turned to the window. The knowledge that her husband had been murdered ate at his stomach. She didn't even know that he'd died. Or maybe the memory was somewhere inside of her, overlooked or hiding. He'd been to a training once on dissociation and what to do when people were under extreme stress. He had many blank spots himself, left over from when he was deployed. Better to let sleeping dogs lie. He decided to back off and allow things to come up on their own. "That sure was some storm last night. Did you hear it?"

"Was it monsoons?"

"I think so."

"I didn't hear anything. They put us down early."

"Down, huh?"

"That's how it feels."

"We need the water," he said. "I just wish it didn't come down all at once."

"Bruce says water is the master, not the slave." Raylene took a handkerchief from her purse and wiped the inside of the window in small circular motions.

"My dad used to say that, too."

"Bruce loves your father dearly. He was brokenhearted when he passed."

"That's nice of you to say."

"Sometimes when you marry, you have to say goodbye to old friendships, but Bruce and your father didn't."

They turned onto Main Street and headed to the south. Because it was tourist season, the roads were busy with people heading in all directions.

"Raylene, my dad used to talk about Bruce's maps."

"He made a lot of them a long time ago, before the government got involved in everything."

"That's what Dad said. Has anyone besides me been asking about them? NPS folks, BLM, collectors, or anything?"

"Well, he doesn't talk to anybody about those maps. He says they just want to go out there to loot the place—oh, look. They're building another motel. All the shit has to go somewhere. I don't think people consider that."

"All the shit, indeed." Dalton laughed.

"We charge them for the food," she said, "but not for the other part of it."

"I can honestly say I've never thought of it that way."

"Well you have to, Patrick. People think the mining business will save them, but there's no market for uranium. And you can't compete with ranching outfits in Florida or California out here. Tourism is the only business anymore."

Raylene was nobody's fool. Dalton didn't understand how she could pull these facts up in an instant but struggle to recall anything else. Her foul language was also a mystery. His own parents died sick but lucid. He wasn't sure which was the blessing and which the curse.

They came to a stop, and he watched her glancing around with a half smile on her face. Dalton thought he'd toss something out and see what took. "Raylene, we found some things missing from Bruce's study." He had talked to her about this before, and he figured any variations in her answer would give him a better sense of what was going on with her memories. "A lot of his pots were gone. I'm thinking about a specific pot you said was from the Swallow Valley, and he kept a book you called the inventory."

"How do you know about that?"

"We were talking about it the other day."

"I don't know why I would have done that. Bruce doesn't like me talking about those things. He says bullshit like that just attracts flies. You should ask him."

Dalton loved talking to this new version of Raylene. "I was hoping to get your help," he said.

"What could I possibly do?"

Dalton had a deception prepared, and he hated himself for it. "Raylene, the library is working on an oral history project, and we'd like to record you talking about some of your favorite places. The library asked for you specifically."

"Oh," she said. "I tried to get something like that started years ago, but there was no money for it."

"Well, I thought we'd go down to that scale model of the monument over at the BLM visitor's center. We can see if that gets the juices flowing."

"What's the BLM got to do with Bruce's things?"

"The folks putting it together thought we might start there, that's all. I was looking for a good excuse to bust you out of that jail for a bit."

Raylene reached across the cab and squeezed Dalton's wrist. "Those things you're asking about are gone because Bruce has been putting them back."

Dalton was still trying to work out what that meant. She had said it before and it sat funny with him the whole time. He had never heard of somebody putting things back on their own. Museums, yes. That was happening more and more, but not for individual people, not without the law telling them they had to. Bruce wasn't the kind of man to lick anyone's boots, so why was he doing it? The answer was probably the key to the whole thing, but could he trust her memory of it? He'd have to. "Raylene," Dalton asked, worried to put it out there, "Bruce put in a lot of years finding that stuff. Why would he start—"

"Bruce says when he's gone, people will carry everything off to the four corners of the earth. If we had children, maybe he wouldn't worry. He'd have heirs. But people have been after him to sell, and he hates that."

This version was different from what she'd said the last time. She said Bruce was worried about the meaning getting lost. The way she's saying it now, maybe he was worried about somebody coming after him. The radio crackled. "Sheriff, this is dispatch. I've got LaRae for you."

"Go ahead."

LaRae's voice came through. "I hate to bother you."

"You're okay."

"I've got a call from Pete Ashdown. He came home early from the Freedom Jamboree, and he says somebody stole his backhoe. He wants to talk to you about it."

Dalton looked over at Raylene, who was turned toward the window, leaning forward against the seat belt.

"Is he holding?"

"Yep. He's pretty mad. He's said some salty things—I'm not even sure I know what some of them mean."

"I'll bet."

She patched Pete through and he was already yelling. "Some dumb sons-a-bitches run off with my backhoe, and the trailer, too!"

"Pete, you sure someone didn't take it on a job and forget to tell you?"

"The lock's cut and lying there on the ground. Gate's wide open."

"Okay. I can come down tomorrow and file a report."

"How about you send somebody out?"

"Last time we did that you shot at them."

"They come unannounced."

"Well, I don't have anyone working today who wants to take that risk, Pete. I just don't."

Pete started ranting at him, and Dalton apologized. Raylene turned her head back toward Dalton. "That family would have less trouble if they stopped feeding their young from the table and made them earn their own way," she whispered.

"Here's the thing. I'm driving right now, and LaRae is sitting at the desk on a Sunday, when she's normally supposed to have a day off. I'm going to guess you already called 911 and chewed them a new one when they told you this wasn't an emergency. I could put more people on this, but your taxes would go up, and we both know you're not going to let that happen. So, let's just avoid giving the nanny state any more power than it's already got. We'll see you Monday."

When there was no response, LaRae came back on and said, "I think he hung up."

"Keep a can of pepper spray on your desk. He'll be coming in hot." Dalton said goodbye and replaced the microphone.

"Turn right," Raylene said, knocking on the window with a knuckle.

"BLM office is south of town," Dalton said, pointing straight.

"If it's okay, I'd like to go past the old library."

Dalton pulled a hard turn. "What's on your mind?"

"When I was a girl, I used to spend every day of the summer in that building. The new one is heartless. It's glass and metal and full of computers. I don't like it."

When they came to the building, she asked Dalton to stop. "I used to slide down that rail there. The nasty woman who worked here would scold me and say a lady doesn't let her dress fly about like a kite. That was 1959. I told her some ladies might, but she might not know that, having only read books written for children."

"Was that Caroline Plunkett?"

"Yes, it was," Raylene said.

"I remember her. She liked quiet better than people."

"I believe she did not have the capacity to like anything."

"Why did you want me to stop here if this is the memory it gave you?" Dalton asked.

"Oh, I loved this place in spite of that woman. A lot of life is like that, Patrick. I wanted to have that childhood everything-is-the-first-time feeling back. I would never reread a book back then, because I thought to myself, Raylene, there isn't enough time. Even as a child I knew this world is an hourglass. You can't push any of that sand back to the top." She sat up and looked around. "We can keep going now," she said. "Where were you taking me?"

"To the BLM visitor's center to see that big map of the monument."

"Well, why would you do that?"

"We were going to see what you could remember about the trips you and Bruce would take together out there."

"Bruce who?"

"Your husband, Bruce Cluff, the dentist."

Raylene placed her hand against the side of her head. Dalton sighed and turned the Bronco around. They drove in silence back to where they'd turned off, and he rejoined that road. The radio crackled and the dispatcher came on. "I've got LaRae."

"Put her through."

"I'm sorry to bother you again, but Mrs. Gladstone called in to report a missing person."

"Who?"

"Mrs. Gladstone, she wears all the bracelets, dresses like someone out of the sixties."

"I know that," he said. "Who's missing?"

"Somebody living in one of her trailers. She's from out of town, working for the National Parks. Her name is Sophia Shepard. She was out on the monument, and she was supposed to check in with her but didn't."

"Is it a camping thing?"

"She was out there with a ranger. That Thrift guy stationed at Dellenbaugh."

Dalton let the microphone rest against the buttons of his uniform. He looked around, letting his eyes pause for a moment on Raylene before he checked his mirrors. "She's probably just late, you know. And if she's with a ranger already, I'm not sure there's anything I can do."

"I probably shouldn't be paying attention to this," Raylene said. "It's none of my business, but people not coming back when they are supposed to isn't something to be trifled with."

"Stand by," Dalton said. "Raylene, I don't have the units right now to cover a federal jurisdiction."

"Tell that to the girl's parents," Raylene said in a low voice, her eyes unflinching.

—

By morning, the earth had absorbed most of the rain. Sophia and Reinhardt abandoned their cave with water they bottled from the rain pools scattered across the slick rock. Sophia realized that during her flight from the scene yesterday, she'd been turned around. They'd have to go back to pick up the most direct path to Dellenbaugh Station. She wanted to stay off the road, so they climbed up to the high ridgeline, backtracking her route from the day before. There was a moist granularity to the soil today, which kept the dust down. The air was clear and free of haze, giving the landscape all around the deep focus of a large-format photograph. Directly across from them, the sheer silent cliff faces were streaked with desert varnish. Only a few hours before, they roared with plunging, temporary rivers.

A yellow-headed, blue-bodied lizard drank from one of the tiny tinajas, and it ceased as it heard them, remaining motionless until they had gone by. After a time, they passed a large boulder that had been split by the roots of a pinyon pine. She hadn't seen any of these things during her flight. The return trip was filled with a twofold dread: worry about running into the man who had murdered Paul and anxiety over seeing Paul's body. She did not know if she would search him out or try to stay away.

Sophia stopped when she recognized the view. "Down there. That's where I came up. Everything I told you about happened down there."

"Is it smart for us to go back?" Reinhardt asked.

"Smart? Probably not. But any chance for us to get out of here starts down there. I want to see if anything is left that we can use, and the trail we need to take to get to the ranger station starts here."

Reinhardt nodded in agreement. "I want to inform you that the last of my diarrhea has passed. If you're going to rescue me, it's only fair that you have a clear picture of my physical capacities. Secrets won't save us." Reinhardt's eyes narrowed and he set his jaw. It was clear that he meant for Sophia to reciprocate openness for openness.

"Okay," she said. "I haven't pooped since the day before yesterday."

Reinhardt smiled. "That is not what I meant. My problems are gastro-intestinal. Yours are of another magnitude. But now my problems are yours and yours are mine."

"Whatever," she said, turning toward the cinder cone so she wouldn't have to think about what he just said. "He shot at us from up there."

"Do you think he is up there now?"

"That would be a lot of waiting in a bad storm. He didn't look like an outdoorsman."

"Are you okay physically? May I examine you?"

Sophia stepped back.

"I am a physician," Reinhardt said. She allowed him to take her hands and feel them. He moved from the wrist and forearm, then with one hand he took her pulse. When he let go of her hands, he placed his palm on her forehead, then widened each of her eyes with his fingertips. "You seem well," he said.

"We need to keep moving," she said, walking away.

They hiked down from the cluster of rocks that Sophia ran past on her flight from the gunman. She paused for a moment and vaguely remembered that she had mistaken them for her aunts in Iran. This memory triggered a cascade of other memories, and as her body tensed in preparation for an onslaught of panic, she caught sight of Reinhardt and managed to keep control as they continued down the trail that led to the edge of the palisade.

It was not as she'd left it. The vehicles had all been flipped over like giant mechanical bugs, the windows and windshields crushed flat. The backhoe had been parked across the road at a place with a tree on one side. Several large stones had been pushed into the road, making passage along it impossible.

"I thought maybe you overstated the problem," Reinhardt said. "I had no idea it was so dire."

Sophia refused to respond. Her jaw locked, and her neck seized. She didn't replay the events, but she reviewed them in reverse, flickering slow motion. When the scene had played through, Sophia unslung her day pack and pulled out the map, which had been rolled and flattened and folded. "We are here," she said, showing Reinhardt. "And we need to get there." She pointed to a section in the lower right-hand corner. A crooked double line branched from the main road and showed that the way out was to the southeast.

Reinhardt gasped. "Three days ago, I saw that map. In the diner. Two men were talking about this place and—" He looked down at the wreckage. "And these are them?"

Sophia nodded. "And one more," she said. "Before we begin, we need to find anything we can down there that might help us. Food, water, hats, whatever."

They climbed down and approached the vehicles. They were all inaccessible. The doors wouldn't open, and the windows were cracked but filled with sagging safety glass. She kicked in a window trying to find what she could, but anything useful was gone. She crouched next to her own truck. The vehicle had been shot up, inside and out. Her cooler and water had been taken. Everything was gone, even the shattered phone. She went back to Paul's Jeep, removed the map from her pack, and tucked it under the driver's seat.

"You said he wanted the map. Why hide it here?" Reinhardt asked.

"He's already been through these vehicles. He wouldn't take the time to do it again. Plus, if he finds us, it could buy us some time if we have to come back here to get it."

Sophia approached the turquoise truck, her hand following the upended curves of the wheel wells. The smell of the dead man came upon her all at once. A dozen feet away, he lay sprawled in a thick pudding of blood and soil. His fingers were thick, the tips burst open. A stream of red ants flowed into and out of the cuff of his shirt, the ruddy shimmer of their bodies tracing a path toward a low mound a few paces off. The smell of him became overwhelming as she drew near. She stepped around him in a half circle until she was upwind, which lessened the stench by a few degrees.

"Should we bury him?" Reinhardt asked.

Sophia shook her head. "The other one is down there," she said, pointing down the hill. "We need to focus our energy on getting out of here."

"And the ranger? Should we check on him?"

Sophia did not answer immediately. She was thinking about how far they were from the ranger station and how much longer it would take if they traveled cross-country instead of using the roads. She wondered how much water would be available along the route and how long it would be before it evaporated.

"Over there," she said. "He went over the cliff, there." She pointed, then rose to get some distance between herself and the dead man. Reinhardt walked to the edge of the box canyon and carefully looked over, stretching his neck and scanning back and forth. He shook his head. "I do not see him. It looks like a boulder came loose and is stuck down there."

Sophia joined Reinhardt at the edge. Her insides were pulsing manically.

Where could he be? She saw him go over. Maybe his gray-and-green uniform was working as camouflage. If his body was gone, that suggested a multitude of horrors, timelines in which his body was dragged from the crevice by animals, witches, or worse. She checked the space and saw the boulder Reinhardt mentioned. As they looked together, Reinhardt pointed to the negative space in the cliff wall across from them that matched the size and bulk of the rock below. In tandem, they leaned left and right, straining to see around the giant chockstone. Given the angle of the midday sun, they could only see shadows. Sophia's hand involuntarily reached up and gripped Reinhardt's shirt.

"Perhaps he did not die immediately," Reinhardt said. "We might find his remains somewhere. Perhaps the storm revived him long enough to . . . I do not know."

Sophia scanned the bottom of the small canyon, which ran thirty yards northward, then hooked left and connected to the depression where the other man had been operating the backhoe the day before. She circled back and ran down the slope past the disturbed gravesite, and she crawled back into the space under the fallen rock. There was enough room between the boulder and the ground for a human body, with some to spare. She looked back up at the edge, where Reinhardt stood, haloed in sunlight. Her face flushed. The corner of her eyes swelled, but she fought against the distraction of hope.

"Do you see any blood?" Reinhardt called down.

"No," she called back. "But really. You are, like, the least encouraging person of all time."

"I'm sorry. The last two days have been difficult for me emotionally."

"That makes two of us," she said.

While Sophia began looking for a sign that somebody had walked out, she heard the low crunch of tires on gravel. At first, she thought it might be a rescue, but that thought was immediately replaced by the flash of fear. She looked up at Reinhardt, who froze and pointed. "It's him. From the other day," he shouted. From her position below the road, she couldn't see what was happening, but she heard the car stop. Reinhardt bolted down the incline, and a gunshot tore a chunk of bark from one of the junipers. When Reinhardt met her, they both turned and ran together toward the far end of the canyon wall.

Two more shots ricocheted off the rocks, and they ran without saying anything about how impossible something like this was.

They looked back and saw the man lift a pistol and take aim. Ahead of them the canyon narrowed down to a tight gap just large enough for them to get through one at a time if they turned sideways. They were boxed in, and this was their only way out. Sophia slipped through first, and when she came through to the other side, she saw a pair of boots sticking out from under an overhanging rock. She jumped when she saw them, and crashed into Reinhardt, who was right behind her.

"Water," a voice said. It was Paul. "I need water."

Sophia bent down and helped him sit up.

"Don't," he groaned. "My shoulder is dislocated. And I've broken some ribs."

"But you went over the cliff," she said.

"I sure did," he said. "I hit an overhang halfway down."

Three more shots echoed through the gap.

"Is that guy back?" Paul asked.

They lifted Paul to his feet, and he was barely able to walk. With his good arm around Sophia's shoulder, Paul pointed them toward the dark lava field in the distance. "We need to go there."

"Are you kidding?" Sophia said.

"We'll be okay if we can get there."

The thick lava bed was a few hundred feet away, and they crossed the open ground as quickly as possible, switching their attention between the gap behind them and the directions Paul was giving them. "Go to that sage bush," he said. "It's the second one over. When we get there, you'll see it."

"What?"

"It's a step in the rock, a single flat spot that doesn't look like it's made out of razors."

As they came closer to the steep slope, they just didn't see what Paul was describing. It all looked impossible to climb, like the surface of an inhospitable alien planet. Sophia and Paul tried to find the secret way in, while Reinhardt watched the gap to see if the man was coming through.

"We are wasting our time," Sophia said.

Paul stepped onto the stone crags in one place, backed out, and tried another spot. When that one didn't work, he tried another. The lava was jagged, crowded with fragments and crenellations that would shred a boot to nothing. On his third attempt, Paul found a flat space, stepped from the dry summer grass, and stood in the midst of the clinky heaps of lava.

"We can't go in there. Those rocks are so sharp, they'll tear us apart," Reinhardt said.

"Is this one of those trails you talked about?" Sophia asked.

Paul nodded. "It's the only point of entry on this side. You can't see it, but it's there." He took three more steps to show them. Reinhardt followed, his boots curving across the tops of the dark stone. "No," Paul instructed. "Down in the spaces where the cinders are packed in. Flat spots." Reinhardt moved his feet to the only place that would accept them, then he stood tall and tested the step. Sophia followed, seeing that the path wasn't a structure at all but a change in texture. She couldn't see it, but it was there. Turn one degree off course, and the path would disappear.

Paul climbed slowly to the top of the flow. From there, he stood a story or so above the others and called back down. "None of it is where you'd think to step. We're a lot taller than they were. Take sixty percent of a step and you'll be in the zone," he said, then he disappeared. Reinhardt followed, his arms gyrating. Sophia brought up the rear, and as she disappeared over the edge, the gunman emerged from the gap looking all around, confounded.

Sophia quickly caught up with Reinhardt and Paul, who was draining one of Reinhardt's water bottles.

———

Dalton helped Raylene out of the Bronco and let her take his arm as they went into the BLM building. They passed through the visitor's center with its small room full of posters and kiosks about the history of the early inhabitants, the integral processes of the four seasons, the mission of the Bureau of Land Management, the need to be aware, and instructions for visitors about how they must be prepared for self-rescue.

At the center of this open room was a large rectangular structure that held a three-dimensional relief map that looked like an old photograph taken from the window of an airplane. As they approached it, Dalton figured that if they kept to the scale, he and Raylene would be tall enough to duck buzzing satellites. As Raylene gripped the edge of the map, her head eclipsed a floodlight and cast a shadow across ten thousand acres.

"I've never come in here to see this," she said. "Bruce doesn't have much use for federal government."

Dalton gestured to the model. "How much of it have you seen firsthand?"

"Plenty," she said, then she pointed to the thin stripe of black that led from the square grids of town to the west, then south toward the Grand Canyon. "We've driven that road hundreds of times."

"Where does Bruce like to go?"

"When he was younger, everywhere. The fewer people the better." She pointed to a star-shaped canyon called Giant Gulch. The orange of this narrow, intricate terrain was dulled with white dust from the room. She moved her flattened hand above the open plains. "He liked White Pocket, but his favorite was a place he called Swallow Valley. Paiutes named it Wiiatsiweap because the only way in was with wings." Raylene paused, then tapped her finger in the air. "Believe it or not, all through it there are caves. People rush to the canyons because they are obvious. Bruce always came home with things from unexpected places. He has a sense of where the water used to be, which is where you find the people." She pointed to another spot. "We used to spend a lot of time in Antelope Flats. Just south of there, there are some lovely cliff houses."

"Is that Las Casas Altas?" Dalton asked.

"Yes, that's right. The high houses. There used to be ladders up to the dwellings, but they've been gone for a long time. When Bruce was a teenager, he and some of his friends hiked to the top and came down with ropes—they'd never let you do that today. He said the place was filled with pots, headdresses, carvings, little piles of dolls and whatnot. He said he carried a small red-and-black pot out of there in his shirt, but he slipped when he was rappelling and smashed it to pieces. It cut him so badly he needed stitches, but he kept the pieces and put it back together with model airplane glue. That was his first find. He always regretted using the glue."

"Something like that would get him in trouble now."

"It's all so ridiculous, isn't it?"

"It's all so something, that's for sure," Dalton said.

"Before everyone and their dog started coming through these parts looking for an adventure, Bruce and I would go out together." She stopped talking to find a spot on the map. "There," she said, pointing to a place where a canyon narrowed and the map showed a smooth vertical face. "That is where Bruce proposed to me. It doesn't have a name. He lured me out there for a picnic in the ruins."

"Lured you, huh?"

"I was a good girl then. I didn't just run off into the hills for any old dandy in a bow tie. He promised me fried chicken and arrowheads."

"How was it?"

"The picnic or the proposal?"

Dalton shrugged. "Both?"

"The chicken was dry. Bruce was not." Raylene paused and drifted off. After a time, she began to tremble so much that she had to steady herself. "Something terrible has happened, hasn't it?" she said.

"I'm not sure I understand," Dalton said.

"With Bruce? Something has happened to him."

Dalton sat forward. "Do you remember anything?" he asked.

"Something horrible. In the house. What do you know about it?"

"Not very much, I'm afraid. I'm trying to work it all out," Dalton said, wondering if he should call the Beehive House. If he did, they'd never let him talk to her like this again.

"It doesn't make sense," she said, looking up. "He was taking care of me. He remembered everything for the both of us. All of this. All of Bruce's secrets about the things out here. His collection was our only child. It was always the three of us. Oh, Patrick. My mind comes and goes." She cradled her head in one hand.

"What do you mean, Bruce's secrets?" Dalton asked, knowing he should probably back off.

"There was a day, maybe ten years ago. Bruce saw something that he'd found and traded listed on an auction. He was told it was going to be in a museum, but it didn't end up there. Other people started coming to him with offers to buy his things. Sometimes people would try to sell artifacts to him. More than once, they'd try to sell him a pot he found himself. They didn't know anything about it, or him. Bruce didn't want the money. We always had enough. He loved the history and the adventure––oh, maybe I should sit," she said.

Raylene took a small, lace-edged handkerchief from her purse and dabbed at the edges of her face. "So, this was your plan all along, to jog my memory?"

"Raylene," Dalton said indignantly. "I wouldn't try to––"

"That's a lie and you know it."

From across the room a man named Tyler Gomez poked his head into the room and said, "Hey, Dalton. I got something to ask you." Dalton told Raylene he'd be right back and he crossed the room.

"You work on Sundays?" Dalton asked.

"Not usually. I'm filling in. Yesterday, one of my guys came in from the Antelope Flats section, said he saw a truck with a backhoe on it. When my guys asked them about it, they said they were taking it to their mining claim. I checked the database. There aren't any active claims in that area, but it's mixed up with a lot of inholdings. So who knows. We're going to look into it on our end, but I was wondering if you could keep an eye open on yours."

Raylene cupped her hand along her mouth and offered, "Bruce was talking to someone about Antelope Flats recently, on the phone."

"You're remembering this now?" Dalton asked, turning. "You were just talking about––"

Raylene shrugged. "I didn't remember the call until I heard that man say it."

—

Sophia fell in line behind Reinhardt. Her feet were large for the pathway, and it took precision for her to move without stumbling. Once she found her rhythm, she moved more quickly across the strange trails through the basalt. She wondered what it must have been like to walk across this in yucca sandals. Reinhardt hiked awkwardly but steadily, and Paul led with a slowness that showed how severe his injuries were. The path zigzagged through knee-high boulders, and after a time, she forgot about where to put her feet; they found their own way.

The lava flow extended as far as she could see to the east and north. Beyond these badlands, behind the ripples of searing heat, lay the coarse woolen texture of the dry chaparral. They followed the smooth contours of the trail, which meant it was no random occurrence. Ahead, her companions had stopped, and she noted how the jagged rim of stone fractured the sky. She noticed her muscles relaxing. The ease in her shoulders was unexpected.

Paul gestured to them with a look of excruciating pain, and he put a finger to his lips. She was unsure why they needed to keep quiet. Two shots rang out, but there was no whiz of bullets or ricochet, only a quickly decaying echo bouncing from hill to hill. They all dropped to a crouch and became swallowed up by the stone. From this position they heard incoherent shouting and a third shot. Paul beckoned them to move ahead and led them to a round recess in the lava, the foundation of a room now open to the sky. In the space was a smooth log positioned as a bench.

"We're sitting ducks in here," Sophia said.

"We'll be safe," Paul said, trying to move his injured arm. Sophia looked all around, and Paul noticed she was unconvinced. "This has been a place of refuge for hundreds of years, maybe longer."

"Do the Indian people use it still?" Reinhardt asked.

"Who is your friend?" Paul asked.

Sophia shrugged. "Not a friend. It's complicated. You should have seen him last night, but he's a doctor, so maybe he can look at you."

Reinhardt extended his hand. "I am Reinhardt Kupfer, from Germany." When he saw that Paul couldn't lift his arm, he lowered his. "I am on a . . ."

"A quest," Sophia said. "He thinks he's on a quest."

Reinhardt lowered his head and looked away.

"Aren't we all. Reinhardt, they don't use these trails now. Not in the same way."

"Who were they running from?" Reinhardt asked.

"Other tribes at first," Sophia said.

"Then from us," Paul said, unbuttoning his shirt with one hand. Sophia moved from the log bench to help. She noticed a bullet hole in the breast pocket of his shirt, below his name tag. They both helped him remove his shirt and body armor. "Normally, I wouldn't have had it on, but when my weapon went missing, I had a feeling." Even through his undershirt, she could see a massive bruise spread across his chest, a concentration of black at the center. "It's really hard to breathe."

From this close, she saw just how damaged he was. He was covered in bruises and abrasions. Beyond the obvious, she noticed he held himself differently. His responses were delayed, and his eyes jerked from place to place. He scanned the sky as if it might drop down on him at any moment. But he was not dead. None of them were, and that was something.

"I can help," Reinhardt said. He examined Paul's slumping arm, stopping once during his evaluation to stare at Sophia.

"It's dislocated," Paul said. Reinhardt nodded, feeling the arm and the curve of Paul's shoulder. "I tried to get it back into place myself, but I couldn't."

"Your muscles have contracted. They are looking out for you, but we wish they would relax now that their job is over, right?" Reinhardt asked Sophia to hold Paul around the waist and neck. Paul winced when Reinhardt took the bad arm and lifted it. He sucked air, then modulated his breathing.

"Are you a park ranger, then?" Reinhardt asked.

"Yep," Paul said, eyeing Reinhardt nervously.

"I am a doctor, which we have already discussed. But I am on vacation, which has become something more elaborate than I originally planned."

"Like what Sophia said," Paul acknowledged.

"Yes. Do you and Sophia know each other?"

"We do," Sophia said.

"It's better if our ranger answers." Reinhardt lifted one eyebrow and nodded to make sure Sophia read his subtext. He inspected Paul's arm from the shoulder down, rotating the hand so the palm faced upward. This caused Paul so much pain he closed his eyes. "It's okay to answer my silly questions. I'm only trying to distract you from the pain that will come."

"The guy out there has the lion's share of my attention," Paul said. He looked at Sophia and attempted a smile that shattered when Reinhardt took Paul's arm at the elbow and bent it across his belly. A second later, he lifted the arm, and Paul called out. Sophia let go as the echo decayed. Paul raised his arm and moved it around. His face relaxed. He nodded to Reinhardt and said, "Thank you for coming back to get me."

"She thought you were dead," Reinhardt said. "She was untröstlich."

"What does that mean?" he asked.

Reinhardt thought for a moment. "Heartbroken."

Sophia's eyes narrowed. "I would have picked another word."

"But she is glad you're not dead," Reinhardt said as he sat back down on the log bench. "Wow. I have only done that procedure once before, and I did it incorrectly." After a moment, he said, "Then. I mean to say that I did not do it correctly the first time. I think I did it right today."

Two more shots rang out.

"Why is he doing that?" Paul asked.

"I'm going with, because he's crazy," Sophia said.

"Maybe he is trying to flush us out?" Reinhardt said.

It was difficult to settle on the location of the shots, but it seemed like the man was on the move.

"We may be safe in here, but we can't stay," Sophia said.

"We'll be grilled," Reinhardt said, looking around at the open dark lava and the distant tan hills and the red rock beyond that.

"We are safe. And there's another way out," Paul said.

Paul asked for help replacing his shirt, and Sophia opened up her pack to carry out the Kevlar vest. "We should leave it," Paul said. "It's so heavy."

"Are you kidding?" Sophia said, moving things around in her pack. "We don't have much. A couple bottles of rainwater, pen, a wad of duct tape, notebook, Ziploc bag with matches in it, a thing of sunscreen, now a bulletproof vest."

"I'm glad you have sunscreen. It seems inconsequential, but it isn't," Reinhardt said.

"What do you have?" Sophia asked, unzipping Paul's pack. Inside was an empty water bladder, two clips for his sidearm, a few trail maps, and the blue inventory he showed her at Swallow Valley. "Those guys had Cluff's map with them, the one that goes with this book. It showed a bunch of sites around here, including Swallow Valley. The crazy shooter was after it—"

"I saw that map at a restaurant," Reinhardt interrupted.

"I could really use some ibuprofen," Paul said, looking at each one of them. "Do you have anything like that in your bag, doctor?"

Reinhardt shrugged and unzipped his pack. Inside were his bottles of water, his dead phone, a charging cable, his pemmican wrappers, and the screen-writing book.

"That must be some book," Paul said, "if you haven't ditched it by now."

"It has been important to me," Reinhardt said.

Sophia tried to redirect the conversation before it got too mythological. "The map had a number of sites that are restricted on the federal registry."

"Like I said, Cluff's maps have stuff on them only he knows about," Paul said. "I'll bet somebody found out that he's—" Paul stopped. "It's nothing. Who knows? It's gone now," he said.

"Since I didn't recognize most of what was on the map, I took it."

Paul's face lit up. "What? Where is it?"

"I stashed it in your Jeep."

Paul's head dropped in defeat.

"You know two seconds after he gets that map, we're dead," she said. "I didn't want to give him the satisfaction of taking it from us. Maybe if we don't have it, it'll let us stall him. Plus, the inventory is more important. It has the provenance."

"They kind of work together, especially now that Cluff is gone. I'm not sure it matters at this point."

Sophia drank some water and started to speak but held back, thinking it all through, but the dots were too far apart. "This can't be about money," she said. "None of the items are worth that much. I mean, if we're talking market value."

"It is absolutely about money, but at a totally different scale. There's a plan going around that will shrink the monument boundaries. Probably a dozen plans. There's a race to divvy it all up." Paul moved his body in search of a comfortable position. "You ever have a king cake?" Sophia shook her head.

"For Lent?" Reinhardt asked.

"Yeah. Every year at Mardi Gras, my grandma would make one. Round, sugar on top, a little baby Jesus hidden inside. Find the baby and you've got good luck. A whole lot of people are trying to find where that baby's hiding."

"And the prize isn't pots," Reinhardt said, nodding.

"It's energy. Oil, gas, uranium."

Sophia sighed. "My mother used to say if the Middle East had no oil, it would be poor but peaceful."

Two more shots echoed off the hills.

"Maybe if he keeps doing that somebody will eventually come looking for us," Sophia said.

"I worry about that," Paul said. "I wish we could warn people."

They sat together in silence on the log bench, submerged in the blocky lava with the clouds passing overhead. Here was a ruin of another kind, its history told through absence. It was one thing to consider the domestic life in a pueblo and another to think of those in flight, huddling here for safety. They all waited for another round of shots until Reinhardt asked Sophia for her duct tape, then busied himself making material for a sling to ease Paul's injury. Once it was in place and adjusted, Reinhardt wrapped a second strip around Paul's arm and chest to hold it in place. Paul said it felt better. Reinhardt also applied sunscreen to his own arms and face and told each of them to do the same. "We don't want to survive this gunman only to have a melanoma kill us later."

"I know you're saying we need to go, but go where?" Sophia asked. "Why don't we just get someplace where we can make a call?"

"My phone broke when I fell," Paul said. "Radio's in my vehicle."

"He destroyed everything back there," Sophia said. "And my phone is in a million pieces, which doesn't matter because he took it."

"My phone is dead," Reinhardt said, patting his pack. "And I have photos of the map on it."

"I just need time to think some things through," Paul said.

Reinhardt looked up at the sky, squinted, then took out his book and began reading. Paul leaned over and tried to get a look at the cover.

"Mythstructures for what?" Paul asked.

"Blockbusters," Reinhardt mumbled. "Since we are stuck here, I thought I would pass the time."

"Blockbusters?" Paul repeated.

"As in movies," Sophia said.

"The book was a gift," Reinhardt said. "I know it seems foolish to carry it around after such a chase."

"Anything that tries to help us make sense of this world is a good thing," Paul said. "Plus, the natural world feels mythic to me." Paul looked at Sophia, who seemed as if she might collapse.

"I've been thinking," Paul said. "The guy who's after us is on somebody else's errand. If I arrest him, the trail to his boss will go cold. We need to tire him out. When we can run, we want him to think we're trapped, and when we are near, we have to seem far away. We have to make him believe he is winning." Paul stood and balanced himself. "Let's keep moving before we stiffen up."

They walked on through the nightmare landscape under the punishing midday sun with their heads downward, like pilgrims, watching each step with care. Paul led the way and Sophia followed. Reinhardt stayed between them like a lone calf being led back to the herd. The lava around them looked like a storm-tossed sea frozen in a photograph, but with each step along the path the going became easier. As they walked, their ears strained for the next round of shots that did not come. They began close together, but over time they spread apart, hiking in isolation.

Along the way, Reinhardt noticed a bright gray curve amid the rocks. He looked behind and saw Sophia walking with her head down. Quickly, he stooped and saw that it was a potsherd, glazed in gray and painted with narrow black pinstripes. He picked it up, slipped it into his pocket, and kept walking, letting his fingers rest along its contour. He imagined the look that would appear on Wolf's face when he set it on his desk in the middle of his leather blotter. His body coursed with adrenaline.

Ahead, Paul stopped and looked back and waved to them. When Reinhardt and Sophia caught up, they saw Paul gesturing to an intact pitcher sitting in a natural stone alcove. Its whiteness was stark against the basalt, and it was covered from top to bottom with zigzagging chevrons.

Sophia removed her pack, took out her notebook, squatted, and began to sketch.

"The Paiutes have asked us not to," Paul said.

Sophia closed her notebook and stood. "You're kidding."

"Not kidding. This place is important to them."

"I'm okay with them not wanting us to document anything. I do have a problem with you being the one to enforce it. Your stewardship credentials are up for debate."

"Fair enough."

"Damn right it's fair enough." She threw the notebook in her pack and zipped it shut.

"I feel like we are moving backward through time or like the walls of time have become permeable," Reinhardt said. "Why would they leave such a thing here?"

"It's like a sign for a shop. There's a natural catchment here. It's seasonal. The pot lets people know that there could be water," Paul said. Sophia climbed off the trail a bit and looked over the edge. A natural basin had formed that was half-full from the recent monsoons. "This rock will hold the water for a few days before it drains. Any water you find here will be fresh."

When they had drunk and refilled their bottles, Sophia asked where they were going.

"I have a friend who lives out here, past the lava flow."

"People can live out here?" Reinhardt asked, then he corrected himself. "I know they once did. But it is so empty now. These ruins all seem like something that should have worked but didn't. I meant to ask if people were allowed to live on a national monument."

"It's an inholding. This guy owned the property before Obama made it a monument. When he dies, the property will go to the Park Service. Until then it's private land."

"How far is it?" Reinhardt asked.

"A few miles?"

"Why don't the Indian people have an inholding?" Reinhardt asked.

"That's a really good question," Paul said.

"How do we know this killer won't be waiting for us at your friend's house?" Sophia asked.

"Dreamweaver is extremely private. That's an understatement, actually. He protects himself. You'll see what I mean."

"Wait a minute. His name is Dreamweaver?" Sophia said.

"It's not his *real* name," Paul said. "He sort of gave it to himself in the sixties."

—

Scissors slowed as he came to the narrow gap in the cliff the others slipped through. The rock walls closed in and shot up twenty feet to form a passage just wide enough for him if he turned sideways and held his rifle straight up and down. The tight corridor eventually flared out and opened onto a tawny sagebrush plain that had been almost entirely consumed by a massive bed of lava twenty feet high that rose up like a breaking wave. Behind it stood the collapsed volcanic cinder cone that spawned these heaps of serrated slag. It looked impossible to traverse. Anyone trying to climb up and cross it would have been slowed to a crawl.

He scanned the barren waste, watching for movement. When he found none, he dropped his head to listen, hearing nothing but the drone of wind against itself and the heaving of his own breath. As he approached the imposing, jumbled slope, he looked to the sky for some sign, perhaps birds spooked from their nests, but there was only blank firmament bisected by a pair of contrails. Nothing vanishes, he thought. It's always a trick. You move it, hide it, or never have it there in the first place. He did not know if he was angrier that they had given him the slip or that he could not tell how they had done it.

He fired his pistol twice into the air, hoping to startle them and flush them out. The echo of the shots radiated outward and decayed to nothing. He could chase them, but they would have the advantage of knowing the terrain. From where he stood, he identified a number of vantage points that would reveal their location, but getting there and back would make pursuit impossible. There was the possibility that they hadn't come through the gap at all. The third misdirection. He could see these people getting him to run around that lava like an idiot, while they circled back and stole his car. He shot again, then shouted.

He hiked back through the gap, checking for hiding places along the way. As he walked back through the low area where the Ashdowns had been digging, Scissors spotted the box canyon the ranger had fallen into. There were rock steps that likely broke his fall and made a line of sight from above impossible. While he was piecing together what happened, he heard a shout echoing from the rocks. So, they were hidden, he thought. He ran back through the gap and surveyed the landscape and decided cat and mouse was a losing proposition, and he didn't want to be here when this disaster was discovered.

Scissors made his way back to the vehicles, and at the top of the incline, he looked back to the gap. The cliffs obscured the lava entirely. He decided he wasn't equipped to pursue anyone through this terrain, and if he tried, he would lose. He thought that leaving might draw them out and pressing them would push them farther into the desert, which they knew and he did not. Eventually, they would have to come off the monument, and he would be there to meet them.

He decided to look through the wreckage of the Ashdowns' truck again, trying to find the map, and he came up empty-handed. The girl's truck produced nothing as well. At the ranger's Jeep, he knelt and sorted through the debris that was now collected on the inverted roof. Under some loose glass and stone, he found a folded slip of paper with Sophia's name, address, and phone number on it, which he tucked into his pocket. He'd begin there.

On the way back to his car, he fired his pistol two more times to make them run. The constant jolts of adrenaline would exhaust and demoralize them. When the echoes died out, he stored the weapon and drove away.

—

Dalton drove toward Antelope Flats and Raylene talked. Something about the movement of the vehicle and the familiar landscape opened her up. After a while she asked Dalton to play some Glenn Miller. He responded with Hank Williams, and when the Hank ran out he switched to Patsy Cline. When "Crazy" came on, Raylene said, "I remember now. There was a woman."

"Bruce was having an affair?"

Raylene looked at Dalton like he was an idiot. "The woman was a collector. She'd been calling Bruce because she wanted to get access to places that weren't on the maps anymore, places that most people had forgotten about. Bruce told her he wouldn't do it. He told me she had a reputation."

"Famous or infamous?"

"A bit of both. When Bruce had enough of her pressure, he'd just hang up. A little bit after that—around the first of May—she just showed up during the dinner hour."

"Crazy" ended, and "I Fall to Pieces" came on. Raylene settled back against the headrest and covered her mouth with one hand as she listened to the words. Dalton reached up to turn off the stereo, but Raylene intercepted him with her small liver-spotted hand. "It's okay," she said. "I want to feel it. Sometimes I know what happened and sometimes I don't. I am not sure which state of things I prefer."

"Okay," Dalton said, "but if you want it off or if you want something different, I can do that for you."

"This is better."

The Bronco sailed down a slight hill into a wash strewn with sticks and braided sandy striations from the recent storm. They bounced out of the wash and climbed a hill that gave them a panoramic view of Antelope Flats and the mesas that encircled them. Dalton gripped and re-gripped the wheel a few times.

"What was I talking about, dear?" Raylene asked.

"The woman," Dalton said.

"What woman?"

"We can talk about it later."

They drove on. The songs changing from "So Wrong" to "Strange" to "Back in Baby's Arms." They listened to them without speaking as they passed a lava field to the west that lay in a shattered heap upon the tan grass and sage scrub. The road curved away from the lava field to a cinder cone, then it descended to a cove in the rock, where the road was blocked by large boulders and a backhoe. Through the junipers, Dalton noticed three vehicles turned belly side up with all twelve of their tires pointing skyward.

"Well, what in the world?" Raylene said.

"I think we found Pete's backhoe," Dalton said. He parked and picked up the radio mic. "Kanab dispatch, this is Dalton." When he released the button, there was static. He dialed in the squelch and listened. More static.

"Looks like we're in the repeater's blind spot," Dalton said. He checked the location of his shotgun, then rolled down the windows and got out. "Be right back."

"I'll be a sitting duck in here."

"I'm just taking a look. It doesn't seem like anybody's around."

"Is this thing bulletproof?" Raylene said, knocking on the glass.

"Just between the front and back."

"I didn't sign up for some Wild West show," she said.

"I could always take you back. No sense missing bingo."

Raylene glared at him, no hint of a follow-up smile.

Dalton cracked both of the front windows. "If anything happens, get as low to the floor as you can." Raylene scowled. Dalton walked to the backhoe and noticed blood on the floor of the cab and some streaks of it on the glass. He opened the door and felt for the key, which wasn't there. When he hopped down from the machine, the putrid stench hit him all at once, and he started to gag. He buried his nose in the crook of his arm as he looked for the source.

He ducked under the junipers and came to the inverted vehicles with their crushed cabs and windows. When he arrived at the turquoise pickup, he heard the rustle of feathers, then saw the dark humped backs of six vultures hopping around on a human carcass, their naked heads glistening with blood. The birds scattered when they heard him. Dalton retreated to the road and tried to re-compose himself. He went to Raylene's side of the Bronco and put a hand on the open window. "You'll want to stay put," he said.

"What is it?"

"Won't be sure until the vultures clear out." Dalton looked around the Bronco until he found a bandanna and returned to the vehicles with the cloth over his mouth and nose. A truck and Jeep with federal plates. The other belonged to the Ashdowns. Three vehicles and one body didn't add up. The bullet holes were consistent with a single shooter. He looked for vantage points, like he learned to do in Afghanistan. The cinder cone to the north seemed the most likely spot.

He left the vehicles and followed the backhoe tracks down the incline. The feeding vultures had reconvened and sounded more like pigs at the trough than he ever imagined. As he came to the mound of dirt and discovered the second body, he felt himself slipping into the past.

They were in the Maidan Wardak Province, west of Kabul, in a convoy investigating a Taliban attack that leveled a school. After they left the Kabul–Behsud Highway, they patrolled the neighborhood where the attack had taken place. Before too long they came upon a pack of dogs that scattered when they heard the Bradleys drive in. In the street was a small body, lying in an S-shape, the clothes torn away and the body partially devoured. They parked and fanned out, and Dalton led a group to a nearby house surrounded by a low stucco wall riddled with bullets and spray painted with a Pashto slogan. One of the guys told them it said LONG LIVE THE TALIBAN.

They fell into formation and went through the front gate. Everything was silent except for the chickens clucking behind a wire fence and a red wheelbarrow flipped upside down. One of the guys said something about a poem he had to read in college and somebody else told him to shut up. The windows in the house had all been shot out and when Dalton leaned in to get a look inside, he saw a row of bodies lined up and facedown, the blood gathering into a single pool at a low spot on the floor. More slogans had been painted across the interior of the house, and all he could remember thinking then was why they left the chickens.

As Dalton circled the mound of displaced earth now, he made a mental note of the way the second body was twisted at the waist, and how the head and shoulders were closed up in the dirt like somebody had thought through what they were doing and why. He saw potsherds and corn cobs in the soil, along with bones of those long dead. He inched closer to the newest body and pulled a wallet from the man's back pocket. He stepped away and removed the driver's license. It belonged, as he thought it would, to Byron Ashdown.

Well, Pete, Dalton said to himself, which are you gonna want first, the good news or the bad?

—

They emerged carefully from the narrow maze of stone, everything wrapped in a white phosphorescent flare. The heat of the lava field broke as they left it for the open grassland. A helix of turkey vultures rotated and lifted in the distance like shattered bits of creosote. In front of them, a wide sloping plain populated with rabbit brush, sage, and wizened juniper scrub extended as far as they could see. Behind it was a wide band of green, then deeper still ran a belt of orange and purple cliffs. Beyond that lay the blank white dome of the desert sky.

Paul led them onward in single file. They were grateful for the give of packed soil after spending so long on stone and cinders. Paul lifted his arm and adjusted his sling. Their clothes were crusted in the salt from their sweat, and Reinhardt had fashioned the dust cover of *Mythstructures for Blockbusters* into a hat. He held on to each side of his head to keep it from blowing away.

"Where does your friend live again?" Sophia asked.

"Not far."

"Not far for you, or not far for normal humans?"

"Not far for someone with broken ribs."

"Fair enough," she said. "What do we do when we get there?" she asked.

"Not sure. But he'll be able to help us figure out what's going on."

"Does he have a phone?"

"Not likely, but he'll have internet access or some version of it."

"I don't know what that means," she said.

"Dreamweaver helped invent cyberspace."

"So, he's a hermit Al Gore?"

"No, he's for real. He helped design the internet, ARPANET, or whatever it's called. He had a PhD from Stanford, and he still talks about the network of networks. Working for the Defense Department drove him out here."

"*Had* a PhD? How does that work?"

"In the late nineties he erased himself. He's pretty much a ghost now. I think all that's left is his passport, maybe a social security card. He doesn't talk much about it."

They walked on, crossing the open plain, which now rose gently like the belly of a sleeping giant. They passed a cluster of pink cactus flowers that had run their course and were crumpling in the heat. They passed dead trees and the fanned-out spines of yucca. There was bitterbrush, broom snakeweed, Mormon tea, scorpionweed, red penstemon, and the pasakana, which seemed like it came from another planet altogether. At some distance, an ocotillo's sinuous thorny arms reached skyward. For Paul, the landscape was a kaleidoscope of these familiar names. Sophia knew the shapes, colors, and textures. For Reinhardt, it was a strange loop of unclassifiable and unfamiliar marvels.

As the heat of the day grew, their shadows shrank down to small off-register halos, then turned and grew outward in the opposite direction. They each focused their attention inward, keeping their eyes down to avoid confronting the distance. It seemed at first like they were wandering randomly over the open ground until Sophia noticed they were following a nearly invisible path through the grasses, a trail that followed the contours and took advantage of them rather than cutting straight across. A small lizard ran onto the trail from a tuft of tawny ricegrass, felt her footsteps, then froze. As her shadow fell across its scaled body, the tiny creature turned back and disappeared.

Paul stopped at a wide oval boulder and took stock of where he was. After a few seconds, he left the impressionistic trail at a right angle, and after twenty paces he stopped and motioned for Sophia and Reinhardt to follow.

"We have to stand here, in this exact spot," Paul said.

"All of us?" Reinhardt asked.

"Those are Dreamweaver's instructions." Paul gathered them together with his good arm, then asked Sophia to move a certain flat rock near them. She pulled it to the side, like a manhole cover, and underneath was a large can buried all the way, so the rim was level with the ground. "There's a mirror inside," Paul said. "Can you get it out?" Sophia handed it to Paul, who turned and aimed it toward the green band in the distance, tilting it up and down. "He already knows we're here, or he knows somebody is here, and we want to make sure he knows it's me."

"How would he know someone has arrived? There's nothing out here," Reinhardt said.

Paul squinted and covered his eyes, turned counterclockwise, then stopped. "There," he said, pointing. "It's maybe fifty feet from us."

"What are we looking for?" Sophia asked.

"It's a sensor. Silver. A thin metal rod coming up out of the ground. The thick part is at the top. It looks like a cattail. He's got them scattered all over. They pick up the movement of anything over four feet tall, so jackrabbits and coyotes don't set it off."

"That's not paranoid or anything," Sophia said.

"After all of this shooting, I fear I will be paranoid forever," Reinhardt said.

After a few moments, a series of flashes returned. Paul smiled, "Good. He's there."

"Was that Morse code?" Reinhardt asked.

"Pretty much." Paul handed the mirror to Sophia and asked her to put it back into the can. As they returned to the trail, Paul raked out their footprints with a sage branch. "It wouldn't fool somebody with tracking experience, but it's all part of the instructions. I have to bring the sage with me to prove I did it."

Reinhardt replaced the book jacket on his head. When Paul and Sophia looked at him, he said, "One severe burn is enough."

Again, Paul took the lead, and as he passed Sophia, she stopped him and leaned in. "When I found him, he was delirious with dehydration and diarrhea. I couldn't leave him."

"I get it," Paul said.

Sophia sniffed the air. "Is that watermelon?"

Paul moved the candy to the other side of his mouth. "I saved it."

"For what?"

"For my last meal." Paul turned and started walking.

As they hiked on, the belt of green transformed into a grove of cotton-woods that filled a low spot like an oasis in an illustrated book. They watched two wrens flit across the expanse and disappear into the trees. On a low hill behind the grove was a water catchment, solar panels, and a narrow radio antenna with nearly invisible guy lines securing it to the ground. At the center of the grove was a school bus, and on one side it was fitted with a screened-in porch set underneath a corrugated metal roof. As they drew closer, they noticed more of the cattail sensors and an abundance of bird calls from the interior of the grove of trees. Somewhere a rooster crowed, and a human voice growled at it to keep quiet. They passed into the delicious shade, and the coolness of it washed over them in waves.

The bus doors opened and Dreamweaver descended the stairs in unlaced boots and tan cargo shorts. A gray checkered bathrobe fluttered behind him like a cape, his pale chest covered in thick, curly white hair.

"Paul Thrift, what the hell?" Dreamweaver bellowed. "This kind of intrusion will not stand!" Paul held up the sage branch. Dreamweaver dropped his chin. "At least you've kept to the protocols, but who are these spies?"

"We're all in some trouble, friend," Paul said.

"I hope it's the right kind of trouble," Dreamweaver said, smiling. His teeth were perfect except for a single gap on the right side where a canine should have been. He threw his arms open to draw Paul into a bear hug, but Paul held up a hand.

"I've got some broken ribs."

Dreamweaver turned his head and glanced at him out of the corners of his eyes, then he sized up Sophia and Reinhardt. "How did the Spider-man break his ribs?" he asked.

"Spider-man, huh?" Sophia asked.

"I didn't pick the name," Paul said.

"It was gunshot wounds," Reinhardt said, "or maybe the fall."

"Did you shoot back?" Dreamweaver asked, wiggling a finger into one ear. When Paul said that he didn't return fire, Dreamweaver made a grunting noise, then removed the finger. "You were wearing your armor, I guess."

Paul nodded.

"You know how I feel about guns," Dreamweaver said.

"Last refuge of a scoundrel. We've had that conversation before," Paul said.

"I know Big Brother requires you to carry one. I'm just saying." Dreamweaver turned his attention to Sophia and Reinhardt. "A poison dart is faster, quieter, and completely non-corporate."

They looked at each other.

"A dart doesn't have to kill you. Central nervous system paralysis is sufficient force to stop any conflict. Once you paralyze somebody you can still talk to them, and they have to listen. Once you shoot a person, logic goes out the window."

"Anesthesia achieves a similar effect," Reinhardt said. "Though sometimes there can be quite a lot of talking."

Dreamweaver laughed. "I like him. You're from the fatherland? Sounds like maybe Berlin."

"Sehr gut. Sprichst du Deutsch?"

"Ich habe mehr Möglichkeiten, es zu lesen als zu sprechen, aber ich versuche, in der Praxis zu bleiben," Dreamweaver said.

Dreamweaver asked Reinhardt how he managed to team up with the others, and he said Sophia rescued him.

"Ha!" Dreamweaver said. "Turning the tale on its head. The maiden rescues the hombres." He turned to Sophia. "Nice work dismantling ye olde power structures."

Reinhardt turned to the others and flashed his book cover at them with a grin. "This part of our adventure is the rescue from without—"

Dreamweaver nodded, then thought for a moment and nodded again with wide eyes. "That would make me a supernatural guide. I'm good with that. Sit. Let me bring you refreshments." Dreamweaver disappeared into the bus. Reinhardt inserted himself into a bench at the picnic table and rested his head on his arms. Paul lowered himself to the ground and sat in a half lotus and began aligning his neck and spine. Sophia sat backward on the bench opposite Reinhardt and stretched her hamstrings.

The yard was a menagerie of odds and ends. There was a chicken coop attached to a shipping container, a garden protected with military camo netting, a narrow carport with two motorcycles in it, an empty flatbed trailer, four or five spinning windmills made out of hammered copper, strings of prayer flags, a dozen or more blue fifty-five-gallon barrels, one crate that said FRAGILE, and another that said EXPLOSIVES. At the center of the yard was a massive chunk of metallic stone the size of a large pig.

"What's that?" Sophia asked.

"Meteorite," Paul said. "It's why he bought this place. He wanted to own something extraterrestrial. He's been taking chunks out of it and forging tools with the metal."

Dreamweaver returned after a time with a serving tray of Mason jars full of cucumber water. Sophia was hoping for the miracle of ice, but she knew such a luxury was a ways off. There was also a plate of unidentifiable orange melon slices, a bowl of nuts, and a second bowl heaped with jerky. He set it all on the table. "Water, sugar, protein, fat, salt. Should take the wilt out of you hothouse flowers," Dreamweaver said.

As they all dug in, Paul stood and came to the table. Dreamweaver intercepted him and said, "Eat the damn jerky, son. You aren't going to heal on melon and nuts." Paul looked him in the eye and nodded.

"Good." As they ate and drank, Dreamweaver said, "Questions aren't normally my thing, but neither is homicide, attempted or otherwise . . . so, I've got to ask. What the hell happened to you people?"

Sophia looked at Paul, who didn't speak immediately.

"I was rescued from my own bad judgment. I think that is a different story from theirs," Reinhardt said.

"Fair enough." Dreamweaver turned to Sophia and she recounted the tale of the Ashdowns, meeting them once and then again. She told of the map and the man who killed them, then explained about Paul's arrival and how he was shot, how she fled and found Reinhardt and returned to find Paul alive, then she relayed the story of how they escaped through the lava flow.

"Let's back up to the map." Dreamweaver's eyes landed on Paul. "Any chance it belonged to Bruce Cluff?" Dreamweaver asked.

Paul looked down and nodded. "It's his."

"Which one?"

"It's the one with Antelope Flats, Las Casas Altas, and Swallow Valley," Paul said.

Dreamweaver squinted as he thought. "Makes sense," he said. "There's been all kinds of action since the president tweeted about shrinking the monuments. The guys who used that map to go pot hunting had no idea how much money they could make selling it to the people getting ready for the auctions or that they were at the epicenter of an oil, gas, and government hootenanny."

"I don't know if you heard, but Cluff died," Paul said.

Dreamweaver nodded. "Breaks my heart. But he didn't kill himself. I don't buy a word of it. Smells like the work of corporate assassins."

"I heard the two dead grave robbers talking about the maps," Reinhardt interjected.

Dreamweaver locked eyes with Reinhardt. "From the spirit world?" he asked.

"What kind of question is that?" Sophia said with a dismissiveness she immediately regretted.

Dreamweaver rolled his eyes. "You can call it multidimensional space, string theory, quantum entanglements, Rudra's roar, or whatever blows your hair back. Just don't make your limitations of consciousness my problem, okay?"

"I am not offended by your question," Reinhardt said, "but I am not talking about metaphysics. I saw them at a restaurant fighting over the map, saying all these same place names. It seems like the man who came after us was actually after them. I have a photo of it in my dead phone."

Dreamweaver paced back and forth for a time, then said, "We won't need your copy. This is some D.C.-level capitalist horseshit, so why bring in small-time old boys like the Ashdowns?"

"What are your friends online saying about the retractions?" Paul asked.

"Everybody's talking about the energy angle: shale oil, fracking, natural gas. But good old-fashioned bubbling crude isn't in anyone's long game. People have the numbers on that. Some say he's just amping up his base. I've got no love for government, less for corporations, man. You know that. What are Parks folks saying, Paul?"

"They think it's a play to dismantle the whole parks system. Privatize everything. Roll back the EPA, Clean Air Act, water—everything down the tubes," Paul said.

Dreamweaver pounded the table and cursed, then he sat back and stroked his wide white beard.

"What do you think is going down?" Paul asked.

"Uranium," Dreamweaver said, growing calm, folding his hands across his belly.

"There's no market for uranium. Production is down around here," Paul said.

"That's right. It's all coming from Kazakhstan, Canada, and Australia, man. How do you think the president plans to fend off North Korean missiles? With his comb-over? I'll bet he's angling to rebuild our nuclear capacity. I mean, it's probably not his idea. He can't think that many steps ahead."

Reinhardt leaned forward. "To me what you are saying does not sound crazy, but it should."

"It's probably the Russians putting that in his head. I can't believe it's come to this. I've stopped reading science fiction. It's not necessary anymore."

"How did we go from pot hunters to warheads?" Sophia asked.

"Everything is connected," Reinhardt said, weaving his fingers together. He looked to Dreamweaver for confirmation, who nodded.

"The dead are pawns," Dreamweaver said. "Follow me."

He led them into the bus, and when they climbed the stairs, Sophia noticed how cool it was. "I thought it would be like a furnace in here," she said.

Dreamweaver pointed to a ramshackle contraption in the corner covered with a thousand copper fins. "Physics sends the hot air back to its brothers outside. They hate being separated. It's a good deal for everyone."

The bus still had its steering wheel and driver's seat, but the rest had been gutted and redone in the fashion of a ship's interior. The workmanship was exquisite. Wood strips curved along the interior. The knobs and vents were fashioned from brass. The original bus windows had been removed and reglazed with wood stiles and muntins. The glass itself looked as if it had been stolen from another age, warping the view just enough. The furniture was an eclectic mix of styles, at times Victorian, but also modern. On the walls were various maps, one of which was nearly identical to Cluff's map, without the marks showing what had been returned. Reinhardt tapped Sophia and pointed to it. She shushed him, but noticed a line of small unburnished pots with simple red designs on a narrow shelf. They were in amazing condition. "Where did these come from?" she asked.

"I made them," Dreamweaver said, walking past a bed at the far end of the bus that was draped lavishly in linen. Clustered nearby was a compact array of old computer and electronic equipment. He seated himself at the console and started reaching around, flipping switches like a pilot. The equipment came on slowly, amber lights and small square displays with their pulsing sine waves. The main monitor flickered on. It was the only piece of new equipment they could see in the whole menagerie. Dreamweaver had them turn around and cover their faces while he logged in. After the system whirred and chugged, they all heard a dial tone, then a chromatic sequence of telephonic whines followed by a beep-dong-beep and an alien array of cavitations: the buzz of a chainsaw, a spray of water, a broken klaxon, then silence.

The only thing that appeared on Dreamweaver's screen was code. He worked in a terminal window that occasionally showed recognizable words. He used no mouse, his fingers racing across the keyboard instead. Between processes Dreamweaver scratched under his beard and muttered to himself as he went deeper and deeper into the system. He checked some numbers in his small notebook and kept going.

"What are you looking for?" Sophia asked.

"Truth."

Sophia looked at Paul, who shrugged.

"I'm just guessing at the coordinates for the sites you said were on Cluff's maps. I don't trust online maps anymore. The USGS has been erasing cultural sites from their GPS data. It is essentially useless. I mean, this is nothing new, but now it's worse. I've got a buddy who found a database with proposed parcels for the retraction of the monument." He shook his head. "There's entries for the whole country. By the way, Alaska is a nightmare." He typed and searched and eventually wheeled over to the bookshelves on the opposite side of the bus and pulled a volume called *Four-Corners Geology*, thumbing through it as he scooted back. "Paul, look at this." He pointed to three places on a multicolored map showing the mineral layers. "There's uranium all through the parcels that are set to go up for auction." He snapped the book shut and tossed it on the bed, then pointed to some needlework hanging near his workstation. It showed a tiny fish about to be swallowed by a larger fish, about to be swallowed by an even larger one. "I hate to get all Deep Throat on you, but we've got to follow the money, and that's going to take a little doing."

Paul hung his head, and Sophia found a chair and sat down. Reinhardt said, "Somehow I thought this was going to be an inner journey."

Dreamweaver looked up at him. "There is no inner self. The exterior world is likewise an illusion. The way that can be named is not the true way, my friend. Perhaps the mystery of mysteries conceals itself in the word 'way.' If only we will allow these names to return to what they leave unspoken. All of it is *way*, man. All of it. There's no nouns, only verbs."

Reinhardt nodded, but he didn't follow.

"That's from Martin Heidegger, your countryman. He knew a lot more than he was able to articulate." Dreamweaver pushed his chair back from the console. "I'm going to data mine this cesspool, but in the meantime, you all need to stay hidden. But not here. I can't have that. Let me hit up some friends in Short Creek. For the moment, you can camp in the grove, but that's got to be short-term."

As they filed out of the bus, Dreamweaver asked Paul to stay behind. "Hey, brother. You want to tell me what's going on with you? I saw some documents that suggest you're in a whole mountain of trouble."

"It's complicated," Paul said.

"What isn't? I love you, man, but you can't stay. You're much too hot. Don't blindside me. You know how I get."

"I'll fill you in later," he said.

"Hey," Dreamweaver said, looking Paul in the eyes with so much intensity Paul had to look away, "a friend of mine used to say the first duty of a revolutionary is to get away with it."

—

When they arrived back at the public safety building, Dalton helped Raylene out of the Bronco. Once she was on the pavement, she took no help and walked straight through the front doors. As she passed through them, she said, "You didn't have to bring me here. I wouldn't have said anything. And besides, everyone treats me like I'm crazy anyway."

"Raylene, we talked about this."

"You talked. I didn't agree to a word of it." She took hold of the handrail and climbed the steps so slowly Dalton thought she might fall backward. At the top, she saw LaRae and said, "Your boss is in a sour mood."

LaRae looked up and smiled at her. "What flavor of sour is he today?"

"He's gone from sour apples to sourpuss. Something about our field trip. We drove all the way to Antelope Flats, and he wouldn't let me get out. Is there some place I could sit?" Dalton tried to help her to a chair in the waiting area, but she refused, seating herself in the chair next to it.

"LaRae, let's make Raylene comfortable. She said she might like to watch her show. Can we do that on a laptop?"

"We'll manage."

"Is Tanner here yet?"

"He's on his way."

"Send him back when he gets here."

"I've got a billion phone messages for you. One's from Germany." She handed him a stack of Post-its. Dalton took them to his office and started going through them. None were pressing except for the two messages from the real estate people, who said he didn't finish his online profile, and one from the NPS people working with Sophia Shepard. The message said she was on personal time this weekend and hasn't checked in. Dalton circled the license number of the truck with federal plates so he could call it in. There was no message about the NPS Jeep. There were three messages from Pete Ashdown that came in over a two-hour period. LaRae had drawn progressively angrier cartoon faces on each note. Dalton stacked them together and set them aside. The last was the message from Germany. Someone named Wolf Messer wanted to report his friend Reinhardt Kupfer missing. The note said he is not responding to social media.

Tanner knocked on the doorframe. "You ready for me?" he asked.

"Remember how this Cluff and Ashdown stuff hasn't been sitting right with me? Well, I just found Byron and Lonnie Ashdown dead out in Antelope Flats with a couple of trucks and an NPS Jeep that ought to be connected to someone, but there's no corresponding bodies. The vehicles were shot to pieces and flipped upside down like some giant's kid left his toys in the sandbox."

"You call it in?"

"Not yet. I'm still thinking about it."

"If it's on the monument, it's federal jurisdiction."

Dalton nodded. "It is on the monument."

"You look terrible."

"It's a war zone out there, or maybe more like cartel action."

"Weird place for drug trafficking. It's not on the way to anywhere. But Byron could be messed up in anything. Maybe he's a rat."

Dalton unlocked his phone, opened his photos app, and handed it to Tanner, who thumbed through the vultures, upturned vehicles, empty trailer, backhoe, M16, scattered clips, displaced earth, two human skulls, a pile of other bones, shards of pottery. Tanner handed the phone back, then raised his eyes to meet Dalton's.

"See what I mean?" Dalton said. "I've got a lot of loose ends to run down tomorrow. Could you head out there and get a cast of the tire tracks? I've got a missing person report on a park volunteer. I'm starting to think she's in the middle of this somehow. A German tourist has gone missing, too. Raylene says Bruce had been taking all of his Indian stuff back to where he found it. This thing is just a black hole, Chris. We're all gonna end up sucked into it."

Day Nine

High-precision isotopic analyses : The Freedom Jamboree :
Some quid pro quo : Everything's upside down : Back to the
Beehive House : Closed-door stuff

Scissors parked on the street in front of the trailer park. The sun was up but it hadn't broken over the cliffs. He removed the note he'd taken from the ranger's vehicle, which gave Sophia's name, address, and phone number. Her trailer was number nine. He snapped on a pair of blue nitrile gloves and waited until there were no cars in the street before getting out. He opened the trunk, slid a pistol with its silencer into the belt of his pants, and took a small blue pry bar, which he hid along the inside of his arm.

He followed the hedge along the back side of the trailers until he came to number nine. After knocking twice, he pried at the door until it popped open. As he entered the space, he could see that she worked at the small orange built-in table, where there were a few books stacked vertically, a laptop, and a pile of papers held down by a fist-sized chunk of pink quartz. He went through the papers, which were mostly photocopies of academic articles with titles like "Documenting the visitor degradation of Pueblo II NPS archeological sites," "Reconstructing regional population fluctuations using radiocarbon dates: A new case study using an improved method," and "Ethnographic study of the Wïiatsiweap hoax of 1937." Scissors put his finger on the word "Wïiatsiweap," took out his phone, and dialed.

"I'm in her trailer," he said. "She's got an article in here with the word you wanted me to watch for."

"Wïiatsiweap?"

"I wasn't sure how to say it."

"Read me the title."

He did.

"See if there's one in there called 'High-precision isotopic analyses of lead ores from Arizona by PR-DCS-LR: Implications for tracing the production and exchange of glaze-decorated pottery.'"

Scissors struggled to write fast enough. "Hang on. I'm still back at 'isotopic.'"

"Just find it."

He put the phone on speaker and set it on the desk, then went through all the articles and found it near the bottom of the stack.

"It's here."

"Look through the article. Are there any notes? What did she underline?"

He flipped through the pages. "She's got it all the way marked up."

"Is there a computer?"

"Yes, a laptop."

"Take it. I want to know what she's writing."

Scissors took the phone and went into a draped closet. Inside was a roller bag, which he unzipped and threw on the bed. He filled it with clothes and threw in the computer, told her what he'd packed, then asked if she needed anything else.

"Just her. I need to talk to her."

"Well, I'm working on it."

When he realized she'd hung up, he pocketed the phone and made his way out. He heard scratching, and the door bounced a little. A flutey old voice said, "Yoo-hoo," and through the window he saw a woman in a gaudy nightgown walking across the gravel drive with a cell phone to her ear. He ducked quickly to the hinge side of the door, his pistol out.

"I don't know," the woman said. "There's someone moving around in the trailer, but her truck isn't here."

Scissors stepped behind the door just as it opened. A dog burst in and ran to the far end of the trailer. The woman followed. Scissors slipped in right behind her and placed the gun against the back of her head. She went stiff.

He whispered, "Just keep talking. Explain that nothing's wrong."

"Well, apparently, there's nothing wrong," she said.

"Tell them it was just the curtains. Nobody's here."

She repeated what he said. He guided her through the rest of the conversation, then whispered, "Tell them you'll call when she shows up."

"I'll call when she shows up," she said.

"Tell them goodbye now," he said.

"Goodbye now," she said.

He took the phone from her, ended the call, and tossed it on the bed. "Keep your eyes forward and walk to the bathroom."

"But I don't even know who you are."

"What you imagine is better than anything I might say."

"Normal people don't talk like that."

"This isn't a normal situation."

"Killing old ladies won't do a thing for your reputation."

"You keep talking to me, ma'am, and I might have to test your hypothesis."

He pushed her into the bathroom, slammed the door, reached over, and yanked down one of the brass curtain rods from the window above the kitchen sink, which he shoved through the door handle. He replaced the gun in the back of his pants and pulled up the handle on the suitcase. The little dog blocked his way, growling and barking.

"Where were you three minutes ago, you terrible beast," the woman said through the bathroom door.

Scissors looked at the dog, then opened the small oven, and in a single unbroken move, lifted the dog with one hand, shoved it into the oven, and closed the door with the toe of his shoe. The dog's muffled barks brought a smile to his face as he stepped into the dappled morning.

—

From their hiding place behind two boulders, they watched a white Chevy Suburban crest the hill and come to a stop. The vehicle was caked in dirt, dented in two places, and a large round safety mirror hung from the back on a bent aluminum arm.

"That has to be them," Sophia said.

Paul shrugged. "It looks right."

"If your friend would have come with us, we'd know if this was our ride," she said.

"We got more than I expected from Dreamweaver," Paul said.

"I don't think this is the vehicle our assassin would have chosen," Reinhardt said. "It's too appropriate for this place. He is not a country mouse."

The vehicle pulled forward and the window rolled down. A woman with a nineteenth-century-style hairdo, high oval and wraparound side braids, stuck out her head. She wore a Bluetooth headset in one ear and cheap bladed sunglasses. No makeup. She wore a forest-green long-sleeved handmade dress with a Puritan collar. The fabric was plain with no print. The buttons were the same color and nearly invisible. "I'm looking for Dreamweaver's people," she called out.

Paul nudged Sophia. "You go. She won't talk to me."

"What? Why not?"

"I can go," Reinhardt offered.

They both said, "No."

"I'm U.S. government. They don't go for that," Paul said.

"Fine." Sophia stood and stepped into the road.

"He said there'd be three."

Sophia motioned for the rest of them. "They're coming," she said.

"Send the woman out first?" the woman behind the wheel said. "Cowards." She reached out to shake Sophia's hand. "Euphrenia Hamblin," she said.

"Sophia Shepard," she said, and they shook hands. Euphrenia's grip was strong and dry.

Reinhardt emerged from behind the rocks, with Paul following. When Euphrenia saw Paul, she pointed at him with her chin and said, "Dreamweaver didn't say nothing about transporting the federal government."

"Is that going to be a problem? He's hurt, and we're all in a life-and-death situation," Sophia said. "But if you want a rundown, okay. We've got a Fed, a German, and my mother is from Iran."

"Not helping," Paul whispered. He stepped out front. "I hope Dreamweaver explained our situation."

"He did," the woman said, "but it's on me for not asking better questions." Her jaw flexed, making the earpiece move. She drummed her fingers on the steering wheel, then looked over her shoulder into the back of the vehicle. "I can't bring some park ranger across Carver land, especially not during the Freedom Jamboree. It'll be his head first, then mine."

"Wait, wait," Sophia said. "If we turn up dead, this place is going to be crawling with FBI, all kinds of Feds. The German consulate is going to want to know what happened. Same with the National Parks. I'm working on a grant. When I don't check in, they'll all come through this place with a fine-tooth comb."

"What's a consulate?" Euphrenia asked.

"It's his government's U.S. office."

"UN?" the woman asked.

"Not UN, but we are in the UN," Reinhardt said.

"Also not helping," Paul said.

"Why? I see them misunderstanding NATO, but how could they . . ." Reinhardt complained.

"This ain't what I signed up for," the woman said. "I help neighbors, not outsiders."

"I apologize if I am making any assumptions about you from your clothes and manner," Reinhardt said, "but I ask you, which of these do you think was neighbor to the man taken by robbers?"

"What did you say?" the woman asked, lowering her sunglasses. "Are you quoting Scripture?"

"The priest, the Levite, or the Samaritan?" Reinhardt said, nodding.

"Oh," she said, pushing her glasses back up. "You're gonna do it that way, are you?"

"Well, which is the neighbor?" Reinhardt pressed.

"The one who showed mercy," she said through her teeth. "Get in."

The woman called to the children riding with her to come up front and let the guests take the back. A boy and a girl climbed over the seats, the boy riding up front, and the girl riding right behind the woman.

They drove in silence for the better part of an hour until they approached a cluster of a dozen houses, where the road straightened and came to a T. The road here was filled with trucks and tractors and children riding a homemade train pulled by a yellow four-wheeler. There were more people gathered here than any of them had seen in days.

"What's this?" Reinhardt asked.

"Carvertown," the woman said. "It's the Freedom Jamboree."

Paul leaned over and put his head in Sophia's lap. "Cover me," he said.

"Who are these people?" Sophia asked.

"You remember the folks that took over the tortoise preserve in Nevada? A guy blew off his own hand trying to dynamite a boulder so it would block the only road in and out?"

"Oh no," Sophia said.

"This is their celebration of freedom from the long arm of Washington, D.C."

Sophia looked around and saw the place was filled with cowboys, horses, patriotic bunting, "Don't Tread on Me" flags, tables full of food, a dunk tank, speakers on tripods, and a half dozen boys throwing hatchets into a log set up on its end. The road had been blocked off with giant wooden spools.

"Can we get through?" Reinhardt asked.

A fat man pulled up on a four-wheeler wearing a gray Stetson. Euphrenia rolled her window down. The man's face was white and sweat-speckled, and he was breathing through a nasal cannula and supply tube that curled down to an oxygen bottle he kept bungee-corded to the handlebars. He wore thick sideburns, and his plaid shirt was open down to the third button. A liver-spotted hunting dog rode behind him on its hind legs, its paws on the man's shoulders. "Road's closed," he said.

"I can see that," she answered. "Just wondering why, since this is the only road."

"Freedom Jamboree," the man said. "We've been closing down Main Street from here to the schoolhouse since—" He paused to suck in some oxygen. "Since Grover Cleveland was president. We reclaim the road to remind people it was Carvers that built all this, not our government overlords."

"How am I supposed to get home?" the woman asked.

"Y'ain't supposed to. Carvertown is closed. This here's a political statement. I know how you people like to stay out of politics and everything, but it pays to know what's going on."

"We're just minding our own business."

"Hasn't done you all much good," the man said.

"Not sure what you mean," the woman said.

"Your menfolk like to keep you ladies ignorant, don't they?"

The woman looked into the rearview mirror and made eye contact with Sophia, who felt a fire ignite inside her like a welding torch. "We're just trying to get to Short Creek," she sighed.

"I said, this road is closed."

"My kids are sick, and I need to get them home."

"What about those folks in back. They don't look like your people."

"They're cousins," she said.

A voice rang out through a bullhorn. "GOD THE ALMIGHTY HAS MADE OUR NATION. BY DEFENDING ITS EXISTENCE, WE ARE DEFENDING HIS WORK. THE FACT THAT THIS DEFENSE IS BOUGHT WITH INCALCULABLE MISERY, SUFFERING, AND HARDSHIPS MAKES US EVEN MORE ATTACHED TO THIS NATION."

"You see, the speeches have begun. We can't stop them now. You can wait or turn back."

The bullhorn voice continued. "IT ALSO GIVES US THAT HARD WILL NEEDED TO FULFILL OUR DUTY, EVEN IN THE MOST CRITICAL STRUGGLE. THAT IS, NOT ONLY TO FULFILL OUR DUTY TOWARD THE DECENT, NOBLE AMERICANS, BUT ALSO OUR DUTY TOWARD THOSE FEW INFAMOUS ONES WHO TURN THEIR BACKS ON THEIR PEOPLE."

The man stabbed his thumb toward the jamboree. "I think he's talking about your kind, sugarplum."

"I'm sorry, what?" Euphrenia said.

"Might be time for you polygamists to pay us back for draining the aquifer."

"Our wells aren't in Carvertown. Not even close."

"As you are presently trying to cross the aforementioned location, you should think about minding your p's and q's while you are here." The dog riding behind him barked twice. A huge Dodge Ram pulled up behind them and the doors opened.

"Why don't you all step out of the vehicle."

"We will not."

"Citizen's arrest, then," the man said.

The woman calmly turned to her son. "Enoch, why don't you hand me your daddy's Python. I can't reach for it and keep my eyes on this gentleman at the same time."

The boy leaned forward, opened the glove box, and pulled out a large nickel-plated revolver with black grips. The woman took it, cocked the hammer, and pointed it through the window. "This will go right through you, and the dog," she said.

The man's face went white, then he backed up his four-wheeler and waved off the others. Euphrenia put her Suburban in gear and pulled forward, pushing the cable spools out of the way, then she floored it and drove straight through the jamboree. There was room enough for her to speed through the middle of it all. Halfway through, as she hit some tables, food started splattering the side windows. There was a crash as a watermelon struck the hood and burst on the windshield in a spray of red and green. She uncocked the pistol and handed it to her boy and told him to put it back.

When they were clear of Carvertown, Paul said he was sorry for all the trouble. Euphrenia said she'd been waiting most of her adult life to have a reason to do something like that to a Carver, then she turned to her kids. "Not a word, you hear."

"I promise," the little girl said.

After a while the boy said, "That's the best thing I ever saw."

—

It was just after one o'clock when Dalton came into the HooDoo Diner looking for Stan Forsythe. He'd spent the morning doing damage control over what Stan had run in the morning paper. Stan was sitting in his usual spot, eating with one hand and scrolling through his phone with the other. When Dalton sat, Stan jumped and set down his phone but not the fork. The sun caught Dalton in the eyes, so he twisted the blinds until both their faces were in shadow.

"You've got a crime spree on your hands," Forsythe said preemptively, sitting up and wiping his mouth. Dalton set his hands flat on the table. "A suicide, missing people—how many now, three or four?—breaking and entering, a park ranger is under some kind of internal investigation, and Janey Gladstone had somebody lock her in the bathroom of one of her trailers this morning. Put her dog in the oven. Seems random, but I have a theory."

"Of course you do. It's in the paper."

"There's not enough evildoers here in our corner of paradise to heap up this much mayhem."

"I don't know. It's just not a picnic without the ants."

"This has gotta be an outside job."

"Nobody says 'outside job,' Stan."

"What did you come here for? Seems like you should be too busy for a social call."

"I need to put my ear to the rail. What are your crazytown internet friends saying about all this?"

Stan ate a couple fries and looked at Dalton with half a smile. "Am I under arrest?"

"No."

"Well, I think you're coming on a little strong." Stan sucked his Coke dry and tried to catch the server's attention.

"I need to figure out what's going on, or this thing's going to escalate."

"Going to?"

"Stan, for crying out loud. I just need some information."

"In a free market, that information comes at a price."

"You want to turn snitch?"

"I was thinking a little quid pro quo."

"Come on," Dalton said.

"Fine," Forsythe said, inching out of the booth, to show he was serious.

"Okay, what?"

Stan scooted back to his place. "We got Feds coming back through here like they did a few years ago? Do people have to start worrying about losing their property?"

"You know who's in the White House, Stan. Do you think that's what's going to happen?"

"I don't trust any of them. Your answer, please."

Dalton sighed. "No, there's nothing coming at us from the Feds. You think they'd tell me if they were? My turn. Raylene Cluff says some woman was hounding Bruce about his maps. It's been going on for months, maybe longer. What do you know about that?" He leaned forward on his elbows.

Stan's mouth pulsed a little, then he said, "Folks are saying we're going to see the monument downsized. All kinds of people are lining up at the trough."

"What kind of people?"

"Energy people, mostly."

"I need a name."

"There's a lot of chatter going around lately about Ishtar Energy. It's on the rise, run by a woman who used to work in the Obama administration. These operations are all fronts, done with shell corporations. It takes a while to trace them. Bruce told me his phone was ringing off the hook. My turn. Did Bruce kill himself?"

Dalton shook his head.

"Is that no to my question, or no, you aren't going to answer?"

"You're going to have to work that one out on your own or wait for the press release. These energy types, are they the kind of people who'd hire a killer?"

"Of course they would. These people run with the Dick Cheney crowd, even Ishtar Energy. They'll do anything for money. The plutocracy is real. It's a game to them, but you should see their community chest. It's all get-out-of-jail-free cards. Bailouts. Tax write-offs. You don't want to play with these people."

The server came and asked if Dalton wanted anything. He asked for a Diet Coke, to go. Stan shook his cup for a refill, but the woman had already left.

"My turn. What's going on with that fire at the Ashdown place in Cane Beds?"

"Trailer burned down," Dalton said.

"Were they in it?"

"Probably not."

"What about this rumor I'm hearing about how they got into a run-in with a park ranger out by Antelope Flats? The pictures are pretty grisly."

"What the hell? How did you hear that?"

"Remind yourself not to play cards, Dalton. Your poker face is terrible."

"Seriously, how did you hear this?"

"It's all over the internet. Some tourist from California posted a bunch of pictures last night. This is a good game. Let's keep going."

"How long is it going to be before the place is crawling with sickos?" Dalton asked.

"That ship has sailed. It's a snuff pilgrimage now. Geotagged and everything. #nocountryforoldmen," Forsythe said.

"Let me back up. Who's talking about Ishtar Energy? Is this your internet buddies or somebody local?"

"I can't say."

"That's not how this game works," Dalton said leaning forward.

"Look, he's local but he doesn't want anyone to know. But he knows. He's been inside their computer system, says uranium is driving the whole thing."

Dalton took a deep breath and stared at the ceiling, then leveled his eyes at Stan. "If this conspiracy nonsense is coming from Dreamweaver, I swear, I'm going to go supernova."

"You can't tell him I talked to you. Really, you can't. He'll take down my website, or worse . . . Dreamweaver's created a thing he calls porn bots. You don't even want to know what that is."

"I do want to know, Stan, very much," Dalton said.

Stan's face grew red and furious. "He's got this way of, rewriting your website code so all the pictures turn into porn."

"You could get more traffic," Dalton said.

Stan looked around for the waitress. "You think she's gonna get me a refill?"

"So, you know Dreamweaver's crazy, right? With a tinfoil hat and everything."

"The thing is, his tinfoil hat actually shuts down all Wi-Fi and cell signals in a twenty-foot radius. And by the way, crazy is not a synonym for wrong."

"He'd be useless in a trial."

"You'd never get him into a courtroom anyway. He'd be halfway to Cambodia by the time you got out there to pick him up."

Dalton dropped his head into his hands. "Stan, Bruce was a dentist who loved old pots. I'm just trying to figure out what happened to him."

"His pots are in the way of progress. All of us are," Forsythe said. "So, what's your next move? Wait until another body turns up?"

"I don't know."

The server brought Dalton his Diet Coke. "It's on the house. The manager says thanks for keeping it down this time."

—

When they drove out of the orange-and-almond-colored canyons onto the monochromatic plain, the children were asleep, the girl flopped back against the seat, the boy with his head upon the armrest. Euphrenia stroked the boy's hair as she drove. Reinhardt slipped in and out of sleep, rocking with the turning of the road. Paul cradled his hurt arm with the good one, his eyes closed and a meditative look on his face. Sophia watched everyone, her thoughts swirling.

At intervals, Euphrenia lifted her sunglasses, looked back, and caught Sophia's eye.

"Thank you for not abandoning us," Sophia said.

"You can't leave people in the desert. That's the first rule of this place."

"My mother is from a similar land. She always talks about hospitality."

"Where you from?" Euphrenia asked.

"I was born in the States. North Carolina. My mother is from Iran."

Euphrenia nodded. "You said that. Never been over there. Read about it in the Scriptures, though. It's Babylon, right?"

"That's Iraq. We're Persia. It's beautiful. Mountains and desert. It's a lot like Utah."

"We're in Arizona now," Euphrenia said. "Being from I-ran. Does that make you a Muslim?"

Sophia shook her head. "My grandparents are. When my mother left the country, she didn't bring anything with her. It was the Cultural Revolution. She hated what Khomeini's kind of Islam did to women, so it ended for her when she came to the States."

Euphrenia nodded, then turned for a moment to look out the side window. She took off her sunglasses and set them on the console. "Muslims are some of the only other people with families like ours."

"You mean polygamous?"

"That's right."

"I'd like to talk to somebody else who's living this way." Euphrenia took a breath. "Well, I'm supposed to take you to stay with Kimball Tillohash, but he's gone until tomorrow, so we'll have you stay with us. It's probably a good idea you didn't stay another night with Dreamweaver. He doesn't do well with people."

"I wasn't going to say it."

They both laughed.

"We owe Dreamweaver a debt. He helped us get shed of a vexation." The Suburban vibrated across a cattle guard, waking up Reinhardt and the boy at the same time.

"Are we here?" Reinhardt asked.

"Wherever you go is always here," the boy said. "Where you left from is always there."

"Hush, Enoch," Euphrenia said. "Nobody wants to hear it." She stopped the vehicle. "What he can do is get the gate," she said. Enoch hopped out and rode the gate until it was all the way open. When they drove through, he shut it, then rode the rest of the way to the house on the running board, hanging on to the side mirror.

They pulled in front of a massive three-story house with pale yellow siding halfway down one of the exterior walls. The rest of the exterior was bare ply-wood, weathered to gray. A stack of unused siding lay on the ground under the eaves, weighed down at intervals by three large plastic buckets. The windows were small and numerous and set at intervals that must have made more sense from the inside. There was no proper front door, only a series of side entrances marked by large double doors made of steel with narrow vertical windows, the kind of doors common in schools and hospitals. On the far side of the house was a lush and expansive vegetable garden and greenhouse. The rest of the land was dry, mostly untilled dirt the color of unmixed cement.

Euphrenia woke the girl and told her to get some help bringing in the groceries, then she turned and pointed to Sophia. "You can come with me. Enoch will take the men to the bunkhouse to get cleaned up." She switched her attention to the boy. "They can wear some of David Hamblin's clothes, if they fit."

They split off, Sophia heading toward the house, Paul and Reinhardt following the boy down a gravel path toward a barn with a flatbed truck parked in front of it and a Bobcat skid steer parked to one side. The afternoon shadows pulled long to the east.

The interior of the house was clean and open and beige. The kitchen held three refrigerators of different colors and models, and there were two massive stainless-steel sinks. Over one of them hung a spray nozzle like the ones in restaurants. Four girls in matching dresses cut from the same bolt of fabric and wearing nearly identical braids brought in the groceries and quickly sorted the items onto the open shelves. They fawned over two packages of generic sandwich cookies until Euphrenia said, "Whoever opens those is mucking stalls tomorrow."

The room was filled with the cloying but not unpleasant smell of fresh milk. At the long dining table, a small boy in a plaid shirt sat drinking lemonade from a Mason jar, which he held with both hands.

Another woman came through the unlit hallway into the kitchen. She was shorter and older than Euphrenia, with ruddy cheeks and a shock of silver hair flying out of her bun like a solar flare. She looked Sophia over, then set her jaw.

"This is a favor for Dreamweaver," Euphrenia said.

"Is she his girlfriend?" the woman asked.

"Don't think so."

"Daughter?"

"Probably not. They are in flight, Bethany. Dreamweaver asked us to deliver this one and her two friends to Kimball Tillohash tomorrow."

"Where are the others, then?" Bethany asked.

"The men are in the bunkhouse. They will be neither seen nor heard."

Bethany smiled, and her eyes lit up. "We like it that way."

Sophia laughed once, then folded her arms across her chest.

"You'll want to clean up," Bethany said, stepping forward to pinch the corners of Sophia's clothes. "How tall are you?"

"Five seven," Sophia said.

"I think we'll have something for you," Bethany said, then returned down the unlit hallway.

Euphrenia led Sophia up a set of carpeted stairs covered in a clear plastic runner with worn grooves. There was no handrail. The upstairs hall was full of doors, and she was led into an open room at the far end of the house. There were three separate sinks and mirrors. Each cupboard was marked with a strip of masking tape and the name of a different woman handwritten in marker. Beyond that the room had a shower, toilet, and a large bathtub with a sculpted seat and a dozen jets. Euphrenia crossed to the tub and began filling it.

"Oh no," Sophia said. "A shower will be fine."

Without answering, Euphrenia opened a cabinet and took out a bag of Epsom salts. "This will draw out some of the ache." She set the bag down and fetched two towels. "The body is a tabernacle. Caring for it is one of the small joys. Men are more interested in their bellies." Euphrenia sat on the edge of the tub as the water filled. She ran her fingers through the water, watching them pass back and forth. As the water rose, she added the salt and stirred it.

"I haven't had a bath in forever," Sophia said.

"What happened to you and your friends? It's certainly none of my business, but it seems like a calamity."

"I'm not sure, really. A man came after us, we're not sure who sent him or why. This seems like something from a movie, not real life. We're trying to figure it out."

Euphrenia nodded and tested the water, shaking her hand dry when she was done. "Being hunted by a man isn't nearly as rare as it should be. I'll leave you to your bath. You'll want to lock the door. This room is in one of the busier parts of the house."

"You've been too kind," Sophia said.

When the door closed, Sophia undressed, each layer of her clothing stiff with sweat and dirt. She folded each garment into a crude square and stacked them on the counter. Around the scoop of her neckline, at her biceps, and at the ankle there were sharp lines between her exposed skin and the rest of her. She set her wristwatch on top of the pile and lowered herself into the bath. The heat alone released her muscles, but when she remembered the spa button, she was unprepared for what it would do to her. If she had not been sitting already, she would have passed out.

Instead, she ran a soapy hand down her forearm, and cappuccino-colored suds branched down each side. She scrubbed her body, washed her hair, then drifted into a daydream, all around her the dull roar of the jets. She imagined herself in a living room, watching everything like it was a Netflix movie. She did not know the title when she clicked on it, but it had a 95 percent compatibility rating, so she let it begin. It was one of those screwball comedies, with love but not right away. You'd roll your eyes over the bickering, but that's okay, there's always some daffy fight. Think about the great ones: Cary Grant, Carole Lombard, Humphrey Bogart, Lauren Bacall, Spencer Tracy, Katharine Hepburn. There's a third wheel for comic relief and somebody to talk to. Sometimes it's a leopard, sometimes a German doctor. The next part of this impossible recipe is danger. Put them on the run. The audience leans in because it's all so delicious. The star-crossed lovers wander through the seedy underside. It's a cavalcade of weirdos and outlaws. Then suddenly you find yourself in a polygamist's Jacuzzi. It's not a movie, or a myth. It is simply a sentence you never in your life thought you would say, not even to yourself.

There was a knock at the door and Sophia jerked awake. A voice asked if she was okay. She said yes and turned off the jets, stepped out, and wrapped herself in a towel.

"We have fresh clothes for you," the voice said.

Sophia opened the door and an arm passed through a folded stack of clothes that turned out to be a single handmade dress and a pair of dark socks. The dress was unbecoming, but somehow it fit better than any clothes she'd ever worn. As she smoothed down the front of the dress, she realized there were pockets in it. Real pockets.

She wished there was clean underwear and thought for a minute about what it would take to hand wash hers. She abandoned the idea and dressed in what she had, then gathered her filthy clothes into a towel and coiled her hair up into a second one that was by the tub. When she emerged, three girls dressed exactly like Sophia smiled and reached for her hand.

"We could do your hair," one of the girls suggested.

Sophia refused at first, then seeing the dismay on their faces, she smiled and agreed. They led her to a room that had been set up for the occasion with combs and brushes fanned out on a low table. The girls sat Sophia down in a plush burgundy swivel chair. One girl came behind Sophia and removed the towel from her hair and began drying it carefully, dabbing, picking out tangles with the pointed tine of a comb. The other two girls sat cross-legged on the floor at Sophia's feet. One of them folded out a piano keyboard printed on heavy paper and began practicing imaginary scales, humming the notes as she played. The other girl shaped her nails with a wide black emery board. When she saw Sophia looking, she took her hand and started massaging it gently, starting at the center of the palm and working outward.

"Are you girls sisters?" Sophia asked.

"Yes, kind of," said the girl doing Sophia's nails. "We have the same father."

"I see," said Sophia.

"Had," said the girl practicing scales.

"He's dead now," said the one combing hair.

"Passed on," the girl practicing scales corrected. "Now it's just the mothers."

"And us."

"And the boys."

"I'm sorry," Sophia said, remembering what Euphrenia told her. "My great-uncle Zervan was married to two ladies." The girls looked at each other and grinned. "My aunts were Fatemeh and Nahid. I never met them because they lived on the other side of the world. My mother talked about them all the time." These girls reminded her of her own cousins, or really the stories of those cousins. Some wore the veil. Some of those who lived in France and England were punk. Sophia ended up as a person with no particular style at all.

The girl playing imaginary piano said, "Since Papa is gone, you're not here to join the family, are you?"

"Zina," the hair-combing girl snapped.

"Everyone is wondering," she defended. "It's better to ask the truth, right?"

"My friends and I were stranded in the desert, and a man named Dreamweaver helped us get here."

The girls nodded. "Dreamweaver is kind," the one doing nails said.

"And a little strange," Sophia said.

The girls covered their mouths and laughed.

Without asking, the girl standing behind Sophia began gathering her hair together. "May I oil it?" she inquired, and suddenly Sophia smelled a luxurious swirl of rosemary, pine, and a dozen other aromatic notes that reminded her of a mountain rain shower. "We make this here, in the barn," the girl said.

"Yes, please," Sophia said. "I would love to try it."

Once the oil had been combed through, Zina came back and began to braid her hair, humming quietly, and before too long Sophia drifted to sleep.

—

When Dalton finally got back to the office, he googled Ishtar Energy and learned that it was based in Las Vegas, but beyond the slogans about crossing frontiers and powering innovation, he learned very little. Some more digging revealed that Ishtar had been buying up natural gas and oil leases across the Four Corners area. He couldn't find anything about uranium. He sat back in his chair and looked around.

He had an old Army buddy who worked for the EPA in San Francisco, and he wondered if he might know anything. He tried the number he had in his phone, and it worked. After catching up, Dalton asked his question. "I'm working on something and the name Ishtar Energy came up. Can you help me learn a little bit more about them? Their website is useless."

"I can only give you what's in the public record," he said.

"I'll take it." Dalton could hear typing on the other end.

"Only thing that comes up on Ishtar is a 2005 environmental impact statement on a project near a cultural site in central Nevada. It mentions a CEO named Kristine Frangos, looks like she used to work for the Department of the Interior. Doesn't look like anything came of it. You could always get the full report with a Freedom of Information Act request, but since you're law enforcement I'll just send it to you."

"I appreciate that, but I don't want you getting in any trouble."

"There's a lot of closed-door stuff going on around here lately, and I don't like it. We need to kick a little and let in some daylight."

Dalton thanked him. "I need to get out there sometime, catch up, go fishing."

"I'd love to have you."

They hung up and the email came through a minute or so later. He skimmed the report and couldn't make sense of most of it. The name Frangos was in it, along with maps, graphs, charts, and the testimony of geophysicists and archeologists. A lot of it mentioned strategic oil reserves. Dalton googled "Kristine Frangos" and found a two-on-two professional volleyball player from Greece. The other was a CPA living in Bloomington, Minnesota. After that, there was nothing. He thought for a minute about the kind of money it would take to not come up on Google at all.

The phone rang and Dalton answered. "Sheriff, this is LaRae. Someone from the Beehive House called about Raylene, said she went to the bathroom an hour ago and won't come out. She's locked it from the inside, says it's not safe and they need to call Bruce."

"Tell Chris to meet me at the Bronco."

—

On their way to the Beehive House, Tanner said, "Seems like the next stage of this thing is going to involve a psychic."

Dalton chuckled, barely.

"You holding up okay?"

"I had an upsetting lunch with Stan Forsythe today."

"That guy's lucky he's his own boss." Tanner paused. "Is this a good time to talk about those tire tracks at Antelope Flats?"

"Tomorrow could be worse."

"Well they match the ones from the Ashdown place, except there's no spare. He replaced it. Treads almost brand new. I got pictures and a couple of plaster casts. You know, there were people out there taking pictures. I mean, like, recreational photography. I had to put up some tape and run them off."

"Forsythe said something like that was going on."

"I don't want to be a jerk about it, but I almost wish we were back at suicide," Tanner said.

"Don't say that. It's giving up."

"You know what I'm saying," Tanner said. "I should also say we found a rental car, a few miles south of there. I checked, and you'll never guess whose name is on it."

"German guy who went missing?" Dalton said.

Tanner grinned. "That's why you're the boss."

"Any sign of him? His buddy Wolf will not leave us alone."

"He was supposed to be on a sightseeing tour, but he left a couple days ago. The tour company made a point to say he forfeits the rest of his trip."

"God bless America," Dalton said.

They parked and went in. An orderly and a girl with blue hair were waiting for them. "Some woman came to see Raylene today. Dressed real nice," the orderly said, "told us she was one of her kids. Raylene flipped out, saying she didn't have any."

"She doesn't. Where is she?"

The orderly pointed to the bathroom.

"What about the woman?"

"She took off," the girl with blue hair said.

Dalton went to the door and knocked. "Raylene, it's me, Pat Dalton."

"How do I know it's true?"

"We listened to some pretty good Patsy Cline yesterday, didn't we?" he said.

"I know you, and this feels like a trap."

"You told me all about that picnic in the ruins you had with Bruce," Dalton said, then the door unlocked and opened. Raylene was standing there hugging herself. "Could you clear folks out of here?"

"Where's Bruce?" she asked.

Dalton knew that every time she learned what happened her heart broke again in a different place. "He's out on the monument today," he said.

"That man hasn't a lick of good sense. Once he gets all of that stuff put back, maybe I'll see a little more of him."

———

When Sophia awoke, it was dusk, and she was alone. She sat up in the chair and went to the window, where she saw the purple sky and dark clouds and a thin wash of orange in the west. Across the way, the bunkhouse was lit, and she saw Reinhardt move from one window to the next. Paul followed, shirtless, his bad arm across his stomach.

She found her boots and made her way to the front door. The cool air was full of cricket chatter, the unified pulse of the connected ones in the distance and the lone whirring of the isolated ones close to the house. As she crossed to the bunkhouse, one cricket stopped suddenly, and the silence felt like a malfunction. She let herself in and followed the voices to a spare, unfinished room furnished with four folding chairs and an old linoleum-and-chrome table from the 1950s.

Paul's back was to her, and it was covered with bruises, worse than she'd imagined. He raised both arms, and Reinhardt began applying some kind of homemade liniment to Paul's injuries, making him seize when he was touched.

"You doing okay?" Sophia asked.

"This place is Spartan, but now I have seen all the things," Reinhardt said.

"All of what?" she asked.

"All of the promises of my tour company—ranches, relics, and ruins."

"He's been telling me all about it," Paul said, "how he met you at Bryce Canyon, which was the call to adventure. He makes a good case. None of us are in the ordinary world anymore."

Reinhardt smiled and screwed the lid back onto the liniment jar. "Paul Thrift is a tough guy, but he needs to get to a hospital for X-rays and possibly an MRI. I can do very little with what we have here. I will look for a compression bandage." Reinhardt dried off his hands and disappeared through a door.

"It looks really bad, Paul."

"I know."

"I'm glad you're not dead."

"I'm glad you're not dead, either."

They looked at each other for a while, but Sophia's eyes went down to the bruises on his chest. "They've gotten worse," she said.

"I can safely say this is the most pain I have ever felt in my whole life. I'm sorry I got you into this."

"You didn't—" she started to say. "I mean you sort of did, but nobody could have known it would go this way."

"Reinhardt sort of thinks it was fate or something."

"Yeah, fate."

"But really, I'm sorry because I wasn't truthful with you, and I haven't come all the way clean."

Sophia sat cross-legged in front of him. "I'm listening."

"I'm currently on administrative leave pending a disciplinary hearing. I shouldn't have been driving my vehicle or been in uniform. There's no one out here to check, so when you sent me that text, I just suited up anyway."

"Putting that stuff back is serious business, Paul. You know the map those guys had, the one I stashed in your Jeep? The initials PT were written all over it, with dates from, like, a few weeks ago. What else is going on?"

Paul's face dropped and he shut his eyes. "Okay, so . . ." He tried to laugh, but he couldn't. "I have a friend in the regional office in Denver who got a look at the reports I've been sending. They were headed for a Senate committee hearing about the monument rollbacks. I was documenting the artifacts I'd returned with Bruce's help, presenting them as if they'd always been there, and apparently someone in the pipeline flagged them. My friend tipped me off that somebody at the top was planning to bust me for falsifying documents."

"But you were. I'm starting to wonder what they were going to do when they saw my research," Sophia said.

"Bury it. Same as my stuff. Stick it in a box in the basement."

"It would turn into an X-file?"

"Pretty much. When I heard about it, I drove to Denver and barged into a meeting that maybe I shouldn't have barged into. And"—Paul made a grand gesture with his hands—"abracadabra, now I'm under investigation for manipulating federal documents." Paul's eyes fell sad, and he shrugged.

Sophia remembered Dalinda talking about a problem in Denver. "So, Dreamweaver wasn't wrong."

"He rarely is."

"And when you didn't call in for backup?"

"I messed up again. Just trying to save my own hide," he said.

Paul leaned forward suddenly, and Sophia put out her hands to block him. "I'm not going to kiss you, Paul. Read the room, this isn't some kind of rom-com," Sophia said, looking around to see if Reinhardt was near.

Paul pulled a crumpled towel from underneath his butt, sat back, and handed it to her. "Sorry, this was really uncomfortable. And yes, it's definitely not a rom-com."

"How stupid does that make me?" Sophia said.

"Zero percent," he said.

Gunshots rang out from the big house. The first one grabbed their attention and the second sent them to the ground. A tremendous silence followed for a few seconds, then there were shouts. They crawled to the window and saw the silhouette of a man on a ladder falling away from the house. Lights came on at random, the man's legs bicycling in midair like in a Buster Keaton movie.

"I can't see him no more," someone shouted, "but I think I got him."

Reinhardt ran into the room. "It is our assassin," he said.

"Seems like the shots came from inside the house," Paul said.

The man dropped to the ground, rolled with the impact, and disappeared through the brush. Women gathered in the lit windows.

"There's no way it's not him," Sophia said.

Paul turned to Sophia. "You've got to tell them to stay put. Don't follow him."

Outside a boy shouted, "He's run off." Other voices scolded the boy and called him back inside. Through the window they saw someone following the man with the beam of a flashlight until he was gone.

"We should just tell him where the map is," Sophia said. "It's not worth it."

"Then he kills us anyway," Reinhardt said. "Why leave us alive?"

"Reinhardt's right," Paul said.

"Well, it is only an abstraction," Reinhardt said. "I haven't proven the idea empirically. I only know this from television."

"He'll be back. That house is full of kids. We can't stay here," Sophia said.

They heard people coming and turned to meet them. Three women, including Euphrenia, came into the bunkhouse and quietly shut the door. Sophia recognized one of the other women as Bethany. The third carried a double-barreled shotgun, and her left leg ended in an off-color prosthetic foot. "We presume he was here for you," Bethany said.

"I'm afraid so," Paul said.

"I was talking to her," Bethany said, gesturing to Sophia.

Sophia nodded. "It's true."

"Why in the world—never mind, we don't want to know. Did Dreamweaver say anything about this?" Bethany asked Euphrenia.

"He said they were in danger," she answered. "But there was a situation with the Carvers today, one that may have involved David Hamblin's pistol. Perhaps this is the fallout of that indiscretion. If that is true, then this would be my fault."

The third woman said, "We're still in Dreamweaver's debt."

Bethany cleared her throat. "We're pleased to see nobody is hurt, but whatever the cause of this intrusion, I'm afraid you people can't stay. Euphrenia will drive you where you need to go, but we'll need you to leave immediately."

The boy who rode with them earlier ran up, out of breath. "He drove off in a car."

"Get upstairs with your sisters," Euphrenia said, pushing him toward the house.

"He was holding his arm," the boy said, imitating the way it looked.

"I knew I got him," the one-legged woman said.

"The return is often more perilous than the journey," Reinhardt said.

"You shut it," Sophia said. "I'm serious. One more word, and I will not be responsible for what happens next."

PART III

Day Ten

King-size Butterfinger : Keyhole satellites : Outer
space : #herosjourney : Useless to archeologists : Two
old windmills : A breached contract : It's no Hilton :
"Ozymandias" : A low rumble : He could have gone around :
It's a Maslow thing

Scissors bolted the restroom door, then hung a plastic sack from the crank
of a rusted paper towel dispenser. The blue fluorescent lightbulb chat-
tered overhead as he unbuttoned his shirt and peeled it off. He examined
his right shoulder in the dull mirror by turning his knuckles toward the floor.
The skin was crusted in dark blood.

He moved the sack to the crook of his other arm, then took out a small
brown bottle of hydrogen peroxide, uncapped it, and peeled off the seal, placing his trash carefully back into the bag. He dispensed a length of paper towel
and doused it with peroxide, swabbing the wound, which hissed and foamed.
He turned his head to one side to deal with the pain, then he packed the towels
into the bag with everything else. He repeated this process until the wounds
were clean.

He pulled a cheap off-brand multi-tool from the bag, which he sterilized
with disinfectant wipes. He stood in front of the sink and peered inside the
wounds. With his teeth clenched, he dug out each of the three small 20-gauge
balls and dropped them on the floor with a tac-tac-tac.

In this way he administered to himself, being careful to gather the dropped
shot and store them with the other trash. He filled the ravaged holes with

antibiotic ointment and covered each one with its own clear adhesive bandage. When that was done, he pulled a king-size Butterfinger from the bag and devoured it in five decisive bites, then he pulled a new shirt from the bag and switched it out.

He cleaned everything with more wipes, put the last of it into the one bag, and tied it shut. Outside, a man was filling his car with gas while checking his phone. Scissors closed the door and waited for the man to drive off.

When he heard the car pull away, Scissors waited another minute, then came out cautiously, stowed the plastic bag in his trunk, and drove to his motel.

—

They came to a stop in front of a dark house five miles from the state highway. They had driven the entire way from Short Creek without talking. The dawn sky was no longer black, and the stars were nearly gone. There were no neighbors and no lights shining in the valley. Euphrenia sat behind the wheel as they climbed out, dressed in simple clothes with their laundry tied up in grocery-sack hobo bindles, their backpacks slung loose across their shoulders.

"You have to understand," Euphrenia said. "It's not you. They're thinking about the children."

"It's what I would have done," Sophia said.

"This is more than we had any right to ask for," Paul said.

Euphrenia nodded once and rolled up the window. Gravel spat behind her tires, her headlights wandering across the sagebrush as she drove away.

"Back into the frying pan," Reinhardt said, staring into the sky.

Paul adjusted his arm in the new sling Reinhardt had made for him out of a flowered pillowcase, and they all watched the darkness to see if any lights might come up the hill. From this spot, they'd be able to see anyone who approached.

After a time, Sophia asked, "Does this guy know we're coming?"

"Euphrenia said Kimball would be gone, but his truck is right there, so I don't know," Paul said.

They let themselves through the front gate and closed it behind them.

Reinhardt and Sophia separated to let Paul go first. As he approached the house, they saw the curtains part, then close.

"I guess we don't have to knock," Paul said.

In a few seconds the door swung open and a man with long gray hair stepped forward with a pistol in his hands. He spoke through the screen. "Who the hell is out there?" His voice was low and cautious.

"It's me, Paul."

"Dreamweaver sent me a message and told me to hightail it home, which is not the kind of message I was hoping for. You upset that man something terrible."

"We're in a lot of trouble, Kimball."

"Damn right you are." He lowered the gun and re-engaged the safety. The screen door opened and he stepped out. He was wearing a plain white T-shirt and gym shorts. He gestured to Sophia and Reinhardt. "I guess this one is the graduate student, and he's the lost German." He beckoned for them to come in, but he didn't look happy about it. "Quit standing out here in the open." He gestured to the stars with the barrel of the gun. "Keyhole satellites don't miss a thing."

Kimball led them into his small home, set the pistol on the kitchen counter, turned on a single lamp, then thought better of it and switched it back off. He gestured for them to sit, pulled his hair into a ponytail, and dropped into his recliner.

"Kimball is Paiute. Kaibab Band," Paul said. "He also works with me for the Park Service."

"I'm undercover," Kimball said. "And nobody works *with* you, Thrift. You're way out there, and nobody can walk fast enough to keep up. I have a question for you, not rhetorical. Do you know why this guy is after you?" Kimball asked. "The way Dreamweaver tells it, he's probably not a serial killer."

"He thinks we have one of Cluff's maps. The one Bruce was using to keep track of everything he had us putting back."

"He knows?" Sophia said. "I thought this was some big secret project." After a moment she said, "The initials—PT and KT."

Paul shrugged. So did Kimball.

"Knowing about this project and thinking it's a good idea is two different things," Kimball said, his unblinking eyes focused on Paul. "Which map is it?"

"The one that covers Antelope Flats up to Swallow Valley."

Kimball pulled the recliner lever so his feet rose up, then he scratched his chin and swore quietly to himself, drifting from English into Paiute.

"I know," Paul said.

"That ground took the Inter-Tribal Coalition five years to get into the proposal. The only reason for anyone to chase after that map is if they're trying to rework the deal so they can sell everything off."

"I know," Paul said.

"And the whole time we had to sit there and listen to them tell us that using the Antiquities Act to protect our land made us bandits seizing property in the night." His voice hardened and rose in volume. "How are we bandits when it's our home? We're losing White Pocket, Ovatsi, and Wïiatsiweap again," he said. "You don't have to be a genius to know you can't steal from yourself." Kimball shook his index finger. "When Cluff blew up the canyon on the way to Wïiatsiweap, my father wanted to kill that son of a bitch for deciding to jump in himself and protect our land without asking anyone. As per usual, every time something happens out there, they shut Native people out, tell us to mind our own business. You know, like we're not involved. They tell us these aren't our ancestors and then take over the story. They bring us to the table, then turn it around on us. Every time we make some headway, all of a sudden it's another table in another room in another building. And we are the bandits."

"We were just up there," Sophia said. "We can use the archeological work and the courts to stop them."

Kimball looked at Paul. "She's new to this, isn't she?"

Paul shrugged.

"Look at the Keystone Pipeline and Wounded Knee. Look at any of it, and you'll see that the game is rigged. They told us, 'Hey, don't worry, everything up there is already gone. No sense saving land that's already been ruined.' That's all anyone needs to know about white logic." He swore another oath and tightened his fists. "Look, you want to save this place. We're a little sick of saviors, but okay. I want to save it for different reasons. We've been trying to use white people's tools to tear down white people's walls. It works for a little while, then it stops. It always breaks down." Kimball scratched his arm and sat for a moment. "It needs to be said—everything in those ruins belongs to the dead. You shouldn't mess around with it." He sat back in his chair and exhaled. "Once people start taking these things off the land, everything turns upside down. People start falling off. That's what happened to us."

Reinhardt reached down and felt the curve of his pilfered pottery shard with his fingertips, wishing he'd left it in the lava flow. He recalled the warning he'd been given at the gas station. What had the old man told him, that all of this desert was made by water. Now this place is shaped by other forces, he thought.

"You got us down to almost nothing. We're not gone, but it's pretty damn close," Kimball said.

"I know, and I'm sorry," Paul said.

"I know you know, which makes me ask why you brought this trouble to my door?"

"Dreamweaver thought—"

"I know what Dreamweaver thinks. I don't want to talk about that lunatic right now. Why did you decide to come?"

Paul looked at Reinhardt and Sophia. "We had nowhere else to go. You know that."

"I do know. And you should know I don't have time for your white nonsense. I've got my own battles and I don't bounce back from this kind of bullshit anymore." He cranked the recliner forward and stared at Paul. "I'm going to regret this, but tell me what you need, then seriously, I'm done."

"Can you give us a place to rest for a few hours?"

Kimball sighed. "Yes, but you can't stay in the house. I don't need it getting shot up. There's a trailer on the corner of the property."

"Whatever you've got," Paul said.

"Thank you, so much," Sophia said.

"Aho," Reinhardt said.

"Aho?" Kimball turned to Paul. "Who is this guy?"

"He's the German, remember?"

Kimball gripped his forehead for a second, then stood. "Is he saying hello or thank you? Does he even know?" When Reinhardt didn't answer, Kimball walked them through the house, then led them out the back and across the open ground to a travel trailer parked behind a small cluster of juniper trees. Reinhardt looked to the sky for satellites. The eastern horizon was glowing.

"There's blankets and sleeping bags in the cupboards up top. Don't be seen."

"We won't," Paul said.

"I've got to be at work in three hours."

"I owe you one."

"I don't want that responsibility," Kimball said as he turned back to the house. "Seriously. I'm going to catch hell for this."

———

Sophia bolted awake at the sound of a rap-rap-rap on the trailer door. Kimball stood on the other side, dressed in a park ranger's uniform, his hair in braids, the wide brim of his campaign hat shading his eyes. She looked around the trailer. Paul was staring at the ceiling. Reinhardt slept facedown on the upper bunk with one arm dangling over the edge.

"Hey, Paulie. You're in a lot more trouble than maybe you're aware of," Kimball whispered.

"More than the Denver stuff?" Paul said.

"You told me you went out there and barged in on a meeting because of your reports."

"Yeah."

"What you did not say is that you broke in on a meeting with the secretary of the interior, and apparently that didn't sit too well with the muckety-mucks."

Paul looked over at Sophia, who lifted her eyebrows in resignation and shrugged.

"And apparently pictures of your gunfight at Antelope Flats have hit the internet, and some people are saying it's you who did it."

"That's ridiculous."

"They're saying you did it because apparently some BLM guys found

Cluff's missing map in your vehicle and your M16 at the scene with, like, three or four empty clips all over the place. Which seems believable because you're obviously a loose cannon who is trying to set up a smoke screen because you altered reports that were going to Congress. Then you lost your mind in a meeting you weren't even invited to. This is exactly the story they need to prove that this land needs to be in the hands of business guys."

"Those reports were supposed to reset the record." Paul said, then rolled over onto his back.

"Only the victors get to write reports," Kimball said.

"They were the only weapon I had," Paul said.

"Well, you burned all that down. To top it off, somebody on Twitter said you're secretly working for Nancy Pelosi. When they saw your Jeep on the internet, dispatch sent someone down, and they found it all. "They say the truth will set you free, but these days once something hits the internet, it's Katy bar the door," Kimball said. "Truth has no shelf life anymore."

"So, now we're back into the fire again?" Reinhardt asked.

"If there's something worse than fire, this might be it. I was on the computer since you got here. Eventually, I had to stop and get ready. Since it's obvious that I can't really do anything for you, I thought I'd at least bring coffee and fill you in." He lifted a thermos into view, opened the door, and set it inside on the counter. The door piston hissed as it closed.

"Some people think Paul kidnapped you all, or something. You two can fix that part of the story, but I warn you. Don't go out there online and look at anything. It's a dumpster fire. You'll lose heart. I already did," Kimball said.

"We should call the police," Sophia said.

"This is already on its way to the FBI," Kimball said. "Paul might want to turn himself in, but it could be a good idea for you all to split up."

"What do you think we should do?" Sophia asked.

"I don't know. This is your thing. I got you staying out here because I don't need my house getting teargassed."

"Do you think Wïiatsiweap is lost?" Paul asked.

"We've been losing that place over and over again for a hundred years. They stole everything out of there and gave it back empty. They're planning to steal it again. It was always gonna be that way. You all should move on, though. Anyone finds you here, my ass is grass. Who knows about this?"

"Euphrenia and Dreamweaver," Paul said.

"Dreamweaver talks, man. To everybody. Plus, he's crazy. You gotta stay away from him. You know he thinks Indian people came from outer space? Outer. Space." Kimball was close to shouting, but he backed off, said goodbye, and left.

When they could no longer hear his footsteps, Paul said, "I'm sorry."

Reinhardt climbed out of his bunk and poured coffee into mugs he found in the galley kitchen. He handed one to Sophia and Paul, each of whom sat, facing in opposite directions.

"I have one question for you," Sophia said after a long silence.

"Only one?"

"Is Wïiatsiweap the Paiute name for Swallow Valley?" She spelled out the word for him, then said she wanted to be sure they were talking about the same thing.

"It is."

"Have you ever heard of the Wïiatsiweap Hoax?"

Paul shook his head.

Sophia sat up straight. "How about Tom MacNair? Have you heard anything about him? Impresario, con man, provocateur from Glasgow?" Paul shook his head to all of it. "Well, Tom MacNair came through Ellis Island in the 1870s and ended up obsessed with these articles he'd read in the *New-York Tribune* about the pueblos out here. He wanted to see them firsthand, but it took him a decade to save up and make the trip. He sold everything he had and didn't plan on coming back to New York. When he got to Colorado, he found the sites had already been ransacked."

"Oh no," Reinhardt said.

"While he was moping around, he met a guy who said he was selling property that was full of Indian stuff. He must have told a good story, because MacNair bought the land for two hundred dollars, which was almost everything he had left. He got the deed and a map, and when he got there, he discovered he'd bought an abandoned mining claim fifty miles outside of Cortez. MacNair didn't throw in the towel, though. He spent years building a fake pueblo of his own so he could give tours. He'd charge people a dollar for every arrowhead they found. He called the place—wait for it . . .″

"Wïiatsiweap!" Reinhardt shouted. "Ha, I know this one."

"I said to wait for it," Sophia glared at him. "Apparently MacNair got the name from some penny dreadful adventure—"

"Written by Krause, Sigmund F. Krause," Reinhardt shouted. "I read it as a child. His stories of the Indian are very special in Germany. They are why I came."

Sophia and Paul turned and watched Reinhardt do a small victory dance, then they looked at each other, shaking their heads, feeling that somehow, in this moment, they were sitting peacefully in the eye of the storm. Each of them drank in silence when a buzz-buzz-buzz came from Reinhardt's bunk.

"What's that?" Sophia asked.

"My phone," Reinhardt said. "There is an outlet up there, so I charged it."

"Shut it off," Paul snapped. "But it's probably too late."

—

Dalton stopped at the front desk and set down his Diet Coke. LaRae handed him a stack of Post-its and said, "I'm just going to start by saying I'm sorry."

"For what?"

"I didn't put it on a note or anything, but someone from the FBI called and they want to assume control of the whole thing at Antelope Flats."

LaRae watched a smile creep across Dalton's face.

"So, you're not mad?"

"Are you kidding? This is the happiest I've been in two weeks. Can I just send them everything?" he asked.

"I told them when you'd be in, and they said someone would call. They're coming in from Phoenix."

"Vegas is closer. That's weird."

LaRae shrugged. "That's not how it works, I guess. Okay, I thought that was the bad news. You'll see from those notes that maybe I was wrong.

Okay, so the real bad news is Stan Forsythe has been calling, like, every ten minutes."

Dalton read the notes. "So the German isn't dead? He's over at Pipe Spring?"

"Apparently."

"Did you look up these Instagram pictures?"

She told him to come around, and she showed him a series of photos, all with the hashtag #herosjourney. As she clicked through them, Dalton said, "It just looks like somebody on vacation who crashed his rental car on the monument."

"Probably feels different to him," LaRae said. "So, we can put him on the not-murdered list, then. The German consulate would still like you to contact them."

"Okay. It's not like I have anything else to do. Call me when Chris gets in so we can close the loop."

———

Paul and Sophia gathered away from the trailer to talk. They sat on a curve of sandstone that rose from the earth like the back of a whale. They faced to the south, where golden light filled the desert valley, and they looked at the distant escarpment that held the Swallow Valley in secret.

"Back there with Kimball, what was that? It felt like you two were talking on a different frequency than the rest of us."

"It's complicated."

"No reason not to tell me. We're all in this together now."

"I've told you pretty much everything."

"Pretty much is not everything. You barged in on the secretary of the interior?"

"I thought it was going to be someone else."

"It doesn't matter what you thought. Like how returning those artifacts destroys the sites," she said.

"It's the only way to save them. We can't get into court any other way."

"But the site is useless now."

"To archeologists."

"This isn't a philosophical discussion anymore. People are getting killed over this, and I can't figure out why. We will say we've found the real Wïiatsiweap—but you know what that actually means, right?"

"I do."

"People will go up there and find a hoax just like MacNair's DIY pueblo. It's a forgery now because of your stunt with the bowl and the reports."

"I prefer to think of it as repatriation."

"You break a window, you can't glue it back together. Everyone knows that. It's Humpty Dumpty." Paul didn't follow, so she said, "All the king's horses and all the king's men?"

Paul nodded. "It's also called impermanence. The world is in flux. I worry that my whole job is to keep things from changing so the monument matches the photographs. Nature isn't static."

"This conversation is cute, but we're trying to come up with a plan that keeps you out of jail. Did Cluff have any human remains?" Sophia asked.

Paul got uncomfortable and fussed with his arm. "Some," he said eventually.

"Did you repatriate any of them?"

"We got the remains and some ceremonial items to Kimball," Paul said. "Cluff had one stipulation: keep government out of it."

"Neither of you are *non-government*. You know that, right?"

A shout burst through the trees, followed by a single short yelp that sounded like Reinhardt. Before Sophia could respond, Paul was already running south toward the trailer. "Get to Kimball's house and call 911." She took off east, watching Paul over her shoulder as he disappeared into the trees. Her pulse shot up, and she hoped she was running in the right direction. When she brought her head back to the front, she saw a clear space between two juniper trees and headed through it. The gunman appeared from behind one of trunks, his arms to each side. She tried to stop, but she crashed into him. His arms snapped around her, and he clinched her like a bear. She struggled to break free and he grappled her, spun her quickly, and clamped a hand over her mouth as they both dropped to the ground. She felt a prick in her neck, then a burning. She fought back, bit his hand, kicked. But in a few seconds, everything went black.

—

Dalton and Tanner got out of the Bronco in front of Kimball Tillohash's house. The sun was white-hot and the air brittle.

"What's he doing here?" Tanner asked. "Some German tourist can't be friends with Tillohash, can he?"

Dalton shrugged.

They stood at the fence and panned from side to side, slowly, like old windmills. The air around them buzzed with insects. The gossamer filaments of a dozen spider webs lifted on the breeze and blew across the road.

"We gonna sniff him out or set and wait?" Tanner asked.

"A little of both."

They stood for a few seconds, then Tanner pointed at the webs. "That's baby spiders."

Dalton shivered and shook his head. "Don't talk about it."

"Think about what it takes to live like that, just letting the wind take you wherever it wants to."

Dalton sniffed twice, then said, "Karen wants me to sell the house."

"I heard."

"I was going to, since it's just me living there. But watching those things blow around makes me think I'm going to buy her out. Eventually the kids are going to want some place to come back to."

Tanner cleaned his sunglasses. "We came back."

"Yes, we did." Dalton pointed to a duck-shaped sandstone formation. "Last photo this guy posted was of Duck Rock through what looks like a trailer window. It's got to be on Tillohash's land somewhere. Then there were shots of his wrecked car out by Dutch John's Butte, then some coyotes at night. Seems like he was at Entrada Wash for that. Then vacation photos. Bryce Canyon. A chuckwagon dinner. Vegas Airport. Selfies on the plane. Before that, some pictures of him dressed up like an Indian. He had a whole headdress and everything."

"That's weird."

"Well, it's different. The dress-up pictures were from back in Germany."

They heard voices through the bushes. Tanner unsnapped his holster and kept his hand on the grip of his sidearm. They moved together toward the south side of the house so they could see around the trees. They saw two men in plaid work shirts and Carhartts, one with his arm in a sling and the other sitting in a lawn chair holding a bag of frozen peas against his head. They were in the middle of a frantic conversation.

"We're looking for Reinhardt Kupfer," Dalton said.

Paul turned slowly. Reinhardt's hands shot up, and the bag of peas fell to the ground.

"Two for one," Tanner said.

Paul said, "My name is Paul Thrift. I'm ready to go with you, but our friend has been kidnapped. Could you please get this out on the radio?"

—

Sophia woke, trying to gasp. Her mouth was taped shut, her wrists and ankles also bound. She panicked until her brain sensed the trickle of oxygen making it through, which gave her a fragmented sense of the space enveloping her: some steel point digging into her back, her face against a coarse mat, everywhere the smell of fuel. She kicked, and when her feet met the enclosure, the counterthrust bashed her head against a box.

After a minute, an explosion of whiteness. The reaching arms of a tattered black silhouette. A failed scream. Everything black. Then a duration. The smell of onions. A headache. She was no longer in the car. Beneath her was the softness of a bed, strange pillows, and a blanket around her. Two voices: male, female. The female had questions. The male gave short answers.

"You were referred to me as a cleaner, one of the best, but your performance does not measure up to your fee. Everything you're doing now is not work I hired you for, it's you cleaning up your own vomit."

"You wanted me to hire some locals to shake down Cluff—well, it's their vomit. If you would have started with me, we'd be done by now."

"I needed more degrees of separation. And your contract was very specific. I paid you on your terms, and when the situation changed, we renegotiated.

You're asking to be paid in full for failing to deliver the maps. That is—what would you call it?—a shakedown. It's beneath you, Nicholas."

"I was afraid you were going to say something like that."

"And yet you still asked."

Sophia strained to listen, which sent a hot arc of pain through her neck. The conversation halted. She heard them approach and felt them hovering over her. She blacked out again.

A second duration, then the blanket came off and the man sat her up. Orange light slanted through the west windows. The red digits on the alarm clock swam out of focus, then sharpened to read 7:32 p.m. One of them was wearing a Batman ski mask that was too small, the eyeholes stretched out of shape. She was handed a bottle of orange Gatorade with the cap off.

"Scream, and it's lights-out again," the man said.

She nodded, and he pulled the tape off in one clean jerk. The pain of this distracted her from the throbbing in her head and spine. In the silence that followed, he let her drink. It was room temperature but she couldn't stop.

"A little at a time," the woman's voice said.

He took the bottle away, and she fell back to sleep.

After the third duration, she awoke to an argument at full pitch. She lay still, feigning sleep.

"I will not pay you for something you did not produce," the woman said. "You are the one who has breached this contract."

"Breach?" he shouted. "Breach? What are you going to do, call your lawyer?"

"You need to keep it down."

"Silence is the only protection you've got."

"You'd be surprised at the resources I have at my disposal."

"Disposal is alright with me," he said. Sophia heard the click of a gun's hammer, then nothing. She clenched her eyes.

"Go ahead and put a bullet into everyone. We won't bleed money."

"It'll give me some satisfaction."

"You're on a losing streak, Nicholas. Which means it's time to walk away. From what I understand, if you had learned not to double down when your luck turns, you'd still be in a cape and sequins, with a show of your own at the Luxor."

There was another long silence, then the sound of a door opening and slamming shut. After a few seconds, Sophia opened her eyes. The boiling in her head was no longer rolling. The room had stopped colliding with itself. She raised herself on one elbow and looked at the dull, custardy walls and the strange green foliage climbing out of the blue curtains. She rolled over, saw a woman sitting in the upholstered motel chair, her legs crossed at the knees. She wore caramel-colored sling-back kitten heels, and she covered her face with a fox mask made of felt and fur, which she held on a thin, elegant baton. The fine whiskers caught the last of the sunlight.

"I must apologize for the theater," the woman said. "We are finished with that brute."

"Was he planning to kill us?"

"All brutality is, at its core, cowardice. And cowards often bluff."

Sophia tried to sit up all the way, but her head was pounding too much. She fought to get there anyway. Once she was upright, she said, "I've seen him in action."

"Violence lacks nuance. It is a shell game. The noise before the defeat."

"It seems like he's the hands, but you're the brain."

The woman smiled.

"What do you want from us?"

"Us? No, I am only interested in you, Sophia Shepard."

"I'm nobody."

"A clever literary allusion, but I don't buy it. You have a BA in linguistics from Duke, an MA in cultural anthropology from the University of Chicago, and soon you'll have a PhD from Princeton with a dissertation on the mechanics of site degradation occurring on NPS- and BLM-managed cultural sites. I've read your current draft. You're a disruptor."

"You have my dissertation? Who are you?"

"Ms. Shepard, your work is promising. You are arguing for archeology to take a stand against a hundred years of government intervention. You have a reputation as a firebrand, calling out a certain distinguished male scholar last year during a symposium. It's not easy to speak truth to power. We're not even dealing with power here, just quaint, clumsy, ham-fisted ideologies. It's nonsense, isn't it, that we should try to preserve anything unimpaired for the enjoyment, education, and inspiration of the unwashed masses. It's all one great curio shop for them." She bobbed the toe of her shoe and stared at Sophia. The woman's eyes darted around from behind the calmness of the mask. "I would hate for this to seem like some kind of oral defense, but I am intrigued. What do you think our government would have done with your work once you put it out into the world?"

Sophia was too groggy to respond coherently, but she was seething.

"I used to work for the Department of the Interior. Let me help you with that. I can say with absolute certainty that they would have redacted everything, gagged you. Your academic career would have been over before it started. They'd have offered you some G6-level position and stuck you in the basement. And the worst part about it is, when you took the grant money, you agreed to it. This administration has no compunction. They will bury you. It's that simple."

"But I have only been hunted down by you and your pit bull, not the government."

"This is all sleight of hand. The government only cares about what the argument of energy independence will allow them to get away with. It is the latest incarnation of the military-industrial complex. But let's get back to you. I assume you didn't get into this work to serve men in a bureaucracy. When I read your ideas, I see that you still believe in truth."

The woman tilted her head slightly, cocking the mask's ears to one side. Sophia became self-conscious of her clothes, the prairie dress and low-cut hiking boots. Her vision was collecting and solidifying, and she looked at the windows, the locked door, the bolt and chain. During the silence, the air conditioning unit shuddered on.

"Beauty is truth, truth beauty."

"Fancy," Sophia said.

"That is all ye know on earth, and all ye need to know. My recently departed operative doesn't believe in truth. He is a failed illusionist, sawing ladies in half, freeing himself from strait jackets, guessing the correct card. He has told me that people only believe in what they have paid for. I have learned through sad experience that it is impossible to make this equation work in reverse."

Sophia sat a little taller. "This is monologging, right?"

The woman paused, the stillness of her mask amplifying the tension. "I am working on a possible future for you and me, and a way for the two of us to be free of these men and their noise."

Sophia raised her bound wrists. "All this duct tape doesn't feel much like freedom."

"You are a flight risk."

"Abduction is a trigger for me."

The woman laughed, then she rose from the chair. "Let me make you comfortable," she said. With the mask in one hand, she helped Sophia hobble from the bed to the other chair. She opened a leather briefcase, removed a photo album, set it in Sophia's lap, and opened the cover. The first image was a marble relief of a woman's face set atop a frieze of repeating smaller faces. She could see that the work was in the living room of a vast, open, modern home.

Sophia's face froze. "This is the Woman of Wakara. How do you have this picture? Where is it?"

"I own it," the woman said, sitting again.

"Nobody owns it. It was destroyed in 1990 during Desert Storm."

"That is the cover story."

"Explain that."

"Why don't I free your hands so you can continue reviewing these photographs," the woman said.

—

Reinhardt sat in an office chair in the sheriff's department, a paramedic shining a penlight into each eye.

"I'm okay," Reinhardt said. "No need to continue doing that."

"Once an hour," the paramedic said. "Sheriff says you're safer in custody or you'd be in the hospital after getting knocked cold like that."

Dalton came in and spoke with the paramedic, who said Reinhardt had a pretty good lump and probably a mild concussion to go with it. "Don't let him sleep for a while."

Dalton sat in the chair across from Reinhardt. "You're lucky to be alive, Dr. Kupfer. That guy mostly leaves behind bodies. You hear what he said about sleeping?"

Reinhardt nodded.

"Okay. If you need anything let me know. The FBI is working this case now, but just for my own edification, how did you end up in the middle of all this?"

"It's silly to say out loud."

"Try me."

"I was on a quest."

"Who sent you?"

"Me. I sent myself. I was trying to follow my bliss."

Dalton sighed. "Okay. And you don't have any idea why this guy would take Sophia other than she had a map he wanted?"

"That is correct. It's a map of a place called Wïiatsiweap, a city hidden in the cliffs. I knew about it from a book called *The Rifle and the Tomahawk*, by Sigmund F. Krause."

"But the FBI has that map now," Dalton said.

"Tell them to be careful. Apparently, there are some politics involved."

"There's a little politics in everything."

"I am German, so that makes sense to me, but we should try to focus on Sophia. When this man finds out she does not have the map, we could lose her."

"Can you describe the guy who was after you?"

"He was plain with unfashionable clothes, like a golfer."

"Anything else?"

Reinhardt shook his head. Dalton led him back to the holding cell uncuffed. Paul was inside sitting in a half lotus, meditating. As Dalton unlocked the cell door, Paul opened his eyes.

"It's no Hilton, but the security is good," Dalton said.

"Any word on Sophia?" Paul asked.

"Nothing yet. We've got roadblocks at the state line in both directions. I'm going to guess he didn't take off with her across the Grand Canyon."

"He might not have taken her anywhere," Paul said.

"Your friend said he was after Cluff's map. How'd she get hold of it?"

"Should I be talking without a lawyer?" Paul asked.

"You want your girlfriend back?"

"She's not—never mind. She got the map off those Ashdown brothers, right before they got shot."

"With your weapon?"

"Apparently. But I didn't—"

Dalton's radio came alive. "Dalton, this is Tanner. I just picked up a guy on Main Street. He's got a bandage on his shoulder. He's in a pair of boxer shorts and that's it. No ID. Won't talk. I'm just about there."

"He match the description of our guy?"

"Not really. He looks like one of those dudes who had a peyote thing go south on him."

"Not tweaking or anything?"

"Nope. Just sitting there."

Dalton ended the radio conversation and turned back to Paul and Reinhardt. He explained how everything had turned federal and what that meant for him. He explained that the FBI was using the state police and marshals, but leaving the peacekeeping to him. He asked Reinhardt again if he saw the guy who hit him.

"I did not see him, but it had to be the crazy person who was pursuing us," Reinhardt said. "It is difficult to knock someone unconscious with one blow. He got me right in the carotid. I must have hit my head when I fell. I do not think it was luck."

Dalton left them, and Reinhardt lowered his head into his hands. Paul stretched his arm and rotated it. His face was grim. He stood and took hold of one bar and used it to stretch his shoulder. Reinhardt watched him make each movement. "They asked me about you. The story they tell is like the one you have told us, but with more to it. They thought you were the one who did this until Sophia was kidnapped. So, that is lucky."

Paul laughed. "Oh, good."

"But did you help bring these calamities upon us?"

"I don't know, Reinhardt. Maybe. I was just trying to save what's left out here. I thought the end justified the means."

"The world does not change to suit us. You know Sophia saved me, then you saved us, then I put your arm back in its socket, then Dreamweaver, then Euphrenia, then Kimball. Problems will always be with us, but so will the helpers."

"Do you think he's going to call and try to negotiate a trade with us?"

"I don't know, Paul."

They sat in silence for a time, then stood and sat again on different benches. This cycling went on for a while until a door opened and a sheriff's deputy brought in a man who was naked but for a pair of plaid boxer shorts. He entered the room like a disgraced fighter, his head bowed and hands cuffed behind his back. After the deputy pushed him into the cell, the man crossed to the opposite side, where he stood, facing away from Reinhardt and Paul until the deputy left.

The moment the hallway door closed, the man began to hunch and gag, and before the two of them knew what to do, the man spat something heavy onto the floor of the cell. Then he rose, adjusted his posture, and turned theatrically to present himself.

Reinhardt recognized him as the man he'd met on the road.

"It's you," Reinhardt said, looking at Paul for confirmation. "How?"

Scissors tilted his head and smiled. "How, indeed. Paul Thrift, who used up one of his nine lives. How many do you have left?"

Paul stood and took a defensive posture, which he dropped when the pain in his ribs and shoulder flared. Paul pointed to the bandage on the man's shoulder. "So that old woman took a chunk out of you," he said.

"A shoulder for a shoulder," Scissors said, gesturing to the way Paul favored his bad arm.

"I meant how did you know we were here?" Reinhardt asked.

Scissors lifted his eyebrows and said, "You can thank the loudmouth newspaperman at the diner for giving you up. But hush for now. Let's not scuttle our reunion before I get the chance to tell you where Sophia is."

He crossed to the bench and sat and twisted his body to one side and shoved his rear end through the loop of his arms. Once his arms were in front, he picked up the packet he'd spit out. It looked like a condom, which he tore open to reveal a package of small tools and a handcuff key. He quickly released himself and set the cuffs on the bench. He checked the bandage on his shoulder, then turned to Reinhardt and said, "Give me your clothes, and I'll tell you what you want to know."

"My clothes?"

"I can't take his," he said, pointing to Paul's legs. "He's a stork."

"Now, wait a minute," Paul said. "We're supposed to just let you—"

"You have your agency, but if you rat me out, I swear . . . your friend will be lost."

Once the clothing trade was complete, Scissors said, "She is nearby, in a place called the Blue Motel."

"Don't you want the map in return?" Paul asked.

Reinhardt hugged himself and tried not to shiver.

"No," he said. "That is no longer of interest to me. Sophia is with a woman named Kristine Frangos, who is, at the moment, propositioning her. If you hurry, you'll catch them both there. Frangos won't dare try to move her for another few hours."

"Why are you here?" Paul asked.

"Frangos is behind all of this. She has ties that go all the way up. If you hurry, you'll be able to expose her. I can't be the one who does it. Beyond that, I have my own plans to mop things up. The artifacts Cluff had were penny ante compared to what this woman has locked up in her house."

"Why would you help us, after everything you did?"

"Frangos made a lot of mistakes, and she left me exposed. So, I've decided she doesn't get what she wants. Not this time."

"That just leaves more questions," Paul said.

"Too bad. I'm done." Scissors stood and adjusted his ill-fitting new clothes.

He pocketed the key and picked up the tools, which he used to open the lock on the cell door. "Give me fifteen minutes before you start yelling or I'll go straight to the Blue Motel and end it." He shut the cell door, picked the lock to the hallway door, and was gone.

Paul and Reinhardt both looked at the clock. It said 8:17.

"What do we do?" Reinhardt asked. "Wait until 8:32?"

"I say give him three minutes to get out of the building, then we start shouting."

"Good," Reinhardt said. "I'm freezing."

—

Sophia came back from the bathroom and sat in the chair. She reopened the photo album and turned the pages backward and forward while the woman looked on. There were Chinese ritual bronzes, Olmec calendars, sarcophagi, funerary urns, jade masks, a nearly intact Mesopotamian astronomical calculator, Vietnamese copper gongs, and Syrian mosaics. "None of this is possible. One person couldn't—" Sophia said.

"You're right. Not with the resources and restrictions normally available to a museum or university, certainly not a national park. That said, capital is easy to come by. Interesting ideas are not."

"So, let me get this right. You remove artifacts from sites before you—"

"Rescue," she interrupted. "I rescue these things."

"But what you do to rescue the artifacts destroys the integrity of the sites."

"Their destruction is assured, but I am able to make use of magnetometry, ground-penetrating radar, and 3-D modeling. We digitize everything, put time in a bottle."

"Why do the maps matter to you?" Sophia asked.

"I need for there to be only *my* maps, *my* reports. Anything else would undermine the reality I am trying to establish. This way I can keep what matters and sell the rest."

"Without provenance."

"Which is what the market prefers."

"Once it's gone, it's unrecoverable."

"The other option is to squirrel it all away in drawers until everything is lost through neglect. This mad dash to save disappearing people didn't begin with the virtuous Victorian elite. Phrenologists wanted skulls. It was the science of racism. The better angels of the age wanted to save whatever they could before it was gone, by any means necessary. What I'm offering you is the chance to do more than futz around with history, Sophia. Look at those photos, what I have been able to save will stand the test of time. I can throw the land to the jackals, which is all they want anyway. Do you know the poem 'Ozymandias' by Shelley?"

Sophia nodded. She thought of her professor's obsession with it.

"Then you'll know that Ozymandias was the king of kings. How often a man believes he is the alpha and the omega. Sophia, you have seen this a million times. Men build monuments to themselves, and when they have gone, the ruins shout, 'Look on my works, ye mighty, and despair.' How ironic, really. I want to give you the chance to preserve history, and it won't require a vow of poverty or the subjugation of yourself to the venalities of bureaucrats. We will be Amazons."

How strange, Sophia thought. Yes and no to everything. Point by point, she was right about men and bureaucracy. Add it all up, and this woman was some combination of a supervillain and a CEO, the kind of crazy that needs to be locked up. She was as ludicrous as she was terrifying, well dressed, but in the end just banal evil.

Sophia wanted to give this woman a monologue of her own. Instead, to buy herself time, she leaned forward and said, "I'm listening."

———

The exact moment the minute hand clicked from 8:19 to 8:20, Paul and Reinhardt both shouted simultaneously as loud as they could. No one came right away. A minute later, Paul crossed to the door and pushed it open. "Hmm," he said.

"Be careful. They might think we're escaping," Reinhardt said.

Paul crossed to the phone on the wall and dialed 0. "Hello, this is Paul Thrift. I'm back here in holding—"

"How did you reach the phone?" the woman asked.

"That's part of why I'm calling. The guy they brought in just released himself. Bad news is he's the guy the FBI is looking for. We'll be back here, waiting." He hung up and joined Reinhardt on the bench.

Reinhardt's face fell. He placed his hand on Paul's shoulder, and they sat together saying nothing until the sheriff and deputy burst into the room, their guns drawn, their eyes scanning the cell. "Where's the guy?" Dalton asked.

"Like Paul said, he released himself," Reinhardt said.

"He what—how?"

"I'm not sure I can explain what happened. He brought some tools," Paul said.

"But he was nearly naked," Dalton said.

"I think that might have been a distraction," Paul said.

"He regurgitated the tools," Reinhardt said, pantomiming how they came out of his mouth.

"We can keep telling you what happened, but it won't clear anything up," Paul added. "It was for sure the guy who's been after us. He came in here to tell us Sophia is in the Blue Motel. Apparently, he's got a bone to pick with the woman who has her."

"The Blue Motel in Fredonia?" Dalton asked.

"I'm pretty sure that's the one."

"Chris, can you get this to dispatch?" Dalton addressed Reinhardt, "Did he steal your clothes?"

Reinhardt nodded.

"You got that, Chris? He's wearing the German's work clothes."

Tanner nodded and left. Dalton came up to the cell. "Thrift, I don't know what's going on, but you've got a lot of heat on you. I'm going to take your friend so he can help with the description. We'll get this figured out."

"I get it," Paul said, leaning back against the wall.

A low rumble came through the floor.

"What's that?" Reinhardt asked.

A voice came across Dalton's radio. "This is just crazy—there's been a huge accident on the highway, right outside in front of the office. I can see it from my desk. It looks like a tour bus."

"I'm an EMT, I could help you out," Paul said.

"You know they'd string me up if I did that."

"Then take him. He's a good doctor."

———

The tour bus was on its side. They were looking at the wheels and drive train; the roof was facing the other side of the road. Cars were backed up on either side, tourists with their doors open, standing in the summer heat, shielding their eyes, snapping photos, their vacations ruined.

People emerged from the windows that were now facing skyward. They stood atop the wreckage, silhouettes with the sun behind them.

A voice on Dalton's radio told him the volunteer fire department was ten minutes out. He turned to Reinhardt, who was now wearing a pair of running shoes with no socks, shorts, and a Kane County Sheriff's Department T-shirt, and told him to run back to the station and ask LaRae to get the ladder. Dalton cupped his hands around his mouth and shouted to the people on top. "It's higher than you think. Stay put, and we'll get you down."

LaRae was on the radio when Reinhardt got there. "Get the German to the ladder out back."

"What happened?" she asked.

"People said some guy tore out of here in a Buick, cut off the bus, and that tipped it over. And I'm sorry, LaRae," Dalton said, "it looks like he took your Regal."

LaRae stood motionless for a few seconds, with the microphone next to her mouth, then she came around the front of the desk and looked out the front window. When she didn't see what she was hoping to see, she steadied herself on the desk. "Well, shit," she said. "I had that paid off." She took another second to feel the loss, then she gave Reinhardt a key and told him the ladder was locked up out back.

Reinhardt followed her instructions, and with some difficulty, came back through the building with the ladder.

"Oh, honey, you could have gone around," she said.

Reinhardt handed her back the key, she opened the front doors, and Reinhardt made his way to the street. An ambulance had arrived, but no other help was there. Dalton waved him over to a spot near the rear of the bus. They pulled the ladder into place, and people began to clamber down. Reinhardt recognized some of the faces and circled around to the front, where he saw the Ranches, Relics, and Ruins card taped to the glass.

———

"Here's the thing," Sophia said, her voice elevating. "I am still a little bit whacked out by whatever it was your imp stuck into my neck, but I don't think I'm making my point. The artifacts on their own are meaningless. They need a story."

"You're coming across fine—why does an artifact have to mean anything?"

"Because then it's just a thing," Sophia said. "The point is to know more about the people who made it and used it."

"I know you know this, but let's be clear. We favor our own stories over the ones Indigenous people tell. I am interested in beauty for its own sake. Meaning is uninteresting, and our ridiculous need for it has caused us to dismiss many things as unimportant because their meaning does not manifest itself easily: poems, trees, abstract expressionism. How many times have people tried to ascribe meaning to pictographs? They just are, and that's enough."

"Beauty is a construct," Sophia said, aware that she was taking the bait. "We should save all of it, even if it is ordinary, maybe *because* it is ordinary."

"Which brings us back to the eye of the beholder—"

"And the tragedy is that most people have no idea what they are looking at, and so entire cultures have become decorations, fetishes, trinkets to be bought and sold. They love the artifacts, but it stops there. I don't see these people supporting clean water projects or advocating for the thousands of Indigenous women who have gone missing." Sophia interjected. "Call it what you want to, but what you're doing is a textbook case of cultural appropriation."

The woman stopped her with a raised palm, then she moved the mask's stick to her other hand. "Before you say anything else, I want to remind you that we have been talking for thirty minutes, which means we are now playing a different set of roles. I have put an offer on the table and you are arguing theoretical positions."

Sophia quickly considered the situation. She'd been kidnapped so a woman behind a mask could offer her a chance to help rescue invaluable artifacts with what appeared to be unlimited resources. Saying this to herself amplified the ridiculousness of it. "Look," she said, "I'm still getting over being chased, shot at, and drugged. And there's no way I'm going to say anything until I know how you do what you're doing."

"The details are tedious."

"God is in the details, I'm afraid," Sophia said.

"So is the devil." The woman laughed softly. "But let's stop talking about men, could we? Just for a moment, let us talk about what you and I might be able to accomplish together if we could work unimpeded. They would be happy to go on rattling their sabers, issuing sanctions and tariffs. Let them be our misdirection. For them there is only drill, baby, drill. As I have told you—we let them drill, then take what we want out the side door."

"It makes sense, but I need to pee again," Sophia said. "I drank that whole thing of gross Gatorade."

"Right now?" the woman said.

"It's a Maslow thing. I don't follow arguments when I'm in this state."

The woman sighed and gestured to the bathroom. Sophia went inside, pulled the door closed, and locked it.

"Don't lock it," Frangos called out.

"Too late. You have boundary issues," Sophia said, sitting on the toilet.

As she tried to piece everything together, she found herself visited instead by a memory of her mother, sitting at the kitchen table watching CNN on a small white television mounted on the underside of the kitchen cabinets. The correspondent stood in front of a museum in Baghdad, talking about the looting of artifacts from the National Museum. Her mother wept as she watched, and she brought Sophia close and wrapped her in her arms. "My beautiful," she said. "This thing they are doing can never be repaired. They know it, and that is why it is happening." Sophia remembered saying, "But Mama, this stuff isn't from Iran like us." And her mother said, "Borders won't stop them. This way of thinking will destroy everything beautiful in the world, piece by piece." This was the kind of thing the woman out there thought she could use her power and influence to stop.

Sophia finished and sat with the toilet paper wadded in one hand. The woman out there was crazy, but if those photographs were accurate, she was in possession of some of the great lost treasures of the world. She knew she couldn't work for such a person, and she'd never be allowed to work *with* her. She was a megalomaniac, and megalomaniacs don't share. And what would her mother say when she told her that she'd quit her PhD to become this woman's minion? She would fall silent and shake her head.

Sophia stood and flushed and examined herself in the mirror. She looked exhausted. In the high, escape-proof window above the sink she saw a glint and heard footsteps. She stepped onto the toilet so she could see, and outside there were police officers with bulletproof vests and visored helmets, moving in silence, directing each other with hand signals. One of them saw her peering down and stopped. She lifted a finger to her lips and motioned for Sophia to step down. She then put two fingers to her eyes and held them for a second, then nodded, making the "okay" sign.

"You're not trying to escape through one of those windows, are you?" the woman in the other room called out.

"No," Sophia said. "Whatever your guy put into me has destroyed my insides," she said.

"He's a blunt instrument, which is why he is gone," the woman said.

Sophia flushed the toilet again to cover her story, then washed her hands and came back into the main room. The woman had the scrapbook open to another page. "I am particularly fond of this rescue," she said, and she motioned for Sophia to come look.

She checked for hints of police movement outside, wondering how she might be able to stay clear of a firefight. Her pulse was racing, and she knew it was showing.

"We were given access to important cultural sites in Syria during the ceasefire in 2012. We removed key artifacts, which we swapped for fakes. The originals are now in my collection, and the fakes were scattered on the black market, which has—"

The motel door exploded inward and three police officers followed. Two of them tackled the woman to the ground, sending her fox mask spinning in the air, and a third swept Sophia toward the far corner of the room, sheltering her. The woman's plain face was flushed red, her eyes raging. Her face looked strangely expressionless, frozen, ruined.

"Get that binder," Sophia said. "It's all in the binder."

The woman began shrieking and kicking. "You have no idea who I am," she screamed over and over.

"You have the right to remain silent," the officer said. The woman thrashed and kicked, until one of them said, "You need to stay down, ma'am. I'm not going to warn you again." The woman kicked one of the officers in the jaw, and Sophia saw a flash, heard the ticking of electricity, then it was quiet.

Day Eleven

Delegation

Tanner knocked on the open doorjamb. Early-morning yellow light cut through the blinds and striped the walls. "Your vehicle hasn't moved since last night."

"That's right," Dalton said without looking up.

"I brought you one of these," Tanner said, producing a red-and-white thirty-two-ounce soda cup with a few inches of paper wrapper on the tip of the straw. Dalton looked up and smiled. His trash can was full of a half dozen similar cups. The top of his desk was strewn with files, his monitor flagged with Post-it Notes. "This wonderful stuff is going to kill me," he said. "Thank you."

"It won't kill you today," Tanner said, setting the drink within reach.

"How is Sophia Shepard?"

"They gave her something so she can sleep. The FBI is going to take a statement later today."

"What about the other one. The rich lady with the mask?" Dalton asked.

"Haven't heard much. I'm so glad all that happened in Arizona. Sounds like she's some kind of VIP, so the FBI is sweating bullets. Apparently, she's demanding protective custody. She says her man, Nick Scissors, will come after her," Tanner said.

"Stan Forsythe has a theory about her."

"I'm sure he will tell everyone all about it. He's holding court down at the HooDoo. All the usual crackpots. I don't know how we're going to get this particular snake back in the can."

"It's going to take months before we get back to normal," Dalton said. "The day I flew home from Kabul, I took one look around and told the whole country to go to hell. I could do it because I was nobody. It wasn't my problem anymore. When I got home, that place came with me. I was a mess for years. It ruined my marriage. Now I'm somebody, and everything collects on my desk waiting for me to sign off on it. I'd like to hop on an Osprey and take off, just disappear. Turn it off at the end like a movie."

"They don't do them like that anymore," Tanner said. "There's always a sequel. You shouldn't start wanting something that won't happen. Better off being okay with it."

"Dying doesn't even get you out of it. You probably wake up on the other side, and they put you to work. I'm not kidding. I just want a long nap. It's not just the job. I've got a divorce to wrap up, and I've got to work up the courage to tell Karen I'm keeping the house."

"Why don't you take a slug of that soda before you start writing poems or folk songs or something."

Dalton slid his drink closer. Before he could take a sip, the phone rang. Dalton lifted his eyebrows and looked at Tanner, then he answered. It was LaRae. "Hi, Sheriff, I'm sorry about this, but it's Raylene. She said it's urgent. She said she remembered something important."

Tanner shrugged and mouthed the words "See you later," then he left.

"Before you put her through, I wanted to tell you I put out a BOLO for your car."

"You've got a lot to think about. The car can wait," LaRae said.

"You shouldn't have to," he said.

"I'm putting her through now," LaRae said.

"Raylene, how are you?" Dalton said.

"Patrick, could you come and get me?"

He didn't know how to tell her he was off the case or if that would even be something she'd remember or if it would matter. He decided to say that he was going to have a hard time getting away.

"Oh, Sheriff. You can delegate."

Dalton laughed out loud without meaning to. "I'd like nothing better than to run off."

"What if I told you I had the answer."

"To what?"

"To your mystery. I remember it now. I can show you the maps you wanted to see."

"Raylene, we're doing okay with that now."

There was a long silence broken by Raylene telling someone to go away. "If you could pick me up, I could take you right to the maps you're asking about. I'm not sure how long I'll remember because, you know, things come and go, but I know where Bruce kept them. I know where these things are on the monument."

Dalton sized up the papers on his desk. When a notification banner appeared on his monitor from the Arizona State Police, he looked at it, then waited for it to fade.

"Sheriff?" Raylene asked.

"I'll be right there," he said. "It'll take ten minutes."

"Thank you," she said.

He took his soda and walked to LaRae's desk. She looked at him and apologized. He raised his cup and headed out. As he left the parking lot, he passed through the black rubber skids and remnants of brake lights scattered on the road from yesterday's wreck. Out-of-state cars drove past him, headed to the next stop on their vacations.

He parked in front of the Beehive House and went in. Raylene was sitting in the front room, with her purse at her feet, a basket to one side, and something small in her hands.

Dalton waved and signed her out, then helped her stand. She handed him a CD of Glenn Miller songs. "It's called *The Unforgettable*. I pilfered it from one of the gentlemen in here who has been trying to put the moves on me."

"Raylene, your house is just a couple of minutes away. Are we going to need all this stuff?"

She looked away and started wringing the knuckles of one hand with the fingers of the other. Dalton looked down and saw some apples inside the basket, a Ziploc bag of dinner rolls, silverware wrapped up in paper napkins, and two plastic cups stacked one inside of the other.

"Patrick, I feel like we won't need those maps at all today."

"I see," Dalton said, then he helped Raylene stand. When she stooped to pick up the basket, he reached it first.

Day Twenty-Four

Copies of copies of copies

They drove out of town, southward toward the open desert, Sophia driving, Paul riding shotgun, and Reinhardt in the back seat, pressed against the window. The sun was low over the eastern cliffs, and the shadows stretched gently westward. Sophia turned to Paul and whispered, "How does he have so much vacation?"

Reinhardt overheard and said, "Democratic socialism. We also have family leave and still manage to provide the world with the Mercedes-Benz. America does it incorrectly."

Paul said, "He's not wrong."

Sophia scanned the road for antelope, but only found the tall white grasses of high summer. Occasional birds wheeled above them, and ahead of them a red-tailed hawk perched in a dead tree scanning the land beneath. Reinhardt grabbed the front seats and leaned forward into the space between them. "It is amazing that you are free now, Paul," he said.

Paul shrugged. "It helped that I quit my job before they could fire me."

"I still think you didn't have to go that far," Sophia said.

"They wanted to put me on a task force, make me a desk ranger," Paul said.

"Sitting can take two years or more off your life, Paul," Reinhardt said. "The science is compelling."

They drove through the monument to where the road came closest to Dreamweaver's bus. They parked and rolled down the windows, and in a few minutes Dreamweaver's head appeared above a boulder. He scanned the area with binoculars, then threw them a hand signal.

Paul said, "He wants us to get out."

They stood outside of the vehicle with their hands to the side. Dreamweaver descended the hill in desert camo pants and a faded Denver Rockets T-shirt. He had a cardboard tube slung across his back on a length of clothesline like an empty quiver. They allowed him to approach and examine them.

Dreamweaver and Paul clasped arms like Romans. Sophia leaned toward Reinhardt and said, "That thing they're doing right now is fake."

"What is?" Reinhardt asked.

Sophia did the clasp with him. "Romans never did it. It's fake."

"It is still very cool," Reinhardt said. "And it is authentic for them."

Dreamweaver looked up and down the road. "How do I know you weren't followed?"

"We were really careful, man," Paul said.

Dreamweaver stared into the sky. Two vapor trails crisscrossed in the blue expanse. "In any given day, ten thousand satellites cross overhead."

"Do you really think they are watching us?" Reinhardt asked.

"Watching us watching them watching us watching them," Dreamweaver said, spinning his hands around each other like someone showing a child how a machine works. He stopped and grew serious. "I heard that the woman Frangos was found dead in her jail cell. They said she was strangled. No witnesses or anything. She was supposed to go before a grand jury this week. Now nobody is going to know anything about her."

Paul and Reinhardt looked at each other. Sophia kicked a stone across the road. "Is anyone even surprised?" she said.

"That crazy assassin can probably get into anywhere he wants," Reinhardt said.

Dreamweaver unslung the cardboard tube. "Okay, so here's Bruce's map, the one that set everything off. Are you sure you want it? I can keep it at the bus. It'll be safe," he said.

Paul took the tube and slung it across his shoulders. "I want to keep it close," he said. "I went back for the inventory book. This map completes the set."

"Suit yourself."

"I know you told me before," Sophia said, "but every time I start thinking about it, I lose track. So, Cluff gave Dreamweaver a map that's identical to the one that was stol—"

"For backup," Dreamweaver interrupted. "He brought it to me, like, five years ago, in case something weird happened. Insurance."

"I am lost," Reinhardt said. Paul rested his hand on Reinhardt's shoulder to calm him down.

Dreamweaver started gesturing with his hands. "Five years ago, there were two identical maps. Bruce made both. He kept one and gave the other to me. When Paulie started putting Bruce's things back, Bruce made notes all over his copy *and* in that blue book. So, those two tell a very unhelpful story about what people will find out there now that all the stuff Bruce collected is back where it belongs."

"Unhelpful?" Sophia said. "It tells the true story."

"All truths are half-truths," Dreamweaver said, then a thought came upon him. "Okay, maybe not exactly half, but a percentage. Truth is always watered down. Nobody can take it straight. It'll kill you right where you stand."

Sophia's face hardened, and she stared at the ground, then lifted her head back up. "Okay, so when we left with Euphrenia, Dreamweaver went out to your vehicle and swapped the maps—his for the one I stashed?" she asked.

"Correct," Dreamweaver said.

"The FBI have the map from Dreamweaver's wall," Paul explained. "It's completely untouched, doesn't say anything about what I did out there, and it makes everything look like it's always been there. The map we have here with Bruce's notes is the only record of our plan."

"But those forty or fifty years matter," Sophia said.

"I couldn't think of any other way to save this place. Neither could Bruce. Now people will have a map of artifacts they can use to make a case for preservation. If we had a time machine, we could fix it. This is the next best thing," Paul defended.

"A fake is a fake is a fake," Sophia said.

"Authenticity won't mean anything if they tear this place apart looking for oil, or gas, or—"

"Uranium," Dreamweaver said. "Definitely uranium."

"Yeah, or whatever," Paul said. "If you want to call it a fake map, fine. If a fake map points people to real things, then we might just have a shot at saving the monument. A real map that helps them make a case that it's already ruined—that'll just shut the whole thing down. It's a parlor trick. I know that."

"It's postmodern, you know—a copy of a copy of a copy—then the original disappears." Dreamweaver made a puff-of-smoke gesture.

"Plato is spinning in his grave," Reinhardt said.

"You know, this is not even close to the right way to do anything," Sophia said.

Dreamweaver squinted at her until she apologized. "Nobody's going to be wise to what happened. I rode out to Paul's rig and swapped the maps, roughed mine up to give it some patina. Nobody's going to know what the old bastard put us up to. It's possible I made some additions of my own, sites Cluff didn't know about. There's bodies out there, man, people older than anyone has seen before. And there's strange alloys out there, too. Radiating patterns fossilized in the sand consistent with fusion propulsion drives."

"Please say you didn't put UFO stuff on the map," Sophia said.

"Anyway, all of this confusion is going to slow the energy czars down to the speed of federal gridlock."

"There's no UFO stuff, though, right?" Paul asked.

"Why would I put that in there?" Dreamweaver asked.

"A hundred years from now, someone like me will have no idea what really happened," Sophia said.

Paul rubbed his hands together and tried to change things up. "A cool thing is that Sophia is going to wrap up her grant with a full report on Wïiatsiweap.

We're going up there to get more pictures and notes for that. The Senate hearings for retraction of the monument are in a month. It should all time out just right," Paul said.

"At least I don't have to fabricate data," Sophia said flatly. After a pause, she added, "You know I really hate all this Machiavellian garbage."

"We hate it, too," Reinhardt said, the look on his face pure and true.

Dreamweaver handed over the map and stepped back. "You know how this is going to play out, right? You make your report, and there's a public outcry. Because it's an election year, they'll look for some distraction, get people looking the other way. They'll save this place for a season. Build roads, toilets, fences, and signs telling people to keep off the fences. Some social media a-holes will geotag it on Instagram. A million more of them will come. Then they'll close it down, pave it, put a fence around it. The only good that will come from federal involvement is wheelchair access. Joni was right about everything."

Sophia leaned over to Paul and whispered, "Tell me he's not talking about Joni Mitchell."

"He is talking about Joni Mitchell," Paul whispered back, then he said, "Cluff knew this was coming. That's why he called us."

"Yes, he did. There is no government anymore, only the Petrostate."

Dreamweaver hugged everyone, his musk surrounding them, then he walked up the hill and was gone.

They drove to the trailhead and loaded their gear. They hiked without speaking, following the same route as before. The trail took them higher and higher above the valley floor. They rested and took in the long view of the monument, utility lines, lava field, Carvertown, Short Creek, all of it. Sophia led, so she could set the pace, take photographs, and record the trip. Paul brought up the rear, coming ahead only to set up the ropes. Reinhardt stayed between them, giddy at each turn of the trail.

"The difficulty of getting here will surely protect the place," Reinhardt said.

"It might," Paul said as he repacked the climbing gear. He moved slowly and with a little hesitation. "I can see somebody wanting to put in ladders."

"Why not an escalator?" Reinhardt said. He stepped on a small rock with one foot, grabbing the air like a handrail. "You just ride to the top."

They hiked on through the next section, Reinhardt asking questions about the place where Bruce Cluff had used explosives to close off the way. He wanted to know if that could be done again, and Paul said, "Anything is possible." When they came into the amphitheater, the majesty of it crashed over Sophia, and she watched the sensation move across Reinhardt's body like the shadow of clouds parting.

"Worth the trouble?" Paul asked.

Reinhardt could only nod.

"That's why it doesn't really matter what we do with the approach. There's always going to be someone who wants to get here. And there's always going to be someone to sell them the hiking boots to do it in," Paul said.

Sophia set about her work, and Paul helped. Reinhardt followed them for a time, then peeled off and went through the ruins on his own. After an hour, he found them, guided them to the pool of water and gestured to it. "This is all just as Krause described it in *The Rifle and the Tomahawk*. I will show you." He unzipped the top of his pack and took out a book. "I bought this and reread it last week to prepare myself." He rifled through the pages. "Here it is. The main character, Winnetonka, has been chasing cattle rustlers who killed his wife and children. When he catches them, he tries to subdue them and take them to the marshal for justice, but they overpower Winnetonka and threaten his life."

"Oh, Reinhardt," Sophia said. "These books are—"

Reinhardt scowled. "Let me read. 'The rustlers Winnetonka shot died face-up in the white gravel, his arrows pointing skyward from their blood-soaked Confederate shirts, agony etched into their faces like men burning in one of the deepest circles of hell.'"

Paul scratched his chin and tried to keep a kind face.

"Winnetonka spat upon them and continued up the trail to the abandoned dwellings of Wïiatsiweap." Reinhardt smiled and nodded until they acknowledged the word and gestured to the ruins around them. "Winnetonka continued past the silent adobe houses to a small pool fed by a spring. He stripped off his buckskins and dove into the cold water." Reinhardt turned and pointed to the still pool beneath the willows at the base of the cliff. "Winnetonka swam like a giant frog through the darkness, until a bright shimmering spot, like a submerged sun, revealed itself. His lungs burned as he continued through the narrow dark passage. When he emerged on the other side, he quickly burst through the surface into Upper Wïiatsiweap, where he was met by a dozen of his band, who raised their hands to celebrate his victories over the encroaching enemy."

Reinhardt snapped the book shut and looked at them. "You see," he said. "Krause says there is another place, a second world where Winnetonka's people retreated to live in peace."

"I know you love it, Reinhardt, but it's fiction. A potboiler. It's a story written by somebody from somewhere else. Winnetonka isn't even a Paiute name, is it Paul?" She turned to look for backup on this, but Paul had already stripped to his underwear and was wading into the water.

Reinhardt was next, and Sophia followed. The water was not cold and clear, but after she dove, a white portal appeared, and she swam toward it. The walls narrowed around her, and she put her hands on the rocks as she passed through.

When she emerged on the other side, she saw the dripping backs of Paul and Reinhardt. Around them was an entire complex of dwellings three stories high, wooden ladders still leaning against the structures. They were set back under the protection of the cliffs, impossible to see from the air.

Day Seven Hundred Eighty-Four

Epilogue

Sophia grabbed a stack of papers and her briefcase and left her office, almost running. She merged with the throng of students traveling between classes and descended the stairs until she shot out of the building into the upper quad. She looked up at the clock on the carillon tower and saw that she had one minute to be in class.

She hurried along, her thoughts on her lecture, the new-faculty orientation session later that afternoon, and the package of books she'd just received from Paul.

Her phone buzzed as she entered Dunphy Hall. With a free hand, she fished her phone out of her jacket pocket and saw there was a text from Reinhardt. She swiped open the lock screen and read the message.

CHECK IT OUT ☺.

There was a link to a Sotheby's auction web page. Sophia tapped it with her thumb and brought up an image of the aquatic-man pot Paul had returned to Wïiatsiweap. She scrolled and read the text:

NATIVE AMERICAN POTTERY, POLYCHROME POTTERY BOWL, CIRCA 1520, WITH MONSTER AND WATER GLYPH, #642

NATIVE AMERICAN

PUEBLOAN POTTERY

CONDITION: EXCELLENT FOR AGE AND USE

DIMENSION: 9" X 9.5"

ORIGIN: NORTHERN ARIZONA, PRIVATE COLLECTION

She slumped against the wall and kicked it twice. She did not read any further. Students flowed around her. When the halls cleared, she closed her eyes and let her head drop.

"Dr. Shepard, are you okay?" a student asked.

Sophia opened her eyes. It was one of her students. "I'm okay, Terrah. I just got some stupid news."

"I'm sorry."

"It's okay. Tell everyone I'll be right there. If you could get the discussion going, people can start by sharing their reading responses."

When the student left, Sophia's phone buzzed again. It was a phone call from Paul. She answered.

"I just saw Reinhardt's text. Are you okay?" he asked.

"Despondent."

"I'm a total idiot—"

"I won't argue with you about that."

"What I mean is I could have saved you some grief if I told you the pot on that website is a fake," Paul said.

"What?" Sophia pushed off the wall and started pacing. "How is that even—"

"When you told us about Frangos, it gave me an idea. Dreamweaver and I made—"

"Nope. Don't tell me. I don't want to know."

"Do you want to know where I put the original?"

"Seriously, I'm late to class—"

"Sophia, I took it through the water to the other side."

"Does Reinhardt know?"

"Of course he does. It was his idea. He started talking to me about the ultimate boon, being the master of two worlds, and all of that."

"Of course he did," Sophia said.

"I told him to keep his mouth shut," Paul said. "Just remember, we stopped them. The monument is intact. Your testimony did it."

"I've got class. I'm going to have to call you back," Sophia said.

She hung up, took a deep breath, and walked into the classroom.

There was no discussion under way. Everyone was deep into their phones. "Okay, people," she announced. "Put those things away. Let's forget the syllabus today and go in an entirely different direction. I'd like to talk about the problem of authenticity."

Acknowledgments

We say this novel is set on the Utah-Arizona border and that the action unfolds across many jurisdictions. But this story takes place on Native land. So much of American fiction does.

—

Thanks to my agent, Nat Sobel, who saw a certain criminality in my writing and encouraged me to explore it. My editor Jennifer Alton's work and insights transformed this book. This perfect cover comes from Donna Cheng. Thanks to Megan Fishmann, Lena Moses-Schmitt, Katherine Boland, Rachel Fershleiser, Jack Shoemaker, Jordan Koluch, and everyone at Counterpoint Press. They are the champions. And thank you, Dallin Jay Bundy, for being one of my first and best readers.

Before there was a story, there were hundreds of conversations with rangers, American Indian people, archeologists, geologists, biologists, cartographers, morticians, librarians, police officers, historians, curators, writers, adventurers, neighbors, colleagues, students, acquaintances, and friends. Thank you for sharing your time, expertise, and insights. Many thanks to Southern Utah

University special collections librarian Paula Mitchell for her inspired assistance. I am also indebted to Dr. Johnny MacLean for checking my stratigraphy over and over.

I would like to express my thanks to Southern Utah University for their generous support. A faculty development grant helped me travel to gather the first details of this book, and a semester sabbatical gave me the time to revise the manuscript.

Finally, I want to thank my wife, Alisa, for letting me tell her the unformed bits and pieces of this story one hundred million times until they finally came together.

© Sam Davis

TODD ROBERT PETERSEN grew up in Port-
land, Oregon, and now teaches film studies and creative
writing at Southern Utah University. Petersen's previous books include *Long After Dark*, *Rift*, and *It Needs to
Look Like We Tried*. He and his family live in Cedar City,
Utah, on the western edge of the Markagunt Plateau.
Find out more at toddrobertpetersen.com.